A SUN SCORCHED BLOOM

BOOK TWO OF THE MAGIC OF THE WILDFLOWERS TRILOGY

by Megan Shade

A Sun Scorched Bloom. Copyright © 2023 by Megan Shade

Published by: Shade Made Publishing LLC

First Edition

ISBN: 979-8-9878324-1-7

Editing by Sara Coombes: https://saracoombescom.wordpress.com/

Interior art by Lindsey Staton: honeyy.fae on IG for comissions

Cover Art by SeventhStar Art Services

Author's Note: This is the second book in the Magic of the Wildflowers Trilogy and ends on a cliffhanger. It includes adult themes including language, severe assault against a woman, gruesome depictions of violence and death, and sexual content, and is intended for readers 18+.

CONTENTS

To my village,
And especially, my family.
This year has been one for the books—and I still somehow got this book
done. I couldn't have done it without you all.

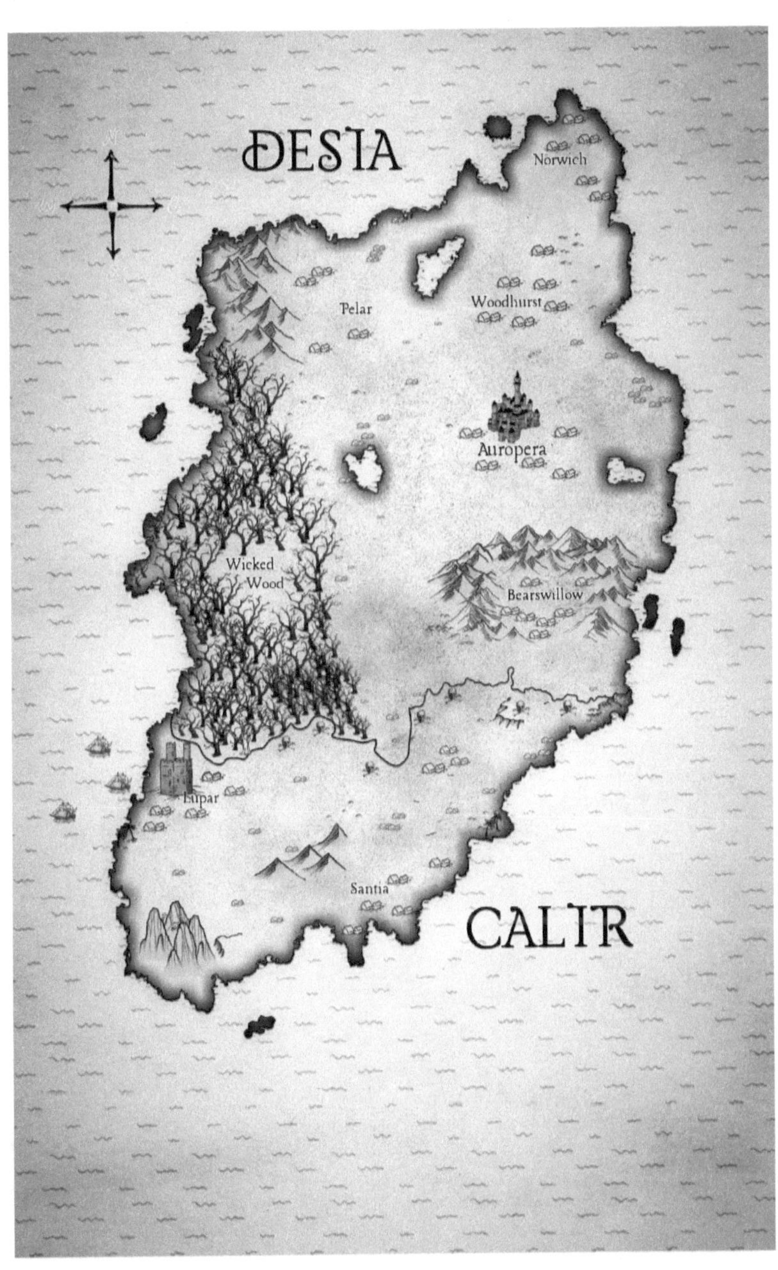

ÐESIA
Norwich
Pelar
Woodhurst
Auropera
Wicked
Wood
Bearswillow
Lupar
Santia
CALIR

BOOK ONE RECAP

Ever since her mother fell victim to the Lonely Death, Azalea (Lea) has tried to find a cure in the petals of the moonflowers. When a pack of fenrir attacks the town, Lea's friend, Thomas, uses his magic to save her, resulting in his arrest for hiding magic from the Black King. Lea is held prisoner by the commander of the Royal Army, Gray, while Thomas is put on trial.

Lea falsely confesses to having magic and is sentenced along with Thomas to a lifetime of servitude. Gray and Lea travel to Auropera, and upon arrival, Lea learns that Gray is the son of the Black King—the Night Prince, Evander Nestruir.

After Alaric, Gray's older brother and Crown Prince of Desia, nearly kills Lea in a brutal attack, Gray confesses his feelings for her. Thomas becomes angry about Lea's relationship with the Night Prince and confesses that he is part of a rebellion led by the unknown Eclipsed King. Thomas tells Lea that the Lonely Death results from a spell that allows the Black King to take power from those who have died.

Gray reveals that he and Lea are mates, and decides that to keep her safe, they must marry. During the wedding, there's an explosion, and Gray forces Lea to flee to the dungeons where the rebellion awaits. Unbeknownst to the rebels kneeling in front of Vincent, Gray slips in the back and quietly confesses to Lea that he is the Eclipsed King and leader of the rebellion.

CHAPTER I

GRAY

"A rebellion to—to *lead*?" Lea stuttered, her eyes wide and body swaying as if the stone floor of the dungeon was shattering beneath her feet. The same stone floor where hundreds of rebels knelt behind them, completely unaware that while they'd been listening to Vincent speak, Gray had entered the enormous chamber and quietly confessed to her that *he* was the one who had orchestrated the entire rebellion.

Gray's eyes flicked to the rebels whose hands remained on their hearts, their thumbs tucked firmly inside their fists and eyes downcast in deference to Vincent, the dark-skinned, heavily tattooed Fae standing at the front of the room. The Fae they *thought* was their new leader, the Eclipsed King.

"How—"

"Shhh—" Gray whispered as Vincent's speech ended, his eyes flicking to Lea and Gray as he inclined his head to the back of the room. Gray nodded, grabbing Lea's hand.

"Rise," Vincent ordered, the clanging of metal and shuffling of feet echoing through the torch-lit chamber and covering the sound of Gray and Lea's footsteps as he pulled her behind the haphazard stacks of oversized wine barrels by the rear wall.

"We don't have much time," Gray said into Lea's ear as he crushed her to his chest in a tight embrace. "Are you hurt?" he asked, running his hands through the hair at the back of her head, then down her shoulders and torso. He pulled back, his eyes scanning her front for injuries. Lea's blue eyes were red-rimmed and brimming with worry, and her long, honey-blonde hair was dotted with ash and soot, but her freckled skin appeared free of anything other than minor scrapes and bruises.

Gray finally exhaled as his heart rate slowed, the panic he'd been feeling since seeing his bastard of a brother, Alaric, trying to kill Lea easing to a persistent apprehension.

"I'm fine," Lea soothed, grabbing his hands and clasping them tight. "I promise, I'm okay. But what's happening? If you're leading the rebellion, why are we hiding?"

Nausea churned in Gray's gut thinking about the confession he would soon have to make to the men and women they were hiding from. "The rebel army can't know. Not yet. I am a Nestruir. The *son* of Brennus Nestruir, the Black King. I may have orchestrated this escape, but there's no guarantee they'll trust me as their leader, or even accept me as part of the rebellion."

It didn't matter to Gray, not one bit. As long as Lea knew the truth, he wasn't too proud to allow Vincent to take the glory for their escape. He'd happily shove down his pride if it meant every rebel made it out alive. "The only thing that matters right now is getting everyone out of here safely—"

The clash of a sword against a shield made Gray pause—three *clangs*—Vincent's sign that Erik was burning away the door hiding the tunnel to the outside of the castle that they'd spent the last year digging.

Dark smoke filled the room, and Gray ripped a strip of fabric from the hem of his shirt, stuffing it in Lea's hand and raising it to cover her nose as the scent of burning wood grew suffocating. "There's so much we need to discuss, and we will, but right now, we have to go," Gray pulled Lea close, pressing a kiss to the top of her head and speaking into her hair.

"The tunnel is enchanted to collapse ten minutes from when the door completely burns away, so run fast. If we get separated, go around the east wing."

Gray sent his shadows floating through the gaps in the barrels and along the floor to where Janelle, Lea's childhood best friend, stood, whipping her berry-dyed purple head side to side. Next to her, Emma's arm was turning red where Janelle's hand squeezed it in a white-knuckled grip. Her curly brown hair was wild and windblown about her delicate, beautiful face, making her look so different from the usually pristine and put-together girl he'd seen working about the castle for so long.

Using his shadows, Gray tugged on Janelle's sleeve, and her shoulders sagged in relief when she saw the trail of darkness leading to where Lea peeked out from behind their hiding spot. Janelle pulled Emma toward them, but Thomas stopped her with a firm grasp of the elbow, his eyes bouncing between Janelle and Lea.

Gray's blood heated in anger. Thomas was always too physical with his demands, so self assured that he didn't think twice before placing his hands on someone. Even through the clatter of the rebels now filing through the hole in the ground, Gray could hear his words.

"Where are you going? We need to leave," Thomas scolded, gesturing to the tunnel.

Janelle inclined her head toward Lea. "We're not leaving her."

Thomas shook his head. "Look, I don't know what's going on, but I still don't trust Evander. We don't even know what he's doing here. I'm getting you out of this place," Thomas whispered.

Gray couldn't decide if he should laugh at Thomas or give in to his fury and kill him. He'd caused more trouble than he was worth since the moment he'd spoken up at the trial. Just minutes ago, he'd seen Gray enter the dungeons—had watched him make eye contact with Vincent and Erik, communicating silently with them. Among everyone in the room, he was one of six people who now knew he was involved in the rebellion, and still, he was too stubborn to believe it.

Thomas attempted to pull Janelle away again, and Lea's anger shot through the bond. *Fury it is,* Gray decided as he stepped out from behind the barrels. With the few remaining rebels focused on making the drop into the tunnel, Gray allowed his shadows to escape in their full glory. They snaked across the stone and floated through the air as Gray lowered his chin, staring Thomas down in an unmistakable challenge. *Pull her away one more time,* Gray thought. *I dare you.*

Thomas's eyes widened as he focused on the darkness that threatened to tear him apart. His face turned a deep red, and he let go of Janelle's arm. "Don't say I didn't warn you," he snapped before glancing at Emma and storming off to join the remainder of the retreating rebels.

Janelle and Emma scurried toward Lea, but as the last few rebels disappeared through the hole in the ground, Gray pulled Lea to meet them halfway and led them all toward Erik. "Be prepared to fight," Gray instructed as they walked. "The fires have been contained to the palace grounds for now, but it won't take long for the king to realize so many of his soldiers are missing. We set off the explosions to the west, and one of my generals was instructed to order every soldier on duty to investigate. The portcullis will be closed and blocked twenty minutes after the last explosion. You have to get out of the castle grounds at any cost. Go straight through town into the forest, the same way we entered Auropera. There's a meeting place roughly eight hundred yards straight south. If you get lost, find someone with a red patch." Gray pointed to the crimson piece of fabric adorning his and Erik's sleeves. "They'll know where to go."

"Okay." Lea swallowed. "Anyone with a red patch. But we won't get separated, right?"

Gray ground his jaw, every fiber of his being recoiling from the thought of not being with his mate as she escaped. But he bore a responsibility to his soldiers, to every man and woman who had shown up here tonight. "I refuse to leave any of our rebels behind to be slaughtered."

Gray grabbed Lea's chin. "Every demon in hell wouldn't be able to keep us apart. If you lose me, I'll find you. I swear it."

Lea's tension flooded through their bond. She wanted to argue. He could *feel* it, but she was holding back.

"Thank you for listening to me," Gray pressed his forehead against hers, his eyes soft as he pressed a kiss to her lips, just for a moment. In the span of three seconds, he tried to convey everything he was feeling through their connection: love, devotion, adoration, protectiveness, and his sense of urgency. The words he was desperate to say danced on his lips, but there was no time to give them voice. Instead, he forced the emotions through the bond, desperate for Lea to know everything he felt. He had so much more to tell her, but not now. Not until they were safe.

Pulling away, Gray watched Erik disappear through the enormous gap where the wooden door had been, at least ten feet by ten feet and still smoldering at the edges. Behind the opening, the wall was hollowed out, and a small hole had been dug into the floor, barely large enough for the biggest of them, Gray, to slide through.

At least three minutes had passed since the door had burned away, leaving only seven for them to escape before it collapsed in on itself. "Janelle, you next," Gray ordered, knowing Erik waited below to help her and Emma down.

Gray moved a strand of Lea's hair from in front of her eyes. "Danger awaits us on the other side of this tunnel, Little Flower. You *will* listen to my direction. If I tell you to run, you *run*. Do you understand? I won't be able to focus on the success of this mission if I'm not confident you'll be safe."

Lea nodded, reaching up to cup his cheek, and Gray felt her sincerity through their bond. "I'll run. I swear. But only if you promise to be right behind me." She smiled at him, and Gray's breath was sucked from his lungs at the beauty of it.

"I love you. Desperately." Gray ran a thumb along Lea's jaw. "Please," he begged, "follow directions this time." Leaning down, he kissed her quickly but fiercely, a promise of what was to come, before pulling back.

Gray didn't even have to search the bond to notice the way Lea's face fell and how her heart thumped wildly in her chest at the loss of his lips from hers. He leaned down, his rough, gravelly whisper brushing against her skin. "The only reason I can pull my mouth from your sweet lips is because if it is on you another second, we will be doing something very different than leading an army away from Auropera."

Lea's face warmed against Gray's cheek as Emma disappeared into the tunnel. Six minutes left.

"It's time." Gray pulled back to look into his mate's beautiful, worried eyes, "Lea, your magic, I need you to—"

"Be careful. Don't use it. I know," she cut him off, pressing her lips together and wringing her hands, nervous energy radiating from her skin.

"No, Little Flower. You are the Queen of Sun and Shadows," Gray rumbled as his own shadows trailed up Lea's body, caressing her neck as they pushed her long hair behind her shoulders. "If you are threatened, I want you to destroy them all."

CHAPTER 2

LEA

Erik caught Lea's arm to steady her as she plunged through the hole and into darkness. Dirt and rocks crunched beneath Lea's boots, and a shiver ran across her skin at the chill coming from the bleak stone tunnel ahead of her. The cold seeped straight into her bones causing bumps to break out across the skin of her neck. It felt like an omen. How had Gray planned all this without her even having any idea? She was completely at a loss for how she had missed so much. He'd promised her he would show her who he truly was, and she'd been too blind, or stupid, to see it.

Gray was beside her in an instant, his hand finding her lower back as if it was a magnet pulling her from Erik's grip. His touch calmed her instantly, and her heart rate slowed.

"Erik, run ahead and help Vincent. We'll find you," Gray ordered, and they clasped each other's forearms, nodding solemnly before Erik turned to Lea.

"Listen to Gray this time, Sunshine." He gave her one of his signature smiles and a wink before turning and disappearing into the darkness.

Just feet away, Janelle and Emma waited, their eyes wide with fear. Lea's mouth cracked open as she prepared to tell them they didn't have to come, that she didn't expect them to follow her blindly into danger once again, but her words got stuck on her tongue when Janelle turned her head and pinned her with a stare.

"I'm going to stop you right there." Janelle stabbed a finger at Lea. "If you try to get me to stay behind, *again*, I'll stab you. I will actually *fucking* stab you. I'm coming. Fucking deal with it," Janelle said with a tone so angry it made Lea flinch.

Emma cleared her throat, giving Lea a contrite smile. "Um... I'm coming, too."

"We're all going, and we're going *now*," Gray pointed down the tunnel, and without argument, Janelle and Emma turned and ran. With a hand on Lea's lower back, Gray urged her forward into the black passage, steadying her as he matched her pace. After a couple breathless minutes, the tunnel sloped upward, the steep incline bringing them back toward the surface of the earth, causing Lea's legs to ache and her lungs to burn.

"Where will we go?" Lea asked through ragged breaths as they sprinted forward, torches illuminating the ground about every thirty feet, just enough so they could see several steps in front of them and no more.

"The resistance is going to Bearswillow, to the cavern. But you and I will go south to Calir. The first step to defeating my father is to find Eudora." The tunnel curved left, the floor becoming more uneven.

"Eudora?" Lea asked breathlessly, struggling to get enough oxygen into her lungs.

"The witch who granted the spell that prevents my family from killing anyone in our bloodline. If we can't convince her to undo it—" The tunnel rumbled, bits of rock tumbling from above their heads. "*Fuck*!" Gray cursed. "Faster!"

Lea stumbled on an errant rock and Gray caught her elbow, lifting her into his arms in one fluid motion. She felt a tug in her chest, and she searched out the bond to feel what was happening in Gray's mind.

Cool relief butted up against fiery anger and intense urgency. She could sense gratefulness, almost like a warm blanket wrapping around her shoulders, mixed with anticipation that caused her heart to pick up its pace. Her head spun with all the emotions flooding into her chest, too many to possibly sort through at once.

Gray's gravelly timbre broke through her moment of introspection as they reached the tunnel exit, a freshly dug hole with a makeshift ladder leading back aboveground. A crash sounded behind them, reminding Lea of a rockslide that had once destroyed the shepherd's cottage back in Bearswillow. The earth shook as pebbles and dirt rained down on their heads. "Read my mind later!" he shouted before pushing her halfway up the ladder. "Move! Now!"

Lea grabbed the rungs, her sweaty hands slipping as she scurried up, and Janelle and Emma clamored to the surface just behind her. The moment Gray cleared the tunnel, the ground shook with a fierceness that made Lea's stomach lodge in her throat. Had Gray known how close they'd been to being buried alive? Lea's eyes watered and she coughed, covering her mouth with her sleeve to protect her from the dust floating up in an enormous plume from the collapsed tunnel.

Without taking any time to catch his breath, Gray ushered them to where the air was cleaner, then pointed to the crumbling stone on the outside of the castle. "We'll circle around the bailey. Stay close to it. The king doesn't know about the passageway, so they'll likely think we're escaping through the western gate we destroyed in the explosion."

Emma twisted her fingers, picking at her nails with shaking hands. "Should we wait to see if anyone else comes?" Her eyes darted nervously back to the exit of the tunnel.

Lea's heart sank. "Elise..." she whispered.

Gray shook his head. "My men will be closing the gates soon. I'm sorry, Emma, but we have to go."

Sniffling, Emma nodded, pressing her lips together as if trying not to cry.

"We'll get her to Bearswillow one way or another," Janelle said, "But it won't help her if we all die. Just—" Her head snapped up so quickly her bones popped. "We need to go. Now."

Crouching low and pressing himself against the wall, Gray edged toward the front gate, ordering them to follow with a wave of his hand. The portcullis appeared in front of them, two guards with red armbands rushing men and women through with hushed whispers and emphatic waves.

Lea could just make out the first houses of the village beyond the castle through the exit when Gray held up a hand, his head swiveling around as he scanned the open area between the side of the castle and the gate.

"Run!" Janelle shouted abruptly, grabbing Lea and Emma and dashing forward. "Close the gate!"

There was still at least a hundred yards for them to get to the wooden bridge that led into town, and Lea's chest squeezed. If they started closing it now, they wouldn't make it.

"Order them to lower it. *Now,* Gray!" Janelle's legs pumped faster, and Lea struggled to keep up.

She pushed harder. If Janelle sensed something was wrong, she couldn't afford to hold them back.

As they sprinted toward the gate, the ground started to shake. Gray looked over his shoulder as the thundering roar of hundreds of feet storming closer mixed with the scratch of metal and clang of swords. Lea followed Gray's line of sight and a jolt of fear shot straight to her lungs, distracting her from the burn she felt with every inhale.

"Close it!" Gray roared, picking the three of them up and increasing his speed to a superhuman sprint. Emma's elbow jabbed painfully into Lea's ribs as his arm wrapped more firmly around their waists.

The two guards jumped at Gray's command, quickly unraveling the ropes from their anchors and pulling, the rugged wooden door lowering with a loud, clunky groan. With the closing mechanism triggered, the guards darted under the gate, then removed their jackets to reveal red patches sewn into the arms of the shirts they wore beneath.

They turned and ran, bolting away from where the gate continued to descend, getting closer and closer to locking Lea and her friends inside. Twenty feet, then fifteen...

Arrows whizzed past their heads as Gray darted forward. Nine feet remained until they were trapped. Gray's breaths were loud and his face red as he strained to carry them all and still get through in time. Lea's skin broke out in a hot, nervous sweat, moisture beading on her neck and dripping down her spine.

Eight feet left, and Lea squeezed her hands tight, her fingernails cutting into the palms of her hands.

Cries of "Halt!" and "Stop them!" rang out from behind. Only seven feet until they were closed off from freedom. If they didn't make it, they'd be facing hundreds of soldiers alone with nowhere to go. It would take too long for the gate to open again. They'd be completely helpless *and* surrounded.

"Hurry!" Lea shouted, her heart hammering in her chest. Six feet remained until the gate closed, the path beyond disappearing inch by inch. *We're never going to make it*, Lea thought. *Unless...*

Reaching inward, she found her shadows. The ones she hadn't used since the night she'd found out the truth of the origin of the Lonely Death. They swirled next to her light, but they felt different somehow. Within her night magic, something felt foreign, like there were two different types of darkness mixed inside her: the difference between the darkness of a waning versus a waxing moon.

Focus! she scolded herself. There wasn't time to overthink things right now. Harnessing the thick layer of urgency and fear pulsing in her gut, Lea forced her shadows outward, gritting her teeth as she grabbed the bottom of the gate and used every bit of her strength to keep it open. It was like using a muscle that had atrophied, somehow physically painful in a phantom limb as she fought against a thousand pounds of wood and metal.

Just as Lea was about to break, Gray dove forward, closing the distance and rolling them under the door. The air was knocked from their lungs as they hit the ground and Lea's shadows faltered, then disappeared altogether, the door slamming shut with a *thud* that caused a fissure to open in the ground beneath it.

Gray scrambled to his feet, pulling Lea with him, then shook out his arms.

"I can't believe we made it," Janelle said, pushing herself to stand as breathlessly as if *she'd* been carrying them in her arms while running.

"It will at least slow them down, but we need to keep going. It won't take long for them to bring ladders and climb the wall." Gray offered Emma a hand as he looked behind him, then forward toward the hilly path that would take them to the village within Auropera. "Janelle? How did you know they were coming? Even I hadn't heard them yet when you warned us." Gray asked, every bit the Eclipsed King as he stared down at Janelle. He appeared to be planning and plotting, his eyebrows scrunching together in concentration.

"I don't know." Janelle shrugged. "I just know things sometimes."

"You just *know things sometimes?* No," he said, his voice stern. "I need to know *how* you knew." Gray stepped forward and put his hand on her shoulder, bending down to look directly in her eyes.

Janelle's gaze flicked to Lea. "I can *sense* it. When someone is coming, or when danger is near. It's a feeling on the back of my neck... It prickles." She absently rubbed the back of her neck. "That's why I'm so good at stealing things—I mean..." she shuffled her feet, "borrowing them."

Gray took a step back, a triumphant smile crossing his face. Even in the midst of danger, the sight of it took Lea's breath away and caused butterflies to fly circles in her stomach. "I knew it." Gray took a step back, motioning Janelle ahead of him. "Janelle will lead from here."

"Ummm... did you hit your enormous head on your way down the big hole?" Janelle's voice was panicked. "I don't even know where we're going!" she argued.

"We don't have time to fight about this. Get us through town, and *fast*. That's an order," he said, crossing his arms and lifting his chin. Suddenly, Gray seemed ten feet tall.

Janelle's eyes opened wide, and she swallowed, giving Gray a look that suggested she thought he had been smoking some redberry root before she let out a resigned sigh and darted across the path toward the village, running straight ahead until they neared the first homes.

"Shit!" Gray hissed under his breath as they crested a small hill and the cobblestone road between the homes became visible. He pulled his sword from his back. Up ahead between the two neat rows of houses, rebels and soldiers clashed, bloody weapons flying and screams of pain echoing. "I was hoping we could escape before the king's soldiers made it here. Run if you can. But be prepared to fight."

"There are so many of them." Lea's magic twisted in her gut.

Gray pulled a dagger from his boot and tossed it to Emma. "I'd hoped that the guards stationed in town would run back toward the explosion to help. Cowards."

Janelle rubbed the back of her neck again. "How are we supposed to get past them?"

"You get past them by listening to your magic, Janelle. Has it ever led you astray before?"

"Magic? No—"

"Now is not the time to overthink this. I need you to get Emma and Lea out of here safely. I am trusting you with my heart, with the person most precious to me in the world. And I am doing it because I *know* you can keep her safe. The best way to keep all of us alive is to get you three out of here as quickly as possible. Avoid danger, avoid fighting if you can. Just get out." Gray quickly glanced around in the moonlight, and Lea wondered what he was able to see with his superior Fae eyesight that Lea and her friends couldn't. "Look for Erik. He knows where to go."

A sensation of eyes on the back of Lea's head made a cold sweat break out on her skin. *Alaric*, she thought, whipping her head around to look for the Crown Prince, Gray's sadistic older brother. He was near, but where? He was nowhere to be seen, but she could *feel* him—feel the malice floating in the air—the undeniable threat of a predator stalking its prey.

As they stepped onto the cobblestone street, chaos erupted. Gray pulled a shiny bronze dagger from his thigh and pressed it into Lea's hand. The tips of dozens of ladders peeked out from over the castle wall and royal guards were climbing over, jumping down to join the fight.

"Let's move!" Gray shouted, urging them forward as Lea's magic sparked at her fingertips. Bits of stone crumbled from the parapet wall as soldiers scurried across. Others planted themselves on top of it, readying their arrows and raising their bows. They were *everywhere*.

Three guards in the navy blue uniform of the Royal Army darted forward with their swords raised. Relief wrapped around Lea's heart as Janelle pulled Emma to the side, dodging their advance and wrenching her backward to hide behind a weathered white fence.

Lea raised her hands and gathered her fire as she stepped forward to join the battle, but an arrow struck the hem of Lea's dress, causing her to stumble. Gray caught her with a hand on her elbow at the same time he speared the second guard on his sword, the man slumping to the ground as deep red blood spurted from the wound. Yanking the arrow pinning her in place, Lea pressed deeper into the well of her magic than ever before and prepared to fight.

But before she could unleash her power, a blast of intense, red-hot fire caused the third guard to collapse in a pile of agonizing shrieks. There was only one rebel Lea knew of who could create such powerful flames.

"Erik!" Lea shouted, turning to look for him in the mayhem. He needed to get to Emma and Janelle. They were vulnerable, except...

Erik's broad form caught her attention only feet from where Emma hid, now alone. Janelle had somehow found a thin, perfectly polished sword and was fighting back to back with Erik, striking down guards as if they'd fought together hundreds of times.

"Duck!" Janelle shouted, and Erik listened, dropping down a moment before an arrow whizzed directly where Erik's right eye had been a moment before. "To the right!" she ordered, and Erik swiped right, opening a ten-inch gash in a soldier's flank.

Lea's mouth went dry as she watched in awe. Janelle had never wielded a sword before, at least that Lea was aware of, but she was fighting as if she had been born holding one. What she lacked in strength she made up for in speed, anticipating the guards' movements before they even seemed to decide themselves. Janelle jumped over an ax that was swung at her knees, and Erik stabbed his sword through her attacker's chest.

Placing her hands on her knees, Janelle took a deep breath before standing again. The guards just kept coming—one after another after another. Sweat beaded along her brow, and Lea felt perspiration break out on her own neck. *She's getting too tired,* she thought as Janelle's movements turned sluggish, her fatigue growing more apparent with every slash of her sword.

On instinct, Lea shot both hands out, flames bursting from her fingertips and exploding in the small space between her friends and the guards attacking them. Janelle hissed, pulling her arm to her chest as the soldiers jumped backward. They fell on the ground as the flames licked at their legs, their wails causing Lea's stomach to drop. She squeezed her eyes shut, trying to block out the sight of the men's tears.

This wasn't what she wanted. What if these soldiers had been given the chance to join the rebellion? Would they have chosen to fight with them instead of against them? What if they weren't actually bad people? Lea's hands began to shake. *I can't do this,* she thought, nausea creeping up the back of her throat.

A nearby rebel with graying hair and smile lines around his eyes fought off two royal soldiers, crying out as a blade nicked his shoulder. Lea stepped forward to help, and one of the soldiers caught her movement, looking up at her with wide, terrified eyes. He was so young—seventeen, if that. Lea's fire fizzled out as if water had been poured directly on it. She couldn't kill him, and yet, despite his fear-filled gaze, he lifted his sword overhead and arced it down directly toward the rebel's neck.

Lea tried to find her power, knew she needed to save the man, but instead of coils of light or darkness, she only found the fear causing her heart to pound erratically. "Dammit!" she hissed as she forced her terror down, searching for her courage and magic. *There*. A small tendril. Demanding it listen, she ordered it toward the young soldier about to deliver a killing blow, but before she could strike, a man with a red armband darted from inside the house and rammed his sword through the guard's gut.

Coward, her subconscious chastised her. Deep down, she knew that her magic was lethal, that she could be helping her fellow rebels by striking down the soldiers fighting against them. But... killing someone? Even if it was the enemy? The idea of it made Lea want to vomit.

A tendril of darkness wound around Lea's arm. "Shield yourself with your shadows!" Gray called from just behind her as he sliced through another guard approaching from the wall behind them. A jolt of sharp confidence pulsed through the bond, waking her magic again. It was as if Gray sensed her hesitation to fight—to kill. "Pull them around you and imagine making them solid."

Gray blasted a charging soldier fifty feet back, throwing him into a hoard of approaching guards in a display of dark power. His shadows floated around her, protecting her as he continued to fight, buying the rebels more time to escape. "Find it, Lea! And use it!"

Protected by her mate, Lea closed her eyes and searched for her night magic. It was harder for her to find, deeper and more elusive inside her than the fire she could now more easily call to her hands. She followed the ball of light next to her heart, branching out until she found a sliver of coolness entwined within. Lea allowed it to emerge, to fill her chest and spread down her arms, dark waves floating from her fingertips. Nausea filled Lea's stomach as she accessed the magic, the feeling so much darker and more dangerous than her light. It felt like sorrow and fear—a terrifying cold vibrating through her bones.

"You're okay," Lea whispered to herself, ignoring the way using her night magic made her skin crawl, knowing that if she wanted to live, she needed to use any power she could muster. Pushing the darkness around her, Lea watched in awe as translucent black tendrils snaked in spirals around her body. They were living things, obeying her, but somehow also moving on their own, writhing and pulsing. The power was intimidating and overwhelming, but somehow also *beautiful*. With her shadows by her side, Lea searched the streets for ways she could help.

Lea's attention returned to where Janelle and Erik fought off a single guard wielding day magic, splashes of fire crashing around their feet. Janelle kept her left arm cradled against her chest as she fought, and Lea cringed at the sight of the charred, black, and blistered skin from her thumb to her elbow.

"Janelle!" Lea shouted, but Janelle held up a hand, silencing her.

"I'm fine. Shield us," Janelle ordered.

Lea wanted to cry, but the adrenaline coursing through her veins made it impossible. She could feel sorry for hurting Janelle later, but she would never get the chance to apologize if Janelle didn't make it through this battle alive.

Picturing her shadows in her mind, she urged them to slither along the ground until they reached her friends' feet, then imagined them surrounding and moving with them as they fought.

She looked for other rebels to shield, but there were few close enough to allow her enough control. It appeared that Gray was keeping the majority of the soldiers from reaching them as the rebellion fled into the woods, while some of the more well-trained rebels fought the guards who had been stationed in town during the explosion. Lea's confidence grew as she watched her mate effortlessly manipulating his shadows into a terrifying weapon while simultaneously using his sword to dispatch his enemies. It was a sight to behold, his movements swift and his bulging muscles on display as he cut through the air, steel and shadows moving in tandem.

A beat of worry overwhelmed her mate bond, and Lea moved toward Gray, sensing he was distracted by his need to protect her. She'd almost reached him when a scream rang out that made her blood run cold. It was the scream of a child—a small one.

Scanning her surroundings, Lea searched for the noise. To her left, a tiny girl stood on the hill behind a home with a shattered front door, the beautiful painted wood in splinters across the front porch and grass. The child was barefoot, looking side to side with wide eyes and walking away from the battle toward the woods behind the houses, with red cheeks and tears so large Lea could see them streaming down her face, even from this distance.

Something exploded in Lea's chest—bravery or foolishness, she wasn't sure—but she didn't have time to examine the feeling. She *had* to help the little girl, refused to let her get hurt, or worse. Lea sprinted toward the child, stumbling over the sharp pieces of broken fence scattered along the ground and trudging up the hill. She scooped up the shivering and sobbing toddler moments before she stepped into the dark, overgrown woods and tucked the girl into her chest. "Shhhh, it's okay now. Let's find your mom, hmm?" she cooed, feigning confidence with a broad smile as she bounced the girl up and down.

"I have her! A little girl! I found her!" Lea shouted as she scanned the village, unsure where the girl's mother was, but hoping she would hear her cries. Her shouts were muffled in the chaos of battle, so Lea walked further up the small hill to allow her a better vantage point. Surely the mother would be frantically searching for her child and would be easy to pick out.

Lea took one step, then froze. Above her, hiding in the dark, dense trees where the woods began, was Alaric. He stood still as stone, only his lips moving as he spoke under his breath. His eyes were manic, full of flames and chaos as he held his hands out toward her. It appeared as if Alaric was in a trance, almost like he was under some sort of spell.

Lea backed away on shaking legs as she pulled the child closer against her chest, which grew tight with pressure and fear. Alaric stopped chanting, and his lips curled, white teeth flashing—but in a smile or a snarl, she couldn't tell.

A cry of terror caused Lea to look behind her on instinct as a familiar voice begged for help. Still hiding behind the rickety white fence, Emma crouched on her knees, her hands covering her ears, her eyes closed tight.

"Leave me alone! Someone make it stop!" Emma screeched.

Lea turned back to Alaric, but he was gone—the smoking leaves on the ground the only evidence that he had been there at all.

Emma shrieked again, and Lea turned, racing toward her, eyes scanning for whatever threat had Emma in such a panic. Her palms were sweaty and her stomach hollow as she reached her friend. Gray's shadows followed and circled around them protectively.

Across the town square and through the remaining rebels and royal guards, Lea made eye contact with Gray. He fought his way closer, striking down guard after guard with one eye on Lea the entire time.

"We need to find her mother!" Lea called to Gray, unable to tear herself away from her friend but knowing that the child was terrified as her tiny body trembled. He nodded, whistling to a nearby soldier and barking orders at him. Gray gestured to the soldier, and Lea handed the toddler off to him, ruffling her hair and pasting a calm smile on her face before the child was pulled away.

With the little girl taken care of, Lea collapsed next to her friend, grabbing her arms. "Emma? What's wrong?" Lea pulled Emma's hands away from her ears, only to be met with eyes so wide her pupils looked like pinpoints.

"They're everywhere, Lea. Everywhere!" Emma screamed, completely in a panic as her eyes jumped all around them. Lea followed Emma's line of sight, confused. The guards had begun to dwindle in numbers. As the battle had raged, so many villagers had joined the rebels in their fight that their numbers had grown exponentially. Gray had caused a wave of death as guards had climbed the castle walls and tried to chase the rebellion, and many of the royal guards had either turned back as they'd witnessed Gray's rampage or had fallen victim to it. The majority of the rebels had escaped into the woods, and some villagers were fleeing toward the woods with small bags in their arms.

"We'll beat the guards, Emma. I know it looks like there are a lot of them, but most have fled or been killed and—"

"I'm not talking about the guards!" Emma sobbed, tears streaming down her face and snot running from her nose as she squeezed her eyes closed tight again, her forehead wrinkling with the effort. "I'm talking about the dead, Lea. I can hear them. I can see them. I can see them *everywhere.*"

CHAPTER 3

LEA

Lea's head swung around so fast that a stabbing pain shot through her neck. *What does she mean, the dead are everywhere?*

There were a few bodies lying in the streets, barely visible through the silver and gold light from the fires and moon. Several dozen royal guards lay dead behind them where Gray fought against the onslaught of men climbing over the castle wall, but his shadows were so thick that it was difficult to see them.

A lantern swinging in the wind crashed to the ground, and Lea flinched at the harsh sound as its fire spread to a nearby patch of grass, illuminating a nearby body—a rebel with a red armband. He was young, and blood dribbled from the corner of his mouth as his glazed eyes stared unfocused at the stars.

A sharp ache hit her gut, and bile rose up the back of her throat as she looked at the broken bodies around her. The smell of death hung in the air, the iron tang of blood hitting her nostrils and making her nauseous. Of course her friend was upset. It was gruesome, terrible in a way that Lea knew she would never be able to forget. But...what did Emma mean she could *hear* them?

Emma had always been in tune with others' emotions. From the moment Lea had met her, she'd been oddly aware of how Lea was feeling. She could always tell what she needed and gladly gave it to her, whether it was space, a laugh, or a shoulder to cry on. It was something Lea had noticed immediately and had been grateful for. She was a remarkable friend. Surely it was just her empathy causing her alarm. It was too much carnage for almost anyone to handle, let alone such a sensitive soul.

"Emma. Close your eyes if you can't look. I'll help get you out of here."

"They're looking at me!" Emma shrieked, her face so pale that the dark circles under her eyes almost looked like bruises. "Make them stop looking at me!" Emma was panicking, rocking back and forth, her bloodshot eyes wide and terrified before she squeezed them shut again to block out the world around her.

"What are you talking about?" Lea could feel the panic creeping into her own voice as she watched her friend seem to curl deeper inside herself. "What do you need?"

"I don't want to see them anymore!" Emma cried. Suddenly, a pair of dainty hands appeared on Emma's upper arms.

"What's happening to her?" Claire asked, soot smudged across her face. *Is Claire part of the rebellion?* Lea had barely seen her since she'd insinuated that Lea was lucky that both of the princes were preoccupied with her... even though one of those prince's attention consisted purely of pain and threats of death. So why was she here now? Claire was far too selfish to risk her life to help those living outside the castle or to fight against the Black King's reign. She was too self-serving. Too... cruel. Certainly, she'd never seemed to really care about Emma, or any of the other servants, for that matter. Lea's suspicions rose. Was it possible she was working with Alaric?

"I don't know," Lea said sharply. "What are you doing here, anyway?"

"I'm fucking leaving with you all. What do you think I'm doing? Emma, get up," Claire spat as if Emma's fear disgusted her. She shook Emma's small, trembling body. "We need to go. The king is on his way."

Emma cried out, tucking her knees beneath her chin and squeezing her eyes more firmly shut.

"Stop!" Lea roughly pulled Claire's hands away from Emma's arms, stepping in front of her to protect her from Claire's less-than-gentle attempt at helping. "You'll hurt her. She's in shock!" Lea's eyes bounced between her mate still fighting a handful of guards and her friend crumpled on the ground, knowing that Emma needed to get to safety or she would be a sitting target for the few royal soldiers that did remain. But she didn't want to leave Gray. Not again.

"How do you know the king is coming?" Lea asked.

"The soldiers running back into the castle were whispering about it. Thank the gods it's night, or I wouldn't be able to hear so far." Claire tapped her ears. "They didn't want to die. Said if the king wanted his son dead, he could do it himself. Now let's move."

Claire has magic? Or is it a trick? "Shit." Lea hissed as she searched for Thomas. He'd be strong enough to carry Emma to safety. Her eyes scanned the streets, heart clenching in fear when she couldn't find him. *Thomas is okay. He must have already made it through town,* she told herself. Taking a deep breath, she turned back to Emma, trying to make a new plan.

Lea could feel Gray's eyes on her as he fought, could sense his gaze sweeping across her body every time he spun and turned, watching over her and assessing for danger. He moved with the grace of a dancer, somehow picking up an older guard with his shadows and throwing him into a patch of fire while simultaneously slicing another man's leg clean off with a single swipe. But even with his superhuman strength and speed, he wasn't invincible. A small cut marred his left cheek, already scabbing over. His shirtsleeve was torn and he was covered in blood splatter—though how much was his, she wasn't sure.

Lea's gut squeezed as Emma let out another soul-shattering scream, so loud Lea was sure that her throat would be raw by morning. *I need to get her out of here.* She looked over her shoulder at Gray, tilting her head toward Emma.

He nodded to her. "I'll be right behind you." Her mate's eyes briefly left hers. "Erik!" he barked. "Take Emma and Lea to the meeting point! I'll find you there!"

Erik scooped up Emma as Janelle stumbled over to them, grabbing Erik's arm. Her eyes were full of pain, her blistered skin now opening and weeping.

Lea reached out to heal Janelle's arm, but before she had a chance, Erik's eyes settled on the burn, flashing with concern as he placed his hand on her injury. The stiffness of Janelle's posture eased as the pain faded and her skin knitted back together. Her arm turned a soft pink, almost good as new, but Lea felt guilt heavy in the back of her throat that she had been the one to cause Janelle that agony.

Janelle placed a hand over Erik's, a silent moment passing between them before she turned back to Lea and pointed to a dark, foot-worn path that wrapped around an old, weathered house. "You need to go around there, behind the tavern. You won't make it if you run straight through town."

Lea turned to look through the village. The streets leading toward the woods were nearly empty now. But who knew what was hiding behind the houses and shops lining the bloody cobblestone street? Alaric could be waiting, or soldiers could be hiding in the shadows behind the houses, preparing to catch those trying to flee.

"The fastest way is straight to the forest." Lea hesitated, narrowing her eyes as her confidence faltered. "I don't know what's happening with Emma, but something isn't right. We need to get her away from here, now."

"If you want to get her out of here fast and *alive*, we need to go this way." Janelle threw her arm backward to point past the dark houses. "We've done things your way until now, and I'm not afraid to tell you that not all your choices have been the right ones. Once again, you're not the only one who loves these people! I do, too. And it's time you listen to me."

Lea's eyes flicked to Emma, who was cradled against Erik's chest, her eyes still shut tight with her hands pressed against her ears. Worry gnawed at her gut, sweat beading on the back of her neck. It went against every instinct to go where Janelle was leading them, where there were far more places to hide and limited sight, where Alaric may be lurking—waiting.

The woods were dark, the gnarled trees threatening in a way she couldn't describe. Was it just fear making her see things? Surely Alaric wouldn't have been so close and allowed her to escape unscathed. But she had seen him—felt his unadulterated rage and fury.

Still, Janelle had never been caught. Not once. And Gray had told them that Janelle would lead them to safety. If Alaric were hiding in their path, Janelle would sense it.

Lea grabbed her friend's hand. "Lead the way." She positioned herself behind Janelle, pushing down her pride and fear, and following her best friend.

Janelle didn't hesitate, turning on her heel and sprinting toward the tavern they'd visited only a few weeks ago, the night Thomas had abandoned them to meet with Vincent. At the time, Lea had been certain he was the Eclipsed King.

The tavern looked the same, except now, the roof was on fire. It appeared the grass that had adorned it had dried from the summer heat, creating perfect kindling to ignite the building amidst the chaos.

Heat kissed the side of Lea's face as they continued to run, darting around the tavern and up the hill before ducking down to squat behind a crop of pointed rocks. Flames flickered off Janelle's face as she thought about their next move, reminding Lea of the many Fire Nights they'd spent together back home, when all they'd cared about was the wine they were drinking and what they would wish for at sunset. How had their lives come to this so quickly?

"We need to wait. Not long, just a minute or two," Janelle whispered as she held a hand up, eyes still scanning the trees and buildings around them.

Lea glanced at the fire spreading closer to them by the second. Her heart pumped harder in fear as smoke rose toward the sky. Scooting back, she sent out a stream of shadows in an attempt to block the flames from advancing toward them. "Janelle, are you sure—"

"Do not finish that question, Azalea. And stop distracting me," Janelle snapped.

Claire shifted, restless as the heat of the fire grew warmer. "Let's go already. We're going to get burned alive."

"Just WAIT!" Janelle hissed, her shoulders rising angrily. Erik placed a hand on her arm, and Janelle leaned into his touch, but her eyes never stopped evaluating their surroundings.

Claire peeked out from behind the rock. "I don't see anyone, and I didn't flee the castle just so I could burn to death right outside it. Let's fucking *go*." She stood from their hiding place, taking one single step forward before an arrow embedded itself deep into her throat. Blood gurgled from the wound and out of her mouth as she stumbled and crashed to the ground with a *thud*, a sickening sound that would haunt Lea's dreams for the rest of her life.

Erik placed Emma on the ground and sprang forward before they could even react. Pulling his sword from its sheath he ran ahead, dodging arrows with ease as they flew straight at his chest. They bounced on the ground as they missed him, and Lea picked one up to examine it. It was long, made of dark wood with a deadly iron tip and midnight blue feathers at its end.

Erik twisted as a twin arrow flew directly past his throat, watching as it struck the rock they were using for cover, inches between Janelle and Lea's heads. A soldier stepped from the treeline—a boy no older than twenty—likely attempting to get a clearer shot. In an instant, Erik set his wooden bow aflame. Fire engulfed the soldier's hands. He screamed as he turned to flee, but there was no escape. Erik killed him swiftly with a slash of his sword to the young soldier's neck before he'd even fully turned, his head severing from his body in one powerful swipe.

Why is it always the head? Lea thought as the urge to vomit into the grass filled her belly.

Blood soaked the ground as Erik held his hands in front of him, sending flames shooting toward the dead guard. It was unnecessary. His spirit was already on its way somewhere beyond the veil, but Erik continued to funnel the might of his power into the corpse at his feet. His muscles were tight as his face reddened with the effort, a look in his eyes Lea had never seen from him before.

"Gods help whoever tries to hurt her..." he whispered to the corpse, the wind carrying his threat to Lea's ears; words spoken softly, darkly, before Erik pulled his flames back inside himself.

Erik ran back to them but stopped abruptly, his eyes wide and face creased with concern. Lea turned, jumping to her feet when she saw Emma standing above Claire's body, her shaking hands held out in front of her.

"There's nothing I can do!" Emma howled at the empty air in front of her, pausing for several seconds before continuing to speak. "I don't know! I can't help you!"

"Hey!" Lea grabbed Emma's face and turned it, forcing her to meet her eyes. "What is happening, Emma? Tell me what you're seeing." Never in her life had Lea seen such terror, such *horror* in someone's eyes. They were bloodshot, wide and frantic.

"Make her stop. *Please*!" she begged.

Tears spilled across Emma's cheeks, tracks of sorrow trailing down her delicate face as Erik returned to them, walking to Janelle and leaning forward to speak into her ear. Did he know what was happening? "Erik, what's—"

"It's Claire," Emma sobbed, grabbing at the sleeves of Lea's smoke stained wedding dress. "She wants me to bring her back! But, I can't! I *can't*!" she shrieked at Claire's body before crumpling into Lea's arms. "I don't know how. Just tell her I can't, Lea."

Lea and Erik shared a look as he moved to grab her again. They needed to get her to safety, but Emma abruptly jumped away, letting out a blood-curdling scream. "I said I *can't*! Don't touch me!" Emma howled as her eyes rolled back into her head and she collapsed. Erik caught her before she could hit the ground and lifted her to his chest. His eyes turned to Lea's for guidance. "What should we do?"

Janelle's head whipped backward to look behind them. "No time for that. Someone's coming. *Run!*"

Without hesitation, they took off, following behind Janelle with complete trust. Lea looked behind her once more at Claire's lifeless body, the flames from battle now licking at her boots as she lay alone in the blood-drenched grass. She hadn't liked her, certainly hadn't trusted her, but Lea was surprised at the sharp sting of sadness she felt at seeing her dead.

This wasn't the first death of the war, but it was the first death of someone she *knew*, someone whose name she had spoken. The thought brought tears to her eyes, her chest burning and making it difficult to breathe. She'd willingly joined the rebellion tonight—and she didn't regret it. But could she survive this war if it meant that all the people she loved might not?

CHAPTER 4

LEA

The night had somehow grown darker, as if the stars had been unable to witness the bloodshed and had hidden beneath a thick sheet of clouds. Lea, Janelle, and Erik stumbled through the pitch black forest, Erik somehow holding Emma tight as they tripped over gnarled roots that seemed to reach toward their feet in an effort to stop their escape. Lea's lungs burned as the scent of smoke and death from the village turned into the damp, earthy odor of the woods, each breath sending pinpricks of fire through her airways. Sweat dripped down her back as she followed behind Janelle, eyes scanning the dark shadows around them for threats.

While every step separated Lea from Gray a little bit more, she kept her connection to him open, searching deep into the corners of their bond for clues to his emotions. Would he be able to find her? She couldn't see any sort of sensible path they were following, now at Erik's lead, but surely Gray would be able to feel her through their bond at the very least. Digging deep, she found the resolve to push through their connection that she was safe. His need for her pulsed against her heart in response—worry that she was running through the dark without him, anxiety that she wouldn't make it safely, followed by a calm wave of reassurance. *You are powerful,* it seemed to say to her. *You will not be defeated*. His confidence in Lea bolstered her movements, sending a zap of energy through her limbs.

Their pace was clipped as they moved deeper into the bowels of the forest. Pumping her legs harder, Lea tried to ignore the burning in her muscles. She'd need to work on her endurance if they'd be traveling all the way to Calir, a journey that would take *weeks*. Escaping the castle was only the beginning. A stab of worry gnawed at Lea's stomach—if she couldn't run through one village without her body feeling exhausted, how were they going to make it to an entirely different kingdom?

Breathing through the pain, Lea focused on the ancient trees enveloping them. They had to be thousands of years old, Lea guessed, based on their size. Their rough, bark-covered trunks were so thick she didn't think that even the four of them could reach all the way around them hand in hand.

Erik turned abruptly to his left, changing course as he passed through a gap between two enormous trunks. He paused, ushering them through the narrow opening before following behind. A brush of power washed over Lea's body—the whisper of something *other* that danced across her skin and spoke to her own magic coiled behind her breastbone.

The rush caused her to stumble, and she tripped, flying into a large clearing filled with rebels. Some were huddled in groups speaking with lowered heads and hushed whispers, while others sat nursing minor injuries near the small fires dotting the open area, providing warmth and a soft, flickering light. None, at least that she could see, appeared gravely injured, but several men and women had blood-soaked patches on their tunics and lacerations on their faces and arms.

No less than forty of the gigantic trees surrounded them, grown so tightly together she doubted she could fit an arm in the gaps between their trunks. They were so tall that she had to crane her head back to look at their canopies, where star-shaped leaves in different shades of deep green rustled in the wind. Along the back of the enormous clearing were more than a dozen horses, fully packed with what she assumed were supplies and weapons. *How long have they been preparing for tonight?*

Safe for the moment, Lea allowed her body to relax, stretching the tight muscles of her neck and arms as she looked toward the entrance. Gray would be here soon. He had to be.

Gray... The air was ripped violently from Lea's lungs. She threw a hand to her heart, and panic filled her chest as she realized her connection to her mate had been severed. She couldn't feel him. *Why can't I feel him?*

Images of Gray lying on the ground, his eyes glazing over as fire burned around him, flashed through her mind. If she couldn't feel him, did it mean... *No. It can't.* A sob tore from Lea's throat as she turned around, tensing her muscles as she prepared her body to sprint back toward town, toward the battle where she had once again left him fighting alone, but a large hand wrapped around her biceps, stopping her.

Erik turned her to face him, and his eyebrows lowered in concern. "Stop right there. I know what you're thinking. He's fine, Sunshine." Erik leaned down to eye level. "Gray enchanted this place himself. No magic can travel through those trees. Not even the bond you're searching for."

Erik's eyes were kind, his anger from earlier only a memory as he gave her a small, reassuring smile. "He'll feel the loss as well and know that you're here safe. It will allow him to concentrate on ending the battle and returning to you."

Lea sucked in a deep breath, nodding as she wiped her eyes with the heel of her hand. *He's fine.* The words became a chant, thumping again and again through her mind along with the rhythm of her racing heart.

"Now," Erik pulled her against his side, "Here's your second lesson. You are strong. This is not the first time we will face combat. Gray is not the type to leave men behind. You might have to leave him, but he will always find you, Sunshine."

Lea's heart slowed, the furious pounding she had felt in her chest easing as she absorbed his words. A shimmering veil sparkled along the border of the trees, so subtle she wasn't surprised she hadn't noticed it in her panic. It was the same magic that had guarded them in the dungeons, the same rush of power that had washed over her as she'd run into the clearing. *Gray will be here soon.* The thought brought her peace. All she could do now was wait for him.

"Good," Erik said as he watched the tension ease from her shoulders. "These people might not know it yet, but you are their queen. After they find out that Gray is behind this movement, they'll be watching your every move, so you better start practicing maintaining a calm exterior. My guess is that they won't trust Gray right away. He's done too good a job pretending to be as wicked as Brennus. But you're one of them. Show them you trust him, and they will follow your lead." Erik clapped her on the shoulder, almost knocking her over before leaving her alone with her thoughts.

Their queen? Lea's heart thumped faster as she schooled her face into a calm expression. It was ridiculous, but if Erik was right and the rebels would be looking to her to decide whether or not to trust Gray, then she needed to remain calm. Forcing herself to turn from the opening between the trees, she peeled her eyes from the place she so desperately hoped to see Gray's enormous, angry form storm through. *I need to busy myself,* she thought. She couldn't do anything to help her mate right now, but she could help Emma.

Among the groups of rebels, Emma was sitting on the hard ground with her knees to her chest. Her face was as pale as the ghosts she claimed to have seen, and she was muttering under her breath with wide, terrified eyes. It sent a shiver through Lea, the idea that spirits might be around them at any moment without their knowledge.

Kneeling next to her was Thomas, and Lea let loose a rattling breath. She hadn't known exactly what had happened to him during the battle, but here he was, in one piece, with no visible injuries. A tiny bit of tension faded from the knot in her stomach as she reveled in the fact that all of her friends were here in the safety of Gray's enchanted hideout.

Lea's heart warmed as she watched Thomas whispering softly to Emma, one hand cupping her cheek as he gently stroked her face with his thumb. Emma appeared to know Thomas was there by the way she leaned ever so slightly toward him. It was an intimate gesture, one she recognized from all the times Thomas had comforted her over the years, and she turned away to give them a moment of privacy.

"Lea," Thomas called, pulling Emma closer. "What happened to her?"

Emma kept her eyes downcast, rocking slightly within the circle of Thomas's arms as she continued to speak to herself.

"Go away. Go away. No, no, no. I don't want to see them again." She muttered, the words nonsensical and her eyes out of focus as if reliving another moment in time.

"Emma?" Lea prodded gently, her voice quiet. But her friend closed her eyes, continuing her rocking.

"Oh my girl, what did you see?" Elise's voice cut through Emma's panicked state as she ran into the clearing and straight to her daughter, kneeling in front of her and grasping her hands. "It happened again, didn't it, my love?"

The spell controlling Emma was shattered as she launched herself into her mother's arms, a devastating sob ripping from her throat as they collapsed together in the soft grass. "Mom! You're here!"

Lea let loose a breath. *Thank the gods.* Elise was here. She would get through to Emma.

"Of course I'm here," Elise soothed as she rubbed Emma's back. "You think I don't know everything that happens in the castle? I can't believe you thought for a single second that I would let you leave without me."

Lea's heart clenched and stuttered, relief that Emma's mother was there butting up against the sorrow of watching her friend suffering clashing in her chest. If only there was a way to take Emma's pain away,

Lea would do it without hesitation. Instead, she took a step back and allowed Elise to comfort her daughter.

"I saw them, Mom. All of them. Claire. The guards," she heaved through tears. "And they *knew* I could see them. They were reaching out to me, begging for help."

"We knew that was a possibility, my love," Elise said, stroking her daughter's face. "We knew it might happen again."

"It *can't*." Emma placed her head in her trembling hands. "*I* can't. I'm not strong enough for this."

"Nonsense," Elise replied, far more sternly than Lea had ever heard her speak. "You are my daughter. I raised you to be kind, and I raised you to be *strong*. There is no weakness in fear, my love. You were given this gift by the gods themselves. Only *you*. It is an insult to them to say that you are not powerful enough to wield it."

A sob burst from Emma's throat, and Elise soothed her hair and whispered soft words of comfort to her daughter.

"Elise," Lea said quietly. "What's happening? How can we help?"

The small Fae looked up at Lea, a brave face attempting to hide the unending worry of motherhood. "As you know, Emma is part Fae."

Lea nodded. She hadn't known for sure how much Fae blood Emma had. It wasn't something they'd discussed, but it stood to reason that, despite Elise being full Fae, Emma was at least part human due to her slightly clumsy nature. She was beautiful in the way of the Fae, delicate and willowy, with smooth, light-brown skin, large eyes, and shiny, curly black hair. But she had never mentioned her father, and it hadn't been something that Lea had cared about. Fae or not, Emma was caring and thoughtful. A one-of-a-kind friend. That was all that mattered to Lea.

"And you also know that, with the king so near, having magic at your disposal is dangerous. *Especially* if yours is a talent that is exceedingly rare." Elise looked around as if still afraid of the king's reach, despite the fact that she was surrounded by those filled with the desire to kill him and end his reign.

"Emma has magic?" Lea asked breathlessly, almost hurt. Had Emma not trusted her to keep her secret safe? But then, Lea hadn't been forthright with Emma about her own abilities, either. Guilt burrowed deep into her belly.

"It appears she does, though we weren't positive. And regardless, her gift isn't one that we wanted to experiment with." Elise tenderly brushed Emma's hair back from her eyes, pausing before continuing to speak. "Years ago, a stable boy fell off his horse. It was spooked by a snake in the grass—an unfortunate accident, throwing the boy onto his neck."

Emma winced as Elise spoke about the child, leaning further into her mother, who immediately began to rub her back. "It's okay, my love." Elise turned back to Lea. "Emma was with me on a walk, only a child."

Emma sniffled, sitting up slowly, and wiping her nose on her sleeve. "I heard his neck snap," she whispered, still clinging to her mother desperately, as if she were the only thing holding her together. "And then I watched his spirit rise from his small, broken body. He sobbed for his mother, begged me to go get her." Tears streamed from her swollen eyes, the sorrow from the memory ingrained in every breath. "I didn't know what to do. So I just—I froze. I just stood there while the boy sobbed and begged for me to help him. I did nothing as he slowly faded away into the wind. It's the only death I have seen, until today. And I will never forgive my own cowardice. I had hoped—" her words were cut off by another sob, and Elise brushed the tears from her face as she comforted her daughter.

"We had hoped," Elise continued, "that it was her imagination. Or a trick of the mind. That maybe the boy had magic himself, projecting his spirit to her in his death. But I always had a feeling." She nodded at her daughter. "She has a gift. Her empathy and ability to see a person's deepest fears and worries and needs... It is not just kindness. She is seeing the very souls that inhabit the bodies we dwell in. In life, *and* in death."

CHAPTER 5

GRAY

The last of the rebellion—*his* rebellion—disappeared into the dense line of trees beyond the city of Auropera as Gray knocked the sword from a young guard's hand. A soldier named Noah that Gray recognized as one of his soldiers knelt at his feet, hands above him in surrender. Gray had considered him for the rebellion on more than one occasion, but something had held him back. Perhaps it was the fact that he looked as if he had just left childhood, and Gray had no way of knowing if this was a battle his soldiers would walk away from. Or maybe it was because he saw something of himself in the boy. Not as he was now, of course, but when he'd been young and naïve—innocent and *good*.

Noah was wet behind the ears and human, but his bravery was obvious. He was the only remaining guard alive on the streets of Auropera, yet his sword was free of blood. He hadn't killed any rebels. *So why is he here?*

The rest of the guards had fled once they'd realized they had no chance of defeating him. A few of his rebels had spread the rumor that the king was on his way—a lie that had caused both his men and the royal guards to flee in fear. Gray, however, knew the truth. The king would have locked himself in his chamber the moment he'd been informed of the explosion in an attempt to save his own skin. But the soldiers didn't know that. They feared Gray, as well as the king, and so they had fled.

Many of Brennus Nestruir's soldiers would seek to join the rebellion in the coming months, Gray expected. Most of the guards had joined the Royal Army for no other purpose than providing for their families back home, their pay allowing for a roof over their heads and food in their bellies. It wasn't loyalty to the cause that had led them to enlist—a fact he would certainly use to his advantage.

Gray's blade pressed harder against the boy's neck, a drop of deep red blood trickling from the small nick. "Where is Alaric? Who gave you your orders?"

Noah's eyes widened. "I—I don't know. We heard the explosion, and we ran to the gates. Prince Alaric found us, told us that to allow you to leave would be to commit treason to the Crown."

Holding his sword firmly against Noah's neck, Gray took a moment to assess him. His body trembled, but he kept his chin high and his eyes locked on Gray's. A mixture of sadness and concern churned in his stomach. He didn't want to kill the young soldier, one who hadn't raised his weapon to harm a single rebel. But at the same time, he couldn't risk bringing anyone with even an ounce of loyalty to his father or brother with him. "And what do you think, Noah?" Gray finally asked.

The boy froze, his brow furrowing.

"Oh yes, I know who you are. Noah Copperton. Human. Eighteen years old. One living parent and three younger sisters. Did I miss anything?"

"No, Commander. But... How do you know—"

"Alaric thinks the army you saw fighting along with me are traitors to the Crown." Gray angled the sword up, raising Noah's chin to meet his gaze, and a fresh dribble of blood spilled from his neck. "I'd like to know. What do *you* think?"

The boy's hands shook as he held them above his head, his arms clearly fatigued from holding them up after carrying his sword during the battle. "I—"

Fire blazed from Gray's left, a sudden surge in the low flames that had been slowly spreading across the dried grass bursting into an inferno that caused his metal breastplate to warm to nearly burning. Gray twisted toward the explosion of fire as a shard of familiar hatred wedged between his ribs. *Alaric.*

"And why, Evander, would it matter if the human believes they are treasonous or not?" Alaric hissed as he emerged through the flames. "Is *he* the future leader of this kingdom? Or is he a soldier whose sole purpose is to follow *my* orders?"

Gray pulled his sword away from Noah's neck and held it out in front of him toward Alaric. "Surprised, brother?" Gray asked with a forced smile as he pulled his shadows from inside his chest and allowed them to burst free. Their long black tendrils snaked along the ground toward Alaric, blending in with the smoke billowing from the grass.

"Surprised?" Alaric threw his head back and cackled, but there was no humor in his eyes. "That you're the Eclipsed King? No." He waved a hand flippantly. "Nothing you could do could ever surprise me. It seems you're not as interesting as you've allowed yourself to believe, nor as discreet."

"You're a terrible liar, you know," Gray said, his taunting tone digging into Alaric's old wounds. It was an old trick of his. Belittle him, poke at his weaknesses, and Alaric would make mistakes in his blind fury. "If you knew I was leading a rebellion, why wouldn't you try to stop me? No. I don't think you're smart enough to have foreseen this."

Flames danced along Alaric's fingertips, a lazy motion, as if he was completely unfazed and unbothered by Gray's comments, but Gray didn't miss how the fire whipped violently as Alaric's jaw clenched. "Well, you've revealed yourself now. Along with every member of your little gang. You know, Father is very unhappy with you and your treasonous band of misfits." Alaric's facade slipped as his eyes flashed black and red. "I've spent my whole life trying to show him your true character. And now? You've done my work for me." He laughed again, an unhinged, terrifying sound. "You've given me the chance to save the day.

I now have the information I need to destroy the rebellion. And more importantly, to destroy *you*. I should thank you, really."

Anger flared within Gray at the callous way Alaric spoke of slaughtering the brave men and women who had pledged to fight alongside him. "You know nothing. Even if you did, I'd rip the tongue from between your teeth before I'd allow you to defeat us. I will kill you, Alaric."

The prince stalked toward Gray, pulling his sword from its sheath. "An interesting threat, when I cannot be killed by your hand. Nor you by mine." A wicked smile crossed his face. "Shame you'll soon find that the same cannot be said for your *mate*."

"You do not speak of her!" Gray seethed. "The curse will be broken, and I *will* kill you. And I'll do it the most painful, horrific way I can imagine. I've had plenty of time to fantasize about how you'll take your last breath, Alaric."

"Not before your *Little Flower* does," Alaric sneered.

Gray lunged with a roar, his sword rising in an arc as it struck with an ear splitting clang against his brother's. Blow for blow, they met each other in speed and strength. Equals in battle, as it had been their entire lives. Where Gray thrust, Alaric blocked. When Alaric swung, Gray ducked. Back and forth they went as storm clouds grew in the sky. Gray's one advantage.

Alaric couldn't use his fire while wielding a sword. Not that it wasn't possible, but he lacked the concentration and mental fortitude to juggle the two tasks. But Gray had practiced that exact thing. He had spent countless hours honing his magic into a weapon that could not be easily conquered. Lightning flashed above their heads, its power growing with each strike, building along with his fury.

"Even your lightning won't protect your mate when I take her. Tell me, does she make the same sounds when she comes as she did when I burned her flesh beneath my fingertips? Those gasps frequent my dreams, little brother."

Wrath—unlike anything Gray had felt before—flared in his chest. He lost control of his power as he went nearly blind with rage. It was only for a second, but it was enough for him to lose focus and slow his movements. Seeing an opening, Alaric struck, his sharp, fiery blade sliding against Gray's wrist. Blood spurted from the wound, deep enough that the tendons in his thumb severed with a snap. The sword fell from his hand as Alaric lunged for his knees, slicing through muscle and sinew as if it was nothing more than warm butter. Gray fell to the ground, blood running down his leg and staining the grass beneath him.

A sudden jolt of power ricocheted through Gray's chest, far more intense than the pain from his hand and legs. His bond to Lea stretched tight before disappearing altogether. *She's safe.*

A smile crossed Gray's lips as the tip of Alaric's sword kissed his cheek, digging into his flesh just underneath his orbital bone. He could take the pain from the cut of a blade as long as he knew that his mate was out of danger.

"So easy to distract. A single threat to that little mate of yours. A human," he laughed. "A *no one.* An embarrassment. And you allow me the upper hand."

"I would find a way to kill us both before I would allow you to harm her." Gray spit blood at his brother's feet.

"It will be me who draws the last breath from her pretty lips. That alone will kill you—"

A *crack* rang out across the square, blood blooming on Alaric's temple as he crumbled to the ground. Behind him stood Noah, clutching an iron-plated shield in his white-knuckled grip. The boy froze for a second, staring at the blood dripping from Alaric's head before throwing the shield to the ground.

"I fucking hate that guy," he spat, reaching down to help Gray to his feet.

Gray rose with a groan, his muscles already knitting back together. Noah handed Gray his sword before kneeling again and placing his hands back above his head.

Gray looked down at Noah, impressed by his courage. "Do you hate the king equally?" he asked casually as he wiped the blood from his face.

Noah looked around silently, as if anxious to speak the words out loud. He nodded. "Let me join you."

Considering his plea, Gray's eyes swept over the boy. There wasn't a whisker on his face, and his muscles were underdeveloped with his youth. His eyes were gentle, like they'd never witnessed violence before this day. "Why did you join the Royal Army?" Gray prodded.

The boy swallowed, pausing before he slowly stood. "If, as I suspect, you are the Eclipsed King," he placed a hand over his heart, thumb tucked into his palm, "then I joined to find you."

CHAPTER 6

GRAY

"To find me?" Gray repeated. How could Noah possibly know he was the Eclipsed King when he could count the number of people who knew his true identity on one hand?

"I'd heard whispers back home, but no one would tell me more. After my father died—"

"Paul," Gray said his name like a eulogy. He remembered when he'd died, leaving Noah's family destitute.

"Yes." Noah's face crumpled. "He died in the fields after being worked to the bone. I lost my youth the day I lost him. It was heatstroke, when I was thirteen years old. He was just trying to harvest enough crops to supply the Black King with cotton and wheat. More and more every year, even as he aged and required more rest. My parents," the boy's voice broke, "they wanted me and my sisters to be educated. Wouldn't allow me to stay home to help my father in the fields. I wrote to the king, begged him to reduce his tithe or let him retire. The letter that was returned demanded double. He died three weeks later."

Gray watched the young man before him try to remain strong, his shoulders squared and the tears in his eyes staying firmly within the bounds of his eyelids. "And why is it you think I'm the Eclipsed King?" Every fiber of Gray's being told him the boy was trustworthy, but the fact that he knew his true identity gave him pause. Was it a trap? Had Alaric known all along?

"I saw you. The week after Father died. I was sitting in a tree near my porch, had been for hours. I couldn't listen to my mother cry for another second. The moon was out, so I saw it clearly when you dropped a satchel near my front door. You were only there for seconds, but the first time I saw you at the castle, I knew it was you."

Gray's mouth went dry, and he struggled to swallow.

"I was scared you'd left something horrible. Something that would upset Mother even more. So I ran to the porch the second you disappeared. But it was gold." Noah's eyes glistened. "A bag full of gold. Enough to feed us and clothe us for *years*. I enlisted into the Royal Army at 16 after hearing whispers of the Eclipsed King, and have tried to work my way up the ranks as quickly as I could to find a way into the rebellion. I've been watching you. You disappear at the strangest times, and you're always writing things down. You have a reputation for the horrible things you've done, but I've never witnessed anything but you doing the just and honorable thing." Noah didn't flinch as he stared the Night Prince directly in the eyes. "I know who you are. And if you'll allow it, I'd like to fight for my father. For every subject of this kingdom worked into their own grave to serve their selfish leader." He stood up taller, banishing the grief from his face. "Please."

Pride swelled in Gray's chest. How he had missed the heart of a lion beating in Noah's chest, he wasn't sure, but he could recognize when he made a mistake. The boy may be young, but he wished to fight this battle with the vigor of Vincent, of Thomas.

"Have you told anyone what you know?" Gray asked.

"I've kept it between myself and the gods," Noah promised, tucking his thumb and placing his fist over his heart.

Gray sheathed his sword as Alaric stirred. "I'd be honored to fight alongside you, Noah." Alaric moaned and turned his head slightly. Gray wished he could sever his head from his body, or plunge a dagger into his wicked heart. But he could feel the curse wrapping around his chest, squeezing until he took a step back. If only Noah would do it of his own volition, he could win what would be one of the biggest battles of the war. Gray's tongue grew thick and painful at the thought, his jaw clenching as the words filled his mind. The curse wouldn't even allow him to ask another to perform the deed.

Noah kept his eyes on Alaric, and Gray wondered what he was thinking. Was he considering killing the Crown Prince of Desia, now that he'd confirmed that Gray was fighting against him? Picking up his discarded sword in a white-knuckled grip, Noah lifted it a few inches, sweat dripping from his hairline. *Do it,* Gray thought, unable to give voice to his order.

Noah's skin paled and his eyes shot to Gray, his eyebrows raised in question. Had he not heard Alaric say that Gray couldn't kill him? Was he waiting for Gray to cut off Alaric's head just as Gray wondered what was stopping Noah?

Alaric moaned again, rolling onto his side. *Dammit!* Alaric couldn't follow them. They were out of time.

"We need to go." Gray called on his storms again as he turned to run. He urged Noah forward and sent thick sheets of rain down around them. Gray held his lightning at bay to prevent Alaric from getting a flash of where they were running, should he fully wake from his unconscious state before they cleared the village.

They didn't speak a word as they ran, sprinting into the forest and jumping over fallen branches and bumpy roots. Noah stayed in step with Gray, his endurance and focus admirable as he sprinted blindly into the dark. His human eyesight wouldn't allow him to see more than an arms-length ahead of him, and yet he didn't stop until they stumbled into the enchanted clearing, through the ward Gray had used a vast amount of power on to ensure that they had a safe place to flee to. Somewhere to heal their injured, and, if necessary, hide, once they escaped.

Gray felt her before he saw her. Felt the bond with his mate snap back into place like a piece of his very own soul returning to him. He released a breath as his eyes scanned her body. There was no visible blood on her besides what soaked the hem of her once white dress, blood she had likely run through in the chaos of their interrupted nuptials. His soul felt light, and the only pain he felt was the slight sting that remained from his own wounds. Nothing indicated that his wife had been injured.

No. His heart dropped. *She's your mate. Not your wife.* He'd moved up his plans for the rebellion to flee Auropera to allow her this choice—the freedom to decide if she wanted to bind her life to his or not. Gray had prayed to the gods for the first time in a century that his efforts would be fruitful, that the intricate timing needed for their escape would allow them to get everyone out safely.

His arms and shadows wrapped around Lea, and warmth flooded his chest as her slight frame crashed against him. She felt like home, soft and comforting, and yet still so fragile. Her relief washed through him as she whispered a prayer of thanks and her hands found his face, wiping the watery blood away with her cold, trembling hands.

"I'm here, Little Flower," he whispered against her cheek before pressing a kiss against her temple. "*We're* here." He allowed himself to hold her a moment longer before pulling away.

The clang of hundreds of swords being drawn and the clatter of soldiers scurrying to their feet caused him to turn, calmly and deliberately, as he forced his shadows to return to his chest. He'd known this time would come. The day he would have to reveal himself as the Eclipsed King and hope that the men and women who hated his family so righteously would believe that *he* was the one attempting to end their rule. And not only that, but choose to follow and help him do it.

Gray raised his chin, meeting eyes with his rebels—the ones he'd hand picked without their knowledge to join the fight against his father. He had one chance to convince them. One chance to make them see that he was so very different from the man they'd thought him to be their entire lives. But as he stared at their furious faces and the way they whispered amongst each other, plotting and planning as the strongest among them inched forward, ready to sacrifice themselves to protect the others, Gray's confidence faltered. After all, he *was* the Night Prince, wasn't he? And one of the very rulers that they had joined the rebellion to kill.

CHAPTER 7

LEA

"Lower your weapons!" Vincent called as he walked with determined strides to stand to Gray's left. "That is an order!"

Erik strode to Gray's right as he moved Lea beside him, the three of them presenting a united front. Mistrust colored the rebels' eyes and their fingers twitched on their swords, their focus darting around as if they'd been cornered.

"Lower them, *now*." Vincent ordered, and had Lea not known better, she would have been certain from his tone that he was the Eclipsed King. "You have followed me, risked everything because you trusted me. I'm asking you to trust me once more." Vincent crossed his arms, pinning every rebel with a stare until their weapon was lowered. Once raised swords were replaced with only accusing stares, Vincent continued.

"You've all believed me to be the leader of the rebellion. And I am one of them. But I am not your Eclipsed King."

Gasps filled the clearing, and despite already knowing this information, goosebumps dotted Lea's arms.

"Over a hundred years ago, I made a pact with Erik and the Fae you know as Evander Nestruir, the Night Prince of Desia. Brennus and Alaric had to die, and we would ensure that would happen. Evander has sacrificed his life to this mission, leading from the shadows, spying on his father and brother to get the information needed for our success."

A nearby soldier, an older man with mud-spattered glasses and receding hair, sneered and turned to whisper in another man's ear. The sentiment was echoed throughout the clearing, expressions of distrust and disgust remaining firm.

An explosion of pride filled Lea's chest. Her selfless mate, giving so much of himself for these people who hated him. And she was certain that he would choose this again and again.

Gray took a small step forward, raising his hands. "I know trusting me won't come easily. I've played the part of dutiful son to King Nestruir for years. Vincent and I," he nodded to the tattooed man, "decided long ago that it was too risky for my name to be associated with the rebellion until we were ready to fight. You all know better than the rest that there are no secrets within the castle walls—that the enemy lurks around every corner. We couldn't risk my father or brother knowing that I was acting as anything other than the Commander of the Royal Army." Gray paused, allowing the weight of his words to sink in.

"Rest assured, my fellow warriors, I have been leading from behind the scenes, planning and waiting for years as we grew our numbers. I have traveled Desia, every inch of its land, to find its weaknesses, to scout for those brave enough to fight alongside us. Our hearts are strong. Our numbers are many. And finally, we are ready!" He met Lea's eyes, nodding at her slightly, and a shiver ran down her spine.

Gray was *leading* the rebellion. Lea still could hardly believe it, but as she thought back through the last several months, connections formed in her mind. His traveling would put him in the perfect position to find members for the resistance, to become more familiar with every hill and valley, each city and town within Desia. It would allow him to rally an army.

Gray had told her that there was more he'd needed to confess, answers that she hadn't been ready to listen to through her anger, and things he couldn't speak of within the enchanted halls of the castle. He had promised her he would show her with his actions that he'd been trying to save the kingdom from the Lonely Death, to save them from the tyrannical rule of his father. Lea choked down the guilt in her throat that she hadn't believed him.

A man abruptly stepped forward—a young soldier, around her age, with wavy red hair and a cautious look in his eyes. His footsteps were soft, tentative as he walked through the shadows to the front of the clearing.

"I'd like to speak, if I may," the man said to Vincent before his eyes bravely met Gray's, despite the fact that he seemed to be shaking ever so slightly.

"Of course, Gregory," Gray said, motioning him forward. The man's head snapped up, his eyes widening slightly.

"You know who I am?" he asked in surprise, his eyebrows raising.

"I make it my duty to know every member who has pledged themselves to my cause. I know the name of every man and woman who stands before me today." Gray looked around, nodding as he named different rebels. "Penelope, Wesley, Cole," he paused, "Thomas." He stopped scanning the crowd as he said Thomas's name, leveling him with a look.

Lea's heart seized in her chest. Clearly, Thomas hadn't known that the man he hated was also the man he idolized—the leader of the rebellion he so passionately supported. She still felt anger toward Thomas for how he'd spoken to her, for implying she was the enemy, but she didn't want to see him hurt. *Don't say anything stupid*, she silently begged her friend.

Thomas remained frozen in place, so still it seemed as if he worried the ground might crumble beneath his feet if he were to move a single muscle.

Gray smirked as he turned his attention back to Gregory. "You're the youngest son of Sarah and Robert—humans. You lost your oldest sister to the Lonely Death three years ago, sat outside her room with your younger sister, Molly, as you waited for death to take her. Then joined the rebellion two weeks later. Did I miss anything of importance?"

Gregory's jaw dropped, his expression turning wary. "You didn't, and while I appreciate that you know about us all," he wrung his hands, lowering his chin slightly, "how are we to believe that you aren't working with your father? That you aren't a spy among spies, ready to report back to the king to dismantle what *we've* been working so hard to build?" Gregory gained confidence as he spoke, his voice growing louder and his face turning red as he practically accused the prince before him of being a traitor and a liar.

"You're a brave man, coming forward to publicly question my motives. If I were working for my father, I wouldn't allow you to speak your concerns. Your throat would be slit before you could make a sound." His words were firm, but not threatening. "You cannot trust my word any more than I can trust that you will not stab your dagger into my back the moment I turn around. I understand your hesitation, but we don't have time to indulge in these questions tonight."

Gray gestured toward Erik. "We created tonight's distraction, but it will only last for so long. For now, you'll just have to trust the man who has been leading you thus far," he nodded at Vincent, who looked around the grove as if challenging them to question him. "You'll have to trust that he wouldn't follow me if I did not have every intention of decimating my father and brother."

Another man pushed his way to the front of the crowd, a rucksack on his back and a small torch in his hand. He cleared his throat, and Lea recognized Joshua, the servant whose arm Alaric had burned to a crisp when he'd helped her gather water. He lowered his chin to Gray slowly before turning to speak to the crowd.

"I can see you are all wary. I, too, would have had the same fears just a few weeks ago, had I learned that the Night Prince was the Eclipsed King we've been following for years, but..." He turned in an arc, locking eyes with each member of the rebellion as they watched him with rapt attention.

"I've experienced his loyalty. If it weren't for him and the woman beside him, I'd be too disfigured to serve alongside you all after Alaric tortured me for his own sick entertainment. Evander saved me, a human, and asked for nothing in return." He took a step forward as he turned back toward Evander, and it didn't escape Lea's notice that he chose not to share the secret of Lea's powers. "I am honored to fight beside you, King Evander, and will do so with the same loyalty you showed me as a servant in your castle," he said as he tucked his thumb into his palm and placed it over his heart.

Gray stepped forward and shook his hand. "And I am honored to fight at your side." Reaching back, Gray grabbed Lea's hand, sending a calming wave of energy through her that slowed her racing heart. "I made a vow tonight, to someone more important to me than the air I breathe, the stars that guide my magic, and the life that floods my veins. I vowed to her that my father and brother would die at my hand. That they would suffer for the evil they've inflicted upon this kingdom."

Lea's heart clenched, his words ringing out as pure truth settled deep into her belly. Raising Lea's hand to his lips, Gray pressed a kiss to her fingers before letting go and taking a confident step forward. "I make that same vow to all of you here today. I will not continue to let my heart beat in my chest while the rest of the kingdom suffers. On my life, death is coming for King and Prince Nestruir!" Thunder boomed somewhere in the distance and the fires flickered, the flames sputtering as if fighting for oxygen.

"I will vouch for him as well!" a young boy Lea didn't recognize stepped forward. "I owe Evander my life, twice over. I will follow him wherever he asks."

"Thank you, Noah. And please, call me Gray." Gray shook his hand.

Several rebels within the crowd placed their hands over their hearts. But still, others remained cautious, a few soldiers appearing to examine the entrance to the clearing as if they were wondering if they could make it back through undetected.

The crunch of dry grass interrupted the tense silence, and Lea looked around for the origin of the noise. One by one, heads turned toward the sound, the crowd parting as Thomas came forward. There was nothing of the boy she had grown up with in the man before her, his serious face lined with fatigue, his shoulders squared and eyes fierce. His hand was on his sword, knuckles white as he approached Gray.

Lea's pulse quickened, her palms growing sweaty. Never in her life had she seen Thomas look so serious, so determined. Erik straightened, moving to place himself in front of Gray, but Gray's shadows floated up to form a wall, blocking off Erik and stopping him.

Thomas paused as he reached Gray, his hand still on his sword, his breathing slow and heavy as he stared at the Eclipsed King, the man he had been fighting against at every turn since his arrival in Auropera. He drew his sword and pointed it at Gray with shaking hands, the tip inches from the mountain tattoo inked across his chest.

"Stop," Lea whispered, her stomach clenching in fear, but Gray stepped forward and took a deep breath, his chest swelling to press against the sword as he met Thomas's eyes. They held each other's stare for a long moment, a silent conversation passing between them. The night was so quiet Lea swore she could hear the fires crackling all the way from Auropera, and she held her breath as she watched the boy she used to consider her best friend come to terms with the events of the evening.

Thomas closed his eyes and dropped his sword, the thud of the metal on the ground a wordless admission of defeat. He knelt before the man who had taken everything from him, who had taken him from his family and home, and stolen the girl he'd loved his entire life.

Pulling the dagger from his belt, he sliced it across his open palm, squeezing it into a fist and letting blood drop at Gray's feet. He tucked his thumb in his bleeding hand and placed it across his chest.

"Yesterday you were my enemy, one I swore I would kill." Thomas met Lea's shocked stare, apologies and regret filling his eyes. "But, I was wrong." He turned back to Gray. "With the blood that runs through my veins, I mark this vow in the earth beneath your feet. If you pledge to do the same, Evander Nestruir, Eclipsed King of Desia, I will fight alongside you, to my death, if that is what the gods decide, to end the rule of the Black King and restore peace to our kingdom."

The clearing filled with tension so thick, Lea felt as if she could barely breathe. She could hear the thump of her heart and the shuffling of feet as the rebels waited to see their new king's response to the man who had admitted he'd wanted to murder him. Every pair of eyes fixed on Evander's face, for surely if Thomas, who hated Gray so much, could believe that there was good in him, then he had to be worth giving a chance.

Please give him a chance, Lea begged silently.

Gray stared down at Thomas, pulling his own dagger from his belt and drawing it across his open palm. Lea felt a mirrored sting of pain in her hand as Gray's flesh opened, but it was nothing compared to the searing agony she'd felt when he'd been injured battling Alaric. Gray held out his fist, allowing his blood to soak into the ground next to Thomas's.

"With the blood that runs through my veins, I mark this vow in the earth beneath your feet. In front of all present here today and the God of the Sun and Goddess of the Moon above, I will fight alongside you, to my death, if that is what the gods decide, to end the rule of the Black King and restore peace to our kingdom."

A cheer went up from the crowd, the ringing of metal echoing and bouncing against the magical barriers surrounding them as one by one, the members of the resistance followed in kind, their blood staining the soil below them in an unbreakable oath. Lea's heart swelled with pride as she stepped forward, pulled the dagger from Gray's hand, and sliced the sharp blade across her palm. She winced as beads of bright red blood pooled in her cupped fist. Turning to Gray, Lea lowered herself to kneel.

A large hand closed around her biceps and she paused, looking up at Gray with wide, confused eyes.

"I told you once that you do not serve me. I meant it then, and I mean it now." He cupped her chin gently, turning her head to look out toward the crowd staring intently at her. "But, by my side, we can serve them together."

Lea couldn't help the tears that pricked her eyes at the sincerity in Gray's words. A smile flitted across his serious face as he continued to twist her body toward the rebels.

Holding out her hand, Lea turned it over and let her life's blood join the scarlet promises dotting the soil. She closed her eyes and opened her mouth to speak, wondering how she had found herself lucky enough to not only be part of the resistance that would change the kingdom, but also to get to stay with Gray.

"With the blood that runs through my veins, I mark this vow in the earth beneath your feet. In front of all present here today and the god and goddess above, I will fight alongside you, to my death, if that is what the gods decide, to end the rule of the Black King and restore peace to the kingdom."

A chorus of gasps met Lea's ears. She opened her eyes to see the blood dripping from her hand was glowing the same silvery-blue she'd seen on the doors of the chapel. Her hand tingled, and her heart pounded erratically in her throat. *What in the gods' names?*

"It's a blessing from the goddess!" Emma called out, pressing her hand to her heart. "I can feel it."

Lea's head swam. What other explanation could there be? She'd only seen that silver blue glow connected to the goddess of the moon. *But why me?* she thought. *And why now?* The possibilities terrified her.

Gray nodded to Emma. "I think you're right. And if my mate has been blessed by the goddess herself, then we cannot lose." Hundreds of heads swiveled back to her, their eyes hopping between herself and Gray. She looked at Thomas, who appeared as if he might throw up at any moment, his face an ashy pale color that reminded her of how he'd looked after she'd tried to make him a potion that would make him invisible as a child.

Hushed whispers bounced between the trees, a mixture of what sounded like prayers and doubtful conversations.

"*Mate*? But... I don't see the mark, my king." Joshua said from somewhere in the crowd.

Gray pulled Lea against his side protectively. "Because we wish to wait for the bond to be sealed until we are safe and away from this evil place. But do not mistake our lack of a mark for a lack of commitment. She belongs to me—is a part of me as deeply as my very soul. Should anything happen to her, I will personally destroy anyone who failed to help her. You will protect your queen, and we will protect you in return."

Destroy them? Lea had no doubt that Gray would do anything to ensure she was unharmed, but surely threatening his soldiers wasn't the way to earn their trust. Clenching her jaw, Lea prepared for the rebels to argue that Gray's focus should be on keeping *them* safe, not her. But, to her utter shock and surprise, one by one, the men and women in front of them bowed their heads in deference to her. All except Janelle, who stuck out her tongue and threw a middle finger in her direction.

"Now," Gray nodded to Vincent, who immediately went to ready the caravan along the back of the grove.

"Deeper inside the forest, there are more horses hidden, along with weapons. We *will* survive this journey, but it will be hard." He looked around, scanning the rebel's faces as if needing to let them know that their safety was important to him. "You will head south to Bearswillow, to a cavern hidden within the Torres Mountains. There, we regroup and await rebels to join us from throughout the kingdom. In the meantime, we train. We prepare. And while we are inside the mountain, you will be safe. I assure you. Elise?" Gray searched the crowd for the plump, older woman.

"Yes?" Elise called from where she still sat on the ground, delicately leaving her daughter's side to stand before him. "Assess the injured, please. I'd like you to tell Vincent who cannot ride alone, so he can assign them to an experienced rider."

Elise bowed her head, promptly turning to the back of the clearing where the wounded were being tended to.

"Those who require a horse or don't believe they can run, see Vincent. Everyone else, you will travel under the cover of night. The supplies are not far. It is imperative that you are quiet, and if you possess magic," the crowd stilled, for they knew as well as he that harboring magic was illegal, "it is crucial that you do not use it until we are safely within the Torres Mountains. The cavern is protected, just as this grove is protected, but there will not be a constant shield as you travel. Find your magic and fold it tight into the deepest recess of your mind. The king will be looking to track it, and he won't need much to be able to find us. I will meet you all in Bearswillow."

Erik bristled, stepping to Gray's side as the rebels moved to follow his orders, picking up their meager belongings and moving toward the horses. "You're not traveling with us? It wasn't part of the plan for me to leave your side, Gray. Wherever you're headed, I'm coming with you." Erik stated matter-of-factly, his voice firm. Gray pulled Lea closer, his eyes softening as he looked at her before speaking.

"You have others that need your protection far more than I do, Erik." Gray nodded to Janelle, who was holding tight to Emma's hand as tears continued to stream down her face. Lea felt Gray's confusion. He didn't know about Emma's magic, but instead of asking, he pressed his lips together, pity clouding his eyes.

"We're going to Calir. I had planned to take care of this prior to leaving Auropera, but with moving our escape up..." he trailed off. "Lea and I will be fine. Together our power far outranks that of my brother, maybe even that of my father. And we both know that he won't track us into the Wicked Wood. We don't need you, but they do," Gray said, inclining his head toward the rebels.

Erik closed his eyes, releasing a breath before glancing over his shoulder. Janelle met his gaze, offering him a shy smile.

Erik turned back to Gray, wrapping his hand around his forearm to pull him into a tight hug. "I will allow you to go without me *only* if you will make a promise. Promise that you will find answers and break the curse. And swear to me that you will bring my queen back safely."

Lea stiffened beside Gray, and she sniffled before leaping into Erik's arms, squeezing him as tightly as she could. Erik's eyes were red and slightly puffy as he returned her hug, holding her like he was afraid to let her go, before finally setting her back down and patting her on the head. Gray had no doubt that Erik loved Lea like the sister he never had—loved her as fiercely as he loved Gray. He pushed down the choking sensation in his chest at his friend's loyalty, at the knowledge he would lay down his own life to protect his mate. Erik's eyes never left Gray's as he waited for his promise.

"As long as the sun rises in the morning, you can know she is safe. Because to allow harm to come to her, Erik, would be to allow darkness to destroy the world."

CHAPTER 8

LEA

Erik allowed Lea to pull away as she twisted to look at Gray. The intensity of his words left no room for doubt that they would both return safely. Lea reached for him, his body warm against her as she pressed herself into his side, her eyes suddenly wet.

"Are you sure we need to go to Calir? Can't we help get everyone to safety first?" Lea asked softly, unsure how much of his plans Gray wanted to share with the rebels who still watched their new king.

"We don't have the time to go with them. The King of Calir, Tanad, is the one who allowed me access to his witch many years ago. If I am to destroy my brother and father, then I have to find a way to break this curse I asked her to place upon us. It is crucial we find Eudora and get her to agree."

"Are you sure they'll allow us passage across the border?" Lea's brows rose in concern. She'd heard of the rivalry between the two kingdoms, one which had nearly led them into war on more than one occasion.

Gray's eyes crinkled around the edges, and it took Lea's breath away. The bright green of his irises contrasted against his soot-covered face, a glimmer of hope in the darkness. "They will more than allow us entry, Little Flower. They are expecting us, prepared to plan our joint attack against the Black King and his tyranny."

"They'll side with us? Support us?" Lea's chest squeezed as her hope grew.

"We have their full military backing. Tanad is every bit as invested as we are in overthrowing my father."

"How can you trust them?" Thomas interrupted. "How can you be so sure that we won't just be trading one king we didn't choose for another?"

"What do you know of Calir, Thomas?" Gray asked pointedly. Thomas's face turned red, but he remained silent, shifting awkwardly from foot to foot in a nervous gesture Lea recognized. He didn't have an answer, and Lea knew why. They knew very little of Calir, of its customs and leaders. Their history wasn't taught, aside from the warning that their border was heavily guarded and to attempt to cross it meant certain death.

"You don't know anything, because my father doesn't allow his subjects this knowledge. Calir is a free kingdom. Magic is unregulated there. Tanad wants nothing other than to allow his neighboring kingdom the same freedoms he allows his own people, as well as to ensure that the Lonely Death isn't able to spread across its borders. He and I have come to an agreement. Now," Gray hesitated, looking toward the moon and appearing to take note of its position, "we need to go. My father will send more guards soon enough. Erik, a word?" Leaning down, Gray kissed Lea's shoulder tenderly. "Say goodbye, my love. Both of our journeys will be dangerous, and who knows how long it will be until we all reunite."

With a nod to Emma and Janelle, Gray turned away, leading Erik to Vincent and speaking in serious, hushed tones, their heads bowed together and jaws clenched. Grabbing Erik's canteen, he dumped water on his face, wiping the grime away from his neck before cleaning off his hands. Water dripped down his shirt, turning transparent enough to see the dark tattoo across his pec, and Lea's mouth ran dry at the sight.

Emma stood slowly, brushing tears from her eyes, and Lea forced her attention back to her friend.

"Please, be safe, Lea," Emma begged before collapsing into her arms. Janelle joined their embrace, the three of them crying together. She didn't want to be separated from them so soon, but Gray was right. If he couldn't get the witch to break the spell, there was no hope of this war ever ending. No one else could ever be a match for the king and Alaric.

"I'll see you both soon," Lea promised, wrapping the words around her heart and tying them in a knot as she sought out Thomas to say goodbye.

He stood only a few feet away, his arms crossed in front of him and his face a reserved calm, but Lea didn't miss the sadness lingering beneath the surface. Frown lines bracketed his eyes, and his shoulders hung as if exhaustion sat heavy upon them. This surely wasn't what he'd expected when he left her room only hours ago, ready to join the rebellion and change the kingdom. Ready to escape not only Auropera, but also the pain of witnessing her relationship with Gray.

It didn't excuse how he had behaved toward her, the cruel words he'd said before still a tiny wedge between her heart and lungs, but it was obvious how much he believed in this rebellion. And it was just as obvious that he loved her.

Thomas appeared years older, more mature. Where he had always been soft and sensitive, he was now hardened and determined, and Lea hoped that his newfound purpose could help keep her friends safe as they traveled back to Bearswillow.

"Protect them," Lea mouthed to Thomas, unable to give voice to the words trapped in her throat.

Thomas nodded, his eyes tight and his Adam's apple bobbing as if there were words that begged to be spoken, before he swallowed them down and put a soothing hand on Emma's back.

Gray turned from Vincent and Erik and walked with determined strides to where Lea waited. "Janelle—" he started.

Janelle jumped, grabbing onto Lea's hand. "I want to come with you. I'm a *great* third wheel. You won't even know I'm there. And I can help you. You know I'm good at avoiding danger," she said firmly.

"You are," Gray agreed. "Which is why I need you with the others. You'll ride at the front with Erik and Vincent. I believe you can be an asset in getting the resistance to Bearswillow safely." Gray gently grabbed her shoulders, turning her around to look at the army preparing for their journey.

Janelle froze, eyes darting between her fellow rebels. "They need you, Janelle." He gestured to the anxious rebels, who appeared to be filled with uncertainty.

"You've made the journey before, and you know Bearswillow well. I need you there to sense what threats are coming."

Janelle paused, taking a deep breath before hanging her head. "Gods dammit, Gray. I really hate you." She looked at Erik, a tight smile pulling at her lips. "Show me my horse, then." She gave Lea's hand one more squeeze, and Lea held back a sob as Janelle refused to look at her, a tear trailing down her cheek.

"This way." Erik placed an arm around Janelle's shoulder and pulled her close. "Have you ridden a horse before, then?" he asked as they walked to the herd in the back.

"Thomas," Gray called to where he sat with Emma against a large tree trunk. Thomas rose quickly, walking to Gray without saying a word.

"Despite our differences, I believe you are committed to this cause. Between that and the magic you hold, I would like you at the tail of the caravan. Ensure we leave no soldier behind."

"I'm honored you'd trust me for the job."

"It is honorable that you are willing to sacrifice your life to help us succeed. But understand that you have had your one chance, Thomas. If you are to fight alongside us in this rebellion, you will not get another. I'm giving you the opportunity to prove yourself and *earn* my trust. Because as of now, you do not have it."

Shame flooded Thomas's eyes, his shoulders hunching slightly forward, and Lea wondered if he was reliving the minutes in which he didn't help as Alaric had beat her in front of him.

Lea felt a stab of sorrow for her friend. "Gray, there's no reason to bring that up. Thomas—"

"No. He's right. I failed you. But I won't ever again." He gave Lea a contrite smile as he added, "My Queen." He turned back to Gray. "I will protect your people. Both of your people."

Gray tilted his head, examining Thomas for several long moments before clapping him on the shoulder. "Then go. Vincent will give you instructions."

Thomas leaned forward, as if wanting to give Lea a quick kiss on her cheek, but he stopped himself, clearing his throat. "Be careful," he warned her. "The woods are not what you expect them to be. Don't be stubborn, and listen to Evander."

He pulled away, glancing at Emma as he passed to await instructions from Vincent.

Lea and Gray stood together, watching as the army began to leave—Vincent, Janelle, and Erik at the front and Thomas at the rear, his sword bouncing against his thigh as his horse trotted forward. Thomas raised his hand in a slow wave as he cleared the magic barrier.

Now that they were alone, the silence in the clearing was startling. The chaos of the night was gone, and Lea became acutely aware of the adrenaline thrumming through her blood. What had happened over the past few hours? How had tonight ended with her fleeing to a different kingdom with the Eclipsed King, when it had begun with a ceremony in which she would vow to tie her life to the Night Prince? Her head spun as she turned toward Gray, her stomach flipping as she found his eyes staring into hers predatorily.

Lea sucked in a deep breath as his eyes darkened. She opened her mouth to speak, but it was quickly claimed by Gray's hungry lips. His tongue found hers as a groan rumbled inside his chest, his hands sliding into her hair and tipping her head back to deepen their kiss before they slid down to lift her legs around his waist. He lifted her quickly, walking her backward.

"You love me," he whispered between kisses, his voice desperate. "Of all the things that have happened tonight, that confession is what has shaken me to my core. All the planning I've done, all the years I spent preparing for the day I would lead the rebellion from this horrendous place, and yet all that has consumed my mind is the way your lips looked as they uttered those words."

He kissed her deeper, pressing her back against the tree as his mouth trailed down her jaw, sucking and teasing as he traced the curve of her neck. "You love me," he breathed, as his forehead found her shoulder, his movements pausing as a shuddering breath racked his body.

Lea grabbed his face, holding it tight between her hands as she lifted it to meet hers. His eyes shone with unshed tears, the relief in his expression shattering her heart. He had played the part of the confident leader from the moment she'd seen him, the moment she'd rushed into his arms in the dungeons below the castle. But now? His stern exterior had been shredded by his need for her. "I love you," she whispered, finding his lips again as he pulled her closer to him. He ground his hips into hers, his thick length pressing against her center as her body wrapped around his desperately.

"I love you," she repeated, needing him to *feel* her sincerity. "I'm sorry I—" she gasped as his strong fingers pulled the neck of her dress to the side and his lips found the top of her breast. She arched into his touch, electricity blazing across her skin.

"I don't want your apologies, Little Flower. The *only* thing I want to hear is the moans of the woman I love as she comes on my fingers." His other hand glided up her leg until he pulled aside her panties in one swift motion, dragging his fingers through her wet folds. His mouth found her nipple at the same moment, sucking hard before softly biting the pebbled tip between his teeth.

Lea felt the rough bark cutting into her back as she writhed in anticipation, crying out Gray's name as his fingers continued to tease at her entrance.

The echoes of an explosion rumbled the ground, fire rising above the trees in the distance somewhere between where they stood and the castle they had fled.

"Dammit." Gray paused, squeezing his eyes shut and withdrawing his hand as he straightened the top of her dress. He pressed a quick kiss to her forehead as he set her on her feet. "We have to go," he said breathlessly, his chest still heaving with the desire coursing through him.

Lea's body refused to comply, to do anything but nod as heat continued to bloom inside her. She allowed Gray to grab her hand and pull her toward Obsidian, quickly unbuckling a rucksack bundled at his side. He yanked a sword from the baggage, and the blade seemed to glow in response as Lea recognized the weapon Thomas had gifted her before the wedding.

"How did you–"

"Erik retrieved your things. I knew you wouldn't want to leave without the letter your mother left you. He found this on your bed. It seemed... important," he said curtly as he strapped it on her hip before hoisting her up onto the horse. "I assume it's from Thomas?"

"It is." Lea confirmed, her stomach twisting in knots. "It was a wedding present."

"It was no doubt intended to kill me should I be the monster Thomas believed I was. But it is a powerful weapon. Do not hesitate to use it," Gray ordered before jumping up behind her and kicking Obsidian's sides. As they raced through the narrow opening to the woods, shimmering magic brushing against her skin and intensifying the ache building inside her, Lea felt Gray pull the pins holding her hair away from her face.

Freedom looks good on you, he'd told her months ago as they'd traveled to the castle. She had been a prisoner, an unforeseen complication in his plans. Had Gray suspected even then that this is where fate would lead them? That only months from that time, she would be racing away into the unknown with her mate at her back, his large palm pressed firmly against her stomach, and her hair once again flying in the breeze behind her?

CHAPTER 9

LEA

Obsidian ran as if he had galloped blindly through these woods a thousand times, dodging branches with the grace of a bird dashing through the leaves of a tree. Rain fell in sheets that washed away the soot and grime from their skin, blocking their sight more than a few feet in front of them. Lea was drenched, her hair sticking to her face and her white and silver wedding dress turning nearly translucent as water soaked through the fabric.

Lightning flashed. Wild, dark gray lightning that seemed to warn anyone who might approach that they would not escape its long, electric fingers. She'd seen this lightning before, this intense power, but it still took her breath away as it crashed protectively around them.

Gray's chest was firm against Lea's back, his arms holding her with a worried defensiveness that peeked through the expression of stern calm he wore on his face like armor. He was afraid. She could feel it without question as she reached toward their bond filled with the buzzing anxiety plaguing his mind.

"We're going to make it, Gray," she whispered, knowing he would hear her despite the wind racing past their ears.

He nodded, nuzzling his lips into her neck. "There is another clearing, a small one, about an hour west. We'll stay there for the night."

Lea's heart raced, thumping erratically in her throat. "Will Alaric be able to find us?"

"He won't expect us to travel toward the Wicked Wood. Even if he does, I've already enchanted it to keep us hidden."

A shiver wracked Lea's body, but from the cold or the danger in his voice when speaking of the woods, she wasn't sure.

"Use your magic to warm yourself," Gray instructed, handing Lea the reins and pulling his cloak around her front.

"But you said to hide our magic, that the king—"

"I can shield us from my father. Not everyone, not the entire rebellion, but the two of us. I've been entering these woods for months, leaving traces of my magic. They won't be able to determine which are recent, and which are pointless trails leading nowhere. We're safe, Azalea. Now, warm yourself."

"I'm fine."

"Your beautiful, peaked nipples are telling me differently, Little Flower," he growled, the desperation in his voice causing them to harden further.

Lea arched against him, pressing her breasts forward as the wet, almost sheer fabric pulled tight across her chest.

"Azalea," Gray rasped, tugging her more tightly against him, his arousal unmistakable as she settled even deeper between his thighs. "Warm yourself," he whispered, lowering his hand to her leg and running his fingers along the goosebumps peppering her skin. "Or I can't promise we will make it to the next grove. It is the worst form of torture to see you shiver, and as much as I'd like to use my body to warm yours," Gray shifted forward, his hard, thick length pressing against her back, "we need to get to safety. Warm yourself, *please.*"

Lea's shivers intensified as his shadows snaked around her body, pushing the fabric of her dress higher and higher, frigid air stinging her skin as he exposed her bare legs. She somehow pulled her attention from the electricity following his touch, the need growing between her legs, and sought out her day magic. It was nestled right next to her night magic in her chest, a bright, warm sensation that she forced into opening its eyes and waking. She allowed it to spread throughout her body, into her fingers and toes, then through her back and into Gray's body, trying to warm them both.

"Good girl," Gray rasped into her neck, his teeth biting ever so slightly against her rain-drenched skin. "Now I can do the wicked deeds I dreamed of doing on our wedding night—all the things I've been longing to do since I saw you standing there as my bride." Gray grabbed her thigh firmly with one hand, his other raising to the low neckline of her dress as his cloak fell away and his shadows wrapped around the reins. He growled as he looked down at her glistening body, circling her peaked nipple with his thumb. The sensation of the lace against her breast coaxed a moan from her throat, and he grabbed the fabric and pulled it down so firmly that the seams broke apart at her shoulders. The dress pooled around her waist as her breasts sprang free, bouncing as Obsidian continued to race into the darkness.

"I dreamt of this as we traveled to Auropera," he rasped. "Alone on the road for so long, with your perfect ass nestled between my thighs. Pictured this in my mind as I came with my own hand, night after night, trying to ease the desperation I felt for you." Gray continued his assault against her neck as he slid both hands upward, cradling her breasts and teasing her with his calloused fingers. Shadows wrapped around her legs, slowly climbing higher.

"I couldn't sleep—could think of nothing else—after watching the way your breasts bounced in front of me with every gallop forward. I pictured my cock between them as they moved up and down. You have no clue what torture I've endured on our journeys together."

"Oh gods, Gray," Lea cried out, the sensation of the rain pelting against her bare chest along with the kneading of Gray's strong fingers causing warmth to build inside her that was separate from her magic. It was a deeply rooted passion—a carnal need. It was a love that could only come from *her* commander.

Lea tried to twist toward him, but Gray's arms pinned her in place as a long thread of darkness snapped across her chest.

"There will be time for that, Little Flower." The shadows crept higher, wrapping across her neck and up to the back of her head, pulling it backward. "Let me savor this. I need to feel your heart beating. I need to feel my mate writhing beneath my hands." With those words, he lowered one hand, pulling her dress up to her waist and exposing her completely. He ripped her underwear off in his fist, tucking them quickly into the saddlebag at his side. *Was he saving her panties?*

As if he could read her mind, he laughed darkly. "A reminder. Of the night we escaped. The night I took my mate, knowing she has seen all of who I am and accepts every dark part of me." He slid his fingers against her already throbbing clit. "Tell me, Little Flower, is it the rain drenching you between your pretty thighs?" He squeezed her nipple, a zap of electricity stealing her breath from her lungs.

"It's you, Gray." She nearly wept at the pleasure building inside her. "Only you."

"*Fuck*," Gray cursed as he slowly swirled his fingers in circles, his shadows pulling her legs further apart to give him access to her throbbing core. Her body clenched, her hips grinding down against his fingers as her head rested back against his shoulder. He continued circling his fingers against her, increasing his speed and speaking words of love and praise into her ear as she squirmed. His other hand caressed her breasts, her nipples, the cold air and sting of the rain against her bare chest causing a bite of pain that only intensified her pleasure.

They continued forward, racing through the darkness toward their safe haven, her body exposed to the elements and under the total control of the Fae behind her. Pressure built inside her and he slowed.

Lea groaned in protest, leaning forward in an attempt to push against his fingers harder, to find release.

"Patience, my love," he rasped.

"I need—"

He increased the pressure of his fingers, his rhythm torturously slow as his shadows caressed her inner thighs. "Do not believe for a second that I don't know exactly what you need." Biting down on her shoulder, he pinched her nipple, hard. "You have no idea how I have burned, how long I've needed to feel this with you. For you to know what I have been working toward, to join me. My queen by my side." He leaned her backward, his mouth finding the hollow between her neck and shoulder. Sucking gently, he circled her swollen nipple, soothing away the sting.

In the back of her mind, Lea realized that she should feel embarrassed. Her beautiful dress was around her waist, her entire body exposed as they fled the kingdom under the cover of night. They were likely being hunted by Alaric at this very moment, but she couldn't find it in herself to care. Despite the danger, she'd never felt so protected.

Gray lifted her head to meet his eyes. "I'm glad you feel safe with me again. It's all I've wanted."

Her expression must have betrayed her, the confusion at him knowing her thoughts.

"Did you forget that I feel what you feel?" He placed a hand over her heart and her pulse thundered.

"And what do I feel?" she asked breathlessly.

"Safe," he repeated as he kissed her deeply. "Passion and fire." Gray sent a cool burst of electricity through his fingers, a zap that caused her to cry out in surprise. "Love." He continued to move and Lea felt as if she might burst, her need too great.

"Please, Gray," she cried out, and a rough laugh laced with desire and darkness vibrated against her back. Lea felt Gray look up, taking in the path before them.

"Whatever you need. *Always*." His movements changed then, less teasing and more intentional. Rough with need, with a singular purpose to push her over the edge. Lea arched against him, pleasure filling every inch of her body, building and crescendoing until she exploded into a million pieces, her mate's name ripping from her throat as her body spasmed. Gray continued to coax out her ecstasy, her orgasm spreading down her legs and onto his fingers.

As she came back down to earth, Lea noticed absently that they'd stopped moving. Wordlessly, Gray led Obsidian into a small circle of trees before sliding off the saddle. Magic passed over her skin, and she shivered, her body singing with its touch.

"Can you stand?" Gray's voice was rough—deep and full of lust. She nodded her head, and he placed her feet onto the soft grass, leaning her against a tree. She looked around, realizing that they were safely inside one of the pockets of the forest that Gray had warded. She relaxed against the tree, breathing a sigh of relief at the knowledge that they were once again tucked inside a magic barrier and undetectable.

A rumble left Gray's chest, and Lea sucked in a breath at his fierce expression. He looked starved, his eyes wide and his breaths ragged. She reached toward their bond to find a searing heat unlike anything she'd ever felt before as he took slow, predatory steps toward her while removing his armor. Despite her bones feeling like gelatin, her stomach clenched.

Her breasts still exposed, Gray hooked his fingers around the dress at her waist and pulled it to the muddy ground. Yanking his shirt overhead in one fluid motion, he wrapped it around her shoulders.

Lea bit down a smile as the fabric stuck to her back, and Gray gave her a questioning look. "I don't think your wet shirt is going to offer me much warmth, Gray," she whispered, her body still on fire for the man standing in front of her. He slowly unbuckled his belt, and Lea's eyes drifted down to the sprinkling of dark hair beginning just below his belly button, at the V of his abs as they disappeared beneath the waistline of his trousers. She felt her breaths growing shallow as she took in the veins in his strong, thick arms. He pushed down his pants, his eyes drinking her in, never leaving her naked body.

"It's not for warmth, though I do hate to see you cold." He stepped forward, pressing himself against her, the feel of his naked body and the heat of his skin instantly causing her blood to boil as need built within her again. Gray leaned down, his fingers caressing the side of her belly, her hip bone, the side of her breast. "It's to protect your beautiful skin as I fuck you against this tree."

Gray grabbed Lea around her waist at the same time he lifted her leg, wrapping it snugly around his hip. She felt his impressive, hard length against her as he pushed her back into the tree, her skin stinging from the rough bark despite his shirt behind her.

His chest heaved with each ragged breath, his cock pushing at her entrance. Lea moaned his name, lifting her other leg and wrapping her tighter around his waist as she tried to pull him closer.

"Say it again," he rasped, his taut body trembling as his love for her overwhelmed their bond. "I need to hear you say it."

Lea looked up at Gray, cupping his face gently in her hands. This fierce Fae, the king of the rebellion, whispered about and feared throughout the kingdom, was baring his soul before her. "I love you," she whispered, trying to push every bit of her feelings toward Gray's magic coiled in her chest. Hoping he could sense that she was done fighting him, that she forgave him for keeping the knowledge of what his father had done from her. That she was accepting him as her mate, fully, here under the stars and moon.

Gray's mouth crashed against hers as he thrust inside her in one swift movement. Lea opened her mouth to cry out but his tongue found hers immediately, swallowing his name from her throat as he kissed her in a way that she'd never experienced before. It was overwhelming—desperate and frantic. His hands squeezed her ass as he plunged in and out, stretching and filling her, claiming her fully. She could feel their bond pulling tighter, twisting around itself like a golden chain that could never be untangled. Not without being consumed by fire.

"Azalea," Gray whispered as he pressed his forehead against hers, his rhythm increasing as sweat beaded beneath Lea's hands. Bark dug into Lea's skin with every thrust, but she didn't care. *Couldn't* care as she felt magic surrounding them, tingling across her skin and wrapping them in a bubble of sparkling, glowing light. "I–" Lea hushed him with a kiss, rocking her hips to meet his every thrust as she silenced what she knew he was going to say, what she felt through the bond. That he needed her forgiveness. That he was sorry—for the lies and the pain he had caused her. For her mother... But there was no room for any of that now.

"I love you," she whispered again against his lips. "There's nothing to forgive."

Gray moaned as she pushed her feelings through the magic around them and the bond between them, soaring as her absolution washed over them. His pace quickened as he pushed her toward the release building inside her again. Thrusting once more, Gray growled out a final word.

"Mine," he said as he pushed into her so deeply, it forced the breath from her lungs. Lea shattered around him, collapsing against the tree as an earth-shattering orgasm pulsed through her. She felt Gray stiffen, spilling into her as he panted her name. "Azalea. Oh, Azalea," he cried over and over, caressing every inch of her body as they came as one, wringing out every ounce of pleasure and joy and love that they could.

"I love you," Lea whispered again as her muscles relaxed, and Gray pulled them to the ground, kissing her deeply.

"And I love you," Gray whispered, his deep timbre rumbling across Lea's skin as he wiped her soaking wet hair away from her eyes. "My mate. My love. My life."

CHAPTER 10

GRAY

A bolt of pain shot through Gray's chest as he looked at Lea's clear, unmarked breast. There was no mark below her collarbone, no symbol above her heart. He'd known there wouldn't be, not with his storms and clouds blocking the moon and stars from seeing their joining. It had been necessary to hide them from the army searching for them, from the soldiers who were likely scouring the woods at this very moment in their mission to find and kill them. It had been an intentional decision, one made to keep her safe.

Even without the need to hide them, linking their lives together as a war approached wasn't something Gray could allow himself to do. But it didn't stop the way his magic writhed uncomfortably in his chest at its inability to join hers fully. To bind itself to the other half of his soul.

They hadn't spoken for several minutes—didn't need to—as Gray held Lea securely against him. Her acceptance of his love had somehow made their bond grow stronger, even without sealing it beneath the elements. He could *almost* hear her thoughts—could feel the contentment radiating off her, the love and relief. Gray swore he might glow with pride, knowing that he had finally made her happy. That there were no longer secrets between them.

Lea shivered, their bodies still soaking wet from the rain that had soaked them to the bone as they'd raced toward safety. It made him restless, uncomfortable in his own skin knowing she was cold, and despite every fiber of his being urging him to wrap himself around her and never let go, he couldn't deny that she would be far warmer if he added a pile of furs and blankets to their body heat. Lea protested as he rose, reaching toward him to pull him back down, but the ease of unraveling her arms from his neck caused reality to crash down on him.

Lea's wrist bones moved beneath his fingers as he wrapped his hands around her forearms and placed them back in her lap. While his bones were as strong as the trunk of a tree, hers reminded him of the long, flimsy branches of a willow. She was so small. So frail. So... *human.* But despite how weak her body was compared to his, the strength of her grip on his heart was staggering. He wouldn't let anything happen to her. It was a duty he was soul-bound to. But in order to protect her, she needed strength for their journey ahead, needed warmth and rest.

"I'm just getting our bedroll. Three seconds, that's all I need. Surely you'll survive without me for that long." He raised an eyebrow with a smirk as he pressed a kiss to her forehead.

"But can *you*?" Lea shot back, reaching her arms out in a stretch that showcased the beautiful peaked curves of her breasts. Gray felt himself grow hard again, cursing under his breath at his rational mind forcing him to get blankets rather than warm her in a far more satisfying way. He stood and hurried toward Obsidian, untying his worn canvas bag from the magnificent black horse's side and unburdening him from his heavy load.

Obsidian whinnied, pressing his nose against Gray's chest before walking to the food and water Gray had readied days prior in hopes that they would make it here safely. It was one of many safe places he'd set up for their journey, not sure which direction they'd be able to flee once his plan was set into action.

"Good boy." Gray patted Obsidian's glossy mane. "Let me know if you sense danger," he instructed him with a scratch under his chin. The horse nickered as if laughing. "You're right," Gray replied, intuitively understanding what his favorite horse was saying. He was already on alert. If he sensed anything, he would let them know regardless of whether Gray had told him to.

Returning to his mate, Gray quickly set up their pallet, along with several thick blankets and furs that he'd packed for Lea's comfort. Tucking her snugly inside, he retrieved his sword from near the tree and placed it next to the bedroll. Always prepared. Always vigilant.

"I'll be right back," Gray said. He wanted to patrol the area once, quickly, just to make sure that his magic had held through the day since he had enchanted their hideaway.

"Join me." Lea begged, pulling back the covers. "I'm still freezing." She gave him a small, sly smile as he took in her bare skin, watching as goosebumps bloomed along her arms and belly.

He couldn't deny her warmth, or anything else. Her chest was splotchy and red, and Gray longed to kiss it, wondering if he had been too rough with her while he'd taken his fill of touching and squeezing her breasts as they'd ridden here. Longing to kiss away any sting that might still be lingering, he crawled in next to her, but Lea stopped him, trailing a finger across his collarbone.

"Where's the mark?" she asked. Lea's eyebrows scrunched together, her thick blonde hair falling across her bluebell eyes as she tried to hide the sorrow brimming there.

Gray settled next to her, a vise tightening painfully around his heart. Every fiber of his body hated the fact that he'd had to prevent sealing the bond. "We're still mates, my love. It's not what you're thinking." He could sense Lea's worry inside his own chest, a restless anxiety that caused his breath to quicken. "It's the clouds. The storm I cast to hide us from Alaric." Gray bent down, brushing a soft kiss where her mate mark would appear someday if they both survived the war. "There can be nothing between us and the moon and sun. Not a branch swaying overhead, nor a bird flying through the sky."

Lea sighed and Gray felt her panic ease, but disappointment remained in the back of his throat, thick and heavy. "We have time. When you're safe. I promise, there is nothing in this world that could keep me from claiming you as mine in every way possible. Someday. But you should know that I won't risk your safety for anything, not even the need burning in my blood to mark you for everyone to see." He pressed a long, lingering kiss to her lips—a pleasure he'd never been afforded before.

Cradling Lea against his chest, Gray listened to her heartbeat gradually slowing as it returned to normal from their... activities. Who the hell was he kidding? It was the most life-changing, soul-moving, primal sex he'd ever had.

Gray felt a tug on the bond. Not an intentional one, he didn't think, but an awareness that his mate needed something. Pulling back to look at her, he found Lea's large blue eyes full of unasked questions.

Gray felt a pinch of pain in his heart at her hesitation to ask whatever was swirling in her mind. Tucking her hair behind her ear, he pulled Lea back down onto his chest, her head fitting perfectly in the groove of his shoulder. "We're away from the castle now. You can ask whatever you'd like. No more secrets."

Lea pressed her lips together, her shoulders finally relaxing. "How long have you been planning for tonight? And did you know we'd be escaping when you asked me to marry you?"

Gray couldn't quite place the bitter taste that spread from their bond to coat his tongue. "I moved up the escape to give you a choice, Little Flower," he said calmly, beginning to run his fingers up and down her arms beneath the thick, soft blankets. "I'll marry you the second we're back in Bearswillow, if that's what you want. But I didn't want to force you into becoming my wife."

"Thank you," Lea breathed.

It had been a sacrifice, one that had potentially risked the safety and success of the rebellion, but it hadn't even been a choice. He would no sooner have forced his mate into marriage than he would have joined his father and brother in their quest for power.

Lea squeezed Gray's hands, a silent acknowledgement that she understood. "I don't even know what to ask. But I want to know everything."

Gray had been waiting for this moment. To be able to tell her what he'd really been doing as he'd traveled the kingdom, the betrayal to his family that he had been planning for nearly a hundred years. He hadn't been able to risk it in the castle. Not with wards and spells to alert his father of anyone speaking treacherous words. For all he knew, they'd only been rumors, but there was too much at stake to allow even a single syllable of his treachery to be spoken within those walls.

Too many people were counting on him—an entire kingdom rested in his tired and blood-soaked hands. So he had suffered silently as the love of his life thought the worst of him—his own mate hating him with enough intensity to reveal a deeply hidden magic inside her that they hadn't even known existed. As she'd hurt and cried and suffered from his betrayal. He thought it might break him, seeing her in pain and being unable to express that he was on her side. That he wasn't the evil monster she believed him to be.

And now, he could finally tell her the reason: Callitia. Gray took a deep breath, fighting against the fury that was slowly building in his veins. He didn't like to speak about her, but his mate had asked to know everything, and he owed it to her to share everything he hadn't been able to before.

"You asked me once... About my reason." Gray pushed the hair from Lea's forehead. "About her."

Lea froze, her muscles tensing and heart skipping a beat, the pounding rhythm vibrating Gray's fingertips as he lazily ran them around her back. "Was there someone—"

He chuckled darkly, interrupting her. "No, Little Flower. Nothing like that. Though, I have to admit, it pleases me to feel your jealousy."

"I wasn't jealous," Lea bristled. But it had been there, dark and acidic.

"You asked me about the Princess of Desia." Gray paused. "My sister, Callitia. Callie."

Lea stilled and a wave of shock flooded through the bond, a splash of the coldest water on the warmest day.

"You said there was no princess."

"There isn't." Gray couldn't help the venom that seeped into his voice. "And as far as the kingdom knows, there wasn't. But she was real. My little sister..." he trailed off, his words heavy and choked with emotion.

A tear trailed down Lea's cheek and she wrapped her arms tighter around his neck as if she could hold him together. It almost made Gray break, his heart clenching painfully. He hadn't even told her his tragic story, but the love and solidarity in her embrace reminded him that he would never be alone again.

Gray kissed her hair, shifting Lea so that he could look into her eyes." She was born long after me, nearly a hundred years. I loved her in a way that, until then, I didn't know was possible. My parents weren't warm. My father trained Alaric and me daily, punished us when we didn't perform to his standards. Rewarded us for our ruthlessness. My mother allowed it. She had no other choice."

"Every mother has a choice, Gray." Lea pressed a kiss to his chest, pulling him out of his cruel memories.

"Her only other choice was death. Defiance was not tolerated. It was beaten out of us little by little as my father molded us into the future leaders of Desia. He was never a father, but a king educating his heirs through violence. But my sister, she was too young for any of that. Too innocent. He had two sons—two heirs, and so he ignored her completely. She was useless to him."

An image of Callie filled his mind, her sweet gap-toothed smile that somehow made her green eyes appear so much bigger and brighter. She'd been only nine the last time he'd seen her happy, her long brown hair flying in the wind as she'd run from him in a game of tag.

"Alaric and I would spend hours with her playing in the woods, indulging her in her games. Her laugh..." The sound still frequented his dreams, the melodic trill of giggles that brightened the somber castle grounds as he'd chased her through the trees, pretending to be a monster. He didn't realize it then, but it had been good practice for all the pretending he would have to do for another hundred years after her death.

Lea curled herself deeper into Gray's side, as if trying to give him some of her strength to get through his memories.

"She was the *only* joy in the castle. Loved by everyone. A little ball of light bouncing through those dark hallways. Until my father extinguished it." Intense anger bubbled along their bond, fueling his own.

"You said the same to me. That you wouldn't let him put out my light." Lea's hand drifted to her chest where her magic slept.

"I'm stronger now." Gray struggled to keep his shadows contained. "I'd sooner let him cut out my beating heart than allow him to hurt you. But back then, I was weak. naïve. I didn't know he was planning on..." Gray couldn't bring himself to say the words out loud.

"But.. why? Why would he kill his own daughter?" Lea asked softly.

"Her magic developed at an early age. Far earlier than is typical. Day magic, and powerful magic at that. She started lighting candles at bedtime when she was only two, trying to avoid sleep in favor of playing." Gray smiled at the memory.

"So he wanted her power?" Lea's voice was filled with disgust.

"It wasn't just that he wanted her power, though that was likely the reason he ultimately decided to take her life. He also feared her."

Lea was silent for a moment. "The Black King feared a child?"

"There was a prophecy, foretold when my father overthrew Queen Emmaline. "*With the blessing of the goddess, evil will fall at her feet, and death will follow where she commands.*" Gray paused, the night around them so silent he swore the gods were listening to his words. "Years later, another prophecy was spoken. *A daughter of the sun and stars will destroy the King of Night and Darkness.* He feared that daughter was his own."

"But she was just a child." Lea's voice broke.

"My father's need for power—for control—is insatiable. It blinds him to reality. He would have been proud of her magic had she been his son—an heir—but as his daughter? She was a threat." Gray paused, tilting his head back and staring up at the dark gray clouds swirling in the black sky. "He slaughtered her in front of me. In front of Alaric. He showed us that day how he steals the magic from the bodies of those he murders." Gray hesitated, his shadows pulsing and yearning to burst from his chest, a lethal look in his eyes. "And I *will* kill him for it."

Lea cupped a hand to Gray's cheek. "I'm so sorry," she said softly, pushing her love down the bond and wrapping it around his heart. Gray felt what she was trying to say immediately—that she understood that there were no words, no apologies that could soothe the violent pain that had remained inside him every day since his sister was taken from him.

"Alaric held me back as my father's sword sliced through her neck. Pulled me away as her blood stained the floor under her tiny body. He was always so eager to please my father, to follow in his footsteps. That was the moment that I knew his heart was as cruel as the king had hoped it would be. That he'd been carved in stone to be the exact future leader that my father envisioned for the kingdom."

"Did he..." Lea trailed off, but Gray knew exactly where her mind had gone.

"Steal her magic? He did. There's a spell, an incantation given to him by a sorceress. She'd been imprisoned under Queen Emmaline's rule for crimes against humans so vile, you would never sleep again if you heard them. My father made her a deal, and the world has never been the same."

Part of Gray almost felt bad for the witch. She was horribly disfigured and had clearly been abused by his father for years. But he would be lying to himself if he said she wasn't third on his list of people whose throats he wanted to rip out with his teeth for the spell she'd created.

"So he doesn't need the Lonely Death to steal magic?" Lea asked, her eyes widening in horror.

"No. As long as the incantation is said before the heart stops beating, it can be done. Though by using the Lonely Death, the kingdom fears a mysterious illness rather than their wicked leader. He chose to slaughter Callie and take her power. My father said it was more merciful this way. That he could kill her instantly rather than allow her to suffer from the Lonely Death for days."

"Gray, I'm so sorry." Lea's grief was thick and overwhelming through the bond.

Gray let the feeling wash through him, tears welling in his eyes. "I tried to fight to get to her. I wanted to kill him, but Alaric held me back. My brother never missed a chance to make our father proud. The king was infuriated by my 'weakness.' He said it was shameful to care more about my sister than the power inside her. And because I was weak, he beat me for months, placed me in the dungeons and starved me. My father," Gray winced, the memory physically painful as a familiar ache squeezed the air from his lungs, "He left her body to rot in the cell with me—a reminder of my weakness, he said. That was the moment I vowed to kill them both."

Gray expected Lea's sorrow to seep into his chest, and he prepared himself for the despair he was sure he would feel from her at his admission. But there was no pity in the emotion radiating from her skin. No, it was purpose, resolve. She crawled onto his lap, straddling him as she stared into his eyes. "I will allow you the killing blow," Lea whispered furiously, "but it will be my face beside yours that bastard sees as he takes his final breath. We won't let him get away with this, Gray. I swear to you, I will help you however I can."

Gray smiled with pride at his fierce, beautiful mate. "I was hoping you would say that, Little Flower." He kissed her deeply, allowing their anger and hurt to merge together until it strengthened into a fiery, deadly point. Gray broke the kiss, pulling back only slightly.

"You doubted I would help you?" she whispered, hurt flitting across her face.

"Never, for a moment, have I doubted you. But I think I will need your help more than either of us initially realized," Gray said, taking a deep breath.

Lea sat silently, leaning into him as if she somehow knew he needed to gather his strength to summon the words that had been dancing through his mind ever since she'd thrown him against the wall with night magic in her fury. She had been so deadly, so beautiful... otherworldly.

"I think the prophecy that my father fears was speaking about you, Azalea. I think that you are the Daughter of the Sun and Stars, Queen of Flames and Shadows, sent to bring peace back to the kingdom; descendent of Queen Emmaline, and true heir to the throne of Desia."

CHAPTER II

LEA

The world went fuzzy as Lea felt Gray's words settle in her stomach.

"That's impossible. I would know. Right? My parents would have known if one of them descended from Emmaline," she stammered. "Surely my mother would have been more powerful. And my father? He doesn't even have magic." He was wrong, of course. And yet, Lea knew there was no explanation for why she had both magic of the day and night, why she and Gray had been chosen as mates when there hadn't been such a thing in hundreds of years.

"Breathe, Azalea. I'm not positive, and it doesn't change anything. *Except* that we need answers."

"Dad might know something..." she trailed off. She didn't even know where her father was. Likely north in Woodhurst, hunting and trading, avoiding the home he'd shared with her mother that caused him so much pain now.

"We're not just going to Calir for their king's help in defeating my father, or to break the curse that would allow me to kill him," Gray said, interrupting her thoughts. "The witch who helped me before will know how to help us find information on who you are and where your magic comes from. She is the one who spoke the prophecy, Azalea."

Gray grabbed her hand, interlacing his fingers with hers and sending her strength as her head began to swim.

"If I am her descendant..."

"Then you are the true Queen of Desia. Rightful heir to the throne. You would unseat Alaric and myself as the next leaders of the kingdom."

Lea shook her head. "I couldn't take your place. I wouldn't want to."

"And I wouldn't lead without you as my queen, regardless. It doesn't matter. Whether you are the daughter of a healer and a trader, or you share blood with the most powerful queen in Desia's history, we will rule together."

"If it doesn't matter, then let's just follow the army to Bearswillow. I don't want to know—"

"We *need* to know, Little Flower." Gray's voice was gentle, but his resolve firm. "Alaric has seen you use your powers—both day and night. If he knows, he will either tell my father or he will try to steal your power for himself. We need to be prepared for all possibilities, and to do that, we need more information."

"What if it's something I don't want to know, Gray?" Lea was terrified of the truth, but why, she wasn't exactly sure. The sound of the rain outside their safe haven pattered against the leaves of the trees as Lea tried to hide her emotions from the mate bond. She didn't want to worry him. Still, she knew he felt them all: uncertainty, fear, curiosity.

Gray placed his forehead against hers, nipping at her lip. "We can handle whatever we learn. You and me together. And we *will* get answers to all our questions. But you won't find them hidden deep in your own mind," he said as he slowly slid his hand up her leg.

CHAPTER 12

GRAY

"**B**ut what if—" Gray cut her words off with a kiss as he threaded his fingers through her hair, pinning her firmly against his chest. "There's time for 'what ifs' another day. Just let me kiss you before we rest. There's been too much worry for one evening."

Lea sighed, melting against him, and Gray felt himself grow hard immediately.

"How can I say no to that?" she asked him with a smile, rolling her hips against his.

Gray leaned up to capture her mouth, his hands sliding down her bare back and finding the arch of her hip bones. Their magic coiled around them as she rocked against him again, already growing wet and beginning to slide up and down his shaft.

"Gods," Gray rasped, bending his neck to take a pink nipple into his mouth. "So beautiful," he murmured against her skin as Lea worked herself against him, her moans a chorus to the melody of an ancient song.

Flipping them over, Gray placed himself against her entrance, staring at her flushed cheeks. He paused, making sure his clouds firmly covered the moon. There were two things he was certain of at that moment. One, he needed to be inside Lea like he needed revenge. He couldn't survive without touching her any more than he could survive knowing that warm blood still ran through the king's veins. And two, he might not live through this war. And he'd be damned if he tied his life to his mate's if there was *any* chance his heart might stop beating.

"Gray, please." Lea writhed against him, pleading for him to fill her. The movement yanked him out of his thoughts. Satisfied that the clouds were covering the moon, he sheathed himself inside her in one long thrust, pushing until he reached her end.

"Yes, more..." Lea groaned as he settled inside, stretching and filling her. The vision of his mate beneath him, bare under the sky and calling for him, filled him with fire. He began to move, slow, deep thrusts that caused his muscles to tighten with restraint. He wanted to claim her again, roughly and savagely, but the way her body undulated with pleasure as he fucked her slow and hard gave him the strength to resist.

Lea's nails dug into his back as he drove deeper, needing to mark himself inside her as much as he longed to mark their bond on her skin. He bit her just below her collarbone, hard, his teeth imprinting into her flesh as she moaned his name. "Oh gods, Gray!" Her voice was filled with ecstasy, and he felt her begin to tighten as he kissed the indentations of his teeth on her skin.

Gray couldn't hold back anymore, couldn't move slowly as their passion became frenzied. Their rapid, pounding rhythm increased until Lea arched beneath him, going still as her walls convulsed around him.

"Gray!" she cried again, and the sound of his name on her sweet, swollen lips caused him to tip over the edge, going rigid as he followed her into oblivion. He kissed the mark he had branded her with, a small bruise blooming beneath her freckled skin. Lea reached up, tracing her fingers along the grooves.

"I didn't mean to hurt you." Gray kissed her skin again, apologizing with affection as he gently pulled himself out of her.

"You didn't hurt me," Lea whispered breathlessly, a blush warming her cheeks. She tilted her head up, placing her mouth just above Gray's heart and looking up at him with questioning eyes, as if asking his permission.

Gray craved her teeth marks with a visceral need he'd never felt before, and his eyes darkened as he lowered his chin.

Lea leaned closer and sank her teeth into his flesh, swirling her tongue against his skin as her teeth cut into him.

Something primal erupted in Gray's chest, an animalistic demand to claim her again. He felt himself growing thick and hard against her stomach and he growled, a low rumble that caused Lea's eyes to flash back to his, a challenge in her expression.

"Wicked girl." Gray thrust inside her once again, their magic answering his movement, so intense the ground shook, and the trees swayed, and Gray wondered if the gods might seal their bond despite the fact that he had hidden them from their view. He needed her so much, he *almost* didn't care. And when she collapsed against him once again, falling asleep almost instantly, he saw only the mark of his passion through his heavy, tired eyes.

CHAPTER 13

LEA

Sleep had never come easier, and Lea woke to the beginnings of orange light creeping into the sky. She wasn't sure if it was the fact that her body was spent from her lovemaking with Gray, or if it was more that her mind could finally relax now that she wasn't at war with herself over loving the Night Prince, despite who his father was and what he'd done. For her to know that Gray had been working for years to overthrow him, to stop him from murdering innocent people, Lea was truly at peace for the first time since she had left Bearswillow.

A fist-sized red and yellow bird flitted from branch to branch above Lea's head, leaves rustling as the branches shook from its weight, and she smiled at the normalcy of it.

"We're still accused of treason and on the run, you know," a gruff, sleep-filled voice said behind her. Gray pulled her closer, kissing her hair as he tucked the furs more snugly around them.

"I'm well aware, thank you, oh mighty Eclipsed King," Lea teased.

"It doesn't feel like you're aware," he scolded, ignoring her teasing. "It feels like you're happy. Relaxed and calm. You should be anything *but* calm."

"Do you not want me to be happy?" Lea forced herself to replace her grin with a frown.

"I've wanted nothing more from the moment I saw you." Gray's voice was rough, and Lea felt tension creep into his shoulders. "But what we're about to do... it's dangerous, Azalea. I need you to remember that. We're fleeing my father and brother, who will both stop at nothing to find us now that we're proven traitors. We're planning for battle, for all-out war," he reminded her.

"There will be plenty of time to be afraid." Lea rolled to face him, curling her small body into his much larger one to capture his warmth. "But we're finally together. There are no more secrets between us. Can you just let me be happy right now, and afraid later? Please?" She pressed a soft kiss to his heart, her lips finding the tattoo of the mountains that surrounded Bearswillow wrapped around a single moonflower that showed his devotion to her.

Gray sighed, pulling Lea on top of him. "I think I'm afraid enough for the both of us, Little Flower. If you want to be happy, then by all means," he sent a zap of electricity through his fingers and straight into her backside, pulling a laugh from her lips as he captured her mouth.

His kisses were slow but deep, and a rumble rattled his chest as her hips moved against him. He had just begun to slide his hands up Lea's thighs when the ripple of morning magic flowed around them, her heart skipping as she was filled with warmth.

Groaning, Gray pulled back. "We need to go. Alaric only travels during the day. We have a decent head start since he doesn't know which direction we fled, but if we want to stay ahead of him, then it's time to ride."

Lea nodded, saluting him with a smirk. "Yes, My King. Let the adventure begin."

"You're going to be the death of me," he said with a forced scowl before tucking the blankets more firmly around Lea's shoulders and rising to gather their clothes. He pulled a dark gray tunic from his pack and slid it over her head, gently freeing her long blonde hair from beneath the collar before handing her a pair of black leggings. They dressed quickly, eating a quick breakfast of bread and dried fruit, and before the sun had even fully crested the horizon, they were racing through the forest, Gray's arms wrapped tightly around Lea as if he worried she might disappear into the foggy morning air.

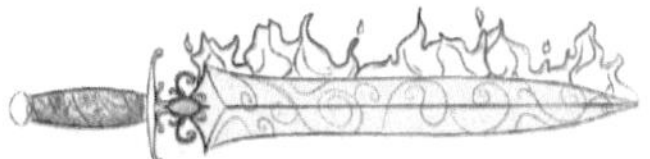

They rode for hours, weaving between trees that grew shorter and thinner the further they traveled. Lea had taken to spending the time looking for different critters, spotting various squirrels, three snakes, and what she thought was a yellow finch before Gray allowed Obsidian to slow. Lea's eyes had grown heavy again, exhaustion urging her to rest her head against Gray's shoulder and sleep, but the brisk pace at which they rode made it nearly impossible. Her mind drifted to her friends, and she sent up a prayer to the gods that they were safe, far away from Auropera and well on their way to the cavern within the Torres.

"Hey," Gray's voice broke through her thoughts. "Are you okay?"

Yawning, she leaned back against him. "Just tired," she replied. "I think all the excitement is finally catching up with me."

Gray looked up at the sky. "I'd like to ride at least until midnight. We need to get to Calir as quickly as possible, and we're only a couple days by horse from the Wicked Wood. Once we're close, it won't be safe to travel at night. We'll avoid entering the woods, go south along the perimeter to be cautious, but there have been reports that the demons that lurk within the wood have recently been hunting outside its borders. It will be crucial that we remain alert at all times."

"Can't we just head straight southwest?" Lea asked. "We could travel through the woods during the day and enchant a pocket of trees to hide us at night, like you did against your brother. It would cut a week off our journey, if not more."

Gray shook his head. "Fae were created to hunt the monsters that now hide in the wood. I have fought them before, Lea. Lost men far more trained than you in their bloody clutches, even in the light of day. I will not risk it."

Lea bit her lip, her hands tightening on the reins as her forehead scrunched. She'd certainly heard the stories, but still, something inside her urged her to enter them.

"I have my sword, my shadows, and my fire. And, I have you." She bumped backward into him. "What could possibly defeat that?"

"The fact that you are pushing the issue tells me you don't appreciate how dangerous those woods are." He ran a hand through his hair in reserved frustration. The horror of memories he was choosing not to share trilled through their bond and across her skin, making her pause.

Lea considered his warning, wishing she had trained harder with Thomas back in Bearswillow. If she had better learned how to wield a sword, to fight with weaponry and hone her instincts, maybe Gray would be more inclined to allow her to fight. Lea yawned again as she spoke. "I was smart enough to escape you back in Bearswillow. And strong enough to fight off Alaric until you got to me."

"You aren't even strong enough to stop yawning." Gray replied, deadpan. "Azalea. There is no doubt in my mind that you are stronger than we realize, smart enough to change the world, and brave enough to try. But until you are properly trained, you will listen to what I tell you. You are *not* ready to face what lies within the wood, and I'm not ready to allow your life to be at risk so soon after leaving Auropera." His words were final, but also made goosebumps spread across her arms. Gray had to know that her life would be at risk again before this war ended. Of course, he wanted her properly trained and ready to face that risk, especially if her life force would soon be tied to his once they sealed the mate bond.

"Fine," she conceded. "I will defer to you. For *now.*"

Gray let a deep breath loose and Lea realized that he'd been preparing himself for an argument.

"I can be perfectly reasonable, you know," Lea reminded him, patting his leg.

A deep laugh rumbled from behind her. "Yes, you were so reasonable when you stormed into the trial with no real plan after I had told you repeatedly I would help Thomas. Or when you shattered a glass just to spite me. Or the time when–"

"I get it," she cut him off. "I thought you were the Black King's loyal Commander, and you were holding me *prisoner*. Plus, it's hard to be reasonable when you make me beg for information. Tell me something to pass the time. Let me in on one of your secrets."

Gray pondered for a moment. "Well, seeing as you now know my biggest one," he said, referring to the small fact that he was the leader of a massive rebellion to overthrow his father, "I'm not sure any of my other secrets matter. What would you like to know?" he asked.

"Your name," she said without even thinking. "You promised me you'd tell me how you came to be called Gray."

"So I did." He kissed the top of her head. "It started as a code name once Erik, Vincent, and I began planning how we could fix the kingdom. It's the color between black and white, the shade between good and evil, dark and light. I knew I would have to do a lot of terrible things for our plan to work. I would have to appear to agree with what my father was doing, pretend to be a devoted son, and play the part of the ruthless commander. I knew I wouldn't be able to step in as my father killed people and stole their magic until we were prepared to fight him. I've tried to keep my darker side from you, but I *have* done bad things, Little Flower. My hands are soaked in blood, even if I am using them to stop a tyrant. My shadows are gray. My lightning is gray. And morally, what I have done lies firmly within the gray."

Lea considered this. "It's the only way to defeat him, Gray." Guilt settled in the back of her throat at using the name. She didn't want him to think about the horrible things he'd done whenever she spoke to him. Didn't want the things that stained his conscience to be connected to the name he used or how he identified himself.

"It's okay, Little Flower." Gray said, and Lea knew he'd sensed her emotions through their bond. "I *am* Gray. It's something I've had to come to terms with, something that I'm not ashamed of or frightened of. He is who I want to be, who I *must* be to finally get revenge and stop the useless slaughter of all those with magic. That's why it's the name I now go by. The Eclipsed King became my code name, and Gray became who I am. It's a way to remind myself that even when I'm doing things I cannot stomach, even when I feel like my soul is damned because I've allowed such vile things to occur as I sit back and watch, I am doing it for a good reason."

"I'm of the light and the dark, too. I have magic of the day and night." Lea grabbed Gray's hand, searching the bond for what he would feel about her confession. "What does that make me?" she questioned.

Gray lowered an arm around her stomach and pulled her tightly against his chest as he leaned down to speak in her ear. A sense of belonging flooded her chest, warmth spreading from her belly through her limbs. It was like discovering something big and important, finding a soul that matched her own, accepting every piece of her.

"Well, Little Flower," he rumbled, allowing his shadows to caress her skin and pull her hair over her shoulder, "I guess that makes you gray, too."

CHAPTER 14

LEA

Lea was freezing, numbed to her very bones, as if a winter chill had found an entryway into her veins and pushed jagged shards of ice beneath her skin. Teeth chattering, she pulled at the covers that had surely fallen off as they'd slept, only to find them wrapped tightly beneath her chin. She burrowed herself deeper into Gray's side, her body shaking as she pulled the blankets above her head and curled into a ball to warm herself.

Gray stirred, pulling Lea more firmly into his arms before opening his eyes sleepily. "Azalea?" He pushed up onto his elbow, worry creasing his face. "You feel like you're on fire." He bolted upright, pulling the covers down enough to place his callused hands against her cheeks. "You're feverish." Concern mixed with the remnants of sleep in his voice as he pulled the covers off of himself, doubling them over Lea's shivering body. "Are you not feeling well?"

Lea shook her head, attempting to sit, but a burning sensation in her chest stopped her in her tracks. Pain seared through the skin below her neck as she tried to speak. She ran a hand up her chest, tears springing to her eyes as her fingers traced pea-sized lumps across her skin. Poison ivy, perhaps, from sleeping on the ground?

She'd seen her mother treat various rashes all her life, had helped treat them with her own hands at her mother's direction, but these bumps felt foreign to her.

Pressing gently on one of the bumps, Lea winced in pain as fluid ran between her fingers. She pulled them back to see fresh blood and a horrified look on Gray's face.

At that moment, Lea knew she should be feeling panic, but instead she just felt tired. *Something's wrong,* she thought through the fog in her mind. Her tongue felt dry as cotton and her head swam with confusion. She'd just been asleep, so how was it possible for her to feel this exhausted?

"Azalea," Gray's voice broke through her rambling thoughts as he pulled the covers back quickly, his hands trembling as he looked down at her chest. "Where is your necklace?"

"Hmm?" Lea absently reached toward her neck, but Gray stopped her hand before she could touch the open sores again.

"Your necklace, Lea! Look at me!" Gray gently grabbed her face, and Lea noticed sweat beading on his brow, shadows floating from the hand now gripping her chin. "Where is it?"

Lea didn't answer, racking her brain about where it could be. Gray laid her down gently before running to the supplies lying on the grass near Obsidian, ripping open bag after bag as he frantically searched through their belongings.

"Janelle," Lea croaked, pushing onto her elbows at a memory of Janelle and Emma's smiling faces as they teased her that her necklace didn't match her wedding dress. *Such a silly worry,* Lea thought as she whispered her friend's name again. "Janelle..." She couldn't finish her sentence. Whatever was on her chest was making it hard to speak. *I need to lie down,* Lea thought through her daze. Collapsing backward, she tried to snuggle back under the covers.

"What do you mean, Azalea? What about Janelle?" Gray rushed over to her, gently pulling her back to sitting. His forehead was creased with concern, his green eyes filled with terror. *Such pretty eyes...* Lea thought as she reached up to touch the dark bags below them.

"I need you to focus. I know you're tired, but I *need* you to answer me. Okay?" The way he was speaking to her reminded her of how Thomas sometimes spoke to his younger siblings. "Think, Little Flower. Where is your necklace? Does Janelle have it?"

Lea looked down at her chest, where the beautiful stones and chain had laid almost every moment of the past year. The sight of her skin caused a wave of dread to flood her veins, burning away some of the confusion and fatigue. Across her breastbone and trailing up her neck were not just bumps, but black welts. They had begun to open, and deep red blood ran in small rivers down to her stomach. A red rash trailed up her throat and across her shoulders where minuscule raised dots were beginning to appear. The pain intensified as she looked at her diseased body, and she was suddenly certain that were she to peel away her skin and muscle, she would find the same black bumps coating the inside of her throat and lungs.

"Emma made such a beautiful dress. She asked—" Lea swallowed down the metallic taste of blood, the effort of speaking causing the wounds in her throat to open. "I gave it to Janelle to wear during the ceremony. I meant to get it back after, but the explosion..."

Gray gathered Lea in his arms and she felt his warmth seep into her, soothing her pain. She opened herself up to him, using precious energy to try to understand what he was feeling. As she closed her eyes and leaned into the bond, she was overwhelmed by his disbelief—his utter terror. He was filled to the brim, absolutely buzzing with panic. His hands found her bloody chest, and he pushed his energy into her, his healing magic closing her wounds and easing her pain just enough to allow her a single deep breath.

"The Lonely Death," Gray breathed. "This isn't happening." His breaths became shallow as his hands traced her body. He looked up at the horizon, the beginnings of oranges and pinks peeking out from above the trees. Lowering her down gently, he pushed every ounce of his power into her skin, pressing his cold, shaking hands against her chest, throat, and shoulders, trying to heal her as much as he could before the sun crested and his magic weakened. "This isn't happening," he said again and again before bolting back toward their sacks.

Lea's mind spun, but she was unsure if it was from the illness or her terror. The Lonely Death had killed her mother, Thomas's father. Little Anthony... And now it was coming for her. The course of illness was unpredictable. She could have two days, maybe three, but however many days she had left, they were numbered. One thing she was certain of was that death would find her.

Gray yanked the box holding her letters and vials from her bag and sprinted back to her. Throwing open the top, he shuffled through the contents until he found Lea's one remaining vial. He uncorked it and held it out toward her; the vial shaking so violently that a drop spilled from the mouth onto the grass. The ground turned black instantly, a tendril of fragrant smoke rising and bringing the sweet scent of the deep blue berries that had grown in her garden to her nose.

"It's the potion of death, Gray." Lea recognized the smell. "Potio mortis." Had her mother expected her to need it? To take herself from this world and travel beyond the veil?

Gray's fingers loosened, about to drop the vial, but Lea quickly grabbed at it, crying out in pain as her sudden movement caused agonizing pain to spread down her arms. Gray scrunched his brows, his nostrils flaring as he replaced the cork, and Lea breathed a sigh of relief. If her mom had thought it might be necessary, she couldn't waste it. *What did you know, Mom?*

Gray stood, roaring at the sky, his head thrown back as his scream rattled the leaves of the trees. He paced, his head in his hands as Lea's own mind spun. How could this have happened? She'd been with Thomas, then Gray, but then there had been chaos...

Fuck. The realization crashed over her. How had she forgotten seeing Alaric in the woods? She'd hoped it had been a dream, a trick of the mind, because surely, wouldn't he have taken the opportunity of seeing her alone to stab her through her heart?

"Gray," Lea whispered, her voice shaking. "It was Alaric, I saw him."

Gray froze mid-stride, swiveling his head to her. "When?"

"During the battle. He was standing in the trees, speaking under his breath. He was just smiling at me, Gray. But he didn't make a move to kill me. Not a single step... I only saw him for a few moments, and it was dark... I thought maybe I was seeing things."

In less than a second, Gray was kneeling at her side, cradling Lea's head between his hands.

"Has he done it before, Gray?" Lea questioned softly, already knowing the answer to her question, but praying all the same that she was mistaken. "Does he know how to summon the Lonely Death?"

Gray pulled her against his chest, refusing to answer as he pressed his lips into her hair. Sobs began to wrack her body, shooting pain through her chest and into her limbs.

"If it can be done, Lea, it can be undone. We will find a way, because I am not living without you. Do you understand me?" He pulled her back slightly, trying to get her to look at him, but her eyes were so heavy they refused to remain open. "Lea!" He grabbed her face. "Open your eyes, Lea!" he ordered, his deep voice full of demand. Her body tried to obey, but sleep pulled at the edges of her consciousness.

"You need to fight! Open your eyes," he begged as his magic tried to fight off the illness attempting to spread through every inch of her. "You will *not* give up, because I will gladly walk into death's embrace before I live a single moment on this earth without you next to me. The world will plunge into darkness without you, My Flower..."

Lea nodded, settling against his chest once again. "I'm tired..." she mumbled, her head lolling forward. "So tired." She couldn't fight it anymore.

"Stay with me, please." Gray's voice broke as she faded into oblivion.

Lea was running, sprinting through dark trees as mud squished between her toes. Where was Gray? She couldn't find him anywhere, but she could *feel* him. The electricity thrumming through her skin told her he hadn't wandered too far. He was nearby. The question was, was he close enough to feel that something was stalking them?

Lea tripped on a root protruding from the ground, crashing into the thick, freezing muck. "*Shit!*" she cursed as her elbow hit something sharp. Where was Gray? The feeling that something was following her grew stronger as the hair on her neck stood on end. A howl rang out from behind her—not the cry of a fenrir, but of something that sounded *almost* human. Something evil to its core.

Scrambling to her feet, she ducked under a branch and threw herself behind a thorny bush, small scrapes peppering her exposed arms and legs. Hissing in pain, she tried to push her day magic toward the cuts, but her light was gone. Where it normally danced and swirled, embracing her heart and pushing light through her bloodstream, there was only a colorless void. She was filled with complete darkness—a black fire ready to destroy. The sensation made her nauseous, and she tried to push away the foreboding energy, but it stuck to the inside of her ribs like hot tar.

Footsteps *squished* nearby, and Lea squeezed her knees to her chest, trying to make herself as small as possible. She worried her thumping heart would give her away and tried to slow it—to force it to beat more gently. Her vision went fuzzy as she held her breath.

It didn't help. She couldn't stop the gasp that escaped her lips as a monstrous figure slowly walked into her line of sight. The man bent down, running his hand against the root she'd tripped over. The root cringed away from his touch, trying to retreat into the ground, but the man was faster as he swiped a finger through the blood that had spilled from her own veins onto the rotting wood. Bringing his hand toward his face, he took a deep inhale, then tilted his head back in a frenzied cackle.

"So careless, to allow yourself to bleed in my presence, *Little Flower*." The sound pulled Lea's stomach into her throat. It was so familiar, and yet, she couldn't place the strange voice that seemed to echo throughout the woods as he spoke.

Lea looked down and clamped a hand firmly against the jagged cut running up her elbow. Blood gushed between her fingers, wet and hot, the stinging of the wound making her eyes water as the blood began to flow so fast she couldn't stem the bleeding.

"Do you not believe I can smell the life draining from your veins? I am Death himself." The man laughed menacingly, a humorless, empty sound that caused pain to bloom throughout Lea's body. Fire erupted in her ribs with every breath, and the skin of her chest and arms burned. *Shit. And why does my neck hurt so bad?*

The demon turned to her as he stood, his green eyes piercing through the dark.

Alaric?

Lea scrambled back, her hands sliding against the slick ground as she attempted to stand. Rough bark scraped her skin as her back hit a tree, and she cried out in pain as she twisted to crawl around it. Escape. That was all that mattered. She felt her airways expand, her blood pumping straight to her muscles. Even the most primal part of her body knew that she needed to flee, but as soon as she turned around, Alaric appeared in front of her again. He crouched down, his head cocked to the side.

"Hello, Little Flower..." he said again, the nickname mocking. Fire sparked at his fingertips as they pressed into her arms, searing her skin. "So nice to see you again. Azalea—"

"Azalea!" She was shaken awake. "Azalea!"

Suddenly, Lea could see again, the world around her a bit brighter than the pitch black she'd been experiencing moments before. It wasn't night at all, but dusk, only minutes before the sun would set.

Lea's nightmare faded away like wisps of smoke as she gasped for air. "Alaric!" She looked around frantically, her hands shaking violently as she reached out for her mate. "He's here! We have to go!" she forced out, her throat burning once again.

"It was a dream, my love. I can't feel Alaric anywhere near us," Gray soothed, rubbing her sticky, sweaty hair from her face as Lea met his eyes. Her heart slowed.

A dream. It was just a dream. Lea shivered, rubbing her arms as she reached out with her senses. Birds still chirped, and the rhythmic hammering of a woodpecker searching for dinner knocked and echoed against the trees. A beetle skittered across the ground near her feet, clicking as it dropped into a small hole. There would be no birds or bugs if Alaric was near. Gray was right. Alaric had only found her in her mind as she'd rested. The only green-eyed Nestruir anywhere near her was Gray, but looking at his eyes now, she hardly recognized them.

They were dull, with dark circles and thick bags betraying the calm facade he was trying to school his face into. His skin was pale, and his hands shook as they cradled her head. It reminded her of when they'd traveled to Auropera, when he'd been so tired after days with her in their village that she had put aside her anger and granted him the gift of sleep.

"You look exhausted," she croaked, weakly tracing the lines above his brow. Her stomach dropped when she looked at her arm. The black welts had spread to just below her elbow and were cracking and oozing blood as she lifted it.

"I'm fine," he whispered as his hands traveled down to her chest. Pain seared through her entire being as the rumble of night magic flew across the grove, and Gray's face immediately creased in concentration. Healing energy flooded into her skin, and she realized the reason for his exhaustion. He'd been trying to heal her as she'd slept throughout the day, depleting himself of magic as he waited for night to replenish it.

"You need to rest," Lea urged, fighting to keep her eyes open.

"I'll rest when I know you're safe," he protested. "The sun is setting. It will replenish my power."

Lea wanted to believe he could save her, but even as he healed her arms, she felt painful sores opening on her stomach. "Gray—"

"I can heal you!" he roared, the bugs and birds that Lea had heard before going silent.

Gray hung his head. "I'm sorry." Gray kissed her hair, so softly it was as if he believed she was made of splintered glass. "I *will* heal you. Do you need anything?"

She shook her head. "The pain's easing," she lied. It was no use, Lea knew that. If anyone would have been able to heal someone from the Lonely Death, it would have been her mother. Only the moonflowers had that power. Lea's eyelids drooped.

"Rest, Little Flower. I've got you," Gray said calmly, but the way his lips trembled as they pressed against her forehead told Lea that he wasn't as confident about her safety as he seemed.

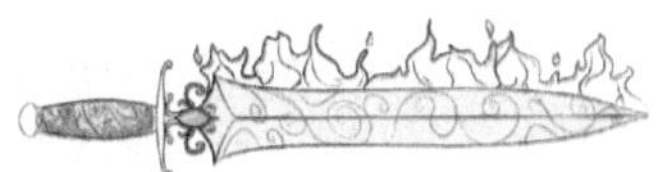

Lea was walking through the forest again, her wedding gown pristine as it flowed softly around her legs. The stars in the fabric seemed to actually sparkle, the same silver-blue tone that she had seen glowing on the chapel doors and in her dripping blood as she'd pledged herself to the rebellion.

What was I doing? Lea thought. She had the vague sense that she was searching for something, but... what? The feeling she was missing something important nagged at the edges of her conscience, like leaving a room and forgetting what you were searching for. *How did I get here?*

Ducking under a bare, low-hanging branch, Lea scanned her surroundings. *There!* A flickering light, dancing just in the periphery of her vision, and Lea knew immediately that it was what she was searching for. The light paused, hovering stationary in the air as if waiting for her full attention before floating into the darkness ahead, beckoning her to follow.

A will o' the wisp, she realized. Lea had heard tales of these mischievous spirits steering travelers from their path into trouble at night, and yet, her feet continued to propel her forward. This spirit didn't seem unkind. It was far too beautiful. She stepped forward, unable to stop walking as she was led around a maze of bushes and tree trunks.

The wisp disappeared as the soothing rippling of a river met her ears. Following the noise, Lea walked toward the long, hanging branches of a willow. It was out of place here in the forest. The other trees surrounding her were taller, almost black, with gnarled trunks and dead, knotted branches, and yet somehow this beautiful, healthy green willow existed amongst them. Water splashed nearby as she stood before the umbrella of branches, the sound of someone wading through the stream beyond causing her to pause.

"Hello? Who's there?" Lea called, and the splashing stopped. *Stupid girl,* Lea chided herself. *Why would you call out your position, alone and vulnerable in the dark like this?* And yet, her body didn't care about the danger as she continued forward.

There was no answer, but still, Lea pulled aside the curtain of greenery. Someone was there, and even though Lea didn't know why, she could feel in her bones that she *needed* to talk to them. The weeping tails of the willow tickled her skin as she walked into the river. Cool, refreshing water rushed against her ankles and light burned her eyes. Blinking back tears, she allowed her vision to adjust, shielding her face from the intense glow. Water sloshed again before a delicate, warm hand gently gripped her chin, pulling her face up to meet the beautiful gaze of a stranger. A tall, delicate woman with silver-blond hair that Lea had seen her whole life memorialized in countless paintings and statues.

Immediately, Lea dropped to her knees as the full power of the goddess of the moon washed over her—a gentle, cool energy that was so pure, it made her want to cry. The goddess didn't speak as she looked at Lea, her hand reaching out toward her chest.

Ouch—what? Blood dripped from the goddess's fingers as she pulled her hand back. Frowning, she bent to dip her hand into the water to let the river carry the traces of red away.

Lea's chest burned, and when she looked down, there were black, bloody welts spreading across her skin. *Are they familiar?* Lea was certain she had seen them before, but where? Each breath she took caused stabbing pain, the sores climbing down her stomach and legs, up her neck, and across her fingers.

The goddess bent down, placing her hands on Lea's head. "It is as I feared." She spoke softly, her voice sweet like honeysuckle wine. "Hold on, Daughter of the Night. He will find a way to save you."

"It hurts," Lea sobbed, the pain becoming so severe throughout her whole body that nausea roiled in her stomach. "I can't—" Breathing became difficult as her lungs filled with blood. She coughed, and the blood drowning her dripped from her mouth and nose. Lea watched in horror as the stream turned a deep red. There was so much blood.

The moon goddess knelt, once again placing a motherly hand on her head. Her voice grew firm, losing its softness and turning demanding. "Hold on. *Fight.* Soon, he will find a way. Do not give in. Do not give up."

Lea gasped for air, desperately trying to get oxygen into her lungs. A roar shook the ground, and she looked up, tree limbs bending and shaking as a feral cry tore across the woods.

"Gods Dammit, help her!" The voice was so familiar, but who was it?

"He will find a way, but you have to hold on. The answer is in your blood. You *must* survive." The goddess was insistent, her eyes wild and face grim as she followed the scarlet trails in the river.

"I can't"—*gasp*—"breathe!" Lea coughed again, blood dripping from her nose.

"Wake up, Azalea. He will save you." The goddess stood, turning to face the moon and waving her hands in an arc across the sky. Her long fingers wiped every trace of clouds and fog away, the moon becoming so bright it showed the true, hideous extent of Lea's sores. Lea gasped, but before she could speak, the goddess flicked her fingers. Thousands of shooting stars flew across the sky. "It's time to accept your fate," the goddess said sadly.

"Are you listening to me!?" That strong, furious voice roared again from somewhere far away. "Save her! Heal her!"

"Get up and go back to him. The answer is in your blood," the moon goddess repeated before fading away into nothing.

Lea splashed the cool water on her face with shaking hands, trying to wake herself enough for her body to obey. But everything hurt so terribly. She would do anything to make it stop.

"I will destroy everything you have created. Both here on earth and in whatever realm you hide. Heal her, or you will be gods of nothing!" She heard fists beat into the ground, the earth shaking. "Please, Little Flower." A phantom hand cupped her cheek. "Come back to me."

The haze in Lea's mind cleared enough to recognize the voice. Gray. Her mate. She would do anything to make the pain stop—*any-thing*—except leave him.

On weak, shaking limbs, Lea pushed herself onto her hands and knees, a scream ripping from her very center as her vision tunneled. *Breathe,* she commanded herself, fighting against a wave of dizziness. She would rise, and she *would* return to him.

In a flash of silver blue light, Lea found herself back in the grove with Gray, struggling to sit up. She sucked in a breath, prepared for the searing pain, but was surprised to find that no blood filled her lungs. Lea looked down at her chest, the black, diseased welts still creeping around her sides to her back. "Gray," she croaked, her body so exhausted she laid back onto her side. "Gray," she tried to say again, but she was so thirsty, her throat so dry that no sound left her lips.

Gray was facing away from her, and he dropped to his knees as he looked up at the sky. It seemed like he didn't know she was awake, but she was too weak to call out to him again.

"Please, don't let her die. Take me. We haven't sealed the bond." Chest heaving, he stared at the stars, at the silent, incandescent moon. "I know you hear me!" Fury crossed Gray's face at the sky's stillness. "If you take her," his voice crackled like fire as shadows twirled into the heavens, reaching toward the gods he begged, "I will follow her into death. But not until I have turned this world to nothing but embers!" Her powerful mate's voice cracked. "Please..." He placed his head into his hands as his anger turned to despair.

Reaching her hand along the ground, Lea watched as Gray's shadows snaked toward her. It was as if they knew she was conscious and watching him, even if he didn't. She wanted to go to him, to comfort him, but the Lonely Death took hold again, pulling her under as Gray turned around, rushing back to her as she faded back into her nightmares.

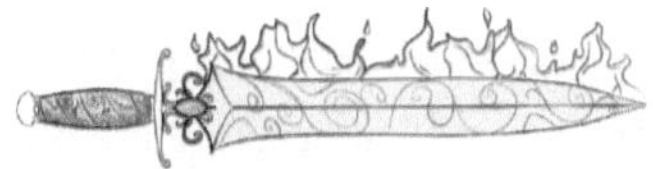

Lea's breaths were shallow, her limbs heavy as she hovered somewhere between dreams and consciousness. Familiar voices filled her mind. Memories, perhaps? Was this her version of her life flashing before her eyes before she took her final breath? She tried to wake—was determined to hold on just a little longer. The goddess had promised Gray would find a way to save her. She only needed to keep breathing. *In and out. In and out,* she chanted in her mind.

Gray... Where was he? She couldn't hear him, couldn't feel his touch. *He's here. He'd never leave you. In and out.* Lea fought to remain conscious as her mind tried to pull her back into a dream. The wind blew, a violent gust that caused her dirty blond hair to blow in front of her eyes, obscuring her view. She could hear people arguing about where to turn, hear the tension in their voices, the frustration. Was it the Royal Army? Had they finally found them?

The wind blew again, pushing her hair back behind her ear. She felt its cool kiss, smelled the sweet fragrance of wildflowers. *This isn't a dream.*

It felt too real, sounded too real. Lea needed to wake up. *Now.* She needed to warn Gray that they were no longer alone. Raising her eyebrows, she tried to open her eyes, but her body was paralyzed. Or maybe, she was just too weak to move. Lea heard the clomp of heavy, powerful hooves moments before she was lifted into a pair of strong, familiar arms, the scent of rain rolling in from a storm comforting her weary soul.

"I'll get us there as fast as we can," Gray soothed. "We'll ride through the night. I won't stop."

"Gray, what's—" The words came out jumbled, incoherent.

"I thought I could heal you once night came, but it just kept getting worse." Thunder crashed as Gray clenched his jaw. "I can still save you. We have to get to Bearswillow and find Erik. He'll marry us. It's the only way." He continued talking, and it seemed to Lea as if he was trying to convince himself his plan would work. "The Lonely Death is specific to my father, but because of my bargain, he can't kill you if you are his daughter, even if by marriage. I can heal you enough to get us there, and then you'll be fine."

Lea tried to reach out to him, to tell him he needed rest. He had never looked so tired, so frantic. His face was sallow and gaunt, his eyes bloodshot.

"It's okay, Little Flower." He pulled them on top of Obsidian gently, kissing her hair as he held her like a small child. Lea's heart shattered as she watched a single tear track down Gray's face. "You can rest," he said tenderly as he spurred Obsidian into a gallop.

They had just passed through the invisible boundary of their refuge when the shuffling of feet and the intensity of anxious voices hit their ears.

Gray pulled his sword in an instant, tucking her beneath his arm.

"I swear to the gods, I will destroy whoever dares to take a single step forward," he roared, black shadows instantly exploding around him, wrapping between the trees and searching out the threat. He looked like the god of death, the embodiment of wrath and vengeance as he kicked Obsidian's side and began to race toward whatever threat hid in the woods ahead. Lea knew he wouldn't wait for them to attack—there was no time. His sword was raised in his white-knuckled fist, and Lea could feel his body buzzing with searing hot fury as he prepared to slaughter their enemy.

Fire shot through the woods from ahead, drawing a line of flames in front of Obsidian that halted them in their tracks before quickly encircling and trapping them. Obsidian reared, letting out an enraged whinny.

"*Fuck!*" Gray shouted as he tried to suffocate the flames with his shadows. He attempted to urge Obsidian through, but the horse refused, stomping his feet in fear and defiance. In the distance, Lea heard several pairs of feet storming through the dense woods. Gray pulled her from Obsidian's back, readying himself to sprint with her through the fire and away from danger, when Lea placed a hand on his cheek and nodded toward the trees.

"Look," she whispered weakly, the action so painful that tears pricked her eyes as blood coated the inside of her mouth. With a whimper, Lea's eyes rolled back in her head, her body going slack.

"Lea!" Gray's eyes dropped to her chest, exhaling as it continued to rise and fall. A stick cracked under a heavy step, and Gray swung his head toward the sound, sword at the ready. The flames extinguished rapidly as five figures appeared through the fog.

"Drop the sword, Gray. We're here to help."

CHAPTER 15

GRAY

A familiar form emerged through the smoke, their hands raised in the air.

"It's just us, Gray," Erik said cautiously.

Gray didn't believe the man standing in front of him was his friend as he stood with his knees slightly bent in a protective stance, his eyes fully black and his shadows swirling around them like a shield. His chest heaved with rage, and he was blinded by panic. Through the bond, Gray could sense that Lea was fading. He was running out of time.

"Erik?" Gray's nostrils flared as his animalistic brain continued to tell him it couldn't be true, that there was no way his Erik was standing before him when he had explicitly told him to lead the rebellion to Bearswillow. His second had never once failed to follow orders. It was a trick of his mind, the gods taunting him with a false solution to his problem. It was too easy.

Every one of Gray's senses told him to run, to protect his mate at all costs. It was his only focus—as ingrained in his body as his own heart beating. His legs shook as he stepped forward just a few feet to get a clearer look. Erik wore the same clothes he'd worn days ago and was covered in dirt as if he'd been sleeping on the ground.

"It's real, brother. We're here," Erik gestured behind him.

Janelle popped her head out from behind Erik at the same time Emma and Noah walked out from behind a tree.

"I don't believe you!" Gray roared. He was seeing things. He had to be. Erik would *never* disobey him.

"Cut the shit, Gray," Janelle snapped. "You're wasting time."

Thunder boomed, a bolt of lightning crackling in the clouds above their heads, ready to strike, but Gray held it at bay. His mind spun, hesitation creeping into his gut. Could it really be true?

Erik crossed his arms and lowered his chin at Gray. "You broke your arm when you were fourteen, trying to scale the wall outside your room. You've watched that woman in your arms for years, loving her so much you stayed away because you thought it was best for her. One time, I shaved your eyebrows off in your sleep after you embarrassed me in the sparring ring. Your father killed my mother."

Gray's mouth went dry. He could count on one hand how many people knew that information.

"It's us, Gray. No tricks. It's real."

As the shadows around them receded, Gray dropped his sword. Lea sagged in his arms as he moved, her head lolling to the side as sleep claimed her once again. She'd done nothing but fade in and out for almost two full days, coughing and crying out as her black wounds had spread. Gray had healed her constantly, his magic weakening to a dangerous level as he'd poured every bit of his power into her, but as soon as he would see her sores scabbing over and beginning to heal, they would open again with a vengeance, weeping and oozing thick, clotted blood.

Gray was glad she had slept, that she wasn't aware of what was happening to her frail human body. He'd been so certain that he could heal her. With the mate bond, he should have been able to, but as her body grew weaker, it became obvious that time was working against them. Lea had begun to mumble nonsense words in her dreams, delirious and confused—a sign of the final stages of the Lonely Death. She was dying, and so he had left, needing to find someone—anyone—who would help them.

"How did you find us? It should have been impossible." Gray had been terrified since the moment he noticed the first wound on Lea's freckled skin. His chest was so full of dread that it climbed into his throat and choked him. But somehow, another sliver of panic worked its way in between his ribs. If they could find him, even through the wards he had placed, then so could his father.

"Emma sensed that Lea was hurt and insisted we turn back. The closer we got, the more she could feel. It's the Lonely Death... isn't it?" Erik's face was pale, his hands shaking slightly.

Gray didn't need to confirm his friend's suspicions. It was obvious by the look on his face that he was completely aware of the danger of what was happening.

"Noah is gifted in tracking. He was able to bring us this far, but you've been hidden behind your enchantments."

"They were too strong for my magic to get through." Noah said, his eyes as big as saucers in his young face as he focused on Lea's oozing, open sores. "I'm sorry, Commander. I've been trying—"

Emma interrupted, speaking for the first time. Her voice was soft but firm, calm and urgent all at once. "We need to hurry, Erik. She's barely hanging on." Emma walked closer, but Erik placed his hand behind him, stopping her.

"You can't get near her, Emma. You have magic," he warned.

"I'll risk it." Emma swung her head to face Erik as if daring him to challenge her. "I see her spirit severing from her mortal body. We have *minutes*."

As if a spell was suddenly lifted, Gray's eyes widened in determination. Erik was here, a length of rope hanging from his sword belt. He'd known exactly what needed to happen. Had come prepared. They could save her. Gray turned to run, Erik fast on his heels. They'd planned for this years ago. If Lea were to ever contract the Lonely Death, there would be only one way to save her.

"You will *not* risk it," Gray shouted over his shoulder at Emma as he reluctantly placed Lea down on the cold, hard ground. Throwing up a shield, he made his shadows thick and firm, blocking the other's access into the clearing. He'd be damned if he allowed the Lonely Death to take one more person Lea cared about.

"We need to heal her enough to wake her, enough that she knows what's happening." Erik said as he wrapped Lea's necklace back around her neck, fastening the clasp. Gray gave him a murderous look as Erik's fingers touched Lea's skin. "Focus, Gray." Erik snapped. "She's going to be in pain as she wakes. You need to stay calm."

"I *am* fucking calm," he snapped.

Erik and Gray knelt beside Lea, both of them placing their hands on her swollen, red skin. They pushed their energy into her body, healing her as much as they could. They pulled the fatigue from her sluggish heart and pushed in light to warm her and darkness to chase away the disease. Lea stirred, moaning in pain as a strangled cry left her mouth.

"I'm here, Little Flower. Stay with me. I know it hurts." Gray laid a hand against her cheek, reaching toward their mate bond. The pain on her face shredded his insides, crushing his lungs and causing searing agony to pound in his skull.

"It's okay," Gray soothed, sweating from the effort of healing her. New sores opened along her arms, and Gray roared in frustration.

Lea cried harder, now fully awake. "It hurts. Make it stop, please."

"We have to do this now, Lea. The pain will go away. Listen." Gray gently turned her face to allow their eyes to meet. "Marry me. *Please.*"

"What?" she croaked, trying to open her eyes.

"Marry me, Azalea. Here, now," Gray rasped.

Lea nodded, a pained smile tipping her lips up as she attempted to lift her arm to cup his face.

Thank gods, Gray said to himself as he gathered her into his lap. "Erik is going to perform the handfasting ceremony. We will be married, and you'll be safe."

Nodding, Lea curled herself into him. A trickle of blood ran from her ears, and panic swelled in Gray's chest.

Lea must have sensed his worry because she forced herself to speak. "This wasn't," her breath rattled, "how I pictured," gasp, "becoming your wife."

She's trying to joke, at a time like this? "Save your energy for our vows, Azalea." He kissed her brow and grabbed her hand, threading his fingers between hers. "Erik? Hurry."

Erik pulled the rope from his belt and wrapped it around Lea and Gray's wrists, tying a firm knot.

"Evander Jonitan Nestruir," Erik spoke so fast, Gray worried Lea wouldn't understand his words in her weakened state. "Do you bind yourself, body, mind, and soul to this woman? Do you pledge to love and protect her until your last breath leaves your tired body?"

Gray could hardly breathe. Despite the magic eating away at Lea's skin, she was the most beautiful woman he had ever seen. The shining light in the vast darkness that was his life, and she was *his*. "I vow it to you, with the gods as my witness," Gray whispered to Lea. His voice cracked with emotion as he continued to stroke her face, trying to hold her pain at bay. The words struck too close to his heart as he held his mate's exhausted, failing body in his arms.

"Azalea Delphinium Astrantia, do you bind yourself, body, mind, and soul to this man? Pledge to love and protect him until your last breath leaves your tired body?"

"I vow it to you," she coughed, blood splatting across Gray's shirt. "With the gods as my witness." She forced out the final words, sagging into his arms in exhaustion.

"As a child of the gods, here to witness your vows in truth and of your own free will, I declare you husband and wife. From this moment on, nothing shall separate you, whether on this earth or beyond the veil. And may the gods annihilate any who try."

The ground shook, Gray's storm clouds vanishing from overhead as the wind picked up, blowing them from the sky. The moon shone brightly, illuminating Noah, Janelle, and Emma hiding behind the smoky entrance to the clearing, safe behind the magical barrier.

The world froze, seconds moving like hours. Hours in which even the gods watched with bated breath to see if they'd said their vows with enough time to stop death. Gray brushed Lea's hair from her face, holding his breath as he waited for her ashen face to flush with blood. Slowly, her body started to knit itself back together, her wounds scabbing over and her breathing becoming even once again.

"You're okay," Gray said, a guttural sob escaping his throat. He still felt physically ill remembering the moments in the past few hours that he hadn't known if she would survive. His body ached, fully expended from all the magic he had poured into Lea, desperate to save her, but he didn't care. He squeezed her tighter, embracing the feeling of her strength returning. She'd been so weak—he'd hardly been able to feel her through the bond as the illness had progressed. But the brightness in her eyes confirmed she'd come back to him.

"I can't breathe," Lea sputtered, and panic settled like a rock in Gray's gut.

"That's impossible." Gray's blood pounded in his ears. *What went wrong?* "The spell won't allow you to die. What are you feeling?" Gray began to lift her from the ground, but Lea wiggled backward.

She sucked in a deep inhale. "I'm okay." She leaned back into him. "You were squeezing me too tight." A small smile danced on her lips as Gray released his grip on her, allowing her to take a deep, restorative breath.

A barking laugh erupted from his chest. The whirlwind of his emotions was too much. He wanted to drizzle down warm rain to wash the blood from Lea's skin, to rejoice and weep and never let her go, but he also wanted to hand her to Erik and find a way to kill his father. Alone.

Without risking his wife's life. The urge to release his shadows and storms in a powerful gust of rage against him was almost all-consuming.

His *wife*. Gray's heart soared, then sank. It was more than he'd ever let himself hope for. And unless he was willing to tie her life to his, the most he might ever have.

"She's okay, Gray." Erik patted him on the shoulder firmly before dropping down onto his butt with a sigh and collapsing onto his back. "She's okay," he said again, this time whispering softly to himself. As sound and life returned to the forest once again, Erik took a deep breath, releasing it slowly as he drug his hands down his face.

Gray was vaguely aware of Janelle and Emma running toward them, collapsing onto their knees to hold Lea's hands. Noah hung behind, standing several feet behind them as if worried he was witnessing something private.

"I'm okay," Lea said to them all, her voice quiet as a soft smile crossed her lips. "Don't worry so much, husband of mine. Or you, my loyal subjects." She offered a weak smile to her friends, and Janelle rolled her eyes.

"Glad to see your sense of humor didn't suffer," Janelle said with a huff, but Gray didn't miss the way her hands still shook.

Placing a hand over Lea's heart, Gray savored the regular, steady beat as his own heart slowed to match its rhythm. She was okay, safe from his father and brother, and he was damn sure going to keep it that way. The urge to seal the bond thrummed through his entire being. He'd be able to hear her thoughts, be able to heal her more easily. But if he died, she would lose her life as well. He couldn't live with that. "I'm sorry," Gray whispered as he squeezed her tighter.

"Commander... look," Noah said breathlessly, interrupting Gray's thoughts as he nodded toward the sky, and Gray shifted to allow Lea to look with him. Above their heads were dozens of sparkling silver-blue stars shooting southwest in a magnificent display of magic. As they watched the beauty in silence, several turned to hundreds, then thousands. The black sky was full of glittering trails of beauty. It was breathtaking, and it reminded him of his mate in a way he couldn't quite place. They were hopeful—barging forward on a path toward something magnificent and important.

"It's a message," Lea whispered, struggling to sit on her own, her body exhausted from the battle it had fought over the past two days. "It's a message for me."

"What do you mean?" Janelle asked, giving Erik a sharp look as he opened his mouth to speak.

"My mother's letter," Lea wiped a tear away with the heel of her still bloody hand. "*There are answers you may someday seek to questions you do not yet know—the stars will guide you to them. Let them.* It's her. I can feel it, *here*." She placed her palm on the middle of her chest, just above where her magic lived. "When I was sick, the goddess showed me these stars. She's telling me it's time to accept my fate."

"Your fate can wait. You need to rest, Little Flower. We'll go to Bearswillow, give you time to heal."

"No, we can't. If we want to win this war," Lea's voice grew in strength and resolve as she nodded to the stars, the incandescent reflection of their light in her eyes, "then we need to follow the stars."

CHAPTER 16

LEA

The shooting stars streaking across the night sky were the most exquisite thing Lea had ever seen, more beautiful even than the flowers from her garden or the shimmering magic that bent the trees and filled the air every sunrise and sundown. They were calling to her, forcing her eyes toward their faraway destination and urging her feet to follow.

"This war has been underway since my father took the throne. A few more weeks won't change the outcome. Erik, where are your horses? We'll leave for Bearswillow immediately," Gray barked at his second, interrupting the peace of Lea's stargazing.

"The horses need to rest. We rode them nearly straight through the day and night to get to you in time," Erik said, ignoring Gray's snappy tone as he stuffed some nuts and dried berries into his mouth. He held out his hand, offering some to Janelle, then Emma.

"And we're not going back to Bearswillow," Lea argued, trying to squirm from Gray's arms to stand. She couldn't very well argue she was strong enough to fight her way through the Wicked Wood when she was a puddle in Gray's arms. "I already told you, we have to follow the stars."

"We're going to the cavern! *That* is what we *have* to do!" A snarl left Gray's throat as he held her closer, refusing to let go, his chest rising and falling as frustration pulsed through the bond.

"Gray..." Erik warned, raising his hands out in front of him. "Now is not the time. We talked about this. You said you'd be prepared."

Lea looked back up at the sky, but her focus remained on Gray and Erik's conversation. *What is Erik talking about?*

Gray's fingers tightened around Lea's arm and leg, squeezing so hard it was as if he worried she would disappear if he didn't hold her close enough. Tension radiated off his skin, mixing with something fiery and furious that she couldn't quite identify.

"Let me have her, Gray. Take a walk." Erik maintained eye contact with him, stepping forward with his arms outstretched. "We can discuss this when you've calmed down."

Gray took several slow, shaking breaths before speaking in deliberate, staccato sentences. "Make Azalea a fire and a pallet to lie on. Emma," he snapped, his rapid breathing causing his nostrils to flare, "I'd like you to stay close to her. Let me know if she starts to feel wrong to you. Sick again, or tired. Anything that seems different at all, you will find me."

Emma nodded. "Of course. She feels stronger now, but I agree. She needs to rest."

Gray thanked her gruffly before turning to Janelle and Noah. "I'd like you to come with me. We will do a sweep of the area and assess for threats to ensure it is safe for Azalea to recoup before we return to—" he cleared his throat and rolled his neck and shoulders—" before we discuss the next steps."

Lea worried about the argument that was about to ensue, that her headstrong friend would tell Gray to go fuck himself and that she was not his soldier to boss around.

"Let me know when you're ready to go," Janelle said instead, discreetly winking at Lea before going to help Erik build a soft pallet. Emma patted Lea's knee before stepping a few feet away, giving them some privacy. Lea's nerves faded enough for her to breathe deeply, but that hum of worry and anger still circulated around her heart, a steady stream of powerful emotions surging from the bond.

Looking up, she took in the desperation on Gray's face. Dark purple bruises shadowed his eyes, and his tangled hair was haphazardly pulled into a bun. She traced the lines bracketing his mouth, his lips turned down into a frown. Needing to soothe them away, she placed her palm against his cheek, and he leaned into her touch and closed his eyes. "I'm okay," she reminded him gently.

Through the bond, Lea felt Gray try to suppress the surge of primal need that flooded through him—the fiery urge to take her away and hide her from the world.

"You almost died, Azalea. Do *not* tell me that you're okay," Gray whispered heatedly, almost brokenly. "If you won't take this seriously, I will chain you to my side and drag you back to Bearswillow. I promised you I would keep you safe. Do *not* forget that I keep my promises."

Lea's mouth cracked open, but she had no words. Gray *had* promised her that, and she knew how he felt about keeping his word. But there were more important things in life than being safe. Every fiber of her being was certain she needed to follow the stars, that something important was waiting for her wherever they led. But the absolute grief and terror on his face over what had almost happened—it caused a painful lump to settle in Lea's throat. The last thing she wanted was to hurt him, to add even one more line of worry to his rugged, handsome face.

"Go, Gray." Erik appeared at their side, holding his arms out toward Lea. "Go patrol the area. Calm down."

Tensing, Gray bared his teeth at his friend. "Are you *my* commander now?" he growled.

"No. But I'm the only one here with sense at the moment. And I'm the only person you've ever been able to trust unconditionally. If you want to do what's best for her, then allow her to rest, and go calm down."

Taking several steadying breaths, Gray shoved past Erik without a word and tenderly placed Lea down on a soft pallet of furs next to the crackling fire, pulling a thick wool blanket snugly around her shoulders and bending down to kiss her hair.

"We're not done with this conversation, Azalea," he said gravely before turning and stalking through the trees, calling sharply for Janelle as he retreated.

Lea watched in awe as he trudged away, his heavy steps causing the trees to tremble as shadows seeped out from him in every direction. The night around her lightened a bit as he left, as if the sun was beginning to rise, but Lea knew it was just her husband's rage calling the darkness to him that caused her to be able to see more easily.

Husband, The word brought a lightness to her soul that she wouldn't think possible after being so close to death. But it was true. She was alive, and married to her mate. The other half of her soul. Lea placed a hand to her chest where her necklace laid, smoothing the black piece of star Gray had gifted to her with her tired fingers.

As the wind softly blew through the clearing again, the crickets resuming their chirping and the frogs beginning their nightly song, Erik's shoulders relaxed. He turned to her, giving her a beaming smile as he came to sit at her side.

Noah cleared his throat. "If you're okay, I think I'll gather some firewood? Give you some time to talk. Or... I don't know. Rest." He raised his eyebrows in question.

Erik tilted his head, but nodded before turning back to Lea. "Now that he's your husband, you'll have to learn how to handle him. I'll teach you," Erik teased.

"I'm not sure he's the kind of Fae that can be *handled*, Erik. But you can teach me how to try. What's happening? He's so furious. I can still feel his rage through the bond, but he needs to listen to me. We *have* to go through the woods. I've never been more sure of anything."

"I agree with your crazy plan, for once." Erik sat beside her on the cold ground, stretching his hands out toward the fire for warmth. "Gray's not angry with you. He's not himself, Sunshine. Not right now."

"Because he's the Eclipsed King?" Lea questioned nervously, wringing her hands. It would be quite the burden to lead a rebellion against your own family, to feel a personal responsibility for the safety of all of your followers.

"No. Gray's the same man as the Eclipsed King as he was when you knew him as the Commander, or Gray, or Evander. It's the mate bond that's making him act erratic." Erik pulled a knife and a shiny pink apple from his coat pocket and began to cut large chunks off, popping them in his mouth. "It hasn't been sealed."

"It hasn't been sealed the entire time I've known him. Why would that make him any different now?" Lea asked.

"Because now you've both acknowledged the bond, confessed your love. You were in grave danger, and your connection sensed that. A Fae male can become..." Erik paused, scrunching his face a bit as he considered his words, "possessive, irrational. The stronger the bond gets, the more intense the need to protect your mate becomes. Gray might think he is above that risk, but he's no different from any other Fae male."

"Except he has deadly magic and the ability to call a devastating and fatal thunderstorm overhead in a second?" Lea joked, attempting to lighten the mood.

"Except with the ability to end the world as we know it," Erik confirmed. "We spoke about it before the wedding. The first wedding." His eyes crinkled at the edges. "I warned him this might happen as you traveled alone, or once you got to Calir and were surrounded by strangers. He was certain he'd be able to control his impulses to protect and isolate you."

"But you knew better?" Lea prodded.

"Gray is the closest thing to a brother I'll ever have." Erik pulled a second apple from his pocket and Lea's mouth began to water. With a chuckle and a quick slice, Erik ripped it in two, handing the slightly larger half to Lea. "I've seen how he is. Not just with you, but with anyone he cares for. Gray loves fiercely. Add in the mate bond..." he sighed. "It's one of the reasons I was so reluctant to allow him to leave without me once we fled the castle."

"Then why did you?" Lea twisted to face Erik. He was conflicted. It was obvious by the way that he stared with tired eyes into the fire, as if answers might be hiding inside it.

"He is my king. My commander." His hand subconsciously traced the scar across his hand. "Emma's the one who reminded me that he is my family first."

Emma smiled sheepishly, looking toward the woods and clearly attempting to pretend that she wasn't paying attention to their conversation as she pushed a stick around the embers of the fire.

The stars called Lea's eyes back to the sky, and she heeded their command as she laid her head back. She knew that as much as Gray loved her, it would be difficult to convince him he needed to put her at risk in order to follow her hunch. And to be fair, it *was* a risk. Lea hadn't missed the direction the stars were pointing them in, hadn't missed how they shot directly southwest, past the moon and the star of Altair, straight toward the Wicked Wood.

Was it some cruel cosmic joke that they were being led straight into the horrible wasteland full of nothing but danger? Her mother's words clanged against her skull. *There are answers you may someday seek to questions you do not yet know—the stars will guide you to them. Let them. Let them.* The words were the beat of her heart. *Let them. Let them.* Yes, it would be dangerous, but the way her magic squirmed inside her—the desperate feeling in her chest that urged her to stand and heed the sky's calling—it demanded to be answered.

She was certain that this was her fate, her adventure. She'd been naïve, a foolish girl, too busy living in the past and focusing on herself to recognize that things needed to change. The sting of Thomas's words the day before her failed wedding to Gray were sharper than talons in her mind, digging deeper and deeper as their truth settled into her very marrow. He'd warned her that change was coming, that the king couldn't continue to go on unchecked. Gray had been risking his life for hundreds of years to save the kingdom, to fight against and destroy his own family so that every Fae and human living in Desia could have a better life. And she hadn't even been brave enough to join the rebellion on her own.

There was no excuse, but if she was being honest with herself, she knew it was because deep down she couldn't join a cause that she thought would end in the elimination of the Nestruir family. Not when that family had included Gray.

It had been easy to fixate on her grief over losing her mother, her anger at being forced to leave Bearswillow along with Thomas and serve the king. Easier still to focus on Alaric's hostility toward her and his constant presence in the back of her mind. And all the while, the king was stealing magic. Ruthlessly slaughtering the innocent, all for the sake of attaining power he didn't even use.

All the attacks from the south had supposedly been dealt with by Gray and Erik, but Gray had said that King Tanad of Calir would be waiting for them—that he would help them. Why would he do that if his kingdom had been attacking them for centuries? It didn't add up, and Lea started to wonder if there had ever been attacks at all, or if Gray and his battalion had simply been patrolling the woods as an excuse for Gray to meet with the King of Calir.

"Are the threats to the south real, Erik?" Lea's voice broke through the silence, raspy as it scraped across the scar tissue from her healed wounds in her throat.

Erik laid down beside her near the fire and stared at the shooting stars. "There is still a lot you don't know. The attacks to the south aren't from Calir, if that's what you're asking. The demons within the wood, however..." he pondered for a moment. "They're spreading further east, venturing beyond the boundary we've spent centuries pushing them into. We don't know why they're becoming increasingly bold. Gray thinks they can sense that villages and towns are becoming weaker, less protected by the magic we have tried to keep from being discovered. People like you. Like Thomas, and the others in your village... The demons can smell you, taste that you're different and a potential threat. It provides some measure of protection, but the more the king kills, the less magic lives throughout the villages to warn them away, and the bolder the monsters get."

"But what is it they want?" Lea shivered as a chill shot down her spine.

"They simply crave death. They are mindless killers, built for ripping through flesh and rotting minds. Some can make you go mad just at the sight of them, and others..." Erik shuddered, and Lea's hands clenched at her sides in fear at the enormous Fae's response to thinking about what dwelled within the woods. "I've seen grown men weep, cry out for their mothers as their intestines were ripped from their stomachs. I've seen lifeless bodies hanging from trees, so high in the branches it would have been impossible for them to have climbed."

"But you and Gray have always survived." Lea prodded, desperate for an ounce of comfort. For something that she could hold onto to know that they could survive this.

"We have, as have many others, but at what cost? Half our men quit the patrols after their first time in the Wood, choosing less danger and less pay so they never have to return."

An uncomfortable chill ran through Lea's body, and suddenly she no longer wanted to speak about the evil they might face if they followed what the stars compelled her to do.

"How did you come to be Gray's right-hand man, Erik?" Lea asked, clearing her throat and shaking away the thoughts of demons and monsters. She now understood why Gray was willing to go against his family, but the danger of Erik helping lead this rebellion in secret? It was a gamble, one that could very well end his life far too early.

Erik's eyes shone with sorrow in the fire, glazed over as if remembering a long-gone memory. "Have you ever thought about what motivates men, Lea?"

"I'm not sure I understand exactly what you're asking." Lea lowered her eyebrows.

"Men and women, both Fae and human alike, we do not sacrifice for nothing. Rarely, if ever, is it selflessness that brings us to risk our lives. Vincent—his motivation is *almost* pure. But his is also a sacrifice he makes out of trepidation. He grew up in Calir, was a high-ranking general of their king. He joined our cause out of fear that the Black King's magic would travel beyond their borders. He wants better for his own kingdom than the hell we've been living through in Desia for hundreds of years." Erik threw the core of his apple into the fire, causing the flames to hiss in response. Sparks shot up, but turned to ash with a flick of his fingers, floating back into the fire like snow. "I'm assuming Gray told you his reason?"

Nodding, Lea reached out and placed a hand on Erik's forearm. He'd revealed his reason earlier when trying to prove who he was to Gray. Lea could hear his broken voice as he'd relived the memory echoing in her mind. Even now, hours later, his voice was still too raw, and she knew from the frown on his normally smiling face that his own motivations were something that were hard for him to speak about. "You don't have to talk about it, Erik. Your reasons are your own."

He forced a smile and placed his hand on top of hers. "It's okay, my queen," he teased with a wink. "Do you remember the man always at the king's side? Herald?"

Lea nodded. She'd *never* forget the blond man who had sat to the king's right, the one who had smirked knowingly as Alaric had pinched and burned and tortured her while she served his meals.

"He sired me."

The fire grew taller, the heat so intense that Lea had to pull down the blanket and scoot backward. "Herald is your father?" She tried, and failed, to keep the surprise from her voice. *How did I not know this?*

"He is *not* my father. That title is reserved for men who love and protect their families." Erik took a moment, tracing shapes Lea couldn't see with a stick into the hard ground. "What motivates me, Lea, is revenge." Erik took a deep breath and lifted his hand, watching as sparks and flames danced along his knuckles. "Not long before Gray's sister... When the king..." he sighed, stopping to take a slow breath. "The king was learning to practice his newfound magic," Erik continued. "His ability to steal power from others. I know your pain of losing your mother to the Lonely Death, because my mother was its first victim."

It was as if the fire from Erik's fingers jumped straight into her skin, rage filling Lea from the tip of her toes to the top of her head as a different kind of companionship built between them. The loss of a mother—No. The *murder* of a mother. It wasn't something one could ever fully recover from.

"What happened?" Lea prodded gently, her voice soft despite the fury Lea felt on his behalf.

"The king needed a body to steal magic from, and Herald volunteered my mother. As if her life was worthless. As if she was *nothing*. His motivation was greed; pure and simple. He wished for the power being the king's second would offer. He didn't care that it would leave his son without a mother. Didn't even bother giving me a chance to say goodbye. He locked her in a room with the king so he could watch each step of the disease, each wound appear and sore open. He left her alone as she struggled to breathe, as the life left her body."

The darkness inside Lea coiled tighter, like a viper preparing to strike. "We'll kill him, Erik."

Patting her leg, Erik shook his head as if shaking the memory away. "I know we will, Sunshine. *I* will." He nodded. "And I am grateful that you and Gray will lead us to the day I can take that killing blow. But that begs the question... What motivates you?"

Lea paused, considering his words. It's true. She hadn't joined the cause when she'd thought that she would have to fight against Gray. Even when she'd hated him, she hadn't wanted to see him hurt. But now? "I think it's love," she said softly, feeling foolish. "I'm angry about my mother. I'm furious with the king. But more than that... Janelle has magic. So does Emma, and you. And the people from Bearswillow. I love them too much to allow the king's darkness to destroy them. If we don't fight against him, they'll never be safe. Never." It was the truth. She'd always wanted to be brave. She'd been named for that very virtue and had always felt like she fell short. She didn't want to fight for herself. But for her friends? Her *family?* She'd go beyond the veil happily if it meant they would really get to *live.*

Erik's shoulders relaxed. "I think that's the best reason you could have given me, Sunshine. Which is why we need to convince Gray to follow what the stars are telling you, even if it's dangerous. If the goddess is pushing you to go through the woods, then there's a reason."

"Wait. No," she squeaked, surprised by the fear that threatened to swallow her whole. "Gray and I will go alone." She stuck out her chin, her stomach swirling at the thought of Emma and Janelle traveling with them. "Emma and Janelle. And Noah. He's so young. You'll take them back to Bearswillow, to *safety,* right Erik?"

Erik opened his mouth to speak but was interrupted.

"You're not seriously fucking doing this again, are you?" Janelle stomped toward them, a vein bulging in her forehead. Gray followed stealthily behind her, his shadows only slightly more controlled than before he'd left.

"Janelle," Lea started.

"Nope. Queen or not, I will still fucking murder you. You have needed our help more than once. You likely will again. We go together, or we don't go at all."

"We don't go at all," Gray growled from behind them.

Lea stood shakily, hiding her grimace as she struggled to pretend that she wasn't completely exhausted.

"You said 'we,' Gray. *We* have a rebellion to lead. Did you mean it, or not?" Lea's voice was firm.

A crack of thunder rattled the ground. "Of course I meant it. I still mean it, but—"

"Haven't you ever known something in your soul, Gray?" Lea placed a hand on her chest, right above her magic. "Known beyond a doubt that something was meant to be? That the universe was telling you something and you had no choice but to listen, even if it terrified you?"

"I know in my soul that I love you!" he roared, stalking toward her and grabbing her face between his hands. "I know in my soul that I am nothing if you are gone. I almost lost you, just *hours* ago. And now you're asking me to deliver you to death's door again?" His voice broke as he pressed his forehead against hers. "Please don't make me do this. Don't make me risk your life again," he begged.

The pain on Gray's face, the anguish and fear, it was almost enough to get Lea to agree to go back with him. They could return to Bearswillow, ignore the stars and her gut and pick the safer route. But they wouldn't win this war by playing it safe. Lea took a deep breath. "I'm not making you do anything, Gray. But," she met his eyes, "I am *asking* you to. I'm asking you to trust what I'm feeling, what the stars are telling me. Please." He had to listen. He just had to. The goddess had appeared to her, had spoken to her in her dreams and at the church. She was handing them a map, a way to find answers. Lea had spent so long trying to use the moonflowers to stop the Lonely Death, and she had failed again and again. But here was a different path—a way to finally seize control of her life and save the people she loved.

Gray took several heaving breaths, his shadows trying to break free of his control as they writhed and slithered around Lea's body, as if they could wrap her up and sweep her away to safety. "If we continue on that path and follow the stars to the Wicked Wood, you *will* listen to me. You will obey every command I give you."

"Sir, yes sir," Lea nodded, trying to hide her smile.

"This isn't a joking matter, Azalea." He snapped back, his patience clearly wearing thin. "A single wrong step could lead to death. Making too much noise, picking the wrong place to camp. I need to hear you say it. All of you." Gray turned to Janelle, Emma, and Noah. "Promise me.

Swear to me you will listen to what Erik and I tell you. If I tell you to run, you will leave me and run. If I tell you to hide, you will burrow yourself into the darkest, smallest corner you can find. Swear it."

Lea felt the gravity of her vow as she placed her hand on top of Gray's, silently apologizing for making him feel like she didn't understand his worry. "I swear. I will do as you say. We all will." Lea looked up at her friends and the young boy who so bravely had risked everything to help them find her. Three heads bobbed up and down, a silent confirmation.

Gray sighed, pulling Lea in close. "Then prepare yourself, Little Flower. Tomorrow, we begin our journey through hell."

CHAPTER 17

ERIK

Erik took a deep breath of fresh air as he hiked through the forest with Gray to retrieve their horses. There was still nervous energy running through his veins, as well as a heavy sense of guilt. In the past weeks, Gray and Erik had spent countless hours finding the perfect hiding spots for their escape, knowing that their time was running out. He'd been with Gray, had seen the locations he'd chosen and helped create the pockets of magic-protected forest. And yet, even through his bond to Gray, the blood bond they'd forged ages ago, he hadn't been able to find his king when his mate was dying and he'd needed him most.

Either his memory was failing him, or the enchanted groves had been so well protected that it had been out of his control. He'd known they were heading toward Calir, and that he would likely try to circumvent the Wicked Wood to get there, even though it would add more time to their journey. But which places he had chosen to stop to rest, Erik had no clue. It had been a blind race to find Lea and Gray over the past three days, and the feeling of helplessness that had almost strangled him as they'd searched was not one Erik ever wanted to feel again.

He'd practically had to yank Gray by his collar to get him to leave Lea's side to find the horses and pack them up so they'd be ready to leave at daybreak. They would need to spend as much time traveling during the day as possible before stopping for the night. Moving through the dark in the Wicked Wood was unfathomable, and likely, a death sentence. No. They definitely needed as many daylight hours as the god of the sun would allow them.

Gray walked quietly next to Erik, tension rolling off his shoulders along with the shadows that betrayed his stoic expression. Shadows crawled along the ground, and not for the first time, Erik thanked the gods that Gray had been blessed with night magic rather than magic of the day. While his shadows could be just as devastating as fire, they didn't carry the risk of accidentally incinerating whatever they touched during times of extreme emotion.

And this was definitely one of those times. Erik had no doubt that if Gray could wield fire, they would all have burned up in a horrific inferno. Instead, his furious shadows pulsed and searched for something to devour, deadly silent but magnificently lethal. Even the forest didn't want to risk his rage. The cacophony of bugs went silent as they sensed Gray's presence, and while some might find the complete absence of sound eerie, Erik was grateful for the quiet.

"You have to seal the bond," Erik said finally, his voice echoing through the trees. Gray continued on quietly, seeming to consider his words. *Maybe he'll finally listen*, Erik thought, holding his breath. Gray needed to realize that his irrational behavior only put Lea more at risk. Hope surged in his stomach as the silence stretched on.

Finally, Gray's steps faltered. Erik's hope crumbled into bits of aggravated disappointment as his friend's face hardened before his eyes. Gray had been stubborn since they were children, but ever since he'd spoken to Lea that day in the alley, touched her, it was as if something inside him had awakened. Something feral—animalistic and primal in a way that was unsettling. This wasn't the first time they'd discussed sealing the bond. *Argued*, actually. And Erik knew that it likely wouldn't be the last. It was clear that Gray was beyond his rational ability to think through the decisions he was making with the need to complete the mate bond coursing through his veins, but that wouldn't stop him from trying to make his friend see reason.

Fingers flexing into tight fists, Gray resumed storming toward the horses, averting his gaze. "I told you, Erik, three times now actually, that I will not risk her life to make my own easier. I have a duty to our people to protect them until my dying breath, and I don't plan on breaking that vow."

"Sealing the bond won't change a thing—"

Gray held up a hand, interrupting him. "There is a very high chance that I will not survive this war, and if sacrificing my life is what it takes to destroy my family's horrifying legacy and bring peace back to the kingdom, then that is what I will do. I will wait for Azalea beyond the veil for as long as it takes. I will suffer through every moment happily if it means she gets to live. But I will not bring her with me." Gray's words were determined, almost frightening in his intensity.

Erik studied his friend, his king. Fae didn't age like humans and would still appear in their prime for hundreds of years, if not more. Even so, Gray seemed to have grown older over the last several months. More tired. Weary. It wasn't easy to carry the weight of the kingdom on your shoulders, and yet that was the decision they had both willingly made along with Vincent so many years ago. It wasn't as if he could fault Gray for his stubbornness. Erik would also fight to his death to ensure the king and Prince Alaric's downfall. He and Gray had sworn that oath long ago, spilling their blood and swearing before the gods that they wouldn't stop until the wicked fell. They were bound to their word through blood, magic, and integrity. Even if they hadn't pledged their lives to the cause, Erik knew that they would both make the same decision yesterday, today, and tomorrow.

Erik searched for the moon behind the blanket of thick, gray clouds. Maybe he could pray to the goddess of the moon, ask her to show Gray reason. *Shit!* Erik hissed as he stumbled on a root. A growl of frustration rumbled from his chest. "Call off your clouds Gray, I can't see a damn thing."

"Your eyesight is fine." Gray didn't wait for Erik to catch up. "You're just angry that I want to protect my wife. That I won't give in to your demands."

"I'm not angry that you're ignoring what I'm *asking* of you," he said pointedly. "But I am angry that you're making such a foolish decision when we're about to walk into so much danger. We won't be able to focus if your mating instincts are overtaking your rational mind. You're already not thinking straight, trying to get Lea to return to Bearswillow rather than follow what was obviously a sign from the goddess herself."

"And how do you know it was a sign from the goddess and not a simple meteor shower?" Gray said indignantly, waving his hand and calling more clouds to block out the stars shooting overhead.

"I know it because it's the truth, and so do you." Erik forced his hands to relax, his fingers begging to wrap themselves around Gray's arms and shake some sense into him. "The color of those stars, it's the same color Lea glows when using her magic. It's the same color we saw when she pledged herself to the rebellion back at the castle. The timing of it can't be explained away, Gray. This is the path she is meant to take. That she *wants* to take. If our hunch that she's a descendent of Queen Emmaline is correct, then it is our job to help her fulfill her destiny."

"It is our job to keep her *alive* and *safe*," Gray retorted, his shadows reaching toward Erik of their own volition as he tried to pull them back into himself. Erik took a small step away from Gray, an imperceptible movement, but it didn't escape his friend's attention. Gray took a deep breath, and Erik relaxed as slivers of moonlight began to peek out from the clouds. He knew Gray would never hurt him purposefully, but his magic was a wild thing. Organic, like the dirt under their feet or the water that rushed down from the snow-capped mountains in Bearswillow.

Gray's magic was unruly enough without the mate bond waiting to be forged, but now that Lea had accepted him and confessed her feelings for him, his magic would become even more untamed. If the legends were true, and Erik was finding out firsthand that they were, Gray would be dangerous, irrational, and it wouldn't matter that he'd known Gray for hundreds of years. His singular focus would be to protect his mate from anything he perceived as a threat. Even if that included his oldest and most loyal friend.

"We cannot keep her safe as long as the king and Prince Alaric rule this kingdom, Gray. Even with the spell protecting you right now, she's not safe. Her friends aren't safe. She will never forgive you if something happens to them, not if they're hurt because you stopped her from seeking the answers that she needs."

"Don't you think I know that?" Gray retorted, his fists clenching and unclenching at his sides as they continued walking. "Don't you think I know she'd die for *any* of her friends? That stubborn woman has proved that again and again. You don't think that I am *painfully* aware she would hate me if I stopped her from sacrificing herself for Janelle and Emma? For *you*?"

Erik's chest warmed at the thought. To finally be in the inner circle of his queen, when he had helped watch her with Gray for so long... It was like a family member returning from a long voyage. "And you're not painfully aware that when Lea finds out that you're withholding this choice from her, she might hate you for it, too?"

"I accept the consequences of my decisions." Gray snapped. "I refuse to allow her to die. Just as I will not allow the rest of you to make careless choices. I am the head of this rebellion, and it is my responsibility and my burden to get us all through this war safely. To get every single member of the resistance home to their families. That includes Lea."

"There will be bloodshed, Gray," Erik said sadly, softly. It was inevitable. After all, they had already lost some good men and women in the first battle of the resistance coming out of hiding. They both knew that they would lose many more, even with their best efforts to minimize death.

"And the very idea of that haunts my dreams," Gray rasped, running a hand through his long, dark hair. "But it will *not* be Lea's blood that is shed. I won't seal the bond until we're safe, and if you cannot accept that, then you will be replaced as my second."

Gray would do it, Erik was sure of it. He would do anything to keep his mate unharmed. "We can revisit this when we are safely in Calir, but for now, you need to agree to listen to me if I tell you that you're being irrational. I would die to keep her safe, too. I've sworn it to you, but I will do so again if it means you will *hear* me." Erik reached out and grabbed Gray's arm, stopping him from escaping the conversation and forcing him to meet his eyes. "I swear to you, on the gods and the blood that runs through my veins, I will sacrifice my body, my life, to protect Azalea. If I tell you that you are being blinded by your need to protect her, by the fact that you haven't sealed the bond, you *will* listen to me, Gray. I have never once steered you wrong."

Gray studied Erik for several long moments, his expression hidden on his stony face, the façade that he had perfected over the years of acting the part of the Night Prince naturally falling across his features.

"Would you seal the bond, Erik?" He questioned earnestly. "Would you put Janelle's life at risk by attaching her life to yours? Could you allow that connection, knowing that if you died in this war, she would die alongside you?"

"Janelle and I don't have a mate bond, so your question is irrelevant," Erik responded sharply, grinding his teeth together. The words left a sour taste in his mouth. Janelle was beyond frustrating, never listened to anyone's instructions and blindly acted based on a confusing mixture of impulse and loyalty, but the idea of her dying... Heat flared in his chest. It's not that her loyalty was a bad quality, but Erik feared that it would be the death of her.

"But if she were," Gray pressed. "If she were your mate, would you sentence her to death? Because that is what I will be doing if I seal our bond. I would sentence Lea to death, and I'm afraid that a world without her is not one worth saving at all."

Gray resumed walking without waiting for a reply, and Erik followed slightly behind, considering his words. He understood his logic, his reason, but he was failing to recognize the fact that an unfulfilled mate bond might be a death sentence for her as well. For all of them.

"She'll need to be trained, Gray. Her magic is powerful. It's obvious she is capable of more than either of us knows, but that much power without control? It's dangerous. She needs to be instructed in combat as well, in fighting and weaponry."

"I'll take care of her training, Erik," Gray snapped, stepping closer as his shadows surged along the ground toward Erik's feet.

"I think that's unwise," Erik replied cautiously, knowing his words had the potential to cause Gray to tip over the edge. "It would be better if I trained her. You're too distracted. If you won't seal the bond, then allow me to do this."

Ignoring him, Gray continued walking until they reached the grove where their supplies had been hidden, a nondescript area that looked exactly like every other pocket of trees they'd passed. With determined strides, Gray walked straight to the horses, his jaw ticking as he wrapped a rope from wrist to elbow, securing it in a knot. Erik knew Gray well enough to see that he was thinking, considering his words as he prepared the three horses.

Erik gave him time as he reflected on the journey here. Emma, growing up in the castle, had known the basics of riding and had been sufficient enough in her skills to ride alongside them on her own horse, and Noah had been given one when he'd offered to help track Lea.

Janelle had ridden with Erik, as she'd never been trained in horseback riding. Riding behind her had been difficult, his cock hard and his hands itching to pull her closer. He pushed down the ache spreading through his body at the memory. *Now is not the time to think of such things,* he reminded himself. Not with war on the horizon and Gray so on edge.

Gray tied Noah's honey blonde and white spotted horse to the saddle of the larger horse, a rich, earthy brown stallion with a shining coat, before climbing on and looking at Erik expectantly. Gripping the saddle, Erik pulled himself to straddle the other horse, Cinnamon. It was a feminine name for a stallion, he thought, but it described the horse's coloring perfectly. The click of Gray's heels spurred the pair to trot forward.

After riding in silence for many minutes, Erik waiting patiently as he allowed Gray to work through his stubborn notions, Gray finally spoke. "You may train her in weaponry, and you may train her to use her day magic. I will help her conquer her darkness. That is the most I can agree to." Thunder rolled in the distance, and Erik's jaw almost dropped at Gray's concession. Offering to help train her had been the rational choice, the safe choice, but Erik hadn't expected a rational or safe answer from Gray.

"Okay," Erik agreed with a nod. "We will start her training tomorrow."

CHAPTER 18

LEA

Gray woke Lea just before dawn, shoving a makeshift plate of bark filled with stale bread and fresh berries into her hands. After not eating for so many days, it made her stomach feel sour, but she forced the chewy, tart bites down anyway, motivated by the way the lines of worry on her handsome mate's face eased with every swallow.

Bringing her a bucket of water, Gray gently washed the remaining blood away from her chest and arms, before helping her dress in thick trousers and a soft brown sweater. Her sores had closed completely from the day before, but the memory of the Lonely Death on her skin lingered. Pink welts remained where her wounds had been, the itching almost unbearable as they rapidly healed.

Lea buttoned her tunic, attempting to hide the evidence of her brush with death. Why she bothered, she wasn't sure. It was obvious from the tension in Gray's shoulders and the exhaustion in his posture that he wouldn't be forgetting her brush with the other side of the veil any time soon.

Surprised at how exhausted her body still felt, she allowed Gray to hoist her onto Obsidian. He effortlessly climbed up behind her and Lea immediately felt his arms wrap around her and pull her close as he tugged his riding cape around the both of them snugly.

"It's okay if you need to rest, Little Flower." He pushed her hair back from her eyes, a sweet, gentle gesture. "The Lonely Death might not be able to kill you now, but you're still recovering. There's no shame in allowing yourself to heal."

Lea wasn't sure if that was true. If she was being honest with herself, she'd never felt exhaustion like this before. Not on her journey to the capital, nor after Alaric had beaten her nearly to death. The fatigue she felt now was bone deep, and as relentless as an aphid. Despite the fact that she had done nothing but pass in and out of consciousness for the last several days, her muscles throbbed. Even the deepest breath didn't seem to provide enough oxygen to energize her tired body, and just lifting her arms to braid her hair away from her face had caused them to shake and burn.

As Azalea was about to argue, Emma appeared next to them, leaning forward to scratch Cinnamon behind his ears. "Your body feels weak to me, Lea. It's making *me* tired, sensing how much you need to rest. If you won't listen to Gray, then please do it for me."

Lea sighed as she looked at Emma. There were dark circles beneath her eyes, and lines crossed her forehead and the sides of her mouth. Emma wasn't lying about feeling exhausted. Lea was aware how stubborn she could be, had been forced to be after her mother died and her father had left her alone. But these were her friends, she reminded herself, and she needed to accept that advice from those she trusted was worth considering.

"Okay, I'll rest. But I want you to wake me in a few hours. I don't want to sleep all day and risk being awake all night."

"If that should happen," Gray said, "I can think of plenty of ways to fill our time." Underneath her cloak, Gray's fingers caressed the underside of her breast—his movement hidden from the others. Lea yearned to give in to that feeling, the heat bubbling up inside of her. But not here, and certainly not with an audience.

"Hands to yourself, Commander," Lea whispered with a yawn.

Gray's hand slipped across her belly, pulling her back so she could lean against him, her head falling into the crook of his arm as he held the reins. "Rest, my love."

Lea closed her eyes, allowing the gentle breeze blowing through the trees and the rhythmic, melodic beat of the horses' hooves to lull her into a deep sleep.

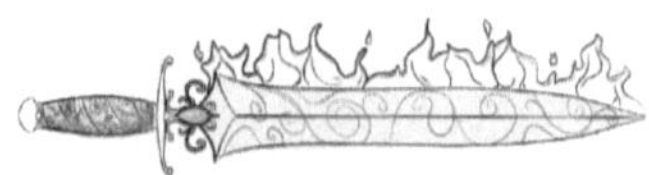

Lea was vaguely aware she was dreaming as she stood in a small area of cleared trees near a rundown cottage that was calling to her from the corner of the clearing. Her stomach twisted as she walked toward the cottage, passing an overflowing garden of moonflowers—stark white instead of the rotting black she was so used to seeing. Reaching down, she trailed her fingertips along the crisp petals, but a gravelly voice made her pause, one that made her stomach churn in anticipation, though the sensation was not entirely unpleasant.

"Azalea?"

Lea was pulled from her dream, opening her eyes to see the beginnings of sunset, a rich orange-red glow radiating across the horizon.

The trees had changed dramatically since she'd fallen asleep, the landscape evolving as she'd wandered the clearing in her dreams. Where this morning there had been average-sized trees with rough, bark-covered trunks and luscious green foliage, the trees that now surrounded them were shorter and skinnier with mostly naked, knotted branches.

A few of the trees held small bunches of dying leaves. They were dry and brown, clinging desperately to the branches in an attempt to survive, and yet, even as she watched, they fell one by one, dropping to the forest floor quickly under the weight of their own death.

"You didn't wake me," Lea croaked. Gray discreetly shook out his arm as she sat up, and she realized that he'd been supporting her body weight on the same arm for the entirety of their ride today. Lea gave him an apologetic smile.

He leaned forward to kiss the back of her head, brushing off her concerns. "I'm fine. Emma said you still felt weak, and you need your strength for when we enter the woods."

"You feel much stronger to me now, Lea," Emma singsonged from behind her. Lea wanted to be angry with them for allowing her to sleep for so long. She didn't like feeling as if she wasn't strong enough to help them during their journey, but she had to admit that she felt much better than before she'd dozed.

As if sensing her thoughts, Erik trotted his horse up next to Obsidian. "If I had to guess, Sunshine, I would say that your sleep last night helped your night magic refuel, and the sun on your face today has helped with your day magic. You need to replenish both after such a severe illness." He looked at her pointedly, as if sensing she was about to argue.

Reaching down deep inside her chest, Lea felt around for her magic. Both her day and night magic did indeed feel stronger, as did her bond to Gray. She hadn't realized before how much the Lonely Death had dulled her senses—that she had been so close to going beyond the veil that even the magic inside of her had started to diminish.

"I do feel better. Thank you all," Lea told them earnestly, her eyes wetting as she thought of the risk and sacrifice her friends had shown by following them here.

"There's nothing to thank us for, My Queen," Noah said, clearing his throat. A blush creeping up his neck.

"No, she can definitely thank us. We were amazing, racing through the forest and finding you. Actually, I demand you thank us. And you can do that by continuing to recover," Janelle said, pointing an accusing finger in her direction. "Because I know you. And I know that the second we get off these horses you're going to try to build camp and do far too much, and you're probably going to fight with all of us about it, and I just want you to know that we all talked, and it's not going to happen. So don't even consider it."

Janelle crossed her arms and looked straight ahead, refusing to look at Lea as Erik slid off the horse.

Lea's heart squeezed in her chest at Janelle's way of showing that she'd been worried. "I'm sorry I scared you, Janelle," Lea told her as Gray and Emma jumped off of their horses. Emma went in search of firewood while Erik unpacked the horses, and Gray went with Noah to enchant the small pocket of trees they had chosen to make camp in for the night.

"It's my fault," Janelle said, her voice cracking. She continued to look straight ahead, refusing to make eye contact with Lea. "I told you to take the necklace off," Janelle said. "I knew it protected you, and I told you to take it off. I didn't think..."

"You didn't rip it from my neck, Janelle. I made a decision. It had consequences, and now I'm fine."

"Okay," Janelle said, with a firm nod, discreetly wiping a tear from her cheek.

"Okay," Lea parroted, knowing that Janelle wouldn't want a mushy acceptance of her unnecessary apology. It was no more Janelle's fault that Lea had taken off the necklace than it was Gray's fault that Alaric had learned the spell to cause the Lonely Death and had found her with just enough time to infect her with it.

Janelle slid off of her horse and walked to Erik, picking up a bedroll and spreading it out on the ground. Gray was at Lea's side in an instant.

Lea bent her knees and stretched her shoulders. She was relieved to find that she felt significantly stronger than she had this morning. She bounced on the balls of her feet, eager to do something to help, but Gray placed two heavy hands on her shoulders.

"I know you don't want to rest more, or sit around while we prepare camp, but before we enter the woods, I want to work on your magic." Gray shot a look toward the sun sinking below the horizon. "It will be night soon and you'll need every bit of strength to control your shadows. It could be the difference between life and death in those woods, Lea. So please, for me, let your body continue to recharge until it is time to train."

Gray's face hovered only inches above hers, sincerity and worry shining in his eyes. It made her heart feel bruised to think about what he had been through the past few days, his fear for her safety, her life. It was because of her and her insistence that they travel through the Wicked Wood that he was experiencing such unease. "Fine," she agreed with a kiss to his worried brow. "I will rest, even though I don't need it, if you swear to me that you will help me train my magic tonight."

"I promise." Gray's relief was evident as he let out a deep exhale, and the lines bracketing his eyes faded. A cool sensation of relief washed through the bond, the strength of Gray's reassurance so strong that she was grateful she hadn't fought back. She walked to where Gray had already set up their bed for the night, right next to the circle of stone where a fire would soon be glowing and warming them.

Gray trudged straight to the edge of the clearing where a fallen tree was lying. The trunk was as thick as her waist and at least ten feet tall. Placing a foot on the middle of the trunk, he bent down, lifting the upper half and pulling so quickly the trunk snapped in two, a reminder of the superior strength of the Fae that she so rarely got to witness. A loud crack rang through the woods, and Lea sat up straighter, her heart picking up speed.

Lifting the tree with ease, Gray carried it to where she sat, placing it behind her to allow her something to lean against. "We're too far from the palace and too close to the Wicked Wood for my brother to search for us here. We should be safe from the demons, but just in case, I have shrouded us in darkness. We're hidden tonight," he said, nodding reassuringly.

Emma approached the small area where Gray had stacked stones to build a fire, arms full of wood. Wordlessly, Erik took the kindling from her and built a small pyre before relaxing back and staring at Lea.

Lea shivered in the cold as she waited for Erik to start the fire. *What is he waiting for?* she thought, scrunching her forehead. She continued to watch him, wondering why he was allowing them to freeze in the cool twilight air, but he simply gestured toward the fire with both hands.

"Well, Queen of Flames? Are you going to keep your subjects warm, or allow us to turn to ice?" Erik raised his eyebrows. Lea looked at the sticks, then to where Erik and Emma sat. They were only inches from the kindling. All Lea could think of was Emma's beautiful curly hair catching flame, or Erik's long sleeve sparking and burning him. "You know I can't control my magic that well," Lea said. "You saw what happened when we were leaving the castle. I hurt Janelle. Her arm—"

"I'm fine," Janelle huffed, waving her arm around excessively to prove her point. "Good as new." But Lea didn't miss the way Janelle scooted a few inches away from the pile of sticks waiting to be ignited. Guilt gnawed at the bones of her chest. It had been an accident, but a gruesome one, and Lea had been lucky she hadn't hurt her friend in a way that couldn't be undone.

"Look, every time I've tried to play with fire, whatever I'm aiming it toward explodes. What if the fire gets too high and gives away our position? Or what if I hurt one of you again?" Genuine fear caused her stomach to churn at the thought of losing control.

"You won't hurt us. Just try," Erik insisted, crossing his arms.

Lea looked to Gray, hoping for support, but he was casually leaning against Obsidian, patting his neck and staring at her expectantly. A small smirk settled on his face, as if daring her to show them what she was capable of.

"Thanks for your help," she said under her breath, knowing he could hear her, before turning back to the fire.

Goosebumps erupted across her arms. The temperature was dropping quickly. "Give me a few minutes," she bargained, "until the sun goes down fully. When my day magic weakens a bit."

"No," Erik said forcefully, startling her. "This is about learning control, and maintaining that control even when you're afraid." There wasn't a hint of the usually jolly Erik in the man in front of her, and Lea shrank back. For him to be so serious... he was afraid for her. "You can do it," he said with confidence.

Gray sent a wave of assurance through her at Erik's words.

Lea stared at the sticks haphazardly stacked into a pyre, taking several deep breaths and closing her eyes as she searched for the warmth bundled inside her chest. She spent a moment unwrapping it from the darkness, focusing only on the light and imagining her power as a thick, lush rose bush. With the flowers pictured in her mind, she imagined pulling off a single rose, a small chunk of magic, and directing it toward the dry kindling before her. A deep blue fire built at the base of the sticks, so hot it made her face sweat as the fire rose a bit higher.

Lea was filled with joy, confidence blooming in her chest at her success. Her happiness was short-lived, though, when the fire immediately shot toward the sky, nearly singeing off Erik's eyebrows as he scrambled backward.

"Control it!" Erik shouted, not yelling in anger or pain or fear, but in encouragement, and his unwavering trust prevented her from shrinking back in defeat. There was no attempt to spring to her aid as he had in the dungeons when her fire had grown out of control, yet the rigid set of his shoulders and jaw betrayed his concern. "Do it now before you give us away."

The fire was too tall, too hot and powerful. Lea's heart beat rapidly and sweat trickled down her spine. She tried to pull it back inside her, but the white-hot heat of the flames seemed to scorch her insides, the pain so severe it nearly made her vomit. She held her hands out in front of her, her skin blistering as she worked to call the fire back into her chest.

Before she could even blink, Gray was at her side. "Help her, Erik," he commanded, a vein bulging in his forehead as he bared his teeth at his friend. Erik was standing in front of him in an instant, blocking his path to her. Gray's hands were trembling, shadows bursting toward the fire, and yet they didn't smother it, the black wisps appearing to bounce off her own magic.

"There's only one way for her to learn how to control her power, Gray, and that is to practice when there is *pressure*. She is safe with us, right here. She'll be fine. You insult my queen when you imply that she needs us to rescue her from her own power."

Lea let his words fill her, his conviction that she could do it. She pulled and pulled the warmth into her veins, and yet the flames only seemed to grow taller. She winced against the intensity of the heat, her blood near boiling.

"Fucking help her! Now!" Gray roared, inches from Erik's face, his shadows still attempting to smother the flames.

"Let her help *herself*!" Erik took another step closer to him, pressing his chest against Gray's in a show of determination. He would not be backing down.

"Be quiet!" Lea snapped at both of them. Her hair stuck to her forehead as heat consumed her entire body. She took several calming breaths, focusing on the hole in her chest where her day magic had been hiding. Her mother's voice floated through her mind, a saying Lea had heard her entire life. *Fear is a thief, my flower. We don't let it steal our strength.* Right now, it was fear that was paralyzing her, making her sloppy and her magic harder to control. But as Gray had told her, she was the master of her power. She couldn't let it rule her. She *wouldn't*.

Pressing her lips together, Lea commanded the heat back inside her chest as the words circled her mind, urging it home. Slowly, the flames died down, enough to stop the scorching burns that had blistered the skin on her hands and arms. She focused on her shadows, finding her darkness and pushing it outward, only allowing a tiny amount to leave her chest. Cold energy left her fingertips, her own shadows floating past Gray's and penetrating the shield surrounding her impossibly hot fire. They absorbed the heat, sucking the warmth away until a fire less than a foot tall crackled in front of her. Lea called the shadows back to her and they obeyed without hesitation, bent to her will far easier than the flames had. Once she was confident she'd tucked every bit of magic back inside her, she lowered her hands.

The skin on her palms was blistered, and it surprised her that her own magic had been able to hurt her.

Even though her skin burned, the pain so severe it brought tears to her eyes, Lea felt grateful. Erik had been right. She'd needed to calm the fire herself, needed some sort of proof that she had it inside her to control the magic she still couldn't seem to make sense of. She had needed some confidence that she could protect herself if she needed to.

Gray attempted to push past Erik, but he created a shield of flames between them. Gray pulled his sword, holding it toward Erik.

"Heal yourself," Erik ordered Lea without turning away from Gray, pulling his own sword.

"Get out of my way, or I send these shadows up your ass, Erik!" Gray threatened, his shadows now attempting to smother the flames that Erik had built.

"She has to do it herself," Erik said, his hands out in front of him and his sword pointed back at Gray. "Do you want her to be able to heal herself? Or do you want her to have to rely on you any time she is injured?"

"I want her to not be injured to begin with! She's too weak for this! She almost died, Erik. Less than twenty-four hours ago. Let me through or I *will* gut you!" Gray seethed, stepping forward and pressing the tip of his sword to Erik's heart.

Lea was exhausted, but she focused on her magic, on healing herself. It wasn't that she thought Gray would actually hurt his best friend, but the way his shadows exploded around them, nearly filling the whole clearing... it wasn't something she was willing to risk. She dove within herself, blocking out Gray's thunderous rage and Erik's arguments, and sent cooling magic down her arms and into her fingers, imagining submerging her hands in a snow-chilled stream, soothing away the burns. Focusing on that cooling energy, Lea pushed away the heat and expelled it from her skin as she took slow, deep breaths. Light filled her veins and the pain faded, slowly, and then all at once. When she opened her eyes, her skin was smooth and unblemished, and even the scars that had remained from the Lonely Death were absent from her body. Her body seemed to glow faintly, the slightest silver-blue radiating from her skin.

Gray and Erik stood in silence, staring at her as they lowered their swords.

"I'm okay," Lea whispered to Gray, utterly drained. "I need to learn to protect myself. Erik did the right thing."

Lightning cracked directly above their head, a flash of light boasting a storm full of rage and fury that threatened to unleash itself at any moment. "Are you in pain?" Gray demanded as he clenched his jaw and his fists. His voice was tight, filled with far more agony than what she'd experienced from the burns on her hands.

"No. I promise you Gray, I'm okay." Lea watched some of the emerald creep back into her mate's eyes, chasing out a bit of the darkness. He stared at her for a long moment before breaking eye contact and raising his sword to Erik's throat.

Shadows wrapped around his neck, holding him in place as Gray lowered his voice. "I do not care if you think she needs to learn to heal herself or not. Maybe she does, but if you keep me from helping my mate again, I will wound you so deeply that it will be impossible for anyone to heal you. Do you understand me?"

Erik returned Gray's furious stare. "She needs to continue to practice, Gray."

"Not *tonight,* she doesn't," Gray spat before shoving his sword into the ground at Erik's feet and stalking off into the forest, thunder and lightning crashing around them as he disappeared into the darkness.

CHAPTER 19

LEA

The sunrise was beautiful, bursting with pinks, oranges, and golds, reminding Lea of the gladiolus growing near her front porch back home. Lea knew she should be feeling dread as they began their journey into the Wicked Wood, but she couldn't help but feel hopeful. So much had changed in her life over the past few weeks. She was hardly the same girl who had walked into the castle after finding out the man she'd spent so much time with was actually the Night Prince of Desia *and* the Eclipsed King, leader of the rebellion against the Nestruir family.

Of course, her stomach clenched at the feeling of danger stalking just behind her, a reminder that she was leading them into a savage, terrible place, but beyond those menacing woods were *answers*. Just on the other side of the terrifying forest was the chance to learn who she was and where her magic had come from.

It was unmistakable where the dangerous part of the forest began—where the wickedness had poisoned the roots and air to allow evil to thrive on its soil. Only feet from where they sat on top of their horses, the ground turned darker and softer, almost as if the dirt itself was rotting. The dark, leafless tree branches seemed to sway as one, left to right, left to right, an inhale and exhale of choreographed evil.

"There's still time to turn back," Gray said as he wrapped an arm around her waist and leaned close to speak in her ear, his breath tickling the back of her neck. "We don't have to go this way."

Despite his soothing touch, Lea could feel his unease even without reaching down the bond. It radiated off him the way a sunburn radiates heat.

At his words, a gust of air blew from behind them, so hard that even Obsidian took a step forward without his master's command. Lea had never once seen Obsidian so much as sidestep a branch without Gray's approval, but even the powerful stallion hadn't been stronger than the intensity of the wind.

Leaning back and resting her head on Gray's shoulder so she could look at him, Lea gave him a confident, if not forced, smile. Trepidation pinched in her chest, but she shoved it down. "We'll be fine. The goddess will protect us. I can feel it." She placed a hand on her sternum.

Immediately, the necklace warmed around her throat, and she lifted her fingers to the piece of star Gray had gifted her without her knowledge so long ago. The piece of fallen sky that had protected her all of those years from the Lonely Death. It pulsed against her skin like the steady beat of a heart, and when she looked down, she noticed it glowed a faint silver-blue. Lea chose to believe it was confirmation from the goddess. She would protect them. *Right?*

Lea swallowed down her doubt. If Gray prodded the bond to find her so uncertain, it was entirely possible he'd try harder to talk her out of going. "Thank you for doing this for me," Lea said, lacing her fingers between his. "Thank you for trusting me."

Finally pulling his gaze from the woods in front of them, Gray's eyes softened. "I would do *anything* for you, Little Flower. I would fight every demon in hell if it meant getting you the answers that you need. But it doesn't mean that I'm not afraid. Do not let your power sleep until we step foot on the soil of Calir. You need to be ready for anything."

A shiver ran down Azalea's spine, and her hair stood on end. "Then it's a good thing I got that magic lesson last night." Lea nudged Gray with her shoulder, trying to lighten the mood.

"Mhmm..." Gray rumbled, obviously not appreciating her attempt at humor. "You are a warrior, Azalea, and you will not be defeated. Hear it like a drum with every step we take. The woods will try to infiltrate your mind, make you think you're weak and desperate. Do not forget that you are the Queen of Flames and Shadows. Do not forget the people behind us who love you. And do not ever allow yourself to forget that you are mine. You belong to me, and me alone. The demons in these woods have no ownership over you." He cupped her cheek. "*Mine*," his gravelly voice traveled straight to her core, their bond stretching taut inside her chest.

"Yours," Lea whispered before leaning up to press her mouth against his. He claimed her lips immediately, deepening their kiss as a possessive groan escaped his throat before breaking it off all too soon. Lea felt the loss of his lips acutely, the buzzing that always accompanied his touch fading away. Lea wanted to protest, but she couldn't blame him for pulling away. They needed every minute of daylight they had to travel south and find a safe place to camp for the night.

"I'll remember. As long as you don't forget that you're also mine," Lea said with a quick peck to his scruffy cheek before turning and facing forward. "Are we ready?" Lea called out to her friends waiting silently behind them. Lea wasn't sure what had come over her, but she knew that she was supposed to lead this charge forward—felt that this was her journey to guide.

"Ready," Noah said, straightening his shoulders and staring into the woods ahead.

"We've been ready, but you guys insist on getting it on no matter where we go, so..." Janelle responded, and Lea heard Erik's contagious laugh travel toward the woods. The trees seemed to shrink back in response to his joy. "We're ready, Sunshine," he confirmed with a chuckle.

"Emma?" Lea called out, only to be met with silence. "Emma?" A lump of fear lodged in Lea's throat as she twisted in her seat in an attempt to see around Gray's massive body, but his hulking form blocked her view. With a huff of aggravation, she grabbed the reins and turned Obsidian to face her friend, taking in her pale face and shaking hands.

The nervous horse beneath Emma shuffled its feet, slowly moving backward as if it understood what was causing Emma's fear.

"What's wrong?" Gray kicked Obsidian's sides, spurring him to trot to Emma. "Emma, talk to me," he said, his eyebrows lowering and his voice deepening. He sounded like the Night Prince once again, the Eclipsed King. His tone had changed from that of a lover's into that of a soldier's.

Emma was rambling, but her words were lost to the wind as her mouth gaped open. Lea focused on her lips, trying to read what shapes they were making. *She's praying,* Lea realized, Emma's eyes fixed on the woods beyond them. Cold dread filled her veins. She'd seen this look before on her friend's face, only days ago.

"Oh, Emma. It's the dead, isn't it?" Lea asked gently, slowly placing a hand on Emma's forearm.

Emma's face paled, her warm brown skin turning a strange shade of gray. "Dozens of them. More..." Emma whispered, her voice shaking. "As far as I can see." Lea turned to look at the forest, at the empty spaces between the crooked, knotty branches of the trees. They were empty, at least to her eyes, but as she stared ahead, her magic felt someone's presence. Her skin prickled as the air became unnaturally cool and the feeling of eyes on her became overwhelming. Lea pulled her sweater tighter, as if it could shield her. They were not alone.

"What do they want, Emma?" Gray prodded, straightening in the saddle and turning Obsidian sideways, blocking the others as he attempted to take control of the situation. Always assessing, always calculating.

"To stop us," Emma breathed. *"Do not enter these cursed woods, lest you wish to join us and wander through the darkness for eternity."*

CHAPTER 20

EMMA

Much of Emma's time on their race to find Lea and Gray had been spent considering the revelation that she could see the spirits of those who had not yet passed beyond the veil. Her entire life, she'd intuitively known people's emotions more deeply than others seemed to. Emma had thought it was simply a strength of hers that she could feel what others did just as they felt it and empathize with their worries and angers and hurts.

Years had been spent explaining away the spirit of the boy who'd lost his life that day. It had been a fluke, or the trauma of witnessing death so young. That's what she'd always told herself, at least. But there was no denying now that what had happened that day would follow her for the rest of her life. Her ability was something heavier than her own shadow, but just as persistent. She would never get away from it.

Emma tried to hide that her hands still sometimes shook slightly from what she had seen when Claire had been killed. Once she'd calmed down, she had reminded herself over and over again that she was not so easily broken, yet she still found it difficult to adjust to this new life so quickly. Not only had she joined a rebellion she hadn't even known existed within the past few days, but she now had to accept that she would never escape death. Anyone who passed would linger, their souls hoping to speak to her, to beg for her to help them, despite the fact that she didn't know *how* to help them. It was a useless gift, and she had prayed to the gods constantly since they'd left Auropera to take the burden from her. Since she'd watched Claire take her final breath, only to rise and demand Emma find a way for her to remain, to *live*.

A different prayer fell from her lips as she stared at the bodies–no, souls—of the countless men in front of her. Most of them wore the black uniform of the royal army, with only a few who appeared to have been villagers, likely from the small pockets of homes that had been built throughout the southern kingdom, not large enough to be considered towns or villages. They were so small that the settlements weren't even named, only groups of eight to ten families, content to be as far away from the capital as possible.

Above their heads, the meteors continued to increase in number, thousands of streaks of silver-blue light racing toward Calir as if urging them forward, the wind suddenly blowing at their backs. It was an obvious sign from the gods to continue on. But how could they go forward when fifty of the dead were warning her that to enter those woods meant certain death?

None of the souls left the confines of the Wicked Wood only feet in front of them. They stood just at the border, staring at her with an intensity that told her they genuinely believed every word they were saying. They had chanted over each other, the same words, but at different tempos and volumes; a muddled melody of darkness and death.

Emma attempted to gulp down her fear and swallow the nausea that was rising up her throat. There were too many of them, too many voices filling her head, and she didn't know how to process it. With a deep breath, she focused on the man closest to them, directly ahead of her horse. He had been a soldier, with red hair cropped close to his head. A horrific gash crossed his eyebrow, cutting into the white bone of his skull. Something jagged had torn through his flesh, leaving strings of skin hanging down his face like ribbons. Looking at the wound, Emma knew that were she to have found him alive with this injury, the wound would have been too severe to ever make him whole again.

Blood crusted his nostrils and the sides of his lips, and Emma shivered at how gruesome his pale face looked. She tried to keep her eyes from looking down, from exploring what the rest of his injuries looked like. Intuition prickled at her skin, a feeling that what she would find on his body would be far worse than the fatal wound on his head, but her eyes disobeyed her. Bile filled the back of her throat as she took in the massive open wound across his abdomen and chest. Sharp bones protruded where his rib cage had been—jagged, broken shards covered in blood. His intestines hung from his belly almost to the ground, and his army trousers were drenched in thick crimson blood. It was sickening, terrifying, but Emma took several deep breaths. It would be cruel to show the disgust she was feeling, the pure revulsion, when this man had died in such a horrific way.

She forced herself to meet his eyes. There had been no dignity in his death, but she could give it to him now by allowing him to speak, by acknowledging what had happened to him.

The others went quiet, now that she focused on the disemboweled man. *Is he their leader?*

"Turn back," he told her hollowly, almost as if the effort to speak pained him, even after his death.

Emma looked at Lea, who stared at her with wide eyes and a face as white as the moon. "We need to get to Calir," Emma told him, trying to keep her voice from shaking, infusing as much confidence into her tone as she could, something she'd practiced her entire life. "The gods have told us that this is our path forward."

The man didn't hesitate. "The gods will abandon you the moment you step onto this cursed soil," he spat. "Even they do not dare venture beyond this boundary."

Emma looked to the man's left, where an older gentleman stood partially hidden by a gnarled black trunk. She'd initially thought that every soul within the woods had been staring at her, as if they had somehow known that she was the one they could communicate with, but no. This man couldn't stare at her. Something had clawed the eyes from his skull.

Horrible scratch marks tore through nearly every inch of his face, with what appeared to be black, burnt skin around the edges of the scratches. A tendon hung from his eye socket, but besides his face, the rest of his body remained unmarred.

"What did this to you?" Emma asked him, her heart racing in her chest. But as he opened his shredded lips, she immediately regretted asking. Somehow, even without his sight, the man knew that it was him to whom she spoke.

"It was nothing more than mist. A dense, black fog that crept around my legs, rendering me nearly paralyzed. The only thing I could move was my mouth. It allowed me to scream as whatever hid inside the fog stole my eyes, my sight. I can still see when the demon uses it. I have seen the death of countless others through my own eyes. The monster... It does not speak. It does not eat. And yet it thrives off of the fear of its victims—off my fear every time it fills my mind with images that no man should have to see."

Emma nodded to him, steadying her hands on the saddle, unsure how to reply to his gruesome confession.

"And you?" She looked directly at a young man to her right, close to her in age with no visible injuries.

"I was sleeping in the army camp," he replied. "I heard the snap of a twig, and then I was gone. In less than a second, my soul was ripped from my body. To this day, I don't know what it was that stole my life—only that I am not the only one among us who met their end this way."

Emma's composure slipped, the sorrow and horror churning in her stomach bubbling up until she couldn't hold it in any longer. She leaned over the horse to vomit onto the ground, her head swimming and throat burning.

The man closest to her, who appeared to be their leader, spoke again. "You're right to be afraid. Nothing good will come of you entering this place." His ominous warning bristled across her skin, sinking into her bones and stealing the color from her cheeks.

"Emma? Are you okay?" Emma barely registered Lea speaking to her.

"Emma?" An unfamiliar hand landed on her arm. "Do you want me to take you to Bearswillow? I can track the way we took and follow the rebellion," Noah said, looking to Gray for what Emma could only assume was his approval.

"I just think..." Emma exhaled a shaky breath as she made a conscious effort to relax her shoulders and calm her mind. "Their deaths were so horrific. Unexpected. The creatures who killed them don't seem to be the kind we're prepared to fight."

"May I address them?" Gray asked.

Emma turned back to the souls and waited for their reply.

After several seconds, the man with the wound on his head nodded. Emma turned to Gray and did the same.

"I am Evander Nestruir. Prince of the Night and son of the Black King."

Emma stiffened as every pair of eyes staring at them from the woods filled with fury.

"We have broken away from my father's reign and plan to overthrow him, but to do that, we need to find answers."

"There is nothing to find here but death," the dead man replied. His anger seemed to have faded away at the thought of the Black King being overthrown, but his wariness remained. Emma relayed the message to Gray, but he continued.

"My wife," Gray smiled down at Lea before looking back toward the woods. "She... We believe that she is the one from the prophecy. The descendent of Queen Emmaline, who will overthrow the king. The gods have told her that this is the way we must travel. It's not a decision I make lightly, but if the goddess herself told her that this is a trial she must face for answers, then I will choose to face the demons of hell to help her. To help all of us get the answers that may save our kingdom."

The dead looked amongst each other, all of them as silent and foreboding as the decaying trees they stood between as they absorbed his words.

"The king's dark magic keeps us here," their leader said finally. "It's because of him that we cannot pass beyond the veil and find peace. We are here to warn those away who seek to find answers, for there *are* answers within this forest, if you can escape the death waiting for you."

Emma told Gray what the man said word for word and Gray considered this for several moments.

"We will overthrow him. Allow us to pass, help us make it to the southern border, and we will end the curse for you. We will find a way to bring you peace. I swear it."

Emma sucked in a breath. What Gray was offering was... difficult, to say the least. She was certain he had no idea how to end the spell his father had put upon these men, not without the witch agreeing to reverse it, and yet she was just as positive that he would find a way to do what he promised them.

"There's a place in these woods that may give you the answers you seek. We are bound by magic, prevented from showing you. But," he took a single step forward toeing the line that separated them from the cursed forest, "If you'll vow that you will kill your father and cleanse the kingdom of every bit of his wicked, evil rule, undo every spell and curse he has placed on this land, then we will do what we can to help you."

Emma relayed the man's offer, and Gray pulled Lea tighter against him as his shadows snaked along the ground. He smiled darkly, every bit a king ready for battle.

"That is a promise that I can easily make you. I will wipe every fingerprint, every trace of him from this world, and not only that, but I will make him suffer while I do it."

CHAPTER 21

GRAY

Anticipation caused Gray's shadows to coil tightly inside him as they approached the line between good and evil, his power crouching low like a wolf ready to spring forward in a vicious attack. He'd crossed over this magical barrier several times, more times than he wanted to remember, and the feeling was always the same. His skin would turn cold and his breath would appear in small puffs of white. The hair on his arms and neck would stand on end, and his hearing and eyesight would sharpen as his body sought out the threats that hid in the Wicked Wood waiting for them. Dread pumped through his veins as they crossed onto the rotting soil.

Shuddering, Gray urged Obsidian around a crater-like divot the size of a horse cart, likely a sinkhole. "Follow my path," Gray instructed the others as he planned out the best way forward. Whirling knots dotted the jagged black bark of the trees that seemed to reach out toward them like fingers. He'd always had a suspicion that those knots were eyes, that the very forest was watching every move they made. Lumpy, irregular roots spread from the bases of the trees like cancerous veins, spreading in large webs and connecting to one another. They twisted like a ball of snakes, so intertwined that the roots blended into a tapestry of death.

Fog floated unnaturally mid-air, long fingers reaching in every direction like smoke bubbling off a cauldron. The woods were as dark as ink.

Despite not having leaves, the long, pointed branches of the trees seemed to cover the sky, causing a strange muted effect that made colors appear dim. But what was most unsettling to Gray was the utter silence. There was no other place in the kingdom he'd experienced anything like it, the air so devoid of sound that he could hear the blood rushing from his heart through his capillaries.

Gray felt Lea shiver and bent down to whisper in her ear. "You need to listen to what you're feeling while you're here. Any sense that something is wrong, anything that doesn't feel normal, you tell me."

Lea nodded silently, and he wondered if she was too afraid to speak. He'd seen it before with soldiers that he had led on missions through these woods. They thought they understood the risk, but ultimately realized they had underestimated that this place had a pulse of its own, one that burrowed inside you and changed your very marrow. Yes, he'd seen many a soldier rendered speechless upon crossing the border between safety and doom. And even though that fear was something he'd experienced before, had tried to prepare himself for, he still felt it just as acutely in this moment. His eyes continued to scan the trees, his Fae senses on high alert.

"Emma?" he called out, unable to see her through the thick, dark fog as she traveled with Erik's horse just behind them.

"I'm... I'm okay," she said, her voice trembling.

"Are the spirits too close to you?"

"They're giving us space, walking behind us."

Gray felt a prickle along his spine and sat up straighter, the feeling of eyes on his skin intensifying.

"Let me know if you need my help, or if they warn you of anything."

Emma didn't respond. He was about to ask if she would like to ride toward the front to avoid the dead's access to her back when Lea shivered.

"We've only just begun our journey, Little Flower. Let me repeat myself. I want to be abundantly clear. It's not too late to turn back," Gray whispered in her ear, praying she would choose this option. He had warned her of the dangers, but *feeling* the dark spirit of the woods was something different.

"I–It's not that. I don't want to turn back, it's just..." She pondered for a moment. "I have a feeling that the worst thing I will find in these woods is that I'm not strong enough to face the answers we're looking for."

An odd sensation skidded across Gray's skin, pushing inside his belly and settling deep in his gut. Uncertainty and self-doubt; feelings he'd never felt from Azalea before, and honestly, it shocked him that the strong-willed, stubborn woman the gods had chosen as his mate would be capable of feeling so small.

"It's normal for you to be afraid, and it's normal to worry about yourself and your friends, for all of our safety while we're in this place, but do not for a second think that you are not capable of facing anything, or anyone."

"You saw me last night, Gray, how much effort it took to control my magic."

"Yet did you control it? Did you do exactly what Erik said you could and heal yourself?"

"You were about to slaughter Erik because you thought I wasn't capable, that it was too much," Lea sighed.

"I was about to slaughter Erik because watching you struggle, feeling your pain, is the worst punishment I have ever faced. Because all my soul wants is to take you as my mate, to protect you as I protect my own life, and the fact that I can't? It drives me to insanity. I wouldn't have risked bringing you here, into this evil place, or risking your life in a war that will likely drown the kingdom in blood if I thought that you were unable to protect yourself. If I truly thought that you didn't have it inside you to be the most powerful warrior among all of us."

"But why would you think that, Gray? I know I have both day and night magic, and I know I'm the first to have both since Queen Emmaline. But I can't call a devastating storm without even trying, and I can't set a field aflame like Alaric can. My powers didn't even reveal themselves until recently. Didn't you say that normally they appear in childhood?" she asked.

Gray tried not to show that her words had struck a chord of uncertainty. It was something he'd spent a lot of time thinking about once her power had revealed itself. One would think the most powerful Fae descendent born in hundreds of years would have come from the womb calling rain clouds with their tantrums, and yet it hadn't been until that night after the fenrir attack that Gray had suspected she had magic coursing through her bloodstream. She should appear Fae, not so fully and wholly human. But the resemblance combined with having both day and night magic? It was something he hadn't figured out yet. Was he wrong about who he thought she was?

She was almost a mirror of Queen Emmaline in the paintings Gray had seen in his father's forbidden books that he and Erik had found in the deepest depths of the castle archives. They had similar hair, similar bone structure of the face, but it was her eyes that struck him the most. It made him question his abilities as a soldier that he hadn't noticed the similarities between those eyes the moment he'd seen her. It wasn't until Lea had shoved him away with shadows she shouldn't be able to command that he'd realized she had the eyes of the long lost beloved queen. Fear had paralyzed him in a way it never had before, because the consequences of possessing the blood of the gods within her, when she had no training and no clue what his father would do to possess that kind of power... He wouldn't even allow himself to think it.

Thunder rolled in the distance as he tried to push down his temper, violence coursing through his body at the thought of his father discovering who his mate may be. It was likely he knew now, or at least suspected. Thank the gods they were married, that she now held the name of his family that would prevent his father or brother from killing her, and yet also prevented her from killing them. To win this war, Gray would have to do the unthinkable. He would have to end the very spell—or was it a curse?—that now protected his mate from death at his family's hands.

Lightning flashed around them furiously, and Gray clenched his jaw, attempting to tamp down his fear. Azalea was his wife. His mate. The other half of his soul, contained in a fragile human body. He would burn the world down if that's what it took to protect her, and as a plan started to form in his mind, Gray wondered if that was exactly what it would take.

CHAPTER 22

LEA

Lea didn't know how it was possible, but it seemed like with every step forward, the woods grew darker, more ominous and threatening. Every crack of a stick or rustle of a branch caused Lea to startle, to reach for her magic on instinct. They'd been riding for hours, and while they hadn't seen anything threatening, she wasn't able to say with confidence that they hadn't been seen themselves.

None of them spoke, not a single word, as they moved forward. The silence was louder than the crowd at the market, louder than the thunder that boomed from her mate's temper. Gray's hand remained firm against her front, his thumb swiping in reassuring arches while his head constantly swiveled as he examined his surroundings. The tension in his shoulders and the tight muscles of his arms betrayed his calm exterior. And yet, through the bond, muddled in with the worry and uncertainty, was confidence.

Lea could feel Gray pulling his power into a ball. It was as if his magic somehow ran deep into his soul—a cavern, a pocket somewhere inside him where his powers slept. She felt him pulling it out, molding it and making it more accessible to ready himself for battle. Lea paid attention as he dug deeper and deeper inside himself, and the magnitude of power she felt radiating from him made her shiver. Had she even seen the full depth of his powers before?

Lea had never felt this immensity of magic from him, but she'd also never searched the bond in this way. She reached for her own magic, considering this a silent lesson on how to tap into her own abilities and powers, but as she tried to dig deeper, she hit a thick iron wall. Impenetrable. Her darkness and shadows still thrummed along with the light inside her chest, that now-familiar hum of magic just waiting to be released, but there was nothing more hiding inside her. Lea was pulled from her thoughts when a zing of alertness shot through her body.

Her hands pulsed a silver blue, her magic flowing into her fingertips of its own volition.

"What is it?" Gray asked her, holding up a hand to pause the others riding behind them.

"I'm not sure," Lea replied. "But I feel something. Something is warning me—" The words had no sooner left her mouth when a whisper met their ears.

"New blood," the disembodied voice said. "What have you brought to us, princccccee?" the creature hissed.

Lea's eyes darted through the dark trees, searching for the source of the voice. Was it possible the creature speaking knew who they were?

"Erik," Gray snapped, and without further instruction, Erik turned his horse, positioning it behind Emma and facing away from Gray.

"Nabis..." Emma whispered. "The dead can see them. About eleven of them, approaching from the south."

"Shit," Gray hissed under his breath.

"We've got this, Lea," Erik called out from behind her. "Get ready to roast some demons, Sunshine," Erik teased with false bravado.

"What is he talking about, Gray?" Lea asked, dread coursing through her veins. Why had Erik singled her out by name?

"It's the demons. Nabis are made of pure darkness," Gray said. "Only fire can kill them. They have no body, no physical form to destroy with a sword. They exist of nothing but black mist and shadows made solid. They can regenerate, rearrange themselves to prevent injury."

"So you can't help fight against them?" Lea was going to throw up. Of all the demons they were going to face in these woods, they had to be creatures that Gray couldn't kill?

"I can help control your powers if you get out of hand. I can call a storm or the wind to bend your flames or douse them. I can distract the nabis, or block their way... But no, I cannot kill them."

"Okay." Lea pressed her lips together, shoving down the anxiety pulsing up her spine. "How do they attack?" Lea asked, trying to get as much precious information as she could in the few moments they had before the nabis appeared.

"Like a viper," Gray said, pulling his sword. "Quick strikes. Their bite contains a poison that paralyzes whatever it touches. A bite to the leg, and you will be unable to run. A bite to the hand, and you won't be able to hold a sword."

Dread filled Lea's gut. What a cruel and telling turn of events that it was because of her that they had entered these woods, and it was now she who had to save them.

"Don't be afraid." Gray placed a hand on Lea's shoulder, squeezing gently. "I'm here with you. As is Erik. We will help you."

"And me," Noah said, his Adam's apple bobbing as he gulped audibly. "I have day magic. Not a lot, but enough to help."

Gray turned. "Did you have any training for the Wicked Wood in Auropera?" he asked.

"No. Not yet. But I can help. I'll distract them, or, I don't know. I can do *something*."

Lea felt a surge of strong emotion from Gray. Impressed. He was impressed by Noah's statement, and Lea had to agree. He was so ready to fight with them. Meanwhile, she was terrified, her hands shaking and her throat dry. But the young soldier nodded at Gray, pulling his sword from his back and positioning himself higher in his saddle.

"You'll protect Janelle and Emma. Do not join the battle unless they're attacked. This is a direct order, Noah."

"Yes, Commander," Noah said obediently.

"Get off your horses," Gray demanded, jumping off Obsidian and grabbing Lea by the waist to pull her to stand behind him. "The nabis won't waste their time trying to harm them if we're on foot. But they will attack them, cripple or kill them to get to us, if necessary. We need the horses to get to Calir quickly."

Erik nodded, lifting Janelle and sliding off his horse before turning and offering Emma a hand.

"They're close," Emma breathed, eyes shifting around nervously.

"Emma, Janelle," Erik said calmly without taking his eyes off the woods. "You both should have some extent of healing magic. Enough to heal yourself from small injuries. I will protect you—" Erik met Janelle's eyes and swallowed, his words thick with some unspoken emotion Lea had never seen from him before, "but if you're injured, I want you to focus on finding your powers inside you and sending them to where you were hurt. Stay close together." Erik reached to his waist, pulling a blade from his right hip, then reached to grab his other dagger from his left side.

"I already took it," Janelle said sheepishly as she held the dagger up in front of her. "Thought I might need it to protect myself. Don't be angry."

Erik looked down at her, the shadow of a smile across his lips. "I'll never be angry with you for defending yourself. Now, stay put." Erik positioned them together just in front of Noah before joining Gray and Lea.

"They're here," Emma rasped as several dark figures stepped through the fog.

CHAPTER 23

LEA

The moment Lea laid eyes on the demons silently floating toward them, the woods grew dramatically darker. It was as if the nabis had repelled any light that had hung in the foggy air as they'd approached. She shivered, but not from the cold, as Gray stepped slightly in front of her.

"What have we here?" the demon asked as they moved closer, not so much walking as gliding. The nabis were tall, and, just as Gray had said, made of shadow. They were darkness itself, a void somehow completely absent of color. Their form was humanoid, and yet somehow not, with bodies that were fuzzy around the edges and wisps of darkness hazy around their figures.

Their fingers were long, with jagged black claws at the end. They had no hair, no facial features, save for a gaping black mouth, only noticeable because it appeared more solid than the rest of its face—a black hole with rows and rows of serrated black teeth ready to sink into flesh. As they approached, they bared those long, sharp teeth, venom trickling down the monster's chins and dripping onto the ground.

"It's been a long while since a group of travelers stumbled our way, hasn't it?" The monster's rough voice was like sandpaper against Lea's skin.

"Oh yes, brother," a raspy voice replied. "Even longer since we've tasted a woman's blood."

"There will be no tasting of our blood," Gray replied as he set his shadows free. In puddles as black as the demons before them, the shadows floated from his tense body across the ground, creeping forward in rivers of darkness. The air surrounding Gray grew darker as he called a storm overhead in a terrifying display of power.

The nabis closest to him chuckled. "And what is it that you believe your shadows can do against us, *Commander*?"

Lea and Gray made eye contact. The monster knew exactly who he was.

"We know more than you would believe," the shadowy figure answered her silent thought. "We can smell it on him—the royalty, the riches. The bloodline. It is all there, hidden under the stench of his fear. But that is not all we know. Take you, for example."

Lea froze. What could this demon possibly know about *her*? As if sensing her question, Gray raised his hand slightly, a silent gesture for her to remain quiet. She searched the bond, hoping to figure out what Gray's plan was. He was curious, but there was a sharp tang of fear surging through him as well.

Muscles tensing, Lea sensed Gray preparing to attack. He gave her a terse nod, and she felt his reassurance flood into her chest. He was ready to protect her; would not allow anything to harm them. It emboldened her. Showing fear would betray her weaknesses, put them all at risk. Raising her chin, Lea stared directly at the creature speaking to her.

"And what is it then that you can smell on me?"

"Hmmm.... Besides the sweat coating your neck, and terror dripping from your pores? I can smell that you are mated to this one." He gestured toward Gray, and he took a subtle step forward. "Such a shame he will be forced to watch as I drain you dry," he taunted.

"I'm sure that would gut you," Gray retorted sarcastically.

"That shows nothing of power," Erik said, flames dancing off his fingertips in a casual display of magic. "I scented they were mated before they believed it themselves. What you are failing to *scent* is that she is more than capable of destroying the lot of you without breaking a sweat."

"Ah, but can you smell that she is not of this Earth?" The nabis took a deep inhale, goading her. "Can you smell the potential she has to change the world? She does." His black face turned to her. "She could." There were no eyes in the dark smoky form, and yet Lea could still feel the monster staring at her. "It does not benefit you, then, that I rather like the world as it is. I do not think I should allow it to be changed."

Without warning, the nabis struck. Lightning fast, just as Gray had told her. The demons jolted toward her, dozens of black serrated teeth snapping inches from her shoulder as Erik sent a blast of flames from behind. The fire parted as it reached her, folding around her body to spare her from both its heat as well as the nabis' attack. The demon hissed, jumping backward as the fire burned away a bit of its darkness. Gray pulled Lea behind him, gripping his sword and widening his stance.

"Move on," he commanded, "and we'll allow you to torment these woods another day. They will burn you into nothing, destroy you, if you continue to fight. There will not be enough left to even send you into the void."

The closest demon laughed—an evil, cackling sound. The others gathered around him, standing in a line just behind where he stood as the demon slowly raised his fist into the air.

"Find your flames, Little Flower," Gray said calmly, "and remember that you are mine. They cannot have you."

The demon's head swiveled to Gray. "I *will* have her, prince," it said as he slowly opened his hand. All at once, so quickly Lea's eyes struggled to keep up, they attacked. Flames rose around them as Erik shot balls of fire at the monsters. Heat warmed her back as a wall of fire blocked Janelle and Emma from the nabis' sight, Noah somewhere behind them, providing their cover. The moment they were hidden, Gray went on the attack. With only his sword, he lunged and parried, swiping wide. The figures grunted as his blade sliced through their dark forms, but without pause, they reorganized and became nearly solid again.

Lea's chest grew white hot, her flames begging to be released, but her arms wouldn't move. What if she lost control again? Hurt Gray or Erik and made it harder for them to fight, putting everyone in danger? Her stomach turned sour, and she searched through the churning bile for even an ounce of courage and confidence.

Erik cried out as a shorter nabis launched at Gray, pushing his hands out and slamming an impressive blast of fire into the demon. "Lea!" he called out. "It's you and me, Sunshine. I need you to focus. I need your help. Dig deep, and aim for their chest!"

Fear still paralyzed her, but she forced herself to breathe, to slow her heart as she searched for the warmth inside her. Raising her hands out in front of her, she sent a prayer to the goddess and unleashed her flames.

They were unruly, with very little control, burning in colors from yellow and orange to a deep red, flicking sparks and ash all around them. Lea focused on aiming them toward the demons as Gray struck at them with his sword, creating a distraction. As Lea's muscles burned with the effort to throw her magic toward the nabis, she began to understand what Erik had meant. Aim for the chest, he'd told her, the largest part of the body, and the easiest to hit.

Two demons shot toward her. Quick lurches meant to disorient. Lea raised her palms and blasted them backward, the demons screaming and hissing as the fire burned away their shadows.

She continued to aim for their chests, and each time her fire struck her target, slamming into the nabis' skin, their silhouette faded. Their darkness became less dense, their forms less sharp.

A shrill scream sounded from Lea's right and she looked over her shoulder to see two demons gliding toward Emma and Janelle. Noah's fire had weakened as he'd fought to cover them. What had been a tall, thick barrier of flames now had bare patches, weak spots with smoking edges.

Through a hole in the wall of fire, Lea watched as Janelle held her dagger in front of her, her face brave and set in determination as she sidestepped in front of Emma. Lea sent her flames hurling toward the monsters approaching them. She didn't have time to worry about her power being too unpredictable, nor about harming her friends. Her entire focus was on destroying the threat as her fury fueled her, and she tapped into that wrath. Flames growing hotter, blue and white fire engulfed the monsters, consuming them whole until nothing remained.

Lea watched in awe as they disappeared, hesitating only a moment too long. She felt teeth sink into her arm and claws scratch her hip. Her scream sounded foreign as she cried out at the intensity of the pain. It was unlike anything she'd felt before, not a stinging or stabbing. Not even a burning. It felt like death—like a cold so severe it threatened to freeze her blood in an instant.

Heat engulfed her as Erik's flames destroyed her attacker, and Lea collapsed to the ground. Only seconds had passed, but the icy pain had already turned into an aching heaviness. She couldn't move her arm, couldn't flex her fingers. Lea tried to stand, but her leg wouldn't move. Everything below the wound on her hip was completely dead to sensation.

"Fuck!" she shouted, touching her shoulder, then her hip, to find a greasy oil-like substance mixed with blood oozing from her arm and dripping down her leg.

Gray was instantly at her side. "*Gods dammit!*" he hissed under his breath. Laying his palms against her wounds, he sent healing magic into her skin. The pain was immediate, excruciating.

"Stop!" Lea cried out, the absolute agony making her vision go blurry.

Gray's brows furrowed, but he removed his hands. "Can you heal yourself, Azalea?"

Lea nodded as she looked up, the heat from Erik's fires causing sweat to drip into her eyes. He continued to fight, and though Erik remained unharmed, his face was red and sweating with exertion. His chest heaved in effort, short of breath, as he fought to keep his flames growing hotter, sending streams of fire dancing around the woods. The battle almost resembled a dance, a gruesome but graceful game of cat and mouse as the monsters dodged his blows with their quick, fluid movements.

As Erik fought against the three nabis, movement caught the corner of Lea's eye. A fourth demon, their leader, who had spoken to them.

"Your power will feed me for years to come—"

Gray moved to strike, arcing his sword toward the nabis's head, but without thought or hesitation, Lea threw her night magic out. There was no effort to aim. She didn't even consider what her shadows would do as she engulfed the monster in darkness, blinding it. An animalistic instinct took over as she let her magic find the evil creature, wrap around it, and push inside to destroy it. Gray had told her only fire could kill them, and yet, she could feel her shadows tearing the icy black form apart, forcing its very essence to bend to her will as it completely disappeared.

□"Gray!" Erik shouted, breaking Lea from her trance, "I'm burning out!" Her shadows faltered as she looked at Erik, and a stab of fear wedged in her heart at his shaking arms. Lea looked back to her mate, an awe-filled expression on his face as his eyes focused on the empty space where the nabis had been moments before. He looked around, ensuring there were no lurking nabis aside from those Erik battled.

□"Go! Help him!" Lea urged, attempting to stand. She grimaced as she rolled to her knees, collapsing onto her stomach as her arm and leg gave out.

□"Don't try to move! Find your fire!" Gray called to Lea as he ran toward Erik, sword arcing in the air at an impossible speed. "You're the only one who can end this, Lea."

□Lea watched Erik and Gray dance around the remaining nabis, lightning fast as they struck and retreated, over and over. They were a mixture of fire and shadows, so entwined with each other that she could hardly tell who the streaks of movement belonged to.

□"I can't! I'll hurt you!" she said with a shaking voice. She didn't trust herself not to lose control, to hit her mate or her friend instead of the demons they fought. They were too close together.

□"You can!" He said with a confidence that made Lea think that just maybe, she actually could.

Lea reached down the bond, fully expecting to feel desperation saturating every fiber of their connection. Instead, she found confidence mixed with a hint of trepidation, but not the full-out panic she'd expected. He couldn't save them, didn't have the tools. But *she* did, and he believed she could. Gray paused for just a moment, looking at her with his chin raised. *You are my queen. Finish this.*

□Gray didn't speak the words aloud, and yet she felt them in her heart, saw them in his eyes. His utter belief in her took Lea's breath away as he raised his sword to continue fighting, a glint of silver cutting through the air. Focusing all her energy on Gray, she thought of warming the metal in his hand. Pictured the blade turning red hot, burning the nabis as he sliced through them.

□Gray flinched when his sword burst into flames, the long silver blade glowing red and orange as fire rose from the weapon. With a quick glance in her direction, Gray laughed, a beautiful, rumbling sound, before launching into his attack. Lea focused on the sword and the sword alone, feeding her magic into it, forcing it to bend to her will and forbidding the fire from spreading beyond the razor-sharp edge.

□Erik's flames dimmed, the well of his magic running dry. "Your sword!" Lea called as a nearby nabis stalked toward him. As if they had rehearsed it a hundred times, Erik pulled his sword at the exact moment Lea commanded it to burst into flames. He stabbed the white hot blade forward as the nabis lurched at his neck, hitting it exactly where its heart would be, if it even had one at all.

□The creature shrieked and attempted to pull back, but Erik was faster. Without the burden of using his day magic, he joined Gray in battle.

□They fought as one, turning back to back as they ducked and struck with their fiery swords, silently communicating.

□"Fuck yeah, Sunshine!" Erik called out as they destroyed what remained of the shadow creatures with ease, the final one evaporating into a fine black mist as Gray decapitated it in one fell swoop.

□"Always with the heads," Lea teased half heartedly as she let her flames wink out, collapsing onto her chest as exhaustion pushed down on her. Making sure her magic was tucked safely away in her chest, she rolled onto her back, resting her head on the cold ground as she looked up at the stars still shooting toward Calir. They'd done it. Their first trial of the Wicked Wood, and it had been as terrifying as Gray had warned her it would be.

"Please," Lea whispered to the sky. "Let this be worth it."

CHAPTER 24

GRAY

It was irrational. Absurd even. But as the final nabis disappeared into wisps of darkness, all Gray wanted to do was claim his mate. He yearned to banish the clouds from the sky and allow himself to be marked with a sun on his chest. It was undeniable that they'd needed Lea's magic to defeat the demons, but he'd worried that she would be unable to move past her fear of hurting her friends. Using her magic made her feel out of control, and Gray knew that she could feel the magnitude of what was inside her and worried that it would be more than she was prepared to wield. Instead of faltering or giving in, she'd found a solution to her problem, even under intense pressure. The nabis were quick, and even as experienced as Erik was with using his magic, he would have had a difficult time hitting only his targets with no mistakes.

To choose such a small target, one that she could latch her magic onto and allow him and Erik to use it to their advantage... It was brilliant. Pride caused his chest to puff out as he dropped himself to the ground, lying on his back next to her. "It was my worst nightmare to face the nabis," Gray told her, grabbing her hand.

"Because you couldn't defeat the monsters on your own and save the day?" A crooked smile tugged at Lea's lips. She'd seen right through him.

"That is exactly why. To face a creature whom neither my magic nor my strength and speed could defeat?" Gray ran a hand through his thick, unruly hair. "It is the thing of my nightmares come alive. But you," he bent down and pressed a kiss to her forehead. "You were brave. That was quick thinking, setting our swords on fire."

"I just knew that you'd spend the whole night pouting if I didn't let you in on the action. You have a bit of a savior complex, you know," Lea teased.

"When it comes to you, absolutely." Gray sat up, helping pull Lea into a sitting position.

"How long does the poison last?" Lea gestured to her limp arm hanging by her side.

"Likely, only another few minutes. Usually once their poison paralyzes you..." Gray trailed off, unable to say the words. He refused to even think about it.

"They kill you?" Lea asked, shuddering.

Gray only nodded, pressing his lips into a grim line. "Come, we need to get moving." Gray looked up at the sky above the dark tree branches. "It will be nightfall soon, and we need to find a safe place to camp."

"Actually," Emma chimed in, stepping forward. "The um..." her eyes flicked sideways, "the men traveling with us say we should stay here. The other demons will sense the nabis and believe whatever they found to either be dead or long gone and not worth their time."

"Emma, they know that they're dead. You can say it," Gray said gently.

"Well, yes, I'm aware." Her cheeks turned pink, and she ducked her head. "I just thought it rude to keep bringing that up."

Gray nodded. "Alright then. Do our esteemed guides have any other advice for setting up camp?"

Emma turned and stared into the woods for several moments. "Stay here, enchant the area to the best of our abilities. If we need a fire, there can't be any smoke. And be ready to leave at first light."

"Easy enough. Erik, are you too depleted to help me shield the area?"

"There's not enough sunlight here. My magic is recharging slower than I'd like." Erik frowned.

"Not to worry," Gray said, pushing his shadows outward so that they snaked toward the trees. "I believe it will be plenty dark enough tonight to refuel mine."

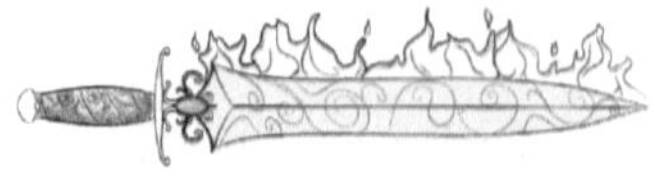

After camp had been set up, five pallets with blankets and furs to protect them from the unnatural chill of the Wood, Gray quickly hunted for dinner.

Lea had insisted she wasn't hungry, but her declaration of not needing to eat had caused his skin to crawl. Gray loved her deeply and entirely, but did she have no sense of self preservation? They'd just fought a demon. Several demons, actually. And there would be more.

"You're eating. Erik, watch her," he snapped as he stormed through the trees. There weren't many animals in the Wicked Wood, but dammit, he was going to find *something*. As if the gods were finally listening, a dark, furry creature darted in front of him. Gray didn't hesitate, decapitating it with so much force his sword sliced six inches into the ground.

Gray picked up the animal from the ground, a foobil, he realized, and quickly skinned it. He'd killed them before while traveling through the Wicked Wood to Calir, and the meat had provided good energy and sustenance. Almost like a squirrel but much larger with thicker, dark fur, it had plenty of meat for them to share.

Stalking back into camp, Gray tossed the foobil carcass to Noah. "Cook this," he ordered as he moved to Lea's side, feeling her forehead and watching for movement in her arm and leg. *Good*, he thought as she used both to scramble backward.

"I'm fine, Gray. I don't have a fever. I feel great," Lea said with a saccharine smile.

"Mmph," was all Gray could manage as he looked to Noah, who was obediently using his day magic to flambé the foobil.

"It's time for another lesson," Erik said to Lea, and Gray bristled.

"Not yet," he barked as he walked to Noah and sliced a thick hunk of meat from the animal and thrust it into Lea's hands with a grunt. "Eat," he ordered.

For once, Lea didn't argue, placing a hand on Gray's arm and sending love and reassurance down the bond. Gray finally exhaled, his shoulders lowering slightly. Being in this forest was going to be the death of him. Why did he agree to Lea's persistence? He should have thrown her over his shoulder and forced her back to Bearswillow, or at a minimum gone around the Wicked Wood to get to Calir.

Noah handed him his own chunk of meat, but it barely registered as he watched some of the color return to Lea's cheeks as she chewed. Once she finished, Gray handed her his water bladder, tipping it up and making sure she drank deeply.

"Enough, Gray," she coughed on the water. "I'm fine!"

"See? She's fine! Excellent!" Erik clapped his hands. "Time for that magic lesson, then!"

"Do you really think that the best time for a magic lesson is in the middle of the Wicked Wood while we're supposed to be hiding for the night?" Lea asked pointedly. "You don't think that might call some attention to us? Especially with my record of chaos?"

Gray's hand clamped down on Lea's thigh. "I agree with Azalea." That familiar protective instinct rose inside him again, the calm he'd felt from her resting and eating immediately consumed by a feral need to destroy any threat that could possibly harm her. If something went wrong, it could alert every monster in this wretched forest of their location.

Erik looked at Gray knowingly. "Before you go all mate-shit crazy on me, remember that you promised me I could train her, and that you would trust me."

"And you promised you would keep her safe," Gray said. Erik rolled his eyes, and Gray considered throttling him, his shadows inching across the ground toward him of their own volition.

Erik kicked at them with his foot, undeterred. "And I will. In fact, what you aren't seeing is that protecting her is exactly what I'm doing. You saw that we needed her today. Had she not lent us her fire, those monsters would have killed us all."

"I would *never* have let that happen," Gray snapped.

"You wouldn't have had a choice," Erik retorted, raising his voice. "She cannot be caught without knowing how to use her magic."

"Now is not the time!" Gray bellowed.

"Now is *exactly* the time!" Erik threw his arms in the air, obviously exasperated. "The best time to practice is when there's pressure. Because any time we will need Lea to use her magic, there *will be* pressure. We don't have time to wait and practice for months on end in a safe, controlled environment. I have enough magic recharged to help her if things go wrong. You can help her with her darkness. But it has to be now."

"Don't I get a say in this?" Lea asked.

"Of course you do," Gray said at the same time Erik firmly said, "No."

"I would like you to practice," Emma said tentatively, looking at Lea with worried eyes. "I'm afraid, and I just think if you could get some confidence, your magic could be an asset in protecting us."

"Let Azalea decide what she wants to do. If she's forced to do it, it will be dangerous." Gray gestured toward Lea. "If you all could feel what I am feeling from her right now, you would never ask her to do this. She's terrified of hurting us, of giving away our location." Gray's face was angry, his jaw clenched as he stared Erik down.

"I want to do it," Lea said quietly.

Gray slowly turned his head toward Lea. "What do you mean you *want* to do it? I know exactly what you're feeling. Do you not remember that?"

"Of course I'm scared. I don't have enough control to not give us away. But I also know Erik cares about all of us, too, and he's right. If I don't practice, if I don't take control of my fears *right now*, how will I be able to help us?"

Gray didn't respond.

"If something like what took place today happens again, I can't be helpless. You have to understand that." Lea held Gray's stare, and Gray couldn't help feeling a small kernel of pride. She was brave, and she, unfortunately, was *right*.

Gray took a deep, steadying breath, flexing and extending his fingers. "Fine," he said through clenched teeth, "but the second any of us sense danger," he gave a pointed look to Erik, "we stop. Do you understand?"

"Sure thing, boss," Erik said, dropping back down on the ground as if there had never been any tension between them at all. "All right Sunshine, let's start small. You need to be able to control how much fire or darkness you're creating." Erik scanned the ground, his head swiveling around until he picked up the smallest twig he could find, only about the length of his pinky.

"I want you to only set just the tip on fire," Erik said.

Janelle raised her eyebrows. "Really? That sounds—"

"Not the time, Janelle." Erik leveled her with a look. "Let Lea focus."

Determination hardened Lea's face, her eyes squinting slightly and her shoulders back. She took a deep breath, and in the blink of an eye, the stick exploded in flames in Erik's hand.

"*Shit!*" he hissed, dropping the flaming wood.

"Serves you right," Gray mumbled under his breath as he flicked his wrist, sending his shadows to suffocate the flames. Erik shook his hand in the air for a moment before picking up another stick.

"Again," he said. On the second try, the flame still engulfed most of the twig, and yet it had stayed away from Erik's fingers. "Good," Erik praised. "Now, make the fire even smaller, just the very top."

Lea exhaled slowly, diminishing the fire, her forehead creased in concentration. The flame grew smaller and smaller before her shoulders dropped and the fire winked out completely.

"Dammit," Lea hissed before meeting Erik's stare.

He picked up a new stick, one even smaller, and Janelle chuckled. "Quiet," Erik told her firmly, but not unkindly. "She can do it."

Gray watched silently, growing less worried as they continued to practice on smaller targets. They were far less likely to attract attention with such an insignificant flame. He sent a reassuring wave of confidence through their bond as she attempted to follow Erik's instructions again.

This time, only the top centimeter of the stick caught on fire. Lea stayed focused, but the tips of her mouth perked up with a proud smile.

"See," Erik said, swinging his head dramatically to look at Gray. "Now, make it burn hotter, Sunshine."

Lea shifted forward, her posture more confident, her movements less tentative. The fire changed from a red and orange color to blue around the edges, and yet she maintained control. As the small branch continued burning, Erik held up a much larger stick in his other hand, roughly the size of his forearm.

"Now," he slammed the stick into the ground so that it stuck straight up into the air, "light this on fire. Top to bottom. But don't let the small one burn out." Lea scrunched her nose, her eyes wary. She shook out her shoulders and arms before raising a hand slightly and focusing on the larger stick. It exploded into flames, and along with it, so did the smaller stick.

"Control it," Erik said through gritted teeth, still holding onto the flaming piece of wood.

"I can't, Erik! Just drop it! Your fingers!" Lea's eyes were wide and brimming with panic.

Indeed, Erik's skin was blistering, the burns spreading from the tips of his fingers to his knuckles.

"No," he ground out. "Control it."

Lea rose to her feet with determined movements and focused on the smaller stick. It only took a second before the flame shrunk, even further this time. Only a few milliliters of flame remained.

"I'm so sorry, Erik—" Lea started, but Erik just held up a hand.

"I'm fine. You did it. Even when you were afraid. Even under pressure."

Lea's shoulders sagged in relief as Erik healed his fingers, his blistered, red skin turning back to a nice, healthy pink.

Gray's stomach churned at the guilt he could feel radiating from Azalea. He walked to her, unable to stop himself from tucking her firmly against his side. Knowing she felt anything but happiness had his fingers itching to rip Erik to shreds. But despite his palpable need to stab his friend for making his mate upset again, Gray knew deep down that this training was necessary. She had to learn to protect herself. Especially if, as he feared, he might not live through this war to be there to protect her.

"Now," Erik said, "I want you to build a fire for us. No wood or sticks or kindling, just a flame that sits upon the ground."

Lea wiped her eyes with the heel of her hand, avoiding everyone's gaze. Her nose was red, and her breathing shallow.

"Hey, you did great." Gray leaned down and spoke into her hair. "You don't have to continue. Only if you want to."

"I just don't want to hurt anyone else," Lea sniffled.

"I think that bastard deserved a little punishment for putting so much pressure on you," Gray teased, forcing a smile. Lea didn't deserve the guilt. Erik had made a choice, knowing Lea would find the strength to control her flames if she feared he'd be hurt.

Lea hiccupped a laugh.

"Actually, Lea," Janelle called out, "if you could make a fire for us, that would be great. I'm freezing my tits off over here."

"You see, it's an emergency, Sunshine. We can't allow our girl here to lose such beautiful breasts, now can we?"

CHAPTER 25

LEA

Janelle blushed, mumbling something under her breath Lea couldn't distinguish.

"Okay," Lea breathed, reaching for her magic again. She stared at the ground, imagining her fire igniting from thin air, but the few tiny sparks that appeared fizzled out. There was nothing for her flames to latch on to, to tether themselves to and hold them in place.

Lea gritted her teeth in frustration, and her face turned red from holding her breath. "Dammit," she hissed, funneling more power into the air in front of her. "It's not—"

A small puff of smoke erupted in front of her. It wasn't much, no more than what accompanied a strong strike of flint, but it was enough to cause a small fire to hover just inches above the forest floor. It was no bigger than her fist, and it wasn't *hers*. Lea reached for her magic, finding every bit of it tucked away firmly in her chest.

Lea's eyebrows shot up in surprise, an expression Erik appeared to mistake for excitement.

"All right!" Erik clapped his hands together with a massive smile on his face. "Time to rest. Lea, keep it burning all night. We need warmth, but using kindling will create smoke and make us a target."

"This is ridiculous," Gray snapped. "She needs to sleep. We all need our energy if we're going to make it through the next few days here. That includes Azalea."

What's happening? Erik didn't do it, and Gray can't create fire...

Someone cleared their throat to her left.

"And she can sleep." Erik was still arguing with Gray. "You know as well as I do that our magic never sleeps, that it comes from a deeper part of us. If she commands it to be so, it will burn through the night."

"And it will drain her!" Gray argued.

"And it will replenish with the dawn," Erik replied calmly, biting into an apple.

Someone coughed, clearing their throat again, and Lea leaned forward, turning toward the sound. Noah was staring at her, a playful smile on his lips. He winked at her, wiggling his fingers. The fire grew just a bit, then receded.

Lea bit down on her lip to keep herself from smiling. He was pulling one over on Erik *and* Gray. If her mate wouldn't sever his head from his body, Lea could have kissed him. Thoroughly relieved, she latched her magic on to Noah's; the fire growing with her own flames now that it had something to hold on to.

Noah's magic diminished, so much so that Lea could barely feel it. But it was there. "In case you need it," Noah mouthed.

"She's not doing it. Not all night," Gray was beginning to rise, so ingrained in his argument with Erik that he didn't notice her relief through the bond. She had help.

"I think she'll be just fine, Commander," Noah pointed toward the perfect tinder-less fire.

"Did I ask your opinion, soldier?" Gray's fury was palpable, but only until he looked at the fire. Gray tilted his head, his eyes narrowing.

"All your arguing is giving me a headache," Janelle said.

"Better than freezing your tits off," Erik replied with a sly smile as he threw her a pointed look.

"I'll do it." Lea nodded, sitting cross-legged and staring into the fire.

"Fine," Gray sat back down. "Noah, a word?" Gray stood without waiting for an answer, stalking away with shadows trailing behind him.

Throwing another mischievous smile at Lea, Noah obediently rose to follow.

"Glad that's settled," Erik said as he crouched in front of her. "Poor kid. It was brave to stand up to Gray like that. Hope he's not too hard on him."

It had been brave, but Erik was wrong about why Gray had pulled Noah away. Through the bond she felt only gratitude. Gray had known the fire hadn't just been of her making. It was the only reason he'd relented in his argument with Erik, and Lea was confident that Gray wasn't scolding him. He was *thanking* him.

"We'll get started on the bedrolls," Erik continued. "Gray's right, you need to sleep tonight. Imagine what you want to happen, and your magic will know what to do. But if you truly need me to take over, I'll be right over there." He nodded to the other side of the fire, patting her knee and leaving her alone to master her flames.

CHAPTER 26

JANELLE

To Janelle's surprise, Lea had kept the fire burning through the night. It had grown a bit since she'd fallen asleep, and Janelle woke up with a sheen of sweat along her back. She'd slept facing away from the fire, preferring not to see her death coming should Lea lose control and destroy them all in a fiery explosion. But somehow she was alive, *and* her tits were warm.

It wasn't that she didn't trust her best friend—she would trust Lea with her life. It was that this was all new. Lea barely knew how to control her powers any more than she did. Janelle wasn't even quite sure what powers she *had*. That prickling sensation she felt on her neck that had warned her of trouble, of getting caught, it had always just seemed to be a part of her nature.

Janelle had assumed that she was simply more aware of her surroundings than most people. But now, looking back, she realized that those sensations had only occurred during the daytime. She never stole at night. Not once, since the night she had tried to sneak some cookies from the white and blue porcelain jar in her dark kitchen and her mother had caught her.

Actually, that wasn't true. The night of the escape she'd felt it. But how? Was the god of the sun watching out for her, or had the goddess of the moon granted her temporary use of her day magic at night? Because since then, there had been no awareness of danger after the sun went down. No prickling, no warnings.

Janelle glanced at Lea, taking in her tired eyes and frizzy hair. It was obvious that she hadn't slept much last night. She'd tried to hide her wide yawns and heavy eyelids when they had all woken to see the fire still going, but Janelle knew that her friend would never admit that her success was not only from her growing magical abilities, but also from her persistence to protect the people she loved.

Lea had always been like that. To a fault, she had made reckless decisions in order to take care of her family and friends. Since her mother's death, she'd deprived herself of sleep, driving herself to near insanity with her persistence in trying to master the moonflowers. One time during that year, when her father had failed to come home again, she'd tried to journey through the mountains north toward Woodhurst with only herself as company. She didn't even pause to consider that she likely would have died in those mountains had Thomas not gone to stop her.

Lea's impulsive actions came from a good place. After all, they only had each other. Their little village was all they had ever let themselves think about. Maybe Janelle should have known she had magic. Maybe Lea had set them all down a dangerous path by choosing to save Thomas in such a headstrong and reckless manner. But they were young, and their world had been small.

It might be unrealistic, but Janelle could only hope that Lea would accept that they were a team. It was no longer up to her alone to carry the burden of protecting others. She had a mate for that now, along with friends who had proved to her that they wouldn't continue to allow her to try to save the day alone. If Lea went down, Janelle fully intended to go down with her.

Janelle brushed her teeth with a small piece of birch, then chewed on some fresh mint Erik had packed in his satchel before they left. She was riding with him again today, and though she now felt more comfortable and steady on a horse, she still didn't think she'd be able to control one herself should trouble arise. At a slow trot, she'd be fine. But at a reckless gallop? She'd likely be killed.

It wasn't just the fact that she wasn't prepared for that kind of action on a horse, or that they didn't have another horse for her to ride that made her feel so comfortable traveling with Erik. Something else made her want to ride with him—a warmth that seemed to surround her and buzz along her skin as he sat behind her. She felt like she was in a bubble, calm and happy, despite the fact that so much danger lurked around them.

If Janelle was being honest, when she'd shown up at the palace—another impulsive decision made by a girl from Bearswillow—she'd had one singular focus: find her friend and get her home. But she couldn't help but feel now like it had been fate.

These people? She would die for any of them. Though Gray did drive her insane with his protective mate bullshit.

"What are you thinking about?" Erik asked, his breath tickling her ear as he placed a hand on her thigh and patted her knee.

Janelle's skin warmed, her heart stuttering as she subconsciously shifted away. She wasn't sure why she did it. Erik was handsome enough, burly and scruffy in a way that made her feel like he'd be able to build her a house with his bare hands. That smile of his was infectious, and she had to admit that it felt good whenever he cracked a joke and her lips tipped up in amusement. But Janelle wasn't good with affection, and if there was one word she could think of to describe Erik, it was affectionate. Not just in the physical sense, though he was far more touchy than anyone else she'd ever met. He had a habit of really making someone feel seen, important. It was like his warm demeanor wrapped you in a bear hug and forced you to feel special, and honestly, it was terrifying.

"I'm thinking about how suffocating your friend up there is being with his new wife." Janelle pushed the thoughts away, uncomfortable with the way her stomach was twisting in knots. "I feel like we're all walking on eggshells to not piss him off. He almost took my head off earlier when I approached him and Lea from behind."

"Ah. You're not wrong," Erik said. "I warned him about this, you know. That if they didn't forge the mate bond, he'd become irrational. A danger to others."

"They need to just seal it already. They never stop touching each other. Can't you enchant a little love grove for them, so they can do the deed? Genuinely, it's disgusting," Janelle said, wrinkling her nose.

It *was* disgusting, but something about seeing them together made Janelle the tiniest bit jealous. Of course, she was happy for her friend. But seeing someone look at her with such all encompassing love and adoration?

Erik sometimes looked at her differently. It wasn't the mixture of thinking she hung the moon and that she was also made of incredibly fragile glass that Gray looked at Lea with. But it was *something*. Maybe. Or maybe it was in her head.

It didn't matter either way. Janelle never needed anyone else to make her feel like a complete person. And yet, wouldn't it be nice if, at a minimum, she had a partner to help her do damage control for the stupid decisions her best friend made?

"I don't know..." Erik pondered, a strange look crossing his face. "Over the top? Sure. If they would just make love under their elements, it would take the edge off. He'd still protect her, of course, but there would be more thought behind his actions. It would be less of an impulse, far more calculated. Still, I think it's a beautiful thing that the gods have blessed them as mates. It gives me hope."

"Make love? Beautiful thing?" Janelle teased. "I think these woods are making you soft."

"Don't be fooled, Janelle." He wrapped an arm around her waist and shifted closer to her, his cock thick and hard against her hip. "My words might be soft, but I have absolutely no problem getting hard."

Janelle's cheeks warmed. She never blushed. Ever. But his words sent something straight into her core that set her entire body on fire. It was stupid, honestly. He was Fae. She was a human who hadn't bathed in days. Her blonde hair was growing roots, her purple hair fading to the edges.

But there was no denying what she felt against her backside, the proof of his desire. For sex, at least. He needed release. They'd been in the woods for days, and Janelle understood better than anyone the need to scratch an itch. Why not do it with her?

Except they were surrounded by people. And not only surrounded by people, but by demons and monsters and things that wanted to eat them alive. Nothing could happen. *For now...* a voice said in her head.

"Shut up," she mumbled.

"What was that?" Erik asked.

"Nothing," Janelle said, continuing to look straight ahead. It wasn't that she didn't want something to happen with Erik, but she wasn't sure she did, either. With other men she'd been with, she'd always known exactly what the extent of their interaction would be. A hook up. A casual fling. Thinking about crossing that line with Erik made her feel as if she was standing on the very edge of the cliff, trying to decide if jumping would be the thrill of her life, or the absolute death of her.

As if sensing her thoughts, Erik shifted back again, resuming their ride as if no tension had passed between them at all.

"Have you ever been in love?" The words left Janelle's lips without her permission, but sitting so close to Erik, watching Gray and Lea and how much they loved each other, she had to know.

"I thought I was, when I was younger. The way I suspect most people feel when they first kiss someone, or the first time they explore someone else's body."

Jealousy twisted in her gut. The thought of him exploring another girl's body made her physically sick. But he was charming. And kind. She had no doubt that girls fell over each other trying to get to him.

"They weren't important," Erik said, his voice soothing. "They didn't challenge me. I suspect many of them wanted me for my position. Second to the Night Prince. There's an allure in having that much power. In having the future king's ear."

Janelle dwelled on this. She couldn't imagine someone trying to *use* a man as kind and joyful as Erik. Spend time with him? Sure. But use him? Never. Even with her temper, along with the tendency to lose her patience quickly, Janelle found herself actually *wanting* to be near him. When she was around Erik, she could rarely stop the tiny smile that pulled at the edges of her mouth. The one she constantly tried to hide. She was tough, after all, and had an image to uphold.

"And you?" Erik asked. "Have you ever been in love?"

Janelle laughed out loud. It wasn't just funny, it was absurd. She had her use for men, and it didn't go beyond the physical. Not since... She shook her head, refusing to think about that night. "No. I have never been in love."

Erik seemed to consider this for a moment, going silent. "Have you never been touched, then?"

Janelle could feel the tension radiating from behind her as Erik waited for her to respond. "That's not what I said," she replied, knowing he wouldn't like her answer, but wanting to be honest with him all the same.

"Did they at least love you well?" he rumbled, his gruff words somehow angry *and* tender.

Janelle shook her head no. "Nothing more than some fun. There wasn't a lot to do in our village." She tried to minimize the truth, that she hadn't allowed anyone in enough to let them do more than fuck her. Any physical contact she'd indulged in had been simply a means to an end.

Erik placed his hand on Janelle's stomach, his palm splayed wide across it. The tip of his thumb rubbed against her hip bone, only inches away from the jagged, raised scar that crossed up the front of her hip and wrapped around her side.

"Fools," Erik growled.

"Maybe I'm not meant for that," Janelle croaked, hardly able to breathe with his fingertips so close to her scar.

"You are meant to be adored. Worshiped. Don't you ever think otherwise, even for a second," he ordered, his words uncharacteristically sharp.

Janelle's skin felt hot, itchy and uncomfortable, as if her thoughts and emotions were trying to break free from her body. She needed to change the subject, but despite her best intentions, she leaned back against Erik instead. She couldn't bring herself to pull away from the feeling of his hard chest against her back and his stubble tickling her temple.

"I'll try to remember that." She cleared her throat. "Anyway. Tell me something about you I don't know. Why are you and Gray so close?"

Erik didn't press the subject, kindly allowing her to move past the moment that had been occurring between them. "It started because my father was the king's closest advisor. We were born only months apart from each other. Our mothers were friends, and we were raised together. We've always been close, but he became my brother the day he saved me." Erik paused, and as much as Janelle wished it was for dramatic effect, she could sense that it was because he needed to gather his strength to continue.

"My father was not a kind man. He was abusive, not only with his words, but with his fists as well. A coward, to attack a child."

Running a hand across his scruffy jaw, Erik sighed as if reliving a memory he wished would remain in the past. "Gray saw bruises in the shape of fingers around my throat when we were twelve years old. His powers had already begun to manifest, but he was nowhere near as strong as he is now. He went to my father in the night, left strangulation marks on *his* throat that did *not* look like fingers. He threatened to kill him should he ever lay a hand on me or my mother again. And the shame my father felt, knowing that a child would be able to fulfill that promise, it kept him from telling anyone.

"The king would have been proud if he'd known that Gray had behaved so ruthlessly. My dad never touched me again. Hardly spoke to me. I returned the favor to Gray, years later, when we made a blood oath to one another." Erik looked down at his palm where a faint scar crossed from thumb to pinky. "I bound myself to him, pledged my life to serve him and help destroy the kingdom our fathers created."

"Men from Auropera seem to have tendencies toward violence against women and children, don't they?" Janelle's words were bitter, angry.

"You better not be speaking from experience," Erik growled. Janelle felt heat at her back, the hand still pressing into her stomach warming to nearly searing hot.

"Just an observation," Janelle felt her stomach churn as Emma held up a hand, pulling the reins with the other to stop her horse. "Something's coming..." Emma said, her eyes wide.

"What is it?" Gray stopped Obsidian and drew his sword in one terrifying, fluid motion, shadows exploding in a shield around them.

"They don't know..." Emma looked around, continuing her silent conversation with the dead.

Erik cursed, and Lea's face paled. And while Janelle was afraid of whatever they were about to face, she couldn't deny the relief that she felt that her deepest secrets could continue to hide safely inside her for just a little longer.

CHAPTER 27

EMMA

"S omething's coming," Johnny, the leader of the dead, said again. "You need to listen, it's not..."

Emma never heard the end of the sentence as a gust of wind rushed through the woods, carrying with it a chill that caused her teeth to chatter painfully. The already cold air dropped at least twenty degrees within seconds. "What the..." Emma turned to Erik to warn him of what Johnny had told her. "Get ready, something's—"

Emma's blood ran cold. Johnny had turned toward her. His usually amicable expression had morphed into one of rage. He dipped his chin, lowering his brows. "You can see us, and yet, you do *nothing* to help us. We warn you. We follow you. And still, you call us the dead. Speak as if we are nothing."

A shiver ran down Emma's spine. "I'm so sorry. I want to help. Really, I do, but I don't know *how*."

"You haven't even tried!" Johnny roared. He bared his teeth in a gruesome smile. "Why do you think we allowed you entrance? Hmmm?" His wounds began to ooze. "You don't deserve our help, you selfish bitch!"

Within seconds, the dead appeared through the trees. Hundreds of them, thousands. There were the soldiers who she'd seen when they'd entered the woods, but there were so many more. And there... still covered in blood, a disdainful snarl on her face, was Claire.

"Claire, I'm so sorry..."

"You left me!" she spat.

"I had to. We were under attack," Emma stuttered as the dead drew nearer. Emma felt eyes on the back of her neck, on every inch of exposed skin. She looked over her shoulder to find that she was completely surrounded. Some of the dead looked emaciated, as if they'd starved to death. Some had fatal wounds and were covered in blood. Others were missing body parts... arms and heads.

"Please, let me know how I can help, and I'll do it," Emma cried as the nearest dead stopped only feet away from her.

"There's nothing you can do for us. Nothing, except join us," the man said with a rattling laugh.

A scream tore from Emma's throat as the mob descended upon her, their hands tearing at her hair and clothing. She gagged on the stench of rotting flesh as pain encompassed her, the weight of the dead climbing on top of her, squeezing the air from her lungs as she fought for her life.

CHAPTER 28

JANELLE

The temperature dropped quickly. Along with the rush of cold air, the snap of footsteps upon dry, crackling branches met her ears.

"We know you're there!" a gruff male voice called through the trees. "If you run, we will be forced to kill you. Do not attempt to use your magic, or we will have no choice but to use our own."

"Shit," Janelle cursed, her stomach sinking. "What do we do?"

"You do nothing." The voice cut straight through Janelle's memories. Sweat broke out along her neck, her stomach jolting and threatening to release its contents. She knew that voice. It lived in the back of her mind, tormenting her.

"Useless, worthless," that voice taunted her in her darkest moments. "Human," it said with disgust.

It couldn't be. Surely if *he* was here, her magic would have warned her of the danger. But there was no mistaking the pure vitriol with which he spoke.

"What are you doing here, Stefan?" Janelle asked with false bravado, squaring her shoulders and tilting her chin up as she waited for the man who had tried to kill her to show himself.

"You're so very predictable, you know." As if reading her mind, Stefan sauntered forward, his steps cocky. He hadn't changed at all. His black Royal Army uniform was pressed and immaculate, and his medium length dark hair was slicked back, highlighting his smarmy eyes. "When the king read off the names of the traitors to our kingdom, I knew that you would be on it," he sneered. "We never got to finish what we started before. Such a waste. So we personally volunteered to find you."

"We?" Janelle felt the blood drain from her face.

The soldier snapped his fingers, and three men emerged, coming to stand behind Stefan. Janelle knew those faces well, but one was missing. Her hand subconsciously rose to the scar on her hip.

"And where's Jakob? Was he too afraid to look me in the eye after what he did?" *Or what he didn't do*, Janelle thought bitterly. She forced her voice to remain steady.

"I did love you, Janelle." Jakob appeared as if out of thin air, stepping forward and placing a palm against her cheek. Janelle flinched, pushing him away.

"What the fuck is happening?" she hissed, wishing in that moment that her magic was something more useful, like the ability to make people explode into a million pieces. "You proved your point already. All of you!" She pointed between them, beginning to panic as Stefan's lips spread into a wide, malicious smile.

"You are a traitor. I will not allow my brother's name to be smeared by his connection to you, worthless human trash."

Janelle cringed. That wasn't the first time she'd heard those words leave Stefan's mouth. But unlike last time, she wasn't in severe agony as he said them while beating her senseless.

"I told you I would find you again."

He had. The night that her lover's brothers-in-arms had discovered them in a compromising position. After Jakob had scrambled off her in shame, they'd started kicking her in the chin. Once she was unable to speak from the damage to her face, his friends had held her up while Stefan punched her repeatedly in her stomach. They'd laughed as they tortured her. And Jakob had stood by, allowing it to happen. That is, until Stefan had pulled a jagged piece of glass from the broken vase on the floor.

"We can't afford a half human bastard child," Stefan had hissed, plunging the shard into her lower stomach and slicing sideways across her hip and side, the searing pain almost as torturous as Jakob's inaction. He'd told her he loved her. And then he'd allowed them to harm her, embarrassed by his relationship with a human.

Janelle had curled into a ball and was bleeding out onto the floor. Satisfied that she'd been taught her lesson, Stefan had looked at her naked body from head to foot with a disgusted grimace on his face before spitting at her feet and walking away. "I will find you again. And I will finish this," he'd promised.

"And I told you I would kill you if you ever tried. *Both* of you," Janelle hissed back, aiming her words toward Jakob.

"And yet I stand before you, as does Stefan, still alive." He grinned. "You won't be able to say the same soon." He shot toward her, wrapping his hands around her throat. Janelle kicked as he lifted her off the ground, scratching at his arms so hard her fingernails bent and bled. Jakob threw her to the dirt, and she gasped in a painful breath.

"But not until we have a little fun," Stefan laughed as the men descended upon her. She felt a blade slice through her skin as a boot kicked her in the eye. Someone ripped at her shirt while someone else stomped down on her leg, cracking the bones in one excruciating blow.

Janelle shrieked, an echo of her screams from the night Stefan and his squad had "taught her a lesson," as they had called it. That she was a worthless human, undeserving of a Fae soldier's affection. Of anyone's affection.

Blood coated her mouth as Janelle pulled her knees to her chest, hoping that death would come swiftly.

CHAPTER 29

ERIK

It was suddenly freezing. Erik saw his breath in a puff of white air, reminding him of the day everything had changed for him. He'd been only a child when he'd come upon his father beating his mother in the early morning hours, just after dawn on a cold winter day. He'd gasped, his terror escaping in a cloud of frosty breath, revealing his location. It had been the first time he had realized that he wasn't safe, and people weren't good. Not even his own father.

He'd sworn to his mother that evening as she'd held a cold cut of meat to his lip that he would never grow up to be like his father. That he would be kind, gentle. That he wouldn't allow his soul to be hardened into that of a killer.

"And yet, how many lives have you taken?"

That voice... It couldn't be. Erik ripped his sword free, the hiss of the metal grinding against the sheath ringing out through the woods. Standing before him was his father, his cropped blond hair and stern expression unmistakable. In his muscular hand was a familiar blade pointing straight at Erik's throat. "You are more like me than you will admit to yourself."

"I am nothing like you. *Nothing*!" Erik shouted, his voice shaking with rage. "I would never hurt someone innocent. And I would certainly never claim to love them!" Erik flew toward his father, grabbing him by his uniform and slamming him into a tree. His father's sword tumbled from his hand as Erik warmed the hilt to near molten, burning his flesh.

In a blind rage, Erik smashed his fist into his father's nose. "I would *never* strike a woman I love! I would never harm a child!" He punched him again. "I would rather die!"

"And yet you strike me!" Herald said through bloody teeth. "Your own father! You're *exactly* like me! You'll destroy the ones you love. Every last one of them. Just wait." The man smiled. Actually *smiled*, as if the thought of his own son becoming a monster was a joyous one.

Erik flew into a blind rage, dropping his sword next to his father's and repeatedly slamming his fists into his jaw. The king's second coughed up more blood as he laughed, completely unaffected.

"Is that all you have? You are *weak*," Herald spat.

Slamming him against the tree again, his father's head cracked against the trunk. Erik wrapped a flaming hand around his throat before closing his eyes and squeezing, unable to look as his father fought for air. He would never be like him, took no pleasure in ending his father's life. But it was necessary. *A swift death is more than he deserves, but I'll settle for it,* Erik thought as his father stopped fighting. He held on tight for another minute, ensuring that he was truly dead, that his heart had stopped beating, before letting go and allowing his father's body to crumple to the ground.

Erik opened his eyes, forcing himself to look at what he'd done.

Disbelief and horror filled Erik's gut as he retched onto the ground. "No, no, no..." Collapsing, Erik screamed, his grief so potent that his roar caused the trees to lean away from him.

"No, Janelle! Wake up!" Erik cried as he lifted Janelle's lifeless body against his chest and roared at the sky.

CHAPTER 30

NOAH

Noah pulled the cloak Erik had lent him around his body tighter. It was suddenly so cold, and he found he was grateful Erik had offered his spare to help keep him warm. It was far too big, but as the chill became almost unbearable, he knew that without it, he'd be miserable.

"Noah," Gray's voice cut through his thoughts. "I think I heard an animal, just up ahead. Can you track it? I'd like to have more than nuts and dried fruit for dinner."

"Yes, Commander," Noah said, a bubble of pride inflating in his chest. He'd wanted to find the Eclipsed King for so long, and now he was actually *helping* him. He could be of service, valuable, and he couldn't help but think that somewhere beyond the veil, his father was proud of him. Noah didn't just want to be part of this war, he wanted to *matter* in it.

Kicking his horse, Maple, in the side, Noah trotted ahead. Reaching out with his powers, he searched for the animal Gray had heard. He let his energy travel outward, along the ground, and up the trees, twisting through the rotting branches up toward the sky, but there was *nothing*. Nothing alive for as far as his magic could reach, and now that he was focusing, Noah could tell that nothing alive had traveled through this part of the woods in weeks, if not more.

He turned Maple around. "I'm sorry Commander, but—" Noah's stomach dropped. Panic unlike anything he had ever felt before caused his hair to stand on end. On their knees with terror-filled eyes were Gray, Lea, Erik, Janelle, and Emma. Several soldiers Noah didn't recognize held gleaming swords across their necks. They were statue still, and Noah had the sinking suspicion that they were simply waiting for the order to kill. While he'd been focused on tracking ahead of them, the Royal Army had found them. Noah drew his sword, his hands shaking.

"You really thought you could escape us?" It was Jordan, a lieutenant for the Black King that Noah had served under. "We suspected that *they* would be traitors, but you?" Jordan tsked. "We had such high hopes. You were moving up the ranks so quickly. So much potential wasted."

Noah called on his flames, imagining them wrapping around each of the guards' hands, hoping that maybe they would drop their swords if he burned them. But Jordan threw up a shield, stopping his magic as if it was nothing.

He sighed. "Again, you betray us?" Jordan stepped forward, jabbing his boot between Emma's shoulder blades and shoving her to the ground. In less than a second, his sword was embedded through her hand, pinning it in the dirt. "I was just going to kill them, but it seems that you need a lesson, soldier."

Emma screamed in agony as Jordan twisted the sword, creating a gaping hole in her palm. "You can kill them. A clean strike. An honorable, painless death. Or I can cut them apart piece by piece. And I assure you," he said with a grin. "It will be anything but quick and painless."

Noah's vision went hazy at the edges. "No. I—Please." He couldn't kill them. He'd never killed *anyone*. He was likely the only soldier in the Royal Army whose sword hadn't been stained by blood. "Please," he begged, jumping off the horse and pushing down the urge to vomit. "You can do the right thing. You can join us."

"It's okay, Noah," Gray said stoically, raising his chin and meeting his gaze.

"No! Please! Don't kill them. Just give me a second!" he begged, staggering forward and dropping to his knees. He looked at Gray, then Erik, pleading with his eyes for them to do *something*. Why weren't they fighting back? Why weren't they using their magic?

"Decide *now*. You kill them, swiftly, or I start carving."

With shaking hands, Noah slowly drew his sword, the metal clanging in its sheath as it scraped free. *Please gods, help me.*

At his hesitation, Jordan raised his eyebrows. "Coward," he spat. "Kill them," he ordered the soldiers as a cruel smile crossed his face. "But take your time."

Noah screamed as he was grabbed from behind. Two soldiers he hadn't seen forced him to his knees, holding his head back by his hair as the guards shoved his friends to the ground and, with their gleaming daggers and swords, began hacking away pieces of their bodies in a bloody massacre.

CHAPTER 31

LEA

"How much longer will we ride?" Lea asked, rubbing her arms. "I'd like to get my cloak when we stop. I'm freezing."

"I was actually thinking the same thing," Janelle called. "I might fall off this horse if these chills don't let up."

Erik scoffed. "As if I would ever let that happen. Though," he rubbed the back of his neck, "I don't feel like myself. Maybe just a few minutes of rest would be good, Gray. It might help us cover more ground in the long run."

Gray rolled his head from side to side, stretching out his shoulders. "Fifteen minutes. We can't afford to lose anything more than that." Pulling back on Obsidian's reins, he stopped the horse abruptly.

An odd sensation pricked in the back of Lea's mind. Something's not right... The Gray she knew would never stop so abruptly without finding a resting spot with a good vantage point before thinking through every possible scenario and assessing the risks.

Lea turned in the saddle, reaching backward to cup Gray's cheek. His *very* warm cheek. What in the gods' names...

"Gray, you're on fire." Lea jumped off the horse, landing with a thud that vibrated up her shins. "Emma, can you come here?" Lea's stomach rolled as she watched Gray slide off his horse. His movements were slow, far less graceful and fluid than she'd become accustomed to. His olive skin had paled, a sheen of sweat causing his strong jawline and cheekbones to glisten.

Lea placed the top of her hand against Gray's forehead, just as her mother had done to her a million times growing up. "He's feverish, Emma."

Emma followed Lea's lead, placing her hand on Gray's sweaty cheek.

"Gods, Emma! Your arm!" Lea felt a shockwave of fear through her chest, her breaths growing shallow. She would recognize those black bumps on her forearm anywhere.

"The Lonely Death," Erik said solemnly.

"Janelle, Erik, stay back." Lea cried out, placing her hands against Emma's hot skin. The disease couldn't touch her... Not now that she had married Gray. Except...

"Open your shirt, Gray," Lea reached toward the top button of his shirt.

"As much as I've been imagining you ordering me out of my clothes today, maybe now isn't the best time—"

"Cut the shit," Lea cut him off, "and open your shirt." He was stalling. The absolute terror she could feel pulsing down the bond told her that he already knew what she would discover when he bared his chest.

He looked down, a deep breath rattling in his throat as he pulled apart the neck of his dirty tunic. Red rashes gave way to oozing, black welts.

"How is this happening?" Lea demanded, her hand going to the necklace at her throat. "What do we do?" she cried out to no one in particular. "Erik, how is this possible?" Lea turned her head to see that Erik and Janelle had dismounted their horse. They were both staring at each other, tears in Janelle's eyes as she took in the bloody, black wounds climbing up Erik's neck. Erik pulled up the hem of Janelle's shirt where a matching rash wrapped around her torso.

"No..." Lea breathed, disbelief causing her thoughts to shut down. "It's not possible." The words became a mantra in her head. "It's not possible. It's not. It can't be."

"I'm so sorry," Gray cupped her cheek, the sorrow in his eyes causing her breath to catch. He'd given up. Her Gray would never, and yet, he *was*.

"We'll fix this. You saved me. You did! When it was impossible, you all saved me! I can find a way to save you, too!"

"Little Flower..." Gray coughed, blood running down his chin and dripping onto his shoes. "There is no cure. We got lucky, saving you. But the rest of us? We're too far away to find anyone to help."

"That can't be true!" Lea was panicking, her hands shaking as she hyperventilated, pushing every ounce of healing energy she could find into Gray's chest, then moving to Emma's arm. Tears rolled from her eyes, blurring her vision. The wounds only grew. "Why isn't it working?" Lea sobbed.

"I'm afraid Gray's right." Emma placed a hand on Lea's arm, her eyes kind, but defeated. "You will get through this, my friend. You are strong, and—"

"Don't you dare comfort me right now!" Lea screamed. "None of you are dying! Do you understand me? I watched my mother die already, Thomas's father... Little Anthony..." a sob ripped from her throat as her darkness writhed inside her.

Gray knelt in front of her, blood now running from the corner of his eye... "I will go beyond the veil knowing you are safe. That is the most precious gift I could be given as I leave this life." Gray pulled her into a tight embrace, comforting her in what just might be his final moments. "I will wait for you. For eternity, if that is what it takes." He leaned back, looking her in the eyes. "Take your time, my love," Gray said as coughs wracked his body. The welts had spread further, wrapping around his throat and down to his fingers. Blood collected beneath where he knelt, every sore on his skin open and weeping.

"This can't be happening! What will I do, Gray?" Lea leaned into him, not caring about the blood and gore. If all she could offer him in his last moments was comfort, then that is what she would give him.

"This can't be happening," she cried again. "It's not real, Gray. Tell me it's not real..."

"It *is* real, Azalea. You need to accept it." Lea froze. Gray's tone had been sharp, dark and bitter. There was no evidence of his kindness, his love for her behind those words. And through the bond, anger. Not sadness, not terror or resignation.. *Anger.*

"It can't be real..." Lea whispered to herself, pulling back from Gray. "It's *not* real," she stood, staring into her husband's eyes for only a second before she held her hands in front of her and exploded the woods into a raging wildfire, eviscerating everything her magic could touch.

CHAPTER 32

GRAY

Shadows traveled across the black forest floor, weaving around fallen branches and the twisted trunks of dying trees as they obediently served their master, searching for threats. Gray shifted on his horse as a rustle sounded from a nearby bush. Whatever had caused it had escaped the notice of his shadows, but not his Fae senses. *Threat.* The word repeated in his mind like a war drum. *Threat. Threat. Threat.*

Growing up, Gray had been jealous of Alaric's flames. They were flashier, perhaps more brutal than his shadows, but as he'd grown he'd learned to become grateful for them. They were a part of him as much as his hands, a muscle he could flex capable of providing him limitless information. If he connected them to his ears, he could hear as far as his shadows could travel. If he focused on his breathing, he could scent a threat from miles away. He could sneak them through tiny holes or underneath doors, use them to gather information or pilfer secret documents.

Immediately, Gray commanded his shadows to seek out whatever was lurking nearby. He *knew* something was there, but he couldn't identify it. It was rare that Gray could be truly surprised when he was using his shadows to their full ability. Which is why the earth tilted on its axis when his father stepped through the gnarled trees.

"Thought you could escape me, did you, boy?" King Brennus Nestruir laughed that wicked laugh that sometimes found its way into Gray's nightmares. He looked younger, filled with vitality rather than the pudgy, lazy, power hungry man he'd become in recent years. His skin was less sallow, his hair thicker, with far fewer strands of gray. He looked strong, dangerous in a way he hadn't appeared to Gray in a very long time.

Gray dismounted his horse, pulling Lea down and pushing her behind him. "Erik!" He motioned to Lea. His priority was her safety, her life. Because if the king was here, it would be for her power. His heart shuddered. His father couldn't have her.

Erik was at Gray's side in a moment, sword drawn.

The king laughed again, throwing his head back and baring his neck as if the idea that Gray and Erik were a threat was nonexistent.

"You know, my son, that I command the power of thousands in my blood. You think I do not know what runs through *her* veins? I do." His voice, or *voices*, echoed off the trees as he took a single step forward. "And I *will* have it."

Time froze. Gray was unable to react, to even say a word to his shadows before his father's magic exploded, circling Lea's throat and lifting her into the air.

Gray's vision turned red. He would destroy the world before he would allow the king to hurt her. His father would never take her magic. As Gray's shadows took control, he grabbed his sword and plunged it into the king's throat. Stalking toward Brennus, he twisted the knife, blood gurgling from the wound. "Let her go, and I'll kill you quickly."

King Nestruir bared his teeth, which were now stained a gruesome red. "You forget, son. I can't be killed." The king tilted his head back with laughter, blood spurting from his neck as the world around them exploded into an inescapable inferno.

CHAPTER 33

LEA

"This isn't real." Lea pushed Gray away, or at least, whatever was *pretending* to be Gray, finding her flames in an instant and coiling them tight. "What are you?"

Gray's eyes shifted, the emerald green turning black an instant before he launched himself at her with a monstrous roar. There was no time to worry about controlling her fire, no time for fear and anxiety to dampen her potential. Lea closed her eyes and channeled every ounce of day magic she held inside her in a giant arc. Throwing a shield of shadows around her friends, she unleashed her fury.

Sweat dripped into her eyes, but her magic continued to pulse from her hands. Gray's doppelgänger wailed, an unnatural, screeching sound, before his skin melted away, leaving a shriveled, pale, childlike figure in its place.

Its skin was paper thin, with blue and black veins that spread like a spiderweb beneath it. There was no hair on its body, and its beady black eyes were unfocused as it took a final rattling breath. She focused her magic on its carcass, the heat nearly unbearable against Lea's skin as it burned in a white-hot blaze.

"Lea!" Gray's voice caused her head to snap up, searching for her mate through her haze of fury and fire. Keeping an eye on the burning monster, she called her magic back into her chest, forcing the flames to suffocate.

The first thing she saw through the smoke and dying red embers was scorched earth. The trees, which had been gnarled and black to begin with, were nearly gone. Jagged trunks still glowing orange jutted out from the barren ground, while ash fell like snow, landing in her hair and on her eyelashes. And through the ash, were pockets of shadows.

She pulled them back, nearly crying with relief as the shadows retreated and revealed her friends, all very much looking pale and terrified, but alive. Erik let out a cry that reminded Lea of a wounded animal as he ran to Janelle, but her focus was pulled away when Gray sprinted toward her. Lea crashed into his arms, pressing her forehead against his chest as Gray tangled his fingers through the hair at the nape of her neck.

"Are you hurt?" Gray wrapped his magic around her like a comforting blanket of shadows, searching for injuries as they prodded and caressed every inch of her body.

Lea shook her head. "What was that?" she asked, pointing to the smoking, cremated remains of the horrendous creature. Noah, his face ashen, grabbed his stomach and turned away, as if the sight of the monster might make him physically ill.

"A tirror." Emma stood on shaking legs. "The dead tried to warn me, but it appeared too fast, invaded my mind before I could hear their message."

"Did you see us all dying of the Lonely Death?" Lea shivered, the image of those black welts fresh in her mind.

"No. It was different for me." Emma's voice was weak, haunted. "It was the dead. There were so many of them, and they were so angry... They wanted to kill me, because I can't help them."

Lea felt a pang of sorrow for her friend. Her worst fear was being unable to help others, even those beyond her help. Her magic was a part of her, a curse that would follow her for the rest of her life. "Gray?" Lea asked, unable to feel anything more than the ferocity of his anger through the bond.

"My father was stealing your magic. He was going to kill you," Gray said through clenched teeth. "I should have known that it was just another damned monster." Shadows floated through the still smoky air, electricity crackling within them as if feeding off the heat. Lightning crashed in the distance as Gray's eyes filled with rage.

"None of us knew, Gray." Erik placed a hand on his shoulder. "Stay calm. We're safe now. She is safe."

"Lea knew," Janelle corrected quietly. "Thank you, for killing it."

Nodding at her friend, Lea took in her appearance. Dark circles bruised the skin beneath her eyes, and a sheen of sweat still glistened on her face. She was pale, and her fingers subconsciously traced her hip and side. Lea cocked her head. She hadn't seen Janelle do that in a long time. It had been a nervous habit once, around the time Lea's mother had died. Something she'd done whenever she was anxious or troubled.

"What did you see, Janelle?" Lea prodded gently. Something wasn't right. Janelle was fearless, but right now? She seemed absolutely terrified.

"I don't—I need to sit down." Janelle paled even further. Erik was at her side in an instant, helping lower her to the ground.

"It doesn't matter what any of us saw," he said reassuringly, keeping a hand on Janelle's back and rubbing in slow circles. "None of it was real. Whatever it was, it can't hurt you."

Janelle nodded, taking slow, steadying breaths.

Gray grabbed Lea's shoulders, turning her to face him.

"Are you sure you're okay?" He ran a finger down the side of Lea's cheek. "How did you know what to do?"

"You were all dying." Lea pulled aside the collar of Gray's shirt, tracing a finger against his unblemished skin. She traced the edge of his tattoo, so grateful that the lines of the mountains were the only hint of black she saw on his chest. "It was the Lonely Death... Every single one of you."

"And you knew it was impossible."

"I thought it was. And then you were unkind, harsh. I knew that if you were dying, you would never make me feel that way." Lea leaned her cheek against his chest. "I don't like talking about this."

"I'm so sorry, Little Flower," Gray bent down and kissed her hair, "if even a part of you thought for a moment that I would let anything take me away from you."

"I'm sorry, too. That you thought your father would be able to steal my magic. That must have terrified you."

"Enough that I didn't realize it was a trick. How did you know how to kill it? You shielded us. The control that must have taken..." Gray gestured to the small patches of ground that were free of soot and embers.

"You all were in danger. I didn't know where you were, or what was happening. It was instinct, I think. My magic just knew what to do." Despite the adrenaline still running through her body and the thumping of her heart against her ribcage, she felt a flicker of pride in her chest. She'd saved them, had erupted the woods into a wildfire without harming a hair on any of their heads.

"Maybe I can help the cause after all. Maybe I can control my magic if I keep practicing."

"I have never once, for a single moment, doubted that, Little Flower." He kissed her again, groaning softly when Lea slipped her tongue between his lips. "I want nothing more than to remove your clothes, inspect every inch of skin with my fingers and mouth to make sure you haven't been harmed... but the smoke." Gray forced himself to pull away, gesturing to the thick, dark air around them as he turned to Erik. "We're a sitting target. We need to leave. Immediately." Gray had become the Commander again. Efficient. Direct. And it did things to Lea that made her want to force Gray to stay and live out his desires.

"Ready the horses." Gray walked to Lea, his shoulder brushing against hers, electricity tingling down her arm where their bodies touched. Gray leaned down to speak into her ear, his breath hot on her neck. His eyes darkened as if he'd heard her thoughts. "Later, Little Flower, when we're alone, you won't be able to stop me."

CHAPTER 34

LEA

They traveled for several hours, all of them silent as they put as much distance between themselves and the smoky site of the tirror attack as possible. Since they'd entered the woods, they hadn't been very talkative. There were times, of course, that they'd had conversations to kill the time, but other times, when the threat of danger breathed particularly close to their backs, they had ridden in deafening quiet.

This was different. No one spoke, not a single word. Their eyes were downcast, all of them lost in thought. Erik's eyes looked particularly haunted as he rode behind Janelle, and Lea wasn't sure if it was her imagination or reality, but she thought she saw him pull Janelle impossibly closer to his chest, almost as if he thought she might disappear.

Once they stopped, Emma dismounted, walking to Janelle and wrapping her in a hug. Lea worried about what Janelle had seen. Based on Emma's reaction, and her unique ability to sense other people's emotions, she was certain that it was something awful. Until today, Lea hadn't thought there were any secrets between them. But whatever it had been, whatever memory she had relived, it was something Janelle had suffered through alone.

Gray had barked instructions to Erik to stay no more than six inches from Lea as he left to set up the wards for their resting spot. He tugged Noah along with him to use his gift of tracking to discern if any other monsters or demons had been anywhere nearby recently, as well as something to hunt for dinner. His protectiveness was getting overbearing, excessive even, but Lea couldn't blame him. She'd almost died numerous times since they'd met, and these woods were the perfect opportunity for the universe to finish the job.

Tonight, they rested under an enormous tree that had fallen some time ago, its thick, dry trunk providing some degree of cover from unwanted eyes. The tree's large branches spread around them, extending like the legs of a spider, creating an almost cave-like umbrella.

Erik had once again tasked her with keeping a fire burning through the night. Gray had, of course, protested, but Erik had reminded him that once again it had been Lea who had saved them today. They needed her, and she needed to train when she was tired. No one was sure how deep her well of power ran, and Erik insisted that it was crucial to learn to channel small amounts of magic even when close to burnout.

"You can still sleep, Sunshine," Erik had reminded her. He'd insisted that if she simply became one with her magic, told it exactly what she wished it to do, her subconscious would continue to control it as her conscious mind rested.

Noah had caught her eye and quirked an eyebrow. *Do you want help?* His expression said. And while Lea appreciated his offer, more than the quiet young soldier could ever know, she shook her head. She needed to do this herself, if only to prove that she could.

Lea knew it was possible. She'd seen Gray shield them as he slept, watched wispy shadows floating around them like a dark, menacing fog. Back in Auropera, he'd sent shadows to lead her back to her room. But still, she worried that if she was not awake to control the small fire burning so close to all of them, a nightmare might find her and she might erupt their little sleepover into another raging inferno.

Staring out into the dark night, Lea snuggled closer to Gray. She hadn't seen him sleep so deeply in quite some time. His face looked younger without the stern, borderline angry expression he always wore.

The lines had softened between his eyebrows and his mouth was slightly open, his jaw finally relaxed rather than clenched tight. Lea couldn't help but hope that she would see this calm expression when he was awake someday, when the war was over and they settled into a peaceful life together.

The crunch of dead leaves pulled Lea from her thoughts. Something was nearby. Lea sat up, rubbing the back of her neck. *It's nothing*...she whispered to herself as she added more energy into the fire, making it burn brighter and illuminating a large circle around them. Nothing was there... No ominous demons had come to kill them, as far as she could tell.

Lea shook her head, trying to clear any paranoia or fear from her thoughts. There was absolutely zero chance that Gray would be sleeping if he had any concern at all that his enchantment would fail, that anyone or *anything* would find them.

As if sensing her worry, Gray opened one eye. "Rest, Little Flower. We've traveled a good distance, and we're not far from Calir. If we leave at dawn, we should cross the border by tomorrow afternoon. But we can't do that if you're losing sleep from fear. My spells are holding firm. I can feel them. They're just as strong tonight as they have been every night."

"I thought I heard something." Lea felt foolish telling Gray something might be near when he was so confident his enchantments were working, but something in her gut told her not to ignore what she was feeling.

"A bird hunting. I've heard owls most of the night. Sleep." He pulled her down, wrapping his arm tight around her chest and tucking her head beneath his chin.

"I'm in awe of you, Azalea. Of what you did today. But your strength and courage doesn't mean that you don't need rest."

He was right. She was utterly exhausted. Never having used that much magic before, her body was fatigued in a way she wasn't used to. Her muscles felt sore, and her movements were sluggish. "But the fire..."

"I'll keep an eye on it for you. Noah is watching as well. Now sleep." Gray kissed the crown of her head and Lea closed her eyes, sleep claiming her so quickly she hardly remembered their conversation when she woke.

It was another *snap* that yanked her from her deep, mindless slumber. Lea closed her eyes to listen more carefully, waiting to see if it was only her imagination. Only a moment passed before she heard it again. *Snap.* Not from the trees, but the ground. It was far too loud to be caused by an owl, or any other nocturnal bird or beast that may be hunting game.

Or maybe it *was* a beast, and they were its prey. As if on cue, several sets of glowing eyes the size of walnuts appeared through the inky black night. They remained outside the perimeter of Gray's wards, but still, they didn't blink as they stared directly at her.

"Gray, something's watching us." Lea sat up quickly, rubbing the back of her neck where her hair stood on end. "There's something here."

Lea turned to look at Gray, wishing that she could have allowed him to get the rest he needed. But even though the creatures were on the other side of the magical barrier... they still knew they were here. Lea shook Gray's shoulder, but he didn't budge. Not a hair moved on his head. "What the—Erik? Something's wrong."

Lea was met with only silence. She scrambled over to where Erik slept, Janelle lying curled within in his arms, but both were as still as stone.

Bile rose in Lea's throat, panic and adrenaline causing her hands to shake. *What do I do?* "Erik!" Lea punched him in the arm as hard as she could, her knuckles popping from the force. She cried out in pain as she ran to Noah, who slept just on the other side of the fire, one hand reaching out toward it. He had dark circles under his eyes, and Lea could tell from the fatigue on his face that he had stayed up to watch the fire. Even through her fear, a pang of appreciation at his loyalty buzzed in her chest.

Lea twisted to find Emma, who had set up her pallet just on the other side of Noah. Her eyes were open, and she was half sitting, as if she had been waking up to warn them when time had simply frozen.

Lea put two shaking fingers to Emma's neck, where the steady beat of her heart happily skipped along. Her chest still rose and fell with deep breaths.

"Who's there!?" Lea yelled out into the night, knowing in her bones that whatever had made those noises was responsible for what was happening. Stepping out from under the cover of the fallen tree, Lea threw a shield of shadows over her friends. She refused to let them be injured, would protect them until her dying breath, if that is what she was about to face.

No one answered, but Lea could still feel something looking at her... *watching* her.

"Show yourself!" She ordered into the night, unwilling to let fear make her cower. She couldn't run, didn't know where to go, even if she was willing to leave Gray and her friends behind. That left only one option. *Fight.*

"Lea, it's me... Don't be scared." A man appeared from behind a tree wearing a green cloak with the hood pulled over his head. Lea knew that voice, but... It had to be another monster, another illusion.

"No..." Lea stumbled backward. It simply wasn't possible for him to be here. She had been sure he'd traveled north, hadn't seen him in months. For him to find her in the middle of the Wicked Wood? It was unfathomable.

"I'll explain everything, but I need you to come with me. Now. It's not safe here."

"I'd rather die than follow you. Do you think me a fool? Expect me to believe you're not just another damned monster trying to lure me to my death?" Flames skipped on Lea's fingertips, her eyes bright with the crackle of the heat coursing through her. It wasn't him. It couldn't be.

The man sighed. "I was afraid you wouldn't believe me. You've always been stubborn." He laughed, a kind, heart wrenching sound, but Lea refused to be tricked. She called on her day magic, allowing it to fill her as she prepared to destroy the imposter in front of her.

"I didn't want to do this, Azalea. But soon, you'll understand..." the man said, pulling his hood down. He took a step forward, and Lea unleashed her fire, an enormous ball of flames launching directly toward her attacker. The man snapped his fingers, and everything froze.

Lea couldn't blink. She could see and smell and hear, but she couldn't move. The ball of fiery magic floated in the air in front of her, still crackling and burning white hot, yet, it didn't move forward. It hung there, only inches from the man's face. He blew out a breath, running a hand through his dark hair.

"Well, you've certainly learned a lot since the last time I saw you." He stepped to the side and walked around the fire still hanging stagnant. "I'm proud of you. But there's a lot you don't know." The man placed a hand on Lea's cheek tenderly. "This won't hurt a bit, but I have to put you to sleep now..."

Lea tried to scream, tried to force her magic to burst through whatever was holding her tongue still, and yet she was completely paralyzed.

"I've missed you so much, my daughter. For now, rest. I'll explain everything when you wake." He touched her temple tenderly, and as the world went dark, Lea fell into her father's strong, familiar arms.

CHAPTER 35

GRAY

Gray woke as abruptly as the snap of strong fingers. He wasn't sure why. All he knew was that something was *wrong—deeply* wrong. Immediately, his arm slid forward to pull Lea against him, to ensure she was safe before he sought out whatever threat had pulled him from sleep, but all his hand found when he reached out was cold, hard ground.

In the blink of an eye, he was on his feet, body thrumming with electricity, building into a mighty strike of lightning just waiting to be released. With every anxious beat of his heart, the energy grew. "Azalea!" Gray roared into the cool night, his throat burning from the effort. Blood pounded in his ears and he was overcome with a wave of dizziness as he desperately searched the camp for his mate. *This isn't happening.* He refused to believe that she was actually gone. He searched out the mate bond, tugging on it sharply. It was there, still thrumming with life, and yet that was all he could feel from it. There were no emotions he could tap into, no hints of where she was or what she was thinking.

"Gray!" His name sounded like an echo, too far away to pull him from his nightmare. Because that was the only explanation. He was living his worst nightmare. She had to be here. He had to find her. Without thinking, he ripped apart their pallet, a large fur bursting into flames as it landed on the fire. He tore a branch from the tree they'd slept beneath, searching its tangled limbs for where she could possibly be. "Azalea!"

he shouted, his vision turning black at the edges as the urge to destroy everything he could reach became overwhelming.

"Gray!" A small hand flapping nervously appeared in his periphery, reaching toward him.

He readied his lightning.

"What's happening?" A voice cut through. He knew that voice. *Right*?

"Wait—Don't touch him!" the worried voice called as he stood, but whoever it was didn't listen, tugging at Gray's sleeve with shaking hands to get his attention.

Threat.

The girl was pulled away just in time, the lightning that had been building within Gray's body exploding outward at her contact. In a flash of violent light, everyone and everything around him went flying backward, crashing into the brittle branches of the spider-like tree with a *crunch*.

Gray swung his head toward them, fully prepared to destroy whoever had dared stop him from searching for his mate—his *life*. All he saw was red, all he felt was pure, all-consuming terror. His eyes were unfocused and black as they slid over the hands that had touched him, searching for weapons as lightning crackled between his fingers.

"I'm sorry," she sputtered, and Gray paused.

"Emma," he breathed, the world snapping back into focus. Emma's big brown eyes were brimming with tears, pleading for him to listen. With every ounce of self control he had, he pulled his shadows back, just enough to see the concern on her face. Concern not for herself, but for Lea, he realized as Emma quickly spoke.

"S-someone took her, Gray," Emma said through tears. "The dead saw it. They don't know where she went, but they said it seemed like Lea knew whoever took her. She recognized him." Noah stood, placing himself between Gray and Emma.

"And she went willingly?!" Gray snapped, ignoring him and focusing on the space behind Emma to where he assumed the dead waited. Gray's fury was palpable, the air actually vibrating with it, but the thought cooled his anger, just a bit. He sent up a quick prayer that it was true—that Lea *had* left willingly with whoever had somehow broken through his wards undetected. He would wring her neck for it, make no mistake, but it wouldn't be the first time that Lea had made a foolish and dangerous decision in the name of saving her friends. But if she had followed someone, it was more likely she was unharmed... for now. Someone who would steal her away rather than killing her outright wanted something from her. And he'd be damned if he wasn't going to find out who and what it was.

"No, not willingly." Emma looked behind her. "They say she didn't want to go. But he used magic to knock her unconscious."

His temporary relief was consumed by a wrath as dark as his soul. The night went black, the moon eclipsed completely by angry, gray storm clouds.

"How in the gods' *hell* did they get close to us? And why was she the only one who woke up?!" Gray was shaking in fury, his shadows already spreading as far as he could control them. They trailed along the ground, twisting through trees and over logs as they searched for their other half.

"Time froze." Emma gulped. "They said the entire forest went silent. Bats stopped in the sky and bugs stopped crawling. They tried to warn me. I was sitting up to tell you and then everything stopped." Emma was crying, her guilt and fear evident in her red eyes and the way her shoulders hung, but it didn't matter. Not Emma's guilt, nor his own failure to protect Lea. No. In that moment, the only thing that mattered was finding his mate and destroying the bastard who had dared steal her from his arms.

"Tell the dead that they will find Azalea, *now*, or they will find themselves rotting in this hellhole for the rest of eternity. If she's not found safely, our bargain is over."

"Gray," Erik warned. "Threatening them might not be the best way to convince them to help."

The forest froze again, but this time, it wasn't from time stopping. It was from the aura of death cascading off Gray's skin. His eyes once again went black. "I will flood this world with darkness so thick it will block out the light. Unless you would like to live the rest of your life in eternal night, you will stop wasting time and help. Me. Find. My. MATE!" A murder of crows scattered into the night as Gray's rage shook the ground.

Erik, Janelle, and Emma stood statue-still. It was as if they were afraid to move, afraid that their actions might strike the match that could actually spark the fire that would destroy the world.

"We need to calm down and think this through, Gray. Who could have taken her?" Erik said.

"Calm. Down?" Gray lowered his chin, his shadows writhing uncontrollably as he took long strides toward Erik. The rage in his chest boiled over, seeping between his ribs and puddling in his gut. He was going to kill him.

"Wait!" Emma cried out, stepping in front of Erik. "Do you remember someone named Lochan?"

Gray froze. "Lochan. I tried to save him, here in these very woods... but—"

"He says it's okay. He knows you tried. And that... he knows where Lea is."

Gray would have given everything to trade powers with Emma at that moment. Would give up every drop of his magic in order to be able to speak to Lochan directly, to ask him to get them to Azalea as quickly as possible.

"Is she okay?" Gray rasped, trying desperately to slow his breathing.

"She was taken to a clearing with a house. He can't say anymore. But he says he will take us as close as he can."

Without a second wasted, Erik was readying the horses, leaving behind everything but their weapons and saddles. He hoisted Janelle up in front of him as Emma mounted her own horse and Noah took up the rear.

"Hurry," Gray begged as thunder boomed. He needed to control himself, to stay calm and precise, but if he lost her...

"Don't even think it." Erik was beside him in a second as Emma kicked her horse's sides and sprinted off through the woods, Obsidian and Cinnamon directly behind her. "We'll find her," Erik reassured him.

"And if we don't?" Gray asked, knowing that there was no possibility that he could live in a world without Azalea. Wondering if he could even live with himself now that he had failed in his responsibility to protect his mate.

"Then I will add my fire to your darkness, and we will destroy the veil to get her back."

CHAPTER 36

LEA

The world went completely silent. The feeling that had been hovering around her shoulders, the presence whispering in her ear that she wasn't safe, that something was coming, disappeared as she woke up in a soft bed of grass, a stark difference to the dead, rotting ground they'd been treading on for days. Sitting up, she pushed her hair from in front of her eyes. She was in a clearing, where the land lived and wildflowers dotted the earth. But... Where was her father?

Had it really been him? She wasn't injured, but surely if it had been another demon who had taken her, it would have simply killed her. And yet, her father had always been exceptionally *ordinary*. Wouldn't she have known if he had magic powerful enough to freeze time? To steal her consciousness?

Pain bloomed in her chest. As misguided as it may be, she *wanted* it to be him. And yet, it couldn't be. Her father may have abandoned her, but surely if he'd gone through the effort to kidnap her, he would have been here when she woke in the strange place. Though oddly, as she looked around, it didn't feel all that strange.

Lea felt as if she had returned home. A sense of calm overcame her, the knowledge that everything would work out settling in her chest as the wind stirred within the clearing. The fresh air wiped away the memory of the cloyingly damp scent of the forest surrounding the grove and seemed to cleanse her hair and clothing of the musty odor. She moved nothing but her eyes, her body freezing and forcing her to take in every detail of the clearing. A cottage sat in the far corner, a full garden surrounding the right side that began at the front gate and wrapped around nearly to the back of the house.

It was overgrown with weeds that caused Lea's magic to tingle in her fingers, begging her to tend to the neglected soil. She ignored the feeling, focusing instead on her surroundings, on what the wind was trying to tell her. A separate garden bed sat on the left side of the house, and she rubbed her eyes as shock and bewilderment flooded through her gut.

She could hardly breathe as her vision tunneled, and her magic writhed in response to what she was seeing. Moonflowers... At least ten vines climbed up several wooden trellises that were in the process of crumbling away. And on those thorny vines were fingernail-sized white petals, *living* flowers, that swayed in the breeze.

Lea began crying without even realizing it, her heart squeezing and fluttering in a strange way. Right in front of her was her very dream come to life. She'd worked tirelessly to see the beauty of those flowers, losing sleep and attempting every combination of variables she could think of. She'd tried planting the seeds at different times, in different types of soil. She'd given the sprouts differing amounts of water and sunlight. And here they were, hundreds of them, just growing in a weed-filled garden bed as if they required no tending at all. *How is it possible?* she wondered.

Lea's feet carried her forward, slowly, as if any movement might startle the moonflowers into crumbling to dust before her eyes as she'd seen them do so many times before.

On shaking legs she walked to the garden, a bed crafted of aged wood with swirling patterns of the moon and stars painted in blue and white across the sides. Lea had been correct that there were ten lines, two neat rows with five plants each. All mature, and all *alive*... Not growing taller or climbing higher, but stagnant, as if stuck in time. In the middle of the neat rows was a statue of the goddess of the moon, her hair flowing behind her with her palms pointed down toward the soil and water dripping from her fingers—the picture of a dutiful goddess, pouring herself into the earth to help it flourish.

Lea took another step forward, her fingers itching to touch the statue. But something was holding her back. The statue glowed a faint silver-blue, and it had an energy about it that made Lea pause. The wind blew harder, wrapping around her arm and lifting her hand. *Follow the darkness...* she heard again. The wind was yet to steer her astray.

With a slow exhale, Lea allowed her palm to be placed on the sun-warmed statue.

Lea's breath was squeezed from her lungs, immense pressure pushing on her chest as the world pitched into night. Her head spun, and dizziness clouded her mind as she was flung forward forcefully, landing on the cold, hard tile of a hallway. Closing her eyes, she waited for the lightheadedness to subside, her knees stinging from the rough impact. *What is happening?* How was it possible for her to be on the soft earth under the moon one moment, then inside a chilly, torch-lit corridor the next?

Her palms ached where they'd hit the floor, and her breaths were ragged as she took in her surroundings. Panic bubbled behind her breastbone, a cold sweat breaking out on the back of her neck. The hard floor. Not the soft dirt, but the cold, *hard* stone floor. The same stone floor she'd scrubbed at least twenty times. She was back at the castle.

Somehow, she was hundreds of miles away from the Wicked Wood and back at the horrible place where she'd been beaten and abused. Had the statue been some sort of portal? Was it a spell? A trap to send her back to where the king and prince likely rested safely in their beds after a long day of stealing magic and commanding their armies to hunt them down?

No, no, no. This can't be happening. Lea was spiraling, and she sucked in a deep breath, trying to slow her heart rate. Would they feel her power? Were they already on their way to find her? Kill her?

Reaching for her magic, she pulled flames to her fingertips, small fires burning as she tried to look more closely at where she was within the castle and figure out how she could escape.

Continuing to take rhythmic, measured breaths, Lea tried to calm her mind. She was standing in a hallway that looked nearly identical to the one Gray had occupied at the castle, and yet, it was different. Rich golden tapestries hung on the walls, displaying proud Fae warriors battling demons, standing between humans and monsters as if their one purpose was to protect them. Others showed extravagant celebrations and feasts with both human and Fae alike, dancing and dining together. One picture, an oil painting framed in a thick, gold frame engraved with suns and moons, showed a human woman, undressed and staring longingly at the Fae male kneeling between her legs.

The painting was beautiful, with delicate brush strokes and incredible attention to detail. It was so entrancing that Lea almost forgot that she was standing in the Black King's castle, for he would never allow a painting like this to adorn his walls. A Fae, in love with a human? He would have Alaric burn such a thing to ashes. And yet, this *was* the same castle she'd spent the last few months in. There was no mistaking it. She had dusted these very windows.

The door to the end of the hallway opened, and Lea was pulled from her thoughts. Holding her breath, she quickly ducked behind one of the tapestries. *Hide!* Her subconscious demanded as a figure shrouded in a black cloak and hood closed the door firmly behind her and walked toward the end of the hallway toward where Lea stood.

Lea tried to make herself smaller, and the figure slowed its cadence, only slightly. Their eyes raked over where Lea had stood moments before, and yet that was the only indication that the person suspected anything was amiss as they continued down the hallway.

Lea waited a beat, then scurried behind the cloaked Fae—a woman, she thought, based on her size and graceful movements. She exited the hallway only to go down a set of stairs that led to the main floor, allowing her outside into a garden that looked so very similar to the one she'd admired from the princess's balcony and Gray's quarters. A sense of déjà vu crashed through Lea's body, and she held her breath in anticipation.

The woman walked directly to a large garden bed in the very middle of the courtyard, and Lea gasped when she saw a statue matching the one she had touched just before being thrown into this dream. Or was it a vision?

The woman lowered her hood and Lea felt a sense of familiarity as she looked at her back. Now that the hood had been removed, her long blonde hair flowed in the wind. Her limbs were thin, and yet remarkably defined with muscle. She moved purposefully, quickly, occasionally looking over her shoulder before returning to whatever she was tending to in the garden.

Lea shivered as fat drops of rain pelted against her shoulders, dampening her hair and causing it to stick to her forehead. The patter of water hitting the ground drowned out the murmurings of the Fae woman as she knelt down in the wet soil, dirtying the knees of the white nightgown she wore beneath the black outer layer. Instinctually, Lea realized what had called this woman into the night. Recognized the sense of familiar anticipation that Lea herself had felt so many times over the past year.

She was waiting for moonflowers to grow.

The woman's hands looked so familiar as they hovered in the air, waiting and ready to pluck the delicate petals once they bloomed. It was a ritual Lea had performed a thousand times before, a well-timed dance that always seemed to end in disaster.

The silence stretched on as they both sat waiting, watching. The stranger's hands shook from the cold, her fingers flexing in frustration as she began chanting. The cadence of it resembled a prayer, one memorized and spoken so often the words rolled off your tongue without any thought, but the language was not one Lea recognized.

The rattle of a door closing caused the woman's head to snap up, but it was the silence that followed, the lack of someone announcing themselves, that made the Fae's eyes turn wary. The woman glanced in Lea's direction. *Does she know I'm here?*

She returned the woman's stare, looking straight into familiar blue eyes that matched her own. *Queen Emmaline,* Lea realized with a gasp. She had to be dreaming. The murdered dead queen had lived hundreds of years ago. It was impossible that she was standing in front of her now. Except, it felt too real to be a dream. She could feel the wind, hear the frogs and smell the mixture of rain and the sweet scent of the flowers that surrounded her. She was all too aware of the shiver of warning that ran down her spine, the way her hair stood on end.

Queen Emmaline looked away and pushed her hands into the dirt, focusing on the moonflowers in front of her, a sudden sense of urgency in her movements. Lea searched the garden but couldn't see the threat that was causing her to act so afraid.

Lowering her head and squeezing her eyes shut, Emmaline funneled all her power into the flowers. The rain continued to fall, and her gaze darted about as she urged the vines to grow more quickly. She closed her eyes, and Lea could tell that her entire attention was now on the moonflowers. The queen needed them for something.

Nothing else could explain her sense of urgency, or why she remained kneeling in the dirt in the rain when she was so clearly afraid. Except, the Lonely Death hadn't been created yet. Not if she was hundreds of years in the past, as she suspected. But hadn't her mother said the petals could cure death itself? Maybe a friend was ill, or she knew death was coming. Maybe she was preparing for something unknown.

Lea watched in awe as the flowers started to bloom, beautiful white buds emerging, and her internal clock began to tick. *You have to pick them!* It made Lea nauseous to watch the queen wait. Did she not know there wasn't time? She had to use them before they turned to ash.

But Emmaline *didn't* immediately pick them. Rather, she gave them several minutes to bloom fully, to completely unfurl as the moon's rays peeked through the clouds. Lea's own hands began to shake in anticipation, her heart pounding furiously, making her chest ache. The queen was wasting time! *"Pick them!"* Lea shouted, but her voice was lost to the wind and the rain.

Emmaline's eyes crinkled in relief as the flowers stopped unfurling, and she plucked the first petal, pulled out a small velvet bag, and began to fill it. She grabbed the flowers by the handful, holding them tight in her fists as she pulled all the buds from the length of the closest vine. It was impossible, *and so, so beautiful.*

The flowers remained white—pristine and perfect. Emmaline's smile was radiant as she placed the petals within the pouch, and Lea was once again struck by a feeling of familiarity. It was her own smile she was looking at, one she'd seen in her reflection her entire life.

Tears filled her eyes as a sense of belonging flooded through her, weaving itself into her marrow along with the certainty that somehow, this woman was related to her.

She was only able to enjoy that smile for a moment, her joy turning to terror as she watched the woman's pretty lips drip red, staining her teeth crimson as she crumpled to the ground in a puddle of blood.

CHAPTER 37

LEA

The queen's body twisted as she fell, allowing her a glimpse of the man who had attacked her, the coward who'd slashed a dagger through the flesh of her throat from behind and stolen away her life. Lea attempted to step forward to help, to stop what was happening, but her feet remained rooted to the earth. She tried to look away, but it was as if her muscles obeyed someone else's command. She had no control as she was forced to watch a cold-blooded murder.

I was meant to see this, Lea thought. She could feel it in her bones. *These* were the answers she searched for, part of the puzzle that had become her life. Focusing, Lea tried to take in every detail as the pristine white petals drifted toward the ground, dropping into the deep red blood along with the queen.

Lea watched in horror, her heart in her throat, as the flowers turned black before her eyes, dissolving into nothing as the blood flowed and bubbled around them. They were gone in an instant, as if the blood had been acid, or like the petals had never existed at all. It physically hurt her to watch the precious flowers die again, agony wedging between her ribs and making it difficult to breathe. Despite the pain, Lea forced her eyes away from the blood-stained earth, her heart thundering as she focused on identifying the queen's attacker.

He was cloaked in black, but was clearly Fae by his imposing stature and muscular build. The man towered above the queen, looking down upon her for several moments before slowly pulling his hood back. Lea's heart pounded in her chest and her eyes widened in surprise, but that surprise was quickly replaced by a feeling of foolishness. She should have known who the murderer was. Erik had told her months ago what had happened to Queen Emmaline.

It was the king, hundreds of years younger and looking far more kingly than when she'd last seen him. Though, if Lea was remembering correctly from Erik's history lesson, before the queen had been murdered, he was not a king, but an advisor and friend to Queen Emmaline's mate. Brennus Nestruir looked down at the blood now coating his boots, a disgusted grimace crossing his face, and Lea's stomach twisted into furious knots.

Leaning over, he whispered something to the queen, something that Lea was unable to hear through the steady patter of rain and the blood roaring in her ears. The king took something out of his pocket, a clean piece of cloth, and dipped it into the blood soaking the ground, saturating it fully before tucking it back away inside his cloak with an evil grin.

The king stayed only another moment, long enough to ensure that the queen had taken her final breath before fleeing away into the night, his blood-stained boot crushing the satchel of petals as he ran. There was no spell to steal her magic, no slow death through the disease he had created, and Lea's shoulders lowered in relief. Had the king known then that he could steal the queen's power, she doubted that there would be any chance that the rebellion could defeat him in the future.

As the king disappeared into the night, Lea watched with tear-filled eyes as the beautiful white petals still growing from the vines turned black and crumbled away into black ash, the wind carrying them off into the dark night. It was a sight that caused painful memories to flash through Lea's mind, her heart stuttering.

She'd watched those petals die again and again as she'd tried to save her mother, and nearly every day since until she was brought to the castle. She'd tried repeatedly to find the right time to harvest them, a way to keep them alive long enough to stop the curse, to cure the disease that she now knew was nothing but a spell cast by an evil man. But every time, they had dissolved into nothing, just as they had moments ago as they'd fallen into the queen's blood.

Still standing frozen in shock, Lea realized two things. Before the king had slain Emmaline, the petals had lived. The queen had shown no signs that she worried they would rot away. There had been an urgency for them to bloom, but she had stuffed them inside the pouch without a second look. Once plucked from the vine, they'd remained plump and white in her fingers as she'd continued to gather more. Had she known the king was coming for her? Had she needed them to save someone? Lea wished she knew.

The second thing she realized, as the rain and wind continued to pelt down upon them, was that the queen's cloak had fallen away when she'd collapsed to the ground. A swollen belly protruded from her nightgown.

The queen was with child, and she appeared to be quite far along. Emmaline's hand rested limply against her stomach, her arm thrown across it as if she could protect her unborn child from the same fate. Lea's heart thundered, pounding against her ribs. The king hadn't just murdered the most beloved queen the Kingdom had ever seen, but also her *heir*. An innocent baby. It was too cruel, too barbaric.

Without thinking, Lea tried to run again, and unlike the last time, her body obeyed. Released from whatever magic had been holding her back, she flew across the ground, collapsing at the queen's side. Emmaline's stomach moved, a kick from the baby stretching her skin as it fought for its life. Without thinking, or even trying, Lea's hands warmed, her palms glowing a faint blue.

Lea placed her trembling palms against the queen's stomach, feeling, praying for movement. She closed her eyes, searching for a thread of life from beneath her fingers. Reaching inside her chest, Lea gathered her light, her healing magic, and pushed it into the queen's skin. She felt a *thump* vibrate along the magic tether—a heartbeat. Then another, followed by a pause, and another *thump*. Sporadic, but still, *there*. Digging deeper into her magic, she forced more healing energy into the queen's belly. *Thump... Thump.*

The heartbeat slowed, the rhythm sluggish and uneven.

"Dammit! Work!" Lea shouted into the night. "Come on!" She tunneled even deeper inside her chest where her magic lived, now searching for her darkness, hoping it could chase away the blackness of death that was preventing her healing magic from saving the baby. Pressing her hands more firmly against the baby inside its mother's womb, she focused on its movement. She could feel the curve of a head, the point of a foot or an elbow. Moving her hands to where she believed the baby's chest to be, she concentrated on funneling her magic into it, into its heart, and yet still she could not seem to penetrate the queen's skin.

Looking around in a panic, Lea searched for a solution. She could not let this baby die. Would not. The weight of its tiny life felt heavy on her shoulders. She had to do something.

Gray had burnt out before, had used all of his magic in the days he'd tried to save her from the Lonely Death, and yet when she had been in danger he had somehow found more, had been able to summon a darkness unlike anything she had ever seen. Reaching down as deep inside her well of magic as possible, she pulled every ounce of healing energy she could find and focused it into her palms, her fingertips. She thought only about the life and the sluggishly beating heart inside the queen's body, wholly absorbed with compelling her magic past her skin.

In the back of her mind, Lea wished that she could have saved the queen as well, but by the amount of blood soaking into the already wet ground, it was clear that she was well beyond saving. Tears pricked her eyes. This had been the beginning. The beginning of the cloud of death that had shadowed the kingdom for the past two hundred years.

Lea felt the baby's heart beat faster, a little stronger. She focused on that beat underneath her fingers, allowed it to course through her body, motivating her to dig even deeper into her magic. Deeper and deeper she went, and—*there,* hidden behind the magic she normally found waiting for her, was something else. It felt unfamiliar, wholly unlike her day and night magic. Whatever it was was wilder and darker, but it was *something.* She pulled from it, wrangling and molding it into what she needed. Lea focused again on the baby, found the firm curve of its head, and directed all she had into healing it.

Sweat beaded on her brow and pain burst behind her eyelids, but none of that mattered when the baby's heart kicked into a normal rhythm. *Yes. Come on.* Lea looked around, searching for a solution. Keeping the baby alive was no good if it was still inside a dead mother. Lea called for help as she searched for a way to remove the baby.

"Someone! Please!" Lea continued to shout, but there was no one around. Even if there had been, Lea didn't know if anyone would be able to hear her cries. She wasn't even sure that the queen had been aware of her presence, though it had seemed that she'd looked at her with that sad, knowing look.

She tunneled further into her darkness, something that she was not yet comfortable with. It felt dangerous and outside of her control. Lea looked up at the sky and screamed, frustration and desperation causing her to shoot her magic up into the air in anger. She had to get someone's attention. A flame like a shooting star lit the sky, traveling up into the wispy clouds.

Clouds.

Closing her eyes and keeping the healing energy flowing into the queen's belly, Lea focused on the sky. She called the largest storm clouds she could imagine, picturing them in her mind and willing them to just *be.* She searched for every ounce of anger in her heart, all the pain that had been caused by the king's actions, the fact that this child she was trying to save would grow up without its mother. Lea allowed the hurt she had fought against since her mother's death to fill her. She thought about all those the king had killed, including Gray's sister and Erik's mother.

So much death. So much destruction. Lea let the fire and electricity rebuild inside her, crackling behind her eyelids and through the base of her skull. She waited, pulling herself deeper into it, honing it into a fine point before letting it detonate into a crash of thunder and lightning that could rival Gray's. Silver-blue streaks crashed all around her, striking the castle and its walls. Needing to get someone's attention, she focused all of her energy on Gray's quarters. *No.* At this point in time, those rooms belonged to the queen.

That *had* to be where she lived. It was where she'd left from, after all. Though Lea wasn't sure why she'd chosen those rooms instead of the king's suite on the other side of the castle. She allowed her lightning to crash into the castle's windows, shaking its thick stone walls as she prayed that one of the queen's ladies' maids would come to check on her in the storm.

"Help! Someone help the queen!" Lea looked up toward the sky, watching her lightning crash in a frenzy, striking the castle, the trees, the ground. A storm that now surpassed any that she'd ever seen Gray create.

Reaching out for the wind in her mind, she called it across the courtyard, pulling it in as if taking a large breath, sweeping and bending the trees and rattling the windows. She crashed another strike of lightning directly onto the queen's balcony, crumbled bits of stone flying into the air from the force of it.

Another deafening crack of thunder boomed, and the balcony cracked, pieces of the railing tumbling to the ground. She pulled her attention back to the baby, realizing its heartbeat had grown sluggish as she'd sent her energy elsewhere. *Stay with me, little one.*

A pair of gardening shears caught her eye in the periphery of her vision. Is this what she would have to do? Cut the baby from her mother's womb with a dirty instrument?

Reaching forward, fingers numb, she grabbed the rusted shears in trembling hands, but dropped them when she heard an ear shattering scream. Lea's head swiveled toward the sound and she sobbed in relief as a woman in a once pristine white uniform, now soaked with rain and muddied at the hem, collapsed at the queen's side. The woman sobbed uncontrollably, placing her hands to the queen's neck, then to her belly.

"Oh, Emmaline!" she sobbed. "I came to find you. The storms... What happened? Who could have done this?"

"It was the king," Lea cried, but the woman couldn't hear her. Lea shifted to the side a bit as the maid crumpled across the queen's body.

"My dear friend," she whimpered, rocking Emmaline's corpse in her arms. All of a sudden, the maid froze.

The woman pressed her hand firmly against the queen's belly, crying out as the baby kicked. Lea searched for the baby's heartbeat again, her shoulders lowering a bit when she found it still beating steadily. But she wasn't sure how much more time the baby had. Exhaustion pulled at Lea's skin, sweat breaking out on her back and neck as she continued to funnel healing energy into the baby. The woman cursed before brushing the queen's hair away from her face.

"I'll be right back. I need to get help. I will save her," the maid promised Emmaline before standing and bolting toward the castle. Tears pricked the back of Lea's eyes, a hard lump forming in her throat. She'd known that the queen was beloved, that the kingdom had missed her dearly after her death, but to see the grief so potent on her lady's maid's face...

Lea hung her head and allowed the storms to settle, focusing only on keeping the baby alive. It was taking more and more magic to keep its heart beat rhythmic and strong. She counted her own breaths, steadying herself and forcing her magic to obey, using just enough to help the baby, but she could feel the chamber of power inside her beginning to empty. She was growing weak.

"Hurry," Lea whispered toward the door, as if the woman could hear her. "Come on, baby," she whispered. "You're a fighter." Lea closed her eyes and waited, praying that the woman would get back in time, praying that her magic was stronger than she believed it to be. Praying for any help she could get. Lea's shoulders began to shake, her hands cramping. There was only a kernel of light left inside her, and she streamed it into a razor-sharp point, directly into the baby's heart.

The heartbeat stuttered, and Lea bit down on her lip, searching the very bottom of her soul, trying to find any ounce of magic left inside her. There had to be more. She was the Queen of Flame and Shadows. Blessed with magic of both the day and night. This couldn't be all she had to offer this child.

Her healing magic disappeared, every last bit of light retreating from her body and funneling into the baby. The chamber that held her day magic felt like an empty husk, aching and pulsing in an unnatural way. All that was left was darkness.

"Dammit! Hurry! Help!" Lea begged. "Someone save her!"

"You save her." A gentle, commanding voice broke through Lea's panic. Standing only a few feet away was a woman, but... Lea looked from her waist length, cascading silver blonde hair to the woman's eyes, a blue so vibrant it was almost startling. She was glowing faintly, and wore a silver crown around her forehead, embellished with hundreds of tiny stars. No, this woman was not of this earth, and this was not a dream.

The goddess of the moon stood before her, ethereal and beautiful in a way that *almost* hurt her eyes.

"What do you mean? I can't save her. I've tried." Lea's voice shook with frustration.

"You do not bow this time?" The goddess cocked her head to the side, and Lea felt a tug deep inside her chest, pulling at her shadows as if coaxing them to return to their master.

"Can you help her?" Lea ignored her question, her reference to the dream in which the goddess had told her to fight, that Gray would save her. *No. It* had *been a dream. Hadn't it?* Lea rubbed at the discomfort beneath her breastbone.

"I can no more interfere here than you can in my realm. Follow the darkness," the goddess urged.

"I don't understand. I don't need darkness. I tried to chase away death with my shadows, but it did nothing. I need healing magic. I need light. Please," Lea begged.

"Follow the darkness..." she said again, placing a hand over her heart and pressing her lips into a grim line.

A bolt of searing pain shot through Lea's chest, and she doubled over as stars dotted her vision. "I have followed the darkness! I followed Gray to the rebellion. I fought to stay with him when I had the Lonely Death! What more can I do!?"

"The darkness is *many* things, daughter. Follow where it leads. It is the key to all."

"I can't," Lea sobbed. "I have nothing more to give."

The goddess floated toward her, grace embodied as she knelt before Lea. She placed a hand against her sternum, the pain burning inside intensifying as her shadows fought to break free. No, not just shadows... Something evil.

"It is only evil, if you use it for evil," the goddess said, reading her thoughts. "You must be strong enough to not allow that wicked urge to conquer you. Follow the darkness," she said again, her hand remaining against Lea's breastbone.

Lea screamed again in agony, her body feeling as if it might explode. Power fought to escape from somewhere deep in her chest, pushing at her bones and skin, making her eyes water and her back arch.

The pain faded as quickly as it had come, and when Lea opened her eyes again, she was once again alone in the garden, her palms pressing down on Queen Emmaline's belly. But there, somewhere deep inside her, a rift had formed. Dark, foreign energy trickled into her chest, like drops of water through a hole in the windowsill. Lea reached toward the tiny crack in the floor of the cavern where her magic lived, prodding it and testing its strength. The sharp pain returned below her sternum as she pushed down, trying to find more of that black power. Lea's light fought to withdraw, the pain so intense Lea retched.

The baby's heart stopped again, and Lea felt its little body writhing as it searched for oxygen.

"I will not let you die." Lea wiped her mouth with her sleeve before returning her hands to the baby's small body and summoning that wicked darkness, pushing down again and tearing into that pain in her chest, crying out in agony as she ripped at the walls that had held her magic neatly contained inside her. A tiny piece of the rift chipped away, and Lea felt dark power rock through her. It felt nothing like the power she had wielded before. It was raw, like she could bend any element to her will, create life or destroy the world, if only she could find more.

She dove deeper, digging and tunneling behind her ribs. Latching on to the darkness, Lea broke out in a cold sweat. It felt like death—all encompassing blackness. In her mind, she grabbed the edges of the fissure with her hands, pulling and pulling until her fingernails broke and her hands bled. With a cry of determination, she forced her way inside the cavern. Energy crackling through her, she pulled every ounce of power she could muster, pushing her arms out to her sides as the hole in the barrier widened, just enough to allow more of the strange energy to escape.

She was night. She was darkness embodied. She was death herself.

CHAPTER 38

LEA

Without hesitation, Lea sought out the baby, grasping the reaper's cold fingers that were trying to pry the baby's soul from its body. She combined the raw, dangerous magic with her darkness, forcing death to release its hold on the infant. Lightning cracked and thunder roared, black clouds eclipsing the moon, the night so dark Lea shouldn't have been able to see her hands in front of her. And yet, somehow, she could.

Someone approached, but Lea kept her eyes closed as she focused only on keeping the baby alive. That unfamiliar power seeped through her fingertips, the baby's heartbeat jolting to attention, beating harder and faster than Lea had felt it before. Keep the baby alive. Make death wait. Do not allow it to win again. Focus. That was all she could do.

"I found her like this," the maid who had left to get help said, her teeth chattering so hard that Lea felt the urge to create a fire to warm her. "Her throat was slit clean open, and her body was cold. She was already gone, but the babe... It kicked me. I swear I felt it kick. Can you help it?"

There was no response for several moments as Lea felt another pair of hands join hers against Queen Emmaline's belly. Another kick, firm and vigorous. Lea felt a fire ignite next to them, burning hot and strong despite the rain pouring around them. *Magic*, Lea realized.

"Gods above," the maid's friend said, and Lea's eyes snapped open.

This isn't possible, Lea whispered in shock. But it had to be, because she knew that voice like she knew the sound of the rain. There, kneeling right next to her with her hands brushing against Lea's, was her own mother.

Adelaide was younger, even more beautiful than Lea remembered her. Her mother would have had to be from a pure Fae bloodline to have survived for as long as she did, to have aged as little as she had. It didn't seem possible, yet there was no mistaking that it was her mother's concerned face she gazed upon. Lea's heart somehow lept and crumbled simultaneously, a mixture of joy and searing longing pounding in her chest.

"Mom," Lea cried, allowing the power of her love for her mother to strengthen her. Death's grip on the baby faltered, and Lea slammed a shield around the baby, refusing to let it take hold again. Her light was eclipsed, but still she forced healing energy into the baby's body. It felt like breathing life into the child, an exhale of pure power.

"Mom," Lea cried again, praying to the goddess to let her mother see her. If she could just give her one more hug, or maybe let her know she was okay, maybe Lea could heal the wound in her heart that still bled from missing her.

Adelaide looked around, and hope warmed Lea's heart, but her eyes quickly moved past where Lea knelt, settling on the same gardening shears that Lea had contemplated using before the maid had appeared. Except she'd have used them without hesitation had they not been so dirty. Adelaide grabbed the shears anyway, pulling them open and hooking the curved edge of the blade against the queen's left hip bone.

"You can't." The maid placed a hand on Adelaide's arm, stopping her. "Infection will rise."

Adelaide's eyes filled with tears.

It doesn't matter, Lea realized as her mother said the same.

"The queen is dead," her mother said as a solitary tear broke free from the confines of her eyelids and rolled down her cheek. "But we can still save her daughter. Look away, if you must." The maid did look away, but

Lea did not as her mother ripped the shears through the queen's flesh, slicing through muscle and fascia. She watched as Adelaide skillfully pushed away the bladder, then much more carefully cut open Emmaline's womb with the same blade, so very careful not to nick the baby.

Lea lifted her hands, allowing her mother to take over the burden of saving the babe. She collapsed in exhaustion as her mother pulled the baby, so very tiny, from her mother's womb. Her skin was a perfect pink, and a wail left her mouth as Adelaide used her apron to wipe the fluid from the baby's face. She hooked a finger into her mouth, expertly clearing her airway before ripping a piece of the moonflower vine away and tying off the umbilical cord.

"It's not possible..." her mother whispered, bundling the baby in her apron and rocking her back and forth. "She should be dead. I should have had to revive her, at the very least."

"A miracle," the queen's maid whispered as she bent down and kissed the queen's hair.

"I don't understand—" Adelaide's thoughts were cut off by the baby's cries. She shushed her gently, placing a finger in her mouth and allowing her to suck.

"Adelaide, Delphine, why are you outside in this rain? What in the goddess's name..." a soft, lyrical voice pierced through the night, trailing off into silence.

"Genevieve, stop. Do not look."

The baby began to wail again.

"Nonsense. What is—" A woman appeared at the edge of the garden. Lea had expected a stranger, another maid. Who else would be wandering the castle grounds at such a late hour? Instead, she watched in horror as Gray's mother, Genevieve Nestruir, rushed toward the queen's body, arms in front of her, with shadows spinning in her hands. Hands that were pointed straight at Lea's mother.

"No!" Lea threw out her own power on instinct, her shadows wrapping around Queen Genevieve's and pulling them away from her mother and the baby. A *snap* resonated through the garden as the queen's eyes widened, her hands clutching her chest as she dropped to her knees.

Unfamiliar magic mixed with Lea's, flinging her backward with the force of it returning to her body. Lea's head cracked against the ground, her vision blurring as she heard her mother's voice once more.

"Genevieve! No!"

Lea's ears rang, pain spreading through her limbs from the wound inside her chest, the crack she had widened as she'd ripped into her own being to find the power hidden there.

"Follow the darkness," Lea whispered as she closed her eyes, giving into the heaviness filling her head, praying for sleep, if only for a moment, to rest.

CHAPTER 39

LEA

Lea woke exactly where she had fallen, the statue of the moon goddess standing next to her, her ethereal stone face staring down with blank eyes.

"Mom," Lea whispered through the lump in her throat. Her mother had been there, had somehow been at the castle when Queen Emmaline was murdered so long ago. It was too much to process, too heavy to dissect. Every fiber of Lea's body ached to see her mother again, so deep it was physically painful. She pressed a hand against her stomach as if it could help hold her together. It was so cruel, to have had those brief moments in which she could see her, hear her, but not speak to her or touch her. Heart aching, she reached out and touched the statue, praying it would take her back, even if just for a moment.

Tentatively, her fingers met the rough, cold stone. "Please," she whispered, holding back tears as she waited. She pushed more firmly, her fingers blanching from the pressure, but the world did not spin, and her feet remained firmly on the ground.

Had she hit her head when she'd fallen? Imagined the entire vision of Queen Emmaline's murder? Of saving the baby? It wasn't possible that it was real, that she had traveled through time and altered the course of history. And yet, without even having to prod, she could feel the crack in the floor of her magic, a trickle of darkness wafting through and swirling in her chest. She ignored it, unable to focus on anything other than the sorrow soaking every inch of her body unlike she had felt since her mother's death.

Lea felt a tickle along her arm, interrupting her thoughts. The moonflowers were growing, wrapping around the trellises and cascading back down where they slowly crept across the dirt. Lea watched in awe as a vine wrapped around her wrist, snaking up her hand and between her fingers.

Her blood-covered fingers. Lea's breaths grew shallow as she examined them. Her nails were cracked, bloody and broken, with sharp, jagged edges. Crimson stained her hands, and she wiped them in the dirt, trying to remove the blood. It *had* been real... Of course it had. But *how*?

With shaking arms, Lea reached forward to pick a moonflower. Had the goddess been trying to help her learn how to wield them? The flowers had remained alive, pristine and white, until they'd fallen into the queen's blood. Even now, she'd never seen them live for so long. They'd always died away within moments of blooming, but now? They almost glowed as they continued to grow, the vines healthy and the flowers vibrant with *life*.

Lea's bloodstained fingers brushed against a petal, soft as a whisper. It didn't recoil, didn't wither away. A flashback of the petals turning into ash filled her mind, and as she plucked the bud off the vine it turned black, crumpling and dissolving into nothing. Tears pricked the back of her eyes as she tried again and again. Why were they blooming if she couldn't pick them?

The moonflowers back at home had always died on the vine after a few moments, but these? They'd obviously been here for *years*. She channeled her light, pushing it into the moonflowers as she tried to harvest the petals, but again and again they died.

Everything had changed, but as the flowers crumbled away into her bloody hands, Lea felt as if she was once again that girl back in Bearswillow who had lost everything, who spent all of her time and energy failing to conquer the illness that had taken so much from her.

Defeated, Lea laid down on her back, staring up at the bright moon in the dark night sky. How long has she been gone? She was overwhelmed, exhausted in a way she'd never felt before. Remnants of the dark, raw power she'd accessed still crackled through her blood, but she pushed it down again. She had needed to use it to save the baby, but the way it made her feel? It had been painful—horribly dark and terrifying, but at the same time, intoxicating in a way that frightened her.

Her head throbbed behind her eyes and at the base of her skull, and Lea sent what little healing magic she had left to soothe it away, but it did nothing to help the pounding headache. She rubbed at her temples, trying not to think about what her ability to use that power had meant, and why it had been sealed away inside her so deeply in the first place. It had almost been as if she'd never been meant to access it at all.

Lea took a deep breath, trying to calm her racing heart. She needed to get back to Gray. He'd know how to help her.

The scent of the moonflowers was intoxicating as she continued to take steadying breaths, unlike anything she had ever smelled before. They were far more potent than any of the ones she'd ever grown. *Just a few more minutes to rest*, she told herself, *and I'll get up and figure out where I am. I'll find a way to get back to him.*

The creaking of door hinges caused Lea to bolt upright, her magic thundering in her chest and begging to be released. Lea's head snapped toward the cabin, taking in every detail on instinct. The windows were shut firmly, and soft white smoke churned from the chimney. The door had opened, only slightly. Adrenaline made her eyesight sharper, and she could see the black outline of someone staring through the cracked door, even through the black of the night.

She readied her magic as she tried to make out the shape. The figure was large and definitely male. The sharp tang of worry filled Lea's nostrils, and she felt a shift in the air as the man inside the cabin shuffled his feet hesitantly.

"Who's there?" Lea called out. "Show yourself. Now!" Lea stood as she sent a bolt of lightning cracking overhead to emphasize her point. She would not be a victim again, was done allowing herself to be caught off guard.

"Azalea, it's just me." Her father stepped out from the doorway, his eyes widening as his foot touched the grass outside of the front door. As soon as he cleared the cottage, he picked up his speed, his long strides bringing him to stand in front of Lea within seconds. He started to reach toward her, but Lea took a step back. Her father lowered his hand, sorrow filling his eyes. "I deserve that." He nodded as if convincing himself. "Look at you," he said breathlessly, gesturing toward her arms where fire licked from her fingers to her elbows. "You seem... different. Your magic, it's *incredible*."

Lea stared at the man in front of her, narrowing her eyes. He certainly looked like her father. Sounded like him, even. There was no prickle of warning that this man was someone to fear. But... how would her father have known where she was? And if it were her father, why would he leave her lying in a garden instead of bringing her inside the cottage? It had to be another demon, another trick. She shuffled back. "You expect me to believe you?" she asked.

"I'm telling you the truth. Are you okay? I heard something inside the house, and I laid you down to investigate, but it was empty, and when I came to get you, you were *glowing*. I couldn't get near you, couldn't step a single foot outside the cottage. I'm sorry I scared you, Bug."

Lea felt as if she had been punched in the stomach. *Bug*. Her father had been the only one who had ever called her that. As she'd grown up, whenever Lea helped her mother in the garden, he'd said she was like a bee buzzing from flower to flower, pollinating and helping them grow.

"If you're my father, tell me something only you would know," she demanded. Was it a demon who could steal her memories? The thought terrified her.

"I know about the moonflower birthmark on your arm." The man touched the inside of his upper arm, exactly where her birthmark inked her skin.

"Which you could've seen while I laid unconscious on the ground," she scoffed. That wasn't good enough. "If you are my father, *prove* it."

"The letter your mother left you. I know that she told you there were things we had kept from you. To let the wind and stars guide you. You clearly listened." He smiled as he stepped forward.

"That letter has been out of my possession *many* times since I went to the castle," Lea argued, and yet her flames receded. How would a demon from the Wicked Wood have found her letter?

"The song your mother used to sing you as a child..."

Lea's chest physically ached at his words. She hadn't thought of the lullaby in a long time, hadn't been able to bear to listen to the words that had soothed her boo-boos and carried her to sleep as a child. Her lips shook as she stepped back. "I don't believe you."

If ever you should laugh, my dear
May that magic echo sing
And when you run in joy through flowers
May your legs fly fast as wings
If ever you should love, my love
Let that love set the world aflame
And if you ever question who you are
There are answers in your name
Winds swiftly blow, rain always falls
And lies often dress as truths
But one thing you can surely know

Is I'll always be with you
Should you ever be afraid, my girl
Find your courage, hidden deep
And if you grow weary in your soul
Let my song carry you to sleep
And if you grow weary in your soul
Let my song carry you to sleep

Her father's chin trembled as he sang the final words, his hands slightly forward, palms in the air as if offering himself to her in his sorrow.

Tears dripped from Lea's chin, watering the ground where the moon-flowers grew.

"If you are my father," Lea's knees shook so violently she thought they might collapse, "then why did you disappear?" A sob burst from her throat. "Why did you leave me?" Lea dropped to her knees as her father rushed forward, cradling her like a baby against his chest.

He'd gone gray at the temples since she had seen him last, and his usually clean-shaven face had become scruffy. But as Lea took shuddering breaths, trying to calm herself, she couldn't mistake the scent of cedar and tanned leather. She squeezed him tighter, hardly believing he was really here.

"Oh, Bug," Lea cringed at the sorrow in her father's voice. "I might not have been home, but I promise I never left you. Not for a moment. You were in my heart, in my thoughts and dreams."

Lea wiped her eyes, swallowing down her anger and hurt. "Then where were you?" she demanded, sitting up straight to put some space between them.

"Let's go inside," her father stood, offering a hand to pull her up. "We have a lot to talk about."

CHAPTER 40

GRAY

Gray had never felt so enraged, so completely out of control of his emotions. The fact that he was unable to find his mate made his heart pound in a way he'd never experienced before. He had felt fury. He'd experienced all consuming fear. But this? It made his body physically vibrate and his shadows yearn to rip the light from the world and consume it whole.

Somewhere deep inside him, so buried away he could hardly feel it, Gray knew that he should be grateful that some of his fallen soldiers had followed Lea. He should be thankful they'd felt loyal enough, even in death, to lead him where she'd been taken. If they hadn't agreed to help them navigate through the Wicked Wood, it was entirely possible that he would have been unable to find her until it was too late. The thought made his jaw clench, and he bit down so hard he tasted blood. He *would* find her. He would rip every tree from the ground, search every inch of this gods forsaken forest, the world, if he had to.

Thunder boomed as Gray's anger built. It was taking too long! Gray bit back his plea for Emma to hurry, trying to stay patient with her. But dammit, they needed to move faster. She was certainly doing her best, but the fact that he was unable to see the dead himself, to demand they move with more urgency—it made him want to murder everyone around him.

His mate. *Gone.* Gray still couldn't figure out how she'd been taken from the safety of his arms. Since Erik, Janelle, Noah, and Emma had found them, Gray had started enchanting their resting spots in a different way. Rather than hiding them completely, he'd made it so nothing and no one that wished them harm would be able to sense them when they were within those shimmering walls he created. It had seemed wise at the time to do this in case of another emergency, in case Thomas or Vincent or Elise had needed to find them.

Through their blood oath, Vincent would be able to track him, if necessary. Gray had thought it was the wise decision, the *safe* decision. So how had he fucked it up so badly? How had he made such a grave mistake? Or had Lea truly known the person who took her, like the dead had said? Gray sparred against his own nature as he tried to control his shadows and storms. Holding the lightning inside him was almost painful as it begged to be released, but he wouldn't allow anything to make it more difficult for them to see where they were going. His raging storm would have to wait.

Commanding the shadows of the forest, Gray pulled them behind him as they raced forward as fast as the dead could run. Gray scoured the bond constantly, hoping to find any flicker of Azalea's presence. If he could just catch a glimpse of her, feel her for a single moment, he was certain that he'd be strong enough to latch onto that feeling and follow the invisible string to wherever she'd been taken.

Taken. The electricity inside Gray grew even wilder as his fury pounded against his ribs. She was captive somewhere. His mate. His magic flared, burning inside him, but he refused the urge to siphon out some of his power to control the chaos inside him. He would not waste a drop, planned on using every bit he could generate to destroy whoever had taken Lea.

Whatever bastard stole her did not have long left to live, and Gray felt a sliver of joy at the idea of ripping the arms that carried Lea away from him off the pathetic creature who had made such a poor decision. To take someone away from their mate? It was unforgivable, a grave error, and the last one whoever had taken her would make.

"Are we close?" Gray asked Emma sharply. Every moment of time that passed caused his panic and fury to build.

"I promise, they're running as fast as they can. But they can't keep up with Obsidian." Emma turned to look into the darkness as they jumped over a fallen tree. "I think we can find it from here. They said if we keep going straight, we'll find a clearing surrounded by green trees." Emma nodded at the invisible men speaking to her. "Right. Okay." She turned back to Gray. "He said it's the only color in that part of the woods, and we won't be able to miss it."

Gray didn't wait to hear another word as he kicked Obsidian's sides, giving permission to his horse to take over at top speed.

"Straight ahead, boy," Gray urged, leaning down and putting his weight through the balls of his feet to allow himself to lift slightly off the saddle. Wind whipped against his face as their speed increased.

Finally, Gray thought, using his shadows like long arms to move hanging branches out of their way and throw tree limbs from their path as they galloped ahead. *I'm coming, Little Flower.* He continued to search for the tether that connected his magic to his mate's, waiting for any hint of Lea's energy, but he was met with nothing but an empty buzzing.

Unable to feel anything other than that Lea was alive, Gray shouted out loud, then down the bond. "I'm coming!" he repeated again and again, not caring that he couldn't feel her. He would force the bond to carry his reassurance to Lea, no matter how far away she was. He would scream loud enough, love hard enough to make the bond bow to his will.

Gray shouted the words again when... *there*. A flicker. The warm, bright energy that made his heart sing. "I'm coming!" Gray roared just as a green clearing came into view ahead. Gray had trained for battle his entire life—had learned the hard way to never go into a dangerous situation blind. It had been drilled into his mind that the smallest mistake could be the difference between life and death, but he didn't care.

Without Azalea, there was no life worth living. And so without assessing the clearing in front of him, without searching for traps or attempting to sense how many men may be lying in wait, Gray flew off Obsidian, pulling his sword from its sheath as he stormed toward the small cottage where he felt Azalea's magic calling for him.

CHAPTER 41

LEA

Her father sat at the table, Lea leaning against a wooden column in the center of the room.

"Talk," she said coolly. He might be her father, but he was basically a stranger to her now. The last time she'd seen him, he'd been loaded down with furs, walking away from their cottage without so much as a glance behind him. It had been months, and it felt like it.

He opened his mouth to speak, but before he could say a word, the door to the cottage smashed open, crashing off the hinges and throwing splinters around the room. Gray's body filled the doorway, shadows filling in the small spaces his massive body didn't occupy, blacking out the view to the outside of the clearing completely. "Where. The fuck. Is she?!" he growled, shadows shooting out with the force of a cannon and slamming into her father.

Lea heard the crack of bone against the wooden planks as her father hit the back wall, a sword against his throat as shadows pulled his head backward by his hair.

"Give me one reason I shouldn't slit your throat right now, Henry," Gray hissed through bared teeth. Lea's father swallowed, a small cut opening beneath his jaw where his Adam's apple moved beneath the razor-sharp edge of Gray's sword. *Has he met my father?*

Dark curls of black smoke began to twist around Lea's ankles, sliding beneath her dress and searching her body for injuries. "Are you okay, Little Flower?" Gray asked without taking his eyes off the man pinned to the wall, his shoulders heaving as he struggled to maintain his composure.

"I would *never* hurt my daughter," he hissed, spitting at Gray's feet. "Can you say the same thing, Night Prince? Murderer!"

Lea's vision flickered and suddenly her father was standing behind Gray, free of his shadows with a dagger pressed between Gray's shoulder blades. "You do not get to speak to her!" her father spat. "Not when *you* murdered her mother! My wife!"

Gray whirled on him, knocking the dagger away with his forearm. It spun in the air and he grabbed it in his left hand as if plucking an apple from a tree. Gray restrained her father with his shadows again, pinning his hands to his sides as the dark wisps coiled tightly around him. Realization washed over his face.

"That's how you stole *my* wife away, then," he said as he threw the dagger across the room. It wedged into the wall with a deep *thud* as Gray placed his sword in the sheath behind his back. "You can freeze time. That's how you escaped with your life when Adelaide had the Lonely Death. I always wondered..."

Lea's mouth went dry. Gray knew her father. Or at least, knew of him.

Henry tried to move his fingers, twisting them around as Gray pinned his arms in place. He was trapped, his nostrils flaring as he drew deep, furious breaths. "Bug? What does he mean, wife?" he rasped, the grief on his face reminiscent of the day her mother had died. It caused a lump to form in her throat and pulled painful memories into her heart. Lea swallowed, pushing down the pain.

"He means exactly what he says. He's my husband." Lea walked on shaking legs to Gray's side, pressing against him for strength. How had things escalated so quickly?

"Even more importantly," Gray shoved her father backward into the chair he had been sitting in moments before, "Azalea is my mate."

Her father physically startled, his face draining of color.

"That's not possible..." her father whispered, so devoid of emotion it was as if his will to live had simply disappeared. "The gods would *never* mate her to you. To someone so evil."

"I'd be careful of what you say next." Erik's flames filled the fireplace, a flickering light warming the room. "Our king here might not harm you, seeing as you are our queen's father, but I will not hesitate to silence you if you disrespect him again."

"Okay, that was hot..." Janelle whispered to Emma, whose cheeks turned pink as she shushed her.

"Not the time, Janelle!" Emma whisper-scolded back.

"Our *queen*?" Lea's dad asked, looking past Gray to where she stood slightly behind him. "I don't understand."

"Have you not heard of the Eclipsed King?" Erik walked to the cupboards and began searching through them. He reached the broken cabinet above the stove, pulling out what appeared to be exceptionally stale crackers.

"That's not him. I've met him. You're lying. Lea, they're lying to you." Her dad tried to stand, but was immediately pushed back down by Gray's shadows.

Lea cringed as she heard his elbow crack against the arm of the chair. "A little more gentle, please?" she asked Gray. She was angry with her father, still felt abandoned and hurt, but she didn't want him to be in pain.

"Oh, Vincent?" Erik said, bits of crackers flying from his mouth as he tried to speak. "Big, tattooed guy? Yeah, he's with us. Any more questions, *kidnapper*?" Erik coughed. "Man, these are dry... Could I get some water?"

Janelle walked to Erik, handing him her water bladder. "Lots of threats against Lea's dad for a guy raiding the pantry. You must not find him too much of a threat."

"Mmmhm." Erik swallowed down big gulps of water. "He won't hurt her. I watched him raise her, if you'll remember. But," Erik stared down the shadow-trapped man, "if you try to take her from us again, my confidence in you ends, and so does my generosity. Did I miss anything Gray?"

"If I let you free, will you behave accordingly and tell us why you're here?" Gray asked, rather calmly for the situation.

"You're planning on overthrowing your father? Stopping the Lonely Death?"

"It is not a plan. It is a reality. Answer my question." Gray snapped.

"And who will lead in his stead? You?"

"Me. And your daughter." Gray wrapped an arm around Lea's middle, tucking her against his side tightly.

"And you trust him, Bug?" Henry's tone went soft.

"With my life. With this kingdom. I trust him with everything I am."

Lea's father hung his head and tried to steady his breath. He pressed his lips together, inhaling slowly. "Then I guess I owe you an apology." He bravely met Gray's eyes. "No more magic. There are things I need to tell you all. To protect Lea."

Gray released him from his shadow's hold. "That is one thing we can agree upon." Reaching forward without letting go of Lea, Gray grabbed a sturdy wooden chair and sat down, pulling Lea into his lap. Lea's cheeks warmed. She'd never so much as hugged Thomas in front of her father before, and now here she sat on the Night Prince's lap.

"Mine," Gray rasped in her ear as Erik plopped onto a soft, deep green couch, Janelle settling beside him as Emma moved to the floor in front of the fireplace. Noah leaned against the wall just behind Henry, his eyes never leaving him as his hand remained on his sword. Lea felt a pulse of pride from Gray, and without a doubt, she knew Gray was thankful that Noah was focusing on protecting her.

"What was so important you had to kidnap my mate rather than come to speak to us during daylight?" Gray asked pointedly.

"It has to do with Mom. Doesn't it?" Lea placed her head on Gray's shoulder, grabbing his hand to ground herself.

"What did you see, Bug?" her father asked gently. "The stars guided you here. They were pointing you right toward this cottage, the garden with the moonflowers. I saw them. I had to bring you here, to this place. The garden. What did it show you?"

"How did you know I would see anything?" Lea's mouth went dry.

"I learned of this place long ago. When I saw the stars pointing you in this direction, I knew the goddess would show you something. What was it?" Her father's eyebrows were lowered, his jaw tight and his eyes bright. He knew more than he was letting on... Who else would have known of this place? And further, who would have known that this is where she would learn the truth?

Lea pushed down her doubts. It didn't matter how he knew. Erik was right. Her father may have abandoned her, but he would *never* hurt her. "Queen Emmaline. Her murder. And then mom was there. But that was hundreds of years ago. You're human. It's not possible that Mom—" Lea couldn't finish the thought as pressure built in her chest, the tightness so intense it made her breaths come in shallow bursts.

Her father's face fell, and he stood to come to soothe Lea, but Gray pulled her closer and stopped him with a deadly look. "Whatever you've kept from her, you will tell her. Now," he ordered sharply.

"Your mother and I... Well I think you know by now that we have magic." He sat back down and placed his head in his hands, taking a deep breath. "We're also Fae."

"But I'm not," Lea whispered. A wave of disbelief crashed over her. And yet, through that disbelief, was a shred of relief. She'd known she was different. She'd had her suspicions.

"I'm sorry, Bug. We should have told you sooner." Henry's voice was brimming with sincerity.

"Don't say it. Please." Lea cut him off, wiping a tear from her cheek. She had wondered for months, ever since suspecting that her mother had possessed magic and didn't tell her. The letter... the lack of resemblance... Lea was human, not Fae. She couldn't have come from Henry and Adelaide.

But that didn't mean she could bear to hear it confirmed. She needed a moment to place a cast of shadows around her heart, to protect it from the truth that was about to shatter everything she'd ever known about herself.

Lea bit down on the bitter despair creeping up her throat before finally raising her chin. "I'm not yours. Am I?" The words physically hurt as they left her mouth, each syllable a razor's cut against her vocal chords. "You're not my birth parents."

CHAPTER 42

ADELAIDE: TWENTY-THREE YEARS AGO

The day Lea's mother found her on a bald in the mountain town of Bearswillow twenty-three years ago, the wind stirred and seemed to bend the long stalks of grass toward a small bundle surrounded by a collection of wildflowers. When Adelaide opened the bundle, she'd found a beautiful baby girl with eyes the color of bluebells and lips the pink of a spring tulip.

The wreath surrounding her, a perfect oval, was filled with hyacinth, bee balm, poppies, lady's bedstraw, and Queen Anne's lace, among many other flowers, with no hints or clues as to who had left this perfect girl behind. Adelaide had been startled, of course, to find a baby so small all alone in the mountains, but what had struck her as the most peculiar was that, despite the warm day and the bright sun beating down on the bald, the baby did not cry. She simply looked toward her new mother, a tiny smile on those tulip pink lips, content to be held once again.

It had been odd to find a baby so close to her home. The baby was at least three months old. Adelaide knew of every birth within the village, for she was the one who attended to them. It seemed impossible that any of the women she knew so well would have hidden their pregnancy, birth, and first several months of motherhood from her, and that she wouldn't have needed any care as she healed or the child grew. It was far more likely that the baby's mother was from a neighboring village, but in that case, was it just luck that she'd been left practically on the doorstep of the village healer?

It had seemed as if this baby was an answer to her deepest prayers. She had begged the gods for a child, had tried for years, but no matter what herbs she drank or magic she used, the only people who sat at their dinner table as night magic swept across the kingdom were herself and her husband. It wasn't until she'd brought the babe home and unwrapped her from her soft swaddle that Adelaide realized that she had been meant to find this child. And while it was possible that this baby was still a gift from the gods, it no longer felt as if finding the girl had been an accident.

As the little girl on the table in front of her stretched her arms, Adelaide caught a glimpse of a small, moonflower shaped birthmark beneath the baby's arm.

"It can't be," she'd breathed, closing her eyes as she thought back to the day she'd cut a baby from her dear friend's corpse. The baby should have been dead. Adelaide had never been able to find an explanation for how the baby had lived, despite the fact that her mother's body had already begun to cool. They'd known that were the baby to stay in Auropera, Brennus Nestruir would find her and kill her. Everyone in the castle knew the rumors of his jealousy, knew that he would do anything to take his friend's place as king.

"You have to take her to Calir," she'd told her friend, Delphine, as Genevieve rushed to collect bread, dried meats, and cheese, as well as several bottles of goat's milk. As they waited for her to return, she pulled a small pouch from her pocket and removed a needle to stitch together the queen's belly, hoping she could use her magic to conceal the scar. "And do not tell a soul who she belongs to. Hide her away. She *will* have magic, and it will be strong. Never allow her to set foot back in Desia, not if she wants to live. Brennus will sense it, and he will find her. And if he finds her..."

Her friend nodded gravely, her face pale. "He will kill her, I know."

Adelaide had wished she could take the baby herself, but she had made Genevieve a promise to help protect her from her husband, and she intended to keep it.

"You have to leave, too." Delphine whispered urgently. "They'll see her scar and know there was a baby. They will know that you're the only one with the skill to pull a babe from a mother's womb."

Adelaide placed a hand on top of Delphine's and nodded. "I *will* leave, I promise. But there is something I must do first. Go."

Delphine rose, the sleeping baby cradled to her chest and the satchel of food across her back. "Where will you go?" she asked Adelaide, her voice choked. "Where will you be if I need to find you?"

Adelaide paused. "Home," she said after a moment. "I think it's time I go home."

CHAPTER 43

LEA

"**Y**ou *found* me?" Lea felt as if she was going to be sick.

"Your mother did. But, yes. We found you, and we loved you immediately, with everything we had."

Gray continued rubbing slow circles on Lea's back.

"And you didn't tell me?" Lea didn't want to cry, but first the vision and now this? She was too exhausted to keep the tears at bay.

"We needed to find answers first." Her father shook his head. "We wanted to be sure of who you were."

"And who am I?" Lea asked. "Who are my parents?"

"What else did you see in the garden, Lea?" Henry asked gently.

"How do you know I saw anything more than what I already said?" Lea shook her head. None of this made sense.

"We're running out of time, Lea. The Lonely Death has crossed the border to Calir. Eudora said that if I could get you here, it would give us answers. So tell me, *please*. What did you see?"

"You know Eudora?" Gray asked, his shadows darkening.

Lea's father nodded.

"And what did you offer her in exchange for this information?" Gray snapped. "The witch does not give without asking in return."

"What I offered her is none of your business. She can help us, but first, I need to know what my daughter saw."

Eudora had told him to bring her here. It made Lea feel as if she was walking on a rope, hanging precariously above a canyon. Lea placed a hand on Gray's arm to ground her. "I saw Mom, she—" The room began to spin. "The queen was pregnant. I used my magic to keep the baby alive, and Mom cut her out. She saved her."

"Your mother sent the baby away with the queen's maid. Delphine. She was meant to raise her in Calir, somewhere she'd be safe. But I think once the baby grew up and Delphine passed, she came back to Desia. I think she wanted to be back inside her own kingdom."

Lea looked around the cottage. Crystals sat in the windowsill, covered in a sheen of dust. A throw blanket was thrown over the arm of the couch, and a clay mug sat near the fireplace.

"Do you think..." She couldn't finish the sentence.

He nodded, understanding anyway. "I think Delphine told her where Adelaide would be, if the girl ever needed help. I think she fell in love and had a child, the granddaughter of Queen Emmaline."

"And you think that Azalea is that child," Gray interrupted, saving Lea from having to speak.

"Yes. Her birthmark. Her magic. There is no other explanation. Our theory was that the queen's daughter knew the king would be looking for her, and wasn't willing to risk your life. So she gave you to us, knowing we would love you like our own."

And they had. They had loved her so well, she had never doubted until recently that she was wholly and completely theirs. But if Lea was being honest, she'd had her doubts as her magic had revealed itself, as Gray had insisted that she descended from Emmaline, but she'd burrowed herself into her denial.

Still, *none* of it made sense. If she really was a descendent of Queen Emmaline, shouldn't she be Fae as well? Or at least have *some* Fae characteristics?

But she wasn't tall or graceful, fast or light on her feet. She didn't have extraordinary eyesight or hearing, and her strength left something to be desired. Either way, she wasn't who she was *supposed* to be, and it felt like she didn't belong to the parents who'd created her any more than the parents who had raised her.

"What happened to her? My birth mother?" The words felt like gravel in Lea's mouth.

"I don't know. I've looked, Azalea. I've searched for her. So that your mother and I could know for sure who you were. Everything we thought? They were just theories, parts of some big puzzle we were missing pieces to. I tried everything to find her, so that we could learn what you might be capable of and how to protect you. But it's as if she just vanished."

"That's what you've been doing? All this time you've been gone?"

"I only left because once your mother died, I didn't know how else to protect you. She had always been so calm, felt so confident you were safe with us. But without her, I didn't know what to do. Your magic was so strong. I wasn't sure how to keep you safe anymore."

"What do you mean, her magic was strong? It wasn't until a few months ago there was any indication that she had any." Gray asked.

"She was already showing her magic the day we found her. Things would fall when she cried. Shadows would reach for her blanket and cover her small body when she was cold. Once, she fell and scraped her knee, and the storm she summoned burned down a neighbors smokehouse when a bolt of lightning hit it. But we didn't want you to be found, so your mother gave you a tonic that dampened your power. You took it every day until she passed."

"The floor," Lea said breathlessly, thinking about the cracked bottom of her well of magic that she had burst through trying to save the baby. Trying to save her own mother.

"What floor?" Gray asked.

"When I was trying to keep the baby alive, in the vision, the goddess appeared. She told me to follow the darkness, so I did. I reached for my night magic and it was like there was something solid blocking the rest of it. I fought against the barrier, ripped into it, and once it cracked—I've never felt anything like it. It was pure power. Nothing like the magic I've wielded before."

"The potion was meant to suppress your magic, to keep you from accessing it. She gave it to you every morning in your tea. She said that pushing down your day magic was easy, but that your shadows were stubborn, that they seemed to be tied to something darker, deeper. Your mother couldn't explain it, but she said she knew she needed to lock whatever that power was away. She said it felt as if it could destroy the world. It took so many tries, so many combinations of ingredients and so much of your mother's magic to make it work. I would have continued to give it to you, but my magic doesn't lend itself to healing. There was nothing I could do."

Lea's stomach squeezed. Something darker, deeper, that was tied to her shadows? Is that why she preferred using her light? Because it didn't pull from that well of magic that felt so beyond her control?

"That's why her magic appeared so slowly. That wall was slowly breaking down, allowing her magic to wake up over time." Gray's eyebrows lowered, his jaw clenching in anger.

"How could you keep all this from me?" Lea asked, suddenly so exhausted. "I understand when I was a child, but maybe it could have helped me with the moonflowers. Maybe I could have saved Mom. And Thomas's dad and everyone else."

"We were afraid, Azalea. Terrified of the king finding you. We just wanted you to live a normal life. This—" he gestured to Gray—"a life of war and danger? It isn't what we wanted for you."

"Even if it can save others in the kingdom from losing someone to the Lonely Death like you did?" Lea reached down the bond, silently asking Gray to lend her some strength.

"I'm a selfish man. I do not regret trying to keep you safe," Henry said curtly. Rubbing a hand across his scruffy face, he softened his voice. "But I do regret keeping this from you. I hope that someday you can forgive me."

It was so much to process. He'd been gone for so long, making her feel unwanted and alone. But even if it was misguided, he had been trying to protect her. Lea rubbed her forehead, pressing against the pain still pounding there. She would have to try to dissect how exactly she felt later.

"How did you find me?" she asked.

"Your necklace. My magic lends itself toward hunting. I spelled the jasper to allow me to track you years ago."

"I didn't even know you and mom had magic!" Lea exclaimed, standing. "And if my vision was true, then mom was alive two hundred years ago. How is that possible? Everyone in town would have known. She'd hardly aged at all from when I saw her in my vision."

"Is it another potion that changes your appearance, then?" Gray asked Henry. "You don't look Fae. I couldn't sense it at all."

"It's the water from the mountains—We don't know why, but when we drink from it regularly, it hides what's in our blood. Makes us appear human, even though we still have our powers. It's why there are so many with magic who live in Bearswillow. It protected us from the king. Let us live our lives undetected."

Erik and Gray made eye contact over Lea's head. "We've always wondered why there were so many humans with magic in Bearswillow."

"It's because most of them weren't human at all," Henry said matter-of-factly. "Our town is small. We protected our own. We weren't the only ones living in Bearswillow who never aged. It was an unspoken agreement amongst the villagers. Protect each other, and don't ask questions. It helped that my abilities to track and hunt helped feed the village."

"And the freezing of time?" prodded Gray. "How does that help you with hunting?"

"I can only freeze it for a few moments, maybe a minute. It allows me to make a clean killing blow, with no suffering to the animal."

"How big of an area can you freeze?" Gray asked, the line between his eyebrows indicating that he was calculating, planning.

Her father leaned forward and placed his elbows on the table, resting his chin on his fingers. "I've never tried to freeze an area larger than this room. And I don't think now is the time to be questioning how you can use me in your battle with your father."

"It is *always* the time to be planning," Noah said from where he still stood against the wall, his eyebrows drawn together. "If we want to win this war, we will need to use everything at our disposal. Every magical ability we have. Is that not what you want?"

"Everything I do and have done is to try to keep Azalea safe." Henry didn't break his eye contact with Gray. "It has had *nothing* to do with this war. So why do you think I will be so willing to abandon *my* fight to keep my daughter alive when your war might be the very thing that kills her?"

Lea lifted her chin. This was her dad. The man who had read her bedtime stories about gnomes and ogres and princesses as he rocked her to sleep. And despite the resentment she felt toward him for leaving her behind, she loved him dearly. He had to help them. If not for the good of the kingdom, then for her. "You'll do it, because I am asking you to. I'm not a child, not anymore. The girl you knew when you left is gone. I will be fighting alongside my mate," she grabbed Gray's hand, "and my friends." She nodded toward Janelle and Erik before smiling at Noah.

He looked around, his jaw working as he appeared to process what she was saying. Running a hand through his hair, he finally exhaled slowly as he stood. "Is there no changing your mind, then?"

Gray cocked his head, like he had expected more of an argument, but Lea recognized the look on her father's face. Defeat. Lea had a mate, someone she loved. And that was something her father could understand. Henry would have done anything in the world for Adelaide, and Lea was sure he had no doubt that his daughter would love just as fiercely. Lea shook her head no, lacing her fingers between Gray's and squeezing.

"Then I guess I have no choice. If you plan on walking into battle, then I plan on being right behind you."

CHAPTER 44

GRAY

Erik had insisted that the rest of their group go back to their campsite to retrieve their supplies, Azalea's father included. He'd balked at the idea, wanting to stay with his daughter, but Erik hadn't given him a choice as he'd slung an arm around his shoulders, offered him a sliver of jerky, and herded him toward their horses. Her father may have been Fae, a revelation Lea would have to unpack later, but he was no match for Erik's size and strength.

It had been decided that Lea's father would go back to Woodhurst where he had connections through his trading, with the aim of recruiting more men and women to fight alongside them. What they aimed to learn in Calir was invaluable information, and Gray didn't trust him. Not yet, at least. While he appreciated that Henry's priority was protecting Lea, he also wouldn't allow him to derail his own plan to defeat Brennus and Alaric.

Gray made a mental note to thank Erik for taking the burden of Henry's presence from his mate. Lea deserved time to process what she'd just learned. And Gray needed time to hold her, to help her through all the intense emotions he could feel flooding their bond.

Lea's grief was so thick it nearly choked him. Though Gray suspected that the idea that Lea's parents might not be of the biological variety may have passed her mind at some point, it didn't ease the sting of having it confirmed. But it wasn't just grief that his mate was feeling. The sharp, bitter bite of betrayal sank into his gut, mixed with a regretful anger that made his heart literally squeeze in his chest.

Not only had they hidden Lea's parentage from her, but her mother had also smothered her magic. Hidden it behind a thick, artificial wall. Gray knew Lea had always felt different, and he couldn't help but echo Lea's feelings of anger and betrayal as he thought about how her parents had hidden the truth. It was well intentioned—Gray knew that—and with time he was sure he would forgive her mother's memory and her father's... well, unorthodox way of learning about his daughter. But had they just allowed Azalea to be herself, they would have been more equipped to both keep her safe *and* fight against his father and brother.

The moment Gray saw those dark shadows explode from her hands in her anger and hatred toward him, he'd known there was a deep well of power hiding somewhere in that tiny body. He had never seen her look so beautiful. Her power was tangible, unlike anything he had ever seen or felt before. It threatened to suck the light from the sky and the soul from his body, had she been able to tap into it.

Staring at Lea as she absently wandered the cottage, he wondered again how he hadn't seen it sooner. The resemblance was there, in her eyes and hair, the way she glowed when she tapped into her powers. But—something had changed. As she traced her fingers from windowsill to desk, across the mantle and to the doorframe leading to what was likely the bedroom, she appeared more graceful. Were her steps softer? Or was his imagination simply allowing her to appear stronger, more invincible, so that he would stop worrying about her fragile human life?

Lea stalled as she reached a tall chest, an ashy oak with a set of drawers at the top and bottom with long, solid doors in between.

"What do you need, Little Flower?" Gray started toward her, but she held up a hand, closing her eyes. Lea inhaled deeply, and Gray watched as shadows drifted from her fingertips. They were soft, almost translucent as they coiled and floated through the air. Small pieces of ash wafted from the shadows, as if they themselves had been made of fire that had been smothered, embers secretly burning and waiting for enough oxygen to ignite once more.

The sight was breathtaking. The way his mate wielded her shadows was so different from his own. They were beautiful. Soft, but powerful. They were magnificent in the same way one would admire a poison. He was confident that those shadows could hide in plain sight, luring you into a false sense of safety before appearing only once they were inside you, consuming you from your very core.

Gray watched with reluctant restraint as Lea's jaw clenched in concentration, her mouth pursing a bit as she chewed on the inside of her lip. Her shadows danced around her, spreading around the armoire and seeping through its small cracks.

A *pop* sounded, and Lea's eyes opened as if she had been startled, but her shadows did not falter. They opened the cabinets and Lea peered inside, shuffling through odds and ends until she pulled a thick, worn leather journal from the back. The cracked cover was a light brown, and when Lea lifted it, at least a dozen pressed flowers slipped from between the pages and drifted to the floor.

As if she had been born welding night magic, she commanded the long tendrils of darkness to pick the flowers up. Lea walked toward the couch as if in a trance—the dead, dried flowers floating through the air behind her.

Gray's heart throbbed. There was nothing he wanted more than to gather his wife in his arms and kiss her pain away. He would use his fingers to pluck the hurt from the center of her, his mouth to whisper into her lungs his absolute devotion. He would gladly offer his shoulders to carry the weight of the truth and loss she was experiencing, and he knew that if he only suggested it, she would allow him to do it.

But he also knew that it would only be a bandage on a wound that would someday have to close. His mate was not weak, and he refused to insult her by doing anything to make her feel like she was incapable of healing herself. But that didn't mean he couldn't stand by her side as she stitched herself back together.

Brushing the journal with her fingers, Lea slowly unraveled the twine and lifted the tattered cover. Gray felt her despair immediately, as sharp as a knife in an artery. Slowly, so as not to startle her, he walked forward, standing behind the couch and placing a comforting hand on her shoulder. He leaned down to kiss the crown of her head, looking at the open pages in her lap.

Sketched in black charcoal was a woman with her child. A woman who looked so much like Azalea, Gray would have thought it was a self portrait. The woman's plump lips were drawn in a gentle smile, her long light hair braided in a simple plait over her shoulder. But it was the baby in her arms that made Gray pause.

He would know those eyes anywhere. At any age, in any universe, in any lifetime. His mate's eyes, wide and naïve, but not in a way that could be considered an insult. They were young, hopeful, unaware of the evils of the world that lurked outside her mother's embrace.

Lea couldn't speak, and she bit down on her knuckle as she tried to control her sobs. Gray had never seen her so fragile and so strong all at the same time.

"It's clear that she loved you," he said gently, running his hands down Lea's arms and resting his chin on the top of her head.

"She's a stranger." Lea cleared her throat, discreetly swiping a tear away. "She gave me away before she even had time to love me."

"She gave you to Adelaide. A woman who she knew was capable of loving you more than her own life. She gave you to someone who would keep you safe. For a mother to give up her child—" Gray winced as the memory of his mother's screams after his sister's death reverberated in his skull—"There is no greater act of love."

"She could have told me," Lea whispered. "I deserved to know."

"You did. But," Gray walked around the couch and angled his body to face Lea. "She just wanted to protect you. I wish my mother had found a way to save my sister."

"That's different." Lea's fingers curled into her palms, her nails cutting into her skin. The scent of metal hit his nostrils, and he reached forward, slowly and tenderly prying open her fingers and sending his healing magic into the crescent-shaped cuts.

"It's not. If I had to make the choice to protect you or allow you to die with me, even if it meant being apart from you, I know what I would choose. Even if you'd hate me for it."

"But I wouldn't want to live that life." She stood abruptly. "I wouldn't *want* to live without you."

"And I refuse to drag you to your death before you are really able to *live*." he lifted the picture, holding it to the side.

"Can you look at this baby, and truly, *honestly* say that she is better off dead, just so that she can stay with her mother?"

"That's not fair," Lea's lips trembled.

"If we had a daughter, if the gods were kind enough to bless us with a child, can you not tell me you'd do exactly the same?"

Lea's hand drifted to her stomach. She wasn't pregnant. Gray would have scented it. And regardless, he ensured the tonic he drank daily would prevent conceiving a child. He would never gamble bringing a baby into this world during a war, would never put them at risk, but the thought of it...

"I'd do anything for my baby," Lea conceded, a tear trailing from the boundary of her eyelashes. "But that doesn't make it hurt less."

Gray grabbed Lea's arms as she collapsed against him, finally allowing the sobs to break free from her chest.

"I know it doesn't, Little Flower." Gray crooned against her hair, soaking in her pain and pushing back every ounce of reassurance and calming energy he could find. He flooded their bond with words he knew Lea wasn't willing to hear at the moment: you are mine, I will never hurt you, you are stronger than you know. But instead of speaking those words aloud, he let her cry out every ounce of her pain on his shoulder, her sorrow soaking through his shirt and wetting his skin.

"Nothing in this life we have lived is fair. Feel it all. Let it mold you. Mourn what you have lost, and when you are ready, forge it into a weapon. Your mother loved you, just as your Mom did. You have a family, Lea. Janelle and Erik, Emma and Thomas. They love you. I think even Noah has become rather fond of you."

Lea sniffled, wiping away fat tears and the snot running from her nose, nodding her head. "I know. I know they do."

"That doesn't mean you can't be sad. But they would do anything for you."

She nodded again.

"And me? I would destroy the world for you. I would leave this cursed place nothing but embers and ash. Extinguish every bit of life to keep you safe. I would offer my soul to the gods, if only to allow you to *live*."

Lea pressed her face against Gray's chest, allowing his strong, muscular arms to envelop her completely. She continued to fall apart, trusting that Gray could hold up the world for her. And dammit, if that would help her, even a bit, he would do it.

"What do you need, Little Flower?" Gray asked quietly, wishing he could take her pain away.

Lea was silent for several minutes, muffling her cries against his chest. She took several long, shuddering breaths before tilting her head to meet Gray's gaze.

Her eyes were swollen, bloodshot and puffy, and Gray trailed the back of his fingers against the evidence of her grief.

"What do you need?" he asked again.

"I need to end this," Lea answered softly. "I need to know exactly who I am, what I am capable of, and I need us to find a way to kill your father and brother so that nothing like this ever happens to anyone else, ever again."

Gray pulled her back toward him, pressing his face into her neck. "Then it's settled, my love. We're not far from Calir. Let's go find a way to take back the world."

CHAPTER 45

LEA

For the hundredth time, Gray asked Emma if the dead sensed anything amiss. Emma had allowed her curly hair to fall in front of her face, turning away slightly as she answered.

"Um... Well, actually, they left."

Gray froze, his jaw muscles becoming more prominent as he clenched his teeth together.

"What do you mean, they *left*?" Shadows pulsed outward as if searching for the deserters.

"They said Lea glowed with the power of the gods. That no demon could touch her. That they feared her, and we were safe."

Gray's head swung toward Lea, his eyelids and chin lowering as he examined her closely. "As beautiful as she is, I don't think that she's glowing."

"The dead said it surrounded her completely, the same light as the shooting stars above us. And that when we walked out of the clearing, they felt the woods churning, heard the monsters inside it fleeing. They retreated to the north."

"And they were so certain that Lea's invisible glowing would keep them away that they were willing to leave us for the rest of the journey?"

"Enough to remind me that they would remember the promise you made to them, and they would be waiting to be set free. They said that they fulfilled their end of the bargain."

"Their bargain is only fulfilled when we pass safely across the border into Calir," Gray rumbled as he pulled Lea tighter against him, his palm sturdy against her stomach as he looked around. He didn't say a word as he focused on their safety, his shadows spreading out as far as he could control them to assess for lurking threats.

It wasn't until they crested a small hill that Gray exhaled deeply, his shoulders relaxing substantially.

Lea shifted forward on Obsidian, her mouth agape and her skin tingling. It was Calir. It had to be.

The line in the ground where the Wicked Wood ended and the kingdom of Calir began was once again unmistakable. But this time, instead of lush, green grass turning into muddy, dead earth, it turned into shimmering sand. It looked as if billions of tiny flecks of gold were mixed into the coarse beige grains.

The landscape was different than anything Lea had ever seen before. Squat trees with thick rough trunks and giant palm leaves at the top dappled the desert, providing shade from the blaring sun. Between the waxy leaves, large purple fruit grew, twice the size of an apple but shaped like an oval. High above their heads, a beautiful blue heron circled lazily, its strong wings outstretched to reveal black-tipped feathers.

"Ahem."

Lea jumped, calling her flames to her fingers when a man with deep brown skin and silver hair stepped out from behind one of the peculiar trees. Though his posture and the stealth with which he walked showed that he was Fae, he wasn't young. There were laugh lines bracketing his mouth and crow's feet around his eyes, which only served to emphasize the turquoise blue of his irises. Gray grabbed Lea's hand, smothering her flames with shadow. "It's okay."

The man did not make another move to walk toward them, but rather leaned casually against the tree and smiled warmly, his hands clasped in front of him. Just past the man, a small river ran into a vast pond, the same flickering gold shimmering in the water as giant winged birds splashed around inside it. They were completely white, not a speck of color on their fluffy, plush wings.

Gray kicked Obsidian's sides and crossed the border, hopping off his horse and striding quickly to the robed man who was patiently waiting roughly ten feet inside Calir.

"My friend," the man said as he finally walked forward, grasping Gray's hand with both of his and shaking it firmly.

"King Tanad." Gray smiled so widely, his eyes crinkled at the edges. "It seems my letter of warning made it here in time."

"It did. Though, according to your letter, you should be crossing my border about two days east of here." He quirked an eyebrow. "Luckily, my trackers felt that you'd changed course. It seems they were correct. I'm glad I heeded their advice. I wanted to be here when you arrived."

"That's very kind of you." Gray clapped the king casually on the shoulder, leading him toward Lea, who still sat on Obsidian's back.

"I was concerned that your decision to travel through the Wicked Wood instead of around it indicated a certain urgency to your arrival," he said, the tiniest kernel of tension slipping into his voice.

"You're not wrong. King Tanad, meet our sudden sense of urgency." Gray placed a hand on Lea's knee and squeezed. "This is my mate, Lea." He grabbed her around the waist and lifted her gently from the horse, tucking her into his side.

Lea bent forward to bow to the foreign king, but Tanad reached out and stopped her, cupping her chin and raising her back to full height.

"So this is the woman I've heard so much about." He slowly twisted her face from side to side, examining her with keen eyes. "Please, do not bow. If I know your mate at all, he might kill me where I stand if he sees his wife submit to another man."

Erik's booming laugh behind them covered up the sound of Gray's growl.

The king looked up at him with a broad smile, reaching into his pocket and grabbing a fluffy chunk of bread. "Good to see you, Erik." He tossed Erik the bread. "I hope you've been practicing your rooksnuff since I last saw you."

Erik jumped off his horse with ease, ripping off a hunk of the bread and handing it to Janelle before tearing a huge piece off with his teeth. "Mhmmm." He swallowed, taking another bite. "I've been a little preoccupied with this whole war thing, but last time was a fluke. You won't beat me again." Erik chuckled as he gave King Tanad a beast of a bear hug.

Tanad's eyes grew sad, the joyous sparkle inside them dimming to a mere twinkle. "And unfortunately, I need you as well. You've heard the Lonely Death has crossed our borders?"

Gray nodded solemnly. "It's true then?"

"Yes. But we'll discuss it more later. There is much to tell you, I'm afraid." King Tanad clapped his hands together, forcing a smile as he looked around Gray's broad shoulders. "And this must be Janelle and Emma, correct?" Tanad closed his eyes for several long seconds before cracking one eye open and looking at Janelle warily. "It appears I'll need to keep my eye on you."

"Oh, you don't have to worry about her," Erik said through another mouthful of food. "She might be a thief, but she's not stupid enough to try to steal from you."

"I'm not a thief!" Janelle cried out, clumsily sliding off Cinnamon. Erik tilted his head at her, raising his eyebrows. "I just borrow things sometimes," Janelle said as a blush creeped up her neck. "But not from you, Your Highness. I swear."

The King winked at her before closing his eyes again. "And Emma," the king said. "I'm sorry for the burden of the gift you carry. It must be hard, seeing those in the worst moments of their existence and being unable to help them." He offered Emma his hand, helping her dismount. "Your soul is kind. I think your gift was given to exactly the right person." He nodded at her slowly, and Emma's eyes watered.

"He can sense people's gifts," Gray leaned down and whispered into Lea's ear. "A very useful power for a king, don't you think?" Lea looked at the man in awe. If he could sense people's powers, would he be able to tell her more about her own? Were there other things he could sense, like why people possessed the power they did? And more importantly, would he be willing to tell her what he felt from her?

"I'm afraid I don't know your name," Tanad said kindly. "But I assume if the Commander here allowed you to join them, you must be a friend." The king shook Noah's hand without hesitation.

"It's Noah," he said, lowering his chin in a bow.

"He's a brave one, Tanad," Gray chimed in, clapping Noah on the shoulder. "And loyal as well. So yes, I would say we consider him a friend."

Noah smiled, a blush creeping up his neck and a dimple Lea had never noticed before pulling in his cheek. Lea's heart warmed a bit. Their circle was growing, her list of friends expanding like the roots of a tomato plant. It felt like the more good people she surrounded herself with, the more joy those roots sucked into her body, nourishing her in a way that was healing for her soul.

"Well," the king clapped his hands together again, interrupting Lea's thoughts. "A friend of Gray's is a friend of mine. Welcome to Calir, Noah." Tanad crooked a finger and a massive cream-colored horse appeared from underneath a nearby tree where it had been lying in the shade. Its hooves were the size of Lea's head, and she wondered if it was to allow the animal better traction in the sand. "I suspect a warm bath and a hot meal are in order. You are our guests, of course."

Gray stepped toward the King. "I'd like to talk about—"

"War and strategy can wait a few hours," Tanad cut him off, holding up a hand. "You've been through so much." He looked at Emma again with kind, understanding eyes. "Let's clean that dirt from your hair and the mud off your leathers before you dirty up our war room, shall we? And poor Erik must be starving. Look at him." He gestured to Erik's broad, muscular body. "He looks malnourished. Have you not been feeding the man? What have you eaten this week, Erik?"

Erik laughed, that booming cackle that brought a smile to Lea's lips every time without fail, as he hopped back up on his horse and pulled Janelle up with him.

"All we had was a foobil! Can you believe it? And I didn't even get my own. We had to *share* it," Erik moaned, holding his stomach as if suffering from hunger pains.

"See?" Tanad raised an eyebrow. "We can't allow your strongest soldier to starve to death. We'll discuss business later," he said with a pointed look before effortlessly mounting his horse.

Lea couldn't help but smile as Gray gave her a leg up to settle into the saddle. It seemed as if her mate had found his match in stubbornness, and she had to say she quite liked it.

CHAPTER 46

LEA

King Tanad's castle was unlike anything Lea had ever seen. As they approached on their horses, Lea was completely awestruck. The castle looked as if a sandstorm had blown it into existence, with sloping walls that drifted down and blended into the sparkling sand that led to a glistening shoreline. Seashells stuck out of the landscape and exterior of the palace, and beautiful turquoise waves rolled onto the shore, starkly contrasting the beige walls of the castle. Had there not been balconies and windows, Lea would've been positive that she was staring at a mountain of sand rather than a palace fit for a king. It was *stunning*. There was no other word to describe it.

Servants and soldiers wandered casually about, their skin tan beneath their lightweight uniforms in various shades of blue. They were barefoot, and Lea wondered if the sand was as warm as the balmy air, or if the salty breeze that was filling her lungs cooled it as it gently blew off the sea.

King Tanad led them through the ornate gold front doors that swung open with a flick of his wrist. They were at least twenty feet tall, with gilded depictions of all sorts of marine life. And somehow, those animals moved. Fish, dolphins, crabs, and various creatures of the sea that Lea didn't recognize slowly swam around on the door as if it was made of water rather than a gold plated entrance to the castle.

"Welcome to my humble home," the king said as they passed an enormous tank that filled an entire wall of the foyer. Unable to resist, Lea raised her fingers to the glass, trailing them softly across where a pink starfish stuck to it. Except—Lea gasped. There was no glass. As her fingers touched the surface, the wet, tiny suction cup feet of the starfish brushed against her fingers. Cool water trailed down her arm, a ripple appearing on the surface of the wall of water.

"Ahh—careful, my dear." King Tanad winked at her. "We wouldn't want too large of a break through the surface. There are some things best kept contained in that tank there." He tilted his head toward where something casting a monstrous shadow lazily swam above their heads.

"Holy shit! I mean—" Noah cleared his throat. "What is that thing? Look at its teeth! They're the size of my hand." Noah took a step away from the tank. "Are you sure that thing can't break through?"

"Chicken," Janelle teased, poking him in the ribs.

"A hakar. The shark's only predator. You're quite safe, though," King Tanad said, waving a hand flippantly. "Though I wouldn't advise sticking your arm in there. If you'd like to play with the fish, there's a tank near the dining room with dolphins. Much kinder animals, dolphins," Tanad mused, stopping when they reached a split in the hallway. To the right was what looked like a statue of a whale floating near the ceiling, while to the left, another wall of water created a tunnel by curling over the top of the hallway like a wave about to crash back into the ocean. "I assume your usual rooms will suit you?" the king asked Gray and Erik.

"Noah, Emma, and Janelle will need their own rooms. If you are able to accommodate that, of course," Erik said, shuffling his feet a bit. He seemed uncertain about his answer, but the king either didn't notice or chose not to acknowledge it.

"Of course. I had the whole wing prepared, so any of those rooms will do. I didn't know how many from your army would be joining us and decided to err on the side of caution."

"We appreciate that." Gray inclined his head.

King Tanad ignored the gesture, waving him off. "Now, dinner will be served in four hours. Does that give you adequate time to rest and refresh yourselves?"

Gray took a breath as if he wanted to argue, his mouth pinching in and his hands coming to clasp behind his back. Lea could feel the thick disappointment that they were not discussing war tactics and ways to kill his father, but also his wariness. They were guests in another kingdom after all, and it wasn't wise nor prudent to make things difficult.

"That will be fine," Gray said graciously, if not a bit gruffly, before they said their goodbyes and walked through the sandstone hallways, up several sets of stairs, and through another elaborate living doorway—this one adorned with an assortment of starfish.

They retreated to their separate rooms, aside from Lea and Gray, but Lea didn't miss Erik's lingering stare as Janelle closed the door to her own quarters. Later, she would ask her friend what was going on. She couldn't imagine a better match for her than Erik, but Lea knew better than anyone that Janelle was strange about monogamy and intimacy. She preferred casual relationships, physical ones, if Lea was being honest. But Janelle had grown so much over the past several months, and Lea hoped that if she decided to entertain the possibility of giving in to the attraction so clearly buzzing between her and Erik, she would have an open mind about something more serious.

Gray closed the door behind them, the click pulling Lea from her thoughts and bringing her attention back to the room. Nearly everything from the furniture to the linens were in shades of white and blue. The bed was enormous, and the bedframe looked as if it had been pulled directly from the sea. It was one large piece of driftwood, with bits of coral still somehow growing in vibrant shades of pink and orange. The back wall of the room was open to the outside, with a view of the ocean that brought tears to Lea's eyes.

She had never seen the ocean before today, had never even thought that it would be a possibility for her. It stretched for miles and miles, and made Lea feel small in the best way. Everything had been so heavy for a long time, so dire and urgent and *big*. But looking at the ocean, she didn't feel big. She felt like just a girl, one of many insignificant people on the earth instead of a possible queen with the only magic that could defeat the Black King.

Lea was still lost in her own thoughts when she felt muscular arms encircling her and Gray's scruffy chin resting on top of her head. She sniffled and swiped away a rogue tear running down her cheek.

"Are you okay? I know the past few days have been hard. Your world's been turned upside down, and you've been so strong through all of it. I'm proud of you for that strength, Little Flower, but I want to make sure you know that you can talk to me. About anything at all. You don't ever have to face anything alone again."

Lea twisted in his arms, pressing her face against his firm chest. "I know that. I do," she said softly. "It's not even learning that my mom and dad aren't..." she drifted off. "I just don't feel like it's possible that *I* am Queen Emmaline's descendent. That I am meant to kill the Black King. I can't be the one from the prophecy. Surely the gods would have chosen someone far more equipped than a girl who had never left her tiny town or used her magic until a couple of months ago."

"The gods do not make mistakes. Not like this, and not when it comes to protecting their kingdom," Gray said as he raised a hand to caress her face, his thumb following the soft line of her jaw. His eyebrows scrunched as he looked out at the ocean for several long, quiet moments before speaking again. "I know I said you can talk to me about anything, and that's true, of course, but hearing you say those words... It makes me feel sick. It's the opposite of the truth. You are *more* than capable of what the gods are asking of you."

Lea laughed out loud. "I'm reckless. How many stupid choices did I make without thought, trying to help my friends when all I did was end up getting them in more trouble? That's the whole reason that we're here, Gray. Because I was too stupid to think things through."

"You are *not* stupid," Gray snapped, a shadow twisting through her hair and gently pulling her head back to meet his eyes. "You may have been reckless at times, but victory requires bravery and sacrifice. You were willing to do both when you broke into that stupid trial to save Thomas. You're loyal, and you have a strong conscience and the self-awareness needed to grow from your mistakes. *That* is why you deserve the power that you've been given."

Gray's eyes darkened, his shadows now pooling around their feet. "Look at my brother and my father. If given the amount of power you have, either of them would have destroyed the kingdom already. The whole damn continent. But I *see* how hard you're working, how you're trying not to lose yourself to your darkness. I can *feel* that you prefer the light. You are good, every piece of you."

Lea thought about that wicked place inside of her, that mysterious magic that felt so wild and unruly. It had *almost* felt evil, and yet she'd used it to save queen Emmaline's daughter, her own mother.

"And what if I'm darker than you think?" Lea asked him with false bravado.

"Then I will join you in the darkness," Gray kissed the top of her head, "and remind you that flowers cannot live without the sun."

CHAPTER 47

GRAY

There were so many emotions flooding the mate bond that Gray could hardly sort through them all. His head swam as he tried to distinguish the different feelings banging around in his skull. There was bitter disappointment, like chocolate so dark it wasn't even sweet, as well as a heavy uncertainty that made butterflies dance in his stomach. There was sharp pain, like a slice of Lea's heart had been cut away from the rest of the muscle, as well as a soothing relief that they had made it here safely. Gray wished he could take all the negative feelings away and leave only the relief. He wanted to use his fingers and mouth and cock to make her forget, if only for a little while.

Lea was still staring quietly toward the ocean, and while he wanted nothing more than to touch and kiss every worry away, he knew that wasn't what she needed. Not right now. She was too lost in thought, too consumed by the revelations that had upturned her world.

Gray's heart ached as he took in Lea's blood-stained hands, muddy clothes, and tangled, matted hair from sleeping on the ground. He might not be able to take away her sorrow, but there were other ways he could take care of her.

Reaching forward to grab her hand, Gray pulled her toward the bathing chamber. It was connected to their room by only a thin wall, with no door to close to separate the spaces, and just like their bedroom, it was open to the rear of the castle facing the shoreline. A large bath sunk into the floor about halfway across the room and ran all the way to the edge of the balcony, with stairs to allow you to step down into the warm water and swim, if that was what you wanted to do. It was private, with walls on either side, but once in the tub, the lip of the water on the balcony appeared to blend into the ocean on the horizon, making it seem like you could swim on forever.

Slowly and tenderly, Gray pulled the band from Lea's hair, combing his fingers through her long, thick locks the best he could before kneeling in front of her and removing her boots. He peeled her socks away, throwing them aside before lifting her feet one at a time and kneading them gently. A groan of relaxation left Lea's throat as he dug his thumbs into her tired arches.

It didn't take long before Gray had her completely bare before him, throwing all of her clothes to the side and removing his own. Lea started toward the bath, but Gray stopped her with an arm around her waist. A tether hung from the ceiling, and he pulled it firmly. Rain fell from little holes above them, warm water that beat against their shoulders and cleaned the grime away from their bodies almost instantly.

Lea laughed out loud, and Gray felt a jolt of amazement at the sound.

"Do you like it?" he asked with a grin.

"How is it possible?" Lea tried to catch the water in her hands. "It's *warm*, and we didn't have to ask servants to haul up thirty buckets of hot water. And it's coming from the ceiling!" She tipped her head back and smiled broadly, letting the fat drops of water soak into her hair and slide across her face.

"You'll be amazed by what you see here," Gray pointed toward a trellis full of purple flowers that continuously bloomed above the bath, dropping fragrant petals into the tub below. "Magic isn't controlled here. It's bountiful, celebrated. Those with different abilities contribute to the kingdom. This is a small bit of water magic."

"It's a miracle," Lea breathed, subconsciously placing her palm on her breastbone where her own magic lived. "Do you think we can really do this?" she asked. "Do you think that Desia could be like this someday?"

"It was once," Gray said almost sadly, pain pinching in his chest as he pulled Lea into his arms. "We'll do everything we can to make sure that it is again," he promised in a deep, rumbling timbre. They remained in each other's embrace for several minutes, allowing the warm water to wash away not only the dirt, but the sadness and confusion muddying Lea's thoughts.

They didn't need soap or shampoo; the water was spelled to clean them completely, but near the large bath was an assortment of oils in short, clear, glass bottles. Gray pulled Lea onto the steps, grabbing a bottle at random and dumping the entire contents into the bathwater. The scents of honey and orange mixed with something earthy that Gray couldn't quite place wafted through the room, the sea breeze carrying it throughout the open space.

The water shimmered from the oil, and Lea didn't hesitate to sink down into it, dunking her head and scrubbing at her face. She was already clean, but Gray understood the urge to rub at your skin when life was hard, to try to wash away everything unpleasant that sat heavy on your shoulders.

Gray followed Lea into the pool, pulling her against his now wet chest and wrapping her legs firmly around his waist. He pushed the wet hair from Lea's forehead before leaning in and kissing her softly, pressing his lips to hers in a whisper of thanks. He had been terrified, if he was being honest, about his plan of escaping with the rebels. What if she hadn't wanted to join them? What if she hadn't been willing to flee the kingdom? And yet, here she was. She had followed him a kingdom away without a moment's hesitation.

Lea didn't hesitate to deepen the kiss, spearing her hands through Gray's long chestnut hair and opening her mouth wide for him. It was all the invitation Gray needed as he lifted her higher and walked them deeper into the water, staying just on the inside of the bath before the ceiling opened up to the sky. There wasn't a cloud in sight, and so to join together under the sun would seal half of the mate bond. Gray knew he would need to talk to her about it at some point, the fact that he wasn't willing to complete the bond until the war was over. But Lea had lost so much already. She was facing enough challenges and sorrow. He didn't want to add to her burden. Not right now. Not tonight.

As Lea bit down on Gray's lip, his hands roamed her body, his thumb finding the underside of her breast and squeezing roughly. Their bond was full of need, their magic desperate to join and find release together. It had been days, far too long, especially for a newly mated pair. But with Lea, Gray couldn't focus if she so much as touched him. It hadn't been safe for him to explore her the way she deserved in the Wicked Wood, but regardless, that had been all he'd wanted to do at night as they'd slept together underneath the thick furs and starry sky.

The starry sky. His magic twisted in his chest at the thought, telling him he was wrong, that he was foolish for refusing to forge the bond with his mate. Almost as if reading his mind, Lea untangled herself from him, standing up so that her full breasts were exposed. She grabbed his hand and looked up at the sun, walking backward with a devilish smile on her face. *Fuck.* The things he wanted to do to that mouth.

Gray took a step forward, almost giving in to that primal urgency, but he forced his legs to stop moving.

"Azalea, I—"

"You don't want to seal the bond."

Dammit. Gray sighed. She saw right through him.

Lea dropped his hand, her eyes glistening with unshed tears.

"Of course I want to seal the bond," Gray said, his heart aching at the pain in the lines of her face. "It's all I can think about. I need you as mine in every way, but—"

"Then why won't you do it? We're safe now. We're here, in a room, alone. Far away from your family. So tell me why."

Gray hung his head, reaching forward and pulling Lea back into the shaded part of the tub. "I won't risk your life," Gray said firmly, almost sharply. "I am leading this rebellion, and I can't ask my soldiers to sacrifice their lives if I'm not willing to do the same. If we're mated, then your life is tied to mine. And if your life is tied to mine and I'm killed..." he trailed off, unable to even say the words.

Lea reached up to cup his face. "If I died, would you not want to follow me beyond the veil?"

"Of course I would, but this is different."

"How?" Lea pushed back from him, anger finally bubbling through their bond. No, not anger. She was absolutely furious. "How is it different, other than you're a stubborn man, determined to get his way no matter what *I* want?"

"The rebellion—No. The *world* needs you. Not just to win this war, but because you're *good*. At the very center of you, you are full of light and all things joyous and *good,*" he repeated. "Who knows what waits for me on the other side of the veil? I'm *not* good, Azalea. I have done not good things. And I refuse to let you die and be dragged to wherever I must repent for those sins."

"Where you go, I go, Gray." Lea's voice was choked, tears welling in her eyes as she crossed her arms over her exposed body.

"No. I won't allow it," Gray snapped.

"You're not listening to me." Lea lifted her chin. "Where you go, *I* go."

"It's not that easy, Azalea. I—" he sputtered. "Look, if I could make sure we were safe, guarantee that you would live, no matter what... Nothing would stop me from making you mine right now. This very second. Can't you understand where I'm coming from?" he asked earnestly, opening his palms toward her and pushing all of his fear and worry and desperation through their connection to show her what the thought of losing her did to him.

"No. I can't understand. Do you plan on dying in this war? Are you so certain it will happen?"

"That's not fair. I can't predict what will happen, but I made a vow to you. To protect you with everything I have until my last breath leaves my tired body. I will not break that vow, Lea. And to seal the bond, that would all but ensure your death."

"You also bound yourself to me. Body, mind, and soul. Do you not understand that there are bigger things to fear than death? I refuse to live a half life, whether you are alive or dead. That is what you are doing to us by not allowing us to join. Don't you feel the ache? Here?" Lea dug her fist into her chest. "It hurts me, Gray. It feels like there's a piece of my heart missing. Do you call that *living*?"

"If your heart is *beating*, then that has to be enough. Just for now." Anger bubbled in Gray's gut. It wasn't fair. Not to him, and not to his mate. Had he done something to deserve the ire of the universe, or his father, or the gods? He faced an impossible choice. But still, he had made it, and there would be no changing his mind. "I won't do it, Azalea. I won't risk you."

Lea pressed her lips together tightly, wiping her eyes with the heels of her hand before walking back toward the stairs. "Then I guess we have nothing else to talk about. Let's get ready to meet the king." Lea kept her gaze away from him as she grabbed a plush towel from a stack on the floor and wrapped it firmly around herself.

Gray followed behind her, the distance between them causing a sharp pain where their mate bond would be. "Please, let me help you," he almost whispered, needing to take care of her. Desperate to find a way to ease the disappointment she was feeling. He understood what she wanted, what she was feeling. He did. But it didn't change the fact that there was no scenario where he was willing to let her die. Anything else that she could ask for, he would give to her. Anything at all, he would find a way. But not this. Not death.

Gray picked up a towel and reached to dry her hair, but she placed a palm firmly against his chest, holding him back. "I want all of you, Gray.

Not just whatever part you're willing to share," she whispered before walking back into the bedroom, leaving him alone in a sea of shadows.

CHAPTER 48

ERIK

Erik had just finished bathing when he heard a tentative knock. Intuitively, as if her soul called to his, he knew exactly who it was. Hurrying to the door, he opened it in one swift motion, enjoying the warmth that crept into Janelle's cheeks as her eyes stared down at the towel slung low around his waist.

"I... I just wanted to..." She cleared her throat. "But I can see your body. *Busy*. I can see you're *busy*." Janelle slapped her palm against her forehead. "Fuck me, I'm gonna go now."

Erik grabbed Janelle's wrist and stopped her as she turned, pulling her forward into the room. "It's just a towel, Janelle," he teased. "If it bothers you that much, I'm happy to take it off." He reached for the corner of the soft fabric.

"Nope. No. That's perfectly fine." Janelle squeezed her arms against her sides as she looked around at his room. It *was* a great room, very peaceful. Maybe not exactly his style, with all the driftwood and light blue fabric—and why were there so many damn pillows? Actually, now that he thought about it, every room in this wing was designed the same—same bed, same table, same rug. So why was she examining it so closely when she'd just come from her own identical one?

Her hair was wet, and she wore borrowed clothes in the style of Calir's dress that hugged her body perfectly. The long skirt draped nearly to the floor and had a slit up the front almost to her hip, its violet hue accenting the tips of her purple hair. The top she wore was cropped, showing a sliver of skin around her belly button.

Erik should have expected the way his cock twitched at seeing her. He should have prepared himself. The clothing here was far less modest, a necessity with how hot it was in Calir during the middle of summer, but still, he hadn't expected to feel quite like *this*. It was as if he was a teenager again, unable to control his body when a girl so much as looked his way.

"Did you need something?" Erik asked thickly, trying to swallow down his desire. Was that what this was? Simply desire? His body craving to touch and taste and explore every inch of Janelle's pale skin?

"Oh, it's nothing. I just got bored." Janelle waved her hands around as if trying to convince them both that was the reason she had knocked. "Emma's sleeping. Poor thing used all of her energy speaking to the dead. She's okay, though," she bumbled. "She was so still, so I held a mirror in front of her nose to make sure she was still breathing."

"I'm glad she's resting." Erik tried not to laugh at how nervous Janelle appeared. Did seeing his bare chest make her as uneasy as him seeing her pale midriff? "Once we start training, we'll need to identify if her magic is of the day or night. That'll let us know the best way to help re-energize her."

"Do you think we should wake her before we meet with King Tanad?"

"I think Emma's gifts lie more in empathy and communication than war and battle strategy. We'll be discussing the best way to kill people swiftly and efficiently so we can end this war. I'm not sure that's what she needs to be hearing right now." Erik felt a familiar sting of pity for Emma. He couldn't imagine having a power so emotionally draining. "I'll have someone bring dinner to her room."

"Yeah, sure. Good idea." Janelle shuffled her feet awkwardly.

"Do you want to come to the meeting, or would you rather stay in and rest?"

"Oh, if you think for a second that I will be missing out on the action, you are sorely mistaken, giant man."

"Giant man?" Erik laughed deeply. "That's the best you can come up with?"

"Oversized rat?" Janelle raised her eyebrows.

"I think I'm more predator than rodent, don't you?" Erik raised his hands, which were glowing with red and orange fire.

"Hmmm..." She tapped her chin. "Bottomless pit," she said with a hint of a smile.

"Well, absolutely, but I don't consider that an insult as much as an observation. It's hard being this strong and manly. I need the protein." Erik extinguished his flames and winked at her as he flexed his arms. He spent hours a day training. Push-ups and pull-ups, sparring, and sword fighting. Even hauling large rocks back and forth across the dungeons to build up his endurance. His muscles had never been so defined, and Erik knew Janelle had noticed based on the way she chewed on the side of her lower lip and skirted her eyes away as his biceps bulged with his arm movement.

Erik and Janelle's time in the Wicked Wood on a horse together had changed things between them. Where before it had been a casual flirtation, Erik now found himself thinking about Janelle almost constantly. And not in the, "Is she trying to steal something from me right now?" way. He wasn't sure when that shift had happened, but it had. And now? He couldn't stop it.

He persistently thought about what Janelle might be feeling or needing, perseverating on if she was cold or nervous, and how he could help her. And despite his best efforts, he wondered what she thought of *him*. Their conversation before the nabis attack told him enough to know that her relationship with sex and intimacy was casual. She'd acted like she had never been in love before, never been hurt before, but Erik suspected that was just another thick layer of Janelle's emotional armor.

Armor he was determined to chink through bit by bit, but for now, he worried that trying to push any sort of relationship—No. Not even a relationship, but the idea of anything deep, anything *real*, troubled her. If she were to pull away, Erik didn't think his heart could take it.

Janelle had hinted she was only comfortable with the physical, but the way her body sang to his, he was certain that once they opened that door, he would never be content with just being friends—with or without the benefits.

Erik was a warrior. His life has been devoted to a cause higher than his own, but he was still a man. And he considered himself a good one. He had no interest in casual sex, though he had partaken in it before. His father had used women. As had Gray's father, and he had no interest in following in their footsteps. What he wanted was to find someone he loved, and make them his world.

He'd enjoyed it then, but with Janelle, he needed more. *This thief is going to steal my heart,* he thought. "Gods. That was disgusting," Erik mumbled under his breath. When had he become so sappy?

"What was that?" Janelle asked.

"Anyway." Erik clapped his hands together in front of him, ignoring her. "Not that you need a reason. You're more than welcome in my bedroom anytime." Erik wiggled his eyebrows suggestively. He might not want to push Janelle away by offering her something serious, but that didn't mean he didn't want her to know how attracted he was to her. "But was there something specific you needed?"

"It's stupid," Janelle said, "and I don't wanna talk about it anymore." She pushed him away and turned to walk out the door, but Erik grabbed her shoulder, electricity buzzing beneath his fingers. "Janelle? Talk."

"Erik, fuck off." She tried to shrug him off.

Now we're getting somewhere, Erik thought. She obviously felt vulnerable, a feeling Erik would bet she wasn't used to. Her anger was her way of pushing him away.

"There's no shame in asking a friend a question," Erik said kindly, letting go of her shoulder.

Janelle crossed her arms. "Who said I had a question? Maybe I came here to tell you that you're an overly jolly giant, and that it's really annoying how happy you always are. Or maybe I came to tell you that you stink from riding for days and I wanted to make sure that you had thoroughly cleaned yourself, because if not, I might be able smell you all the way across the hall, and—"

Erik cut her off. "Do you want to stay here with me?" Erik suspected that was the reason Janelle had knocked on his door. He didn't think the others knew, but Janelle had nightmares. Ever since the tirror attack, she would shake and cry in her sleep, never saying a word or making a peep as tears streamed silently down her face. She was stoic, even as she slept. Janelle was the definition of putting on a brave face. She was a master of pretending that everything was okay, but Erik knew better.

Every night since the attack, he had brushed away salty tears from her cheeks, whispered soothing words into her hair, and woken her gently, so as not to frighten her even more. And on those nights, she would cling to him as if he was the only safe place she could hide in the entire world. But every morning by the time the sun had risen, she'd pulled away again, plastered on a smile or a grimace, and resumed teasing everyone around them.

They'd never discussed it—had never spoken about it. The rage Erik felt thinking about what caused those nightmares made his blood boil, like fire licking the inside of his veins, but it wouldn't help Janelle for him to show his anger. No, he would be Janelle's safe space for as long as she needed, and then, when the time was right, he would destroy whoever it was that had hurt her. Whatever bastard that had made her fearful of showing vulnerability—of loving.

"Well, you see," Janelle was flustered, her cheeks turning an adorable shade of pink, "Being the kind soul that I am, I came over here to see if maybe you wanted to stay in my room. Only because with Gray and

Lea next door, well, you might hear some uncomfortable things." Janelle was speaking fast, her pitch raising higher and higher as she continued. "I thought I'd spare you from being an unwilling third wheel to their mating ritual."

"Is that why you want to share a bed with me?" Erik crossed his arms, purposefully flexing as he did so.

"Forget it, you giant dirt-covered lollipop." Janelle turned and stormed out of the room, slamming the door behind her.

"I'm very clean, actually!" Erik called through the door with a booming laugh. Calmly and quickly, Erik changed into fresh clothes. Well, clothes were a generous description. He put on a pair of thin khaki colored trousers, grabbed his sword belt and two studded daggers, and walked across the hall to Janelle's room. Opening the door without knocking, Erik walked in and placed his belt on a large turquoise trunk at the foot of the bed.

Janelle walked out of the bathroom, her hair now tied into a loose bun. "Excuse me! What do you think you're doing?" she shouted as Erik settled into a large, rather uncomfortable wooden armchair, kicking his feet up and placing his hands behind his head.

"I think you're right," he nodded at her. "I think I will be far more comfortable in here with you tonight."

CHAPTER 49

LEA

Lea and Gray hadn't spoken much since their conversation about fulfilling the mating bond, and the tension was palpable as they walked with Janelle and Erik to meet with King Tanad. Noah had stayed behind, insisting someone needed to stand guard outside Emma's room if she was to be alone. Repeatedly, Gray had told him that they were safe here, but Noah had argued that Emma reminded him of his sister. He'd said it didn't sit right with him to leave her alone in an unfamiliar place while she slept, completely vulnerable, and Gray had relented.

Now Lea wished Noah was there to break the tension. The air was thick with it. Not only between her and Gray, but between Erik and Janelle as well, though, it was a different type of tension she felt buzzing between her friends.

The distance between them was uncomfortable, a wedge inside her lungs that made it difficult to breathe, but Lea couldn't let her feelings go. She wasn't angry so much as hurt. Though she'd suspected Gray's motivations when he'd covered the moon so quickly with clouds on the night of their escape, it felt far more painful to have it confirmed. Though in truth, she'd more than just suspected. Unless Alaric had dragons, blocking out the sky gave them virtually no advantage when they were hiding within the trees and inside his wards.

She'd given him the benefit of the doubt, but today, when he had refused to step into the sun, it solidified Lea's deepest fears. They'd been given a gift from the gods and were the first mates in hundreds of years, but still, Gray would not accept the bond fully.

It wasn't a lack of understanding his motivations that caused her heart to ache, because really, Lea could see where he was coming from. If her fate was to die in the coming war, she didn't want Gray to die along with her either, but she knew Gray well enough to know that he would follow her wherever her soul was taken. So why wasn't she allowed to make the same decision for herself? And why was he only focusing on what the mating bond would do to them in death?

Didn't he realize that it would make life so much sweeter? Lea loved Gray more than she'd thought possible. Looking back, it was absurd she'd ever thought she wouldn't be able to move past what his father had done to her mother. She could no more stop loving him than the waves could stop crashing onto the beach outside their balcony. But with the bond sealed, it would be even better. They would be one in every way that mattered. How could he deny her that for something that might not even happen?

Lea regretted saying she didn't want only what he was willing to offer her, the words sitting like a cold, heavy stone in her stomach. As the four of them walked to meet with the king, their heels clicking on the sandstone floor, Lea felt as if she was going to explode. She couldn't take it anymore. Grabbing Gray's arm, she paused, meeting his turmoil-filled eyes. Erik immediately stopped behind them, and Janelle followed his lead.

"Give us a minute, Erik." Always the obedient soldier, Erik resumed walking without a word, pulling a protesting Janelle behind him.

"I'm sorry about walking out on you earlier," Lea apologized. "I was hurt. I *am* hurt. But that doesn't mean I should hurt you back."

The relief on Gray's face made her heart ache. "So you understand then?"

"That's not what I said, Gray," Lea said, wrapping her arms around his waist and pressing her head against his chest. "I'm asking you to think about this from my perspective."

"I am. I've *tried*. But it's not the same, Azalea," Gray argued.

"It's *exactly* the same. And deep down, you know that. Just promise me you'll think about it?"

Lea could sense Gray was fighting a battle with himself as his jaw clenched and his shadows became unsettled. With a resigned exhale, he folded her into a hug and leaned down to whisper into her hair.

"I will *try* and think about it," he conceded.

"Stubborn man," Lea kissed his chest.

Gray's eyes twinkled, crinkling at the edges. "You're actually calling *me* stubborn?" he asked, his voice teasing.

"Yes," she deadpanned, turning to lead the way down the hall to where Erik and Janelle waited outside a large rectangular entryway. Lea had expected to see the same golden doors that were situated throughout the rest of the castle, but instead, they stood in front of thick, burnt-orange curtains. They shimmered in that telltale way that indicated they were enchanted, and a tickle of danger ran down Lea's spine.

"Do you see that?" Lea asked Gray, wondering what exactly the enchantment was.

"I do. Anyone who wishes King Tanad harm will die a very painful death if they walk through those curtains."

Lea sucked in a breath at the buzz of electricity that seemed to radiate from the doorway, making the hair on her neck stand on end and goosebumps prickle along her skin.

"Well," Erik said, bouncing on the balls of his feet. "See you in there!" With a salute, he jumped through the curtains. Lea held her breath. She knew Erik didn't mean the king any harm, but a sudden painful death? What if the magic was wrong?

As if she had called it into existence, Lea heard a gurgling sound from the other side of the curtain. It reminded her of how Claire had sounded when the arrow struck her through her throat. Erik groaned in pain, and a *thud* made the curtains rustle as something heavy hit the ground. Her stomach dropped as she looked up at Gray, who rolled his eyes.

"Erik!" Janelle shouted as she ran through the curtains without a single moment's hesitation. "Oh! Fuck off, you overcooked ham!" Lea heard, followed by Erik's boisterous laugh.

"Come on, don't be mad! It was too easy. You saw Lea's face when we told her about the magic!"

Gray laughed under his breath, then placed his hand against the small of Lea's back and led them both through the curtains. She felt the pressure of magic, undeniable as it twisted through every inch of her body, searching for her intentions before disappearing all at once.

"That really wasn't nice," Lea told Erik with a pointed look.

"Okay, okay. No more pretending to die. Got it." Erik placed his hand over his heart solemnly, kneeling before her. "My queen." His voice dripped with mock sincerity.

Lea kicked his shoe with a laugh. "Stand up and stop being ridiculous. We have more important things to do." She looked up to observe her surroundings. They stood in a large, circular room, the back wall once again open to a balcony that overlooked the ocean. A wall of clear sparkling magic crossed the opening. It was thick, and appeared exceptionally strong, as if it was meant to keep what was said in the room a secret.

In the middle of the chamber was a massive table shaped exactly like their continent, Desia to the north, and Calir to the south. The table wasn't flat, and definitely wasn't meant for eating at. Instead, it rose and fell along with the dips and hills of the landscape it portrayed.

A pang of homesickness struck Lea's heart as she looked at the jagged Torres Mountain range. It was uncanny how alike they looked. She was looking at a perfect miniature, laid out before them to assist in preparing for war.

Standing over the table was King Tanad, still dressed in his flowing robes and smiling toward them. "I see your sense of humor hasn't changed, Erik. I'm not sure my opinion matters, but I thought it was a rather funny joke."

"Thank you!" Erik said emphatically with a wave of his arms as he walked toward the king. "Remember the time that I–"

"That's enough," Gray said harshly. "We have too much to discuss to reminisce on your old—and might I say terrible—pranks."

Wincing, Lea sent calming energy down the bond. Gray was stressed, and for good reason, but she couldn't fault Erik for trying to lighten the mood. As if sensing her thoughts, Erik winked at her, and Lea smiled. He knew exactly what he was doing.

King Tanad sighed. "Unfortunately, he's right, Erik. Things have grown more dire since you both were last here."

"As it has to the north," Gray admitted, running a hand through his hair.

"Come, let's sit." Tanad gestured to several large driftwood armchairs surrounding the table. Once they were settled, Tanad waved his hand and refreshments magically appeared: a deep purple wine with sweet huckleberries and a single pink flower floating on top for Lea and Tanad and some sort of amber liquid for Gray, Janelle, and Erik. Gray bent forward with his arms on his knees, his expression growing more serious by the second.

"As you can see, our timeline for when we planned our escape with the rebels from Auropera was moved up. There were casualties, but not as many as I expected. By now, the bulk of the resistance should be safely inside the Torres Mountains. Our scouts are traveling village to village to recruit as many people willing to fight with us as possible." Gray's report was succinct, matter of fact.

"And the Lonely Death?" King Tanad asked grimly, his eyebrows pinching together.

Gray gave Lea a sidelong look, reaching over and grabbing her hand. "It is spreading. And quickly."

"Have you confirmed how it spreads?"

"I have. My father casts a spell on one particular person, someone chosen by his scouts. Once infected, the illness will spread to anyone with magic that comes near the original carrier, or anyone they have passed the disease to. Though, if entire villages have fallen, then it seems as if the spell has grown stronger. Just months ago it required very close proximity to spread. But now? It appears that the distance it can infect others from has increased exponentially."

"I had the same concerns," Tanad pressed his lips together. "If it no longer requires contact or being within a few feet of a carrier, it stands to reason that isolation of families in their own homes is now necessary."

Gray nodded, rubbing a hand across his beard. "Agreed. There should be no interaction between non-family units whatsoever. However, that doesn't prevent my father from targeting as many individuals as possible, regardless. The *only* way to stop the Lonely Death is to kill him."

"And Alaric," Lea added, phantom pain throbbing in her chest.

King Tanad nodded, pressing his lips into a grim line as he stood and walked to the table. He pulled several large pins from his pocket. They appeared to be made of copper and were topped with the likeness of a skull. He leaned forward and pressed the sharp metal tips of the pins into the wood representing Calir, a neat, horizontal line just inside the border.

"These are the towns that have been hit with the Lonely Death so far. As you know, magic is not illegal here, and therefore, it is far more potent and common to find than in your kingdom. It is rare to find anyone who doesn't have some sort of power." King Tanad gestured toward the skulls. "These villages were decimated completely. Not a soul was left alive."

Lea covered her hand with her mouth, trying to push down the nausea filling her stomach. "No one?" she asked.

"Not a single soul," King Tanad confirmed. "We've stopped accepting those seeking asylum from Desia across the border. I have put wards in place that will stop anyone attempting to enter the kingdom. It grieves me to do so. To deny your people the chance at safety is not something that I take lightly, but I feel I must in order to keep my own people safe. Our wards should also prevent the king's magic from crossing over our border, unless carried in by a host. My theory is that, prior to closing our border, he infected spies, sent them south, and then planted them in our villages. Aside from you six, no one from Desia has been allowed entrance weeks."

"And has that helped?" Lea asked, wondering how many people had dwelled in those villages.

"It has, to an extent. This final village, here," the king pointed to the seventh skull just south of the border between kingdoms where the land met the sea, "is the only one that fell *after* we implemented those safeguards. It stands to reason that either there is a fault somewhere in my wards, or the king has found a way around my magic."

Lea was going to be sick.

"If that's true, then we have less time than I thought. If he can infect any city he wishes without even sending a host, he could completely eviscerate your kingdom in a matter of months." Gray studied the map and a jolt of determination vibrated through the bond into Lea's chest.

"That is my fear as well," Tanad admitted, his change in tone causing him to appear years older. "It's imperative that we do not allow the king to get his magic past my barriers. There were weeks between the sixth and seventh attack, which makes me believe it's not as easy as we first thought for the king to cast his spell from so far away."

"What do you suggest?" Gray asked.

"You were right when you said isolation was the only way to prevent the disease from spreading. We have asked all those within a three days' ride of the border to interact as family units only. No socializing or mingling, no gatherings. The castle has extra protections, ancient ones from when it was built. I am not concerned about our capital city falling. But I fear my magic is not enough to fight your father's alone. I ask that you ride with me along the border and add your own magic to mine. Reinforce the shield that is already in place. I believe that between the two of us, we should be powerful enough to at least slow your father's progress."

Lea tasted Gray's reluctance in the back of her throat as he squeezed her hand. Swallowing, Lea squeezed back. A thread of worry wound itself around her heart. She didn't want to be separated, but the way Tanad spoke suggested that the journey would be for the two of them alone. But maybe there was something she could do while they were gone... Something that wouldn't just help her pass the time, but would also help further their cause.

"Of course, anything I can do to help." Gray nodded.

"In return, I can offer you my troops. I will not force anyone to join your cause, but most of my men have agreed to fight alongside you. Our new recruits are training, and we are working on gathering supplies. I'd estimate that we will need at least a month and a half to have them armed and ready to leave for Desia."

"That aligns with my timeline," Gray said. "We are training our rebels as well, and Lea's friend Thomas is arming them. We have several steps to take before we're ready to engage. But in the meantime, we're safely hidden. Alaric has no idea where we are, and it will remain that way until we're ready."

"I'd like to help as well." Lea stood, vibrating with energy.

"Do you have an idea, my dear Azalea?" The king asked warmly, almost *knowingly,* as he raised an eyebrow.

"The moonflowers." Lea turned to Gray, her pulse racing. "The cottage isn't far from the border. If you can get me seeds from the garden, I can continue to work on the cure. Maybe with my magic..." She trailed off, afraid to even say the words out loud in fear that she would fail once again.

"You'll have success," Gray finished for her. "And you will." The corner of his lips curled into a crooked smile. Pride resonated through the bond, and Lea's chest and cheeks warmed in response. Her love for Gray grew at his belief in her. *How did I get so lucky?*

"King Tanad, can you spare a scout to gather seeds for my mate?" Gray asked, his face returning to its usual stern and matter-of-fact expression. "You'll find them in the garden in the clearing where Azalea had her vision. I assume you know where that is?"

Tanad snapped his fingers, and a soldier walked through the curtains. His uniform was fitted and was a deep navy that Lea thought resembled what the deepest depths of the ocean would look like. The king gave instructions to the soldier on how to get to the clearing, then asked Lea if there was any particular way the flowers needed to be harvested.

"I'm not sure." She answered, tilting her head and picturing the wreath from home in her mind. "I've always pulled the seeds from the center of the flowers just before I planted them, but I might need to try different combinations to see if it changes anything. If you're able, it'd be best to pull the root of the vines from the ground, and bring them back as whole as possible. And carry as many as you can."

The soldier bowed deeply to her, then to Tanad, before leaving.

With the business of the moonflowers behind them, Gray turned back to the king. "When would you like to leave to reinforce the wall?"

"By morning, if possible," Tanad plucked the skulls from the wood as if he couldn't stand the visual reminder of the death of his people.

"I see." Gray and Erik shared a look. "There is, of course, another reason that we're here."

"Yes, yes. Eudora." Tanad waved his hand flippantly. "She knows you're here, of course, and says that she'll call on you when the stars tell her the time is right. You know how she is, Commander. And you know better than to question her methods."

Gray's eyes darkened, shadows slithering from his fingertips. "We cannot wait for her fickle games to play out. I need to break the curse. Now. Certainly before we return to Bearswillow. And what if the stars tell her to find me while we're gone?"

"Then fortunately, for us, it is not *you* who Eudora wishes to speak to. Our journey will not affect you getting the answers you seek. In fact, it may even be beneficial for you to be absent when Eudora calls upon your mate."

"She refuses to speak to me?" Storm clouds suddenly gathered over the beautiful ocean, the glistening waves dulling as the sun was blocked out.

"She's agreed to speak to Azalea. I'm certain dear Lea will relay the information you are asking for."

Gray looked at Lea warily, his shadows floating up and wrapping around her protectively. "I refuse to leave my mate alone with a witch who demands unreasonable bargains and speaks in riddles. *I* need to learn how to break the curse so I can kill my father. *I* will pay Eudora's price for that information. Not Azalea," he said through clenched teeth. "I am the one who demands answers."

"The witch said how to end the curse is not the answer you *need*," Tanad bridged his fingers together. "That there are other questions that must first be asked."

The underside of Lea's arm tingled, her moonflower birthmark burning as if it was on fire, and she tried to rub the sting away. *Odd*, Lea thought as she sent healing energy to the area. "We need to know if I am the one from the prophecy," she said, still rubbing at the sensitive skin. "If I'm Queen Emmaline's granddaughter, and the true heir to Desia."

King Tanad sat back in his chair, his eyes widening in disbelief. "If that is your question, my darling girl, you need only ask me. This is not the first time we have met, Azalea. Nor will it be the first time that you have met Eudora."

CHAPTER 50

LEA

"What the hell do you mean?" Gray said, jumping from his seat to pace in front of the table, his fingers flexing and extending as he tried to control his shadows.

"I apologize, Commander, but I assumed you knew. The resemblance between them is uncanny, is it not? And as for her magic," Tanad tapped his temple, "it is identical to Queen Emmaline's. It's remarkable, actually, how it feels almost exactly the same."

"Are you referring to the fact that Queen Emmaline had both day and night magic?"

"I'm referring to the fact that Queen Emmaline *and* your mate have primary magic. Magic of the earth—and the sky and the wind and the sea. Power that can create just as it can destroy. It is the magic of the gods, capable of more than we could possibly imagine. Though, as it appears that your mate has been blessed by the goddess," he waved about her body, "her primary magic is tied to the moon. To the darkness."

Lea's mouth hung open, and the room spun as she tried to process the king's words. She'd met the king before, as well as the witch who prophesied the downfall of the Black King? And what did he mean primary magic? Wouldn't that be something she knew about?

But as she dissected the types of power she could feel building inside her, several pieces of the puzzle of who she was clicked into place. She knew she had day magic, as well as magic of the night. The primary magic must be what was hidden so deeply beneath the floor in her chest, the magic that had allowed her to save Queen Emmaline's baby, to force its heart to continue beating until Adelaide removed her from her mother's womb. It was the magic that had rocked through her entire being, the dark, raw, unruly, and wild power that felt like it might consume her whole. It didn't feel as if it could create. It felt like death and destruction, and the more she used her shadows, the more accessible that wicked magic felt.

But what was that small bit of darkness inside her that felt wrong? The foreign shadows that mixed in with her own night magic didn't have the same feeling of pure, unadulterated power like her primary magic did? They felt different. *Other.* Somewhere mixed within them was something that didn't seem to belong to her.

"I don't understand," Lea croaked. With another wave of his hand, a cup of fragrant floral tea appeared in Lea's shaking hands, the sea-horse-patterned china clattering in a high-pitched jingle.

"My dear, not only did I know your grandmother, but I knew your mother. Your birth mother."

Lea nearly dropped her tea as her breath was stolen from her lungs. "My birth mother was *here*?" Lea couldn't believe it. She'd known Emmaline's maid had fled to Calir, but she'd never thought they would have come to the castle.

"She grew up here, actually. I can still picture the day Delphine showed up with a brand new baby in her arms, asking for our help. I hired her as a maid, and she lived here until her death many years ago. She never told me who your mother really was, but I knew. She had the same piercing blue eyes as you. The same eyes as Emmaline."

Lea was dumbfounded. Her birth mother had walked these halls? Had grown from a child to a woman within these walls? "So she had primary magic as well?"

"No. Your mother's power was something different. It was odd, and exceedingly rare. Your mother had the gift of *life*."

"Impossible. No one can create life," argued Erik as Gray sat back, assessing the king.

"Not create, necessarily. She couldn't heal. Couldn't set bones or kill infection, but she could grab a soul locked in the reaper's grasp and hold it at bay. She couldn't bring back the dead, but she could hold death off long enough for the healers to do their work. It was remarkable, actually. She helped many soldiers survive what should've been fatal wounds, saved countless mothers during birth, as well as children suffering from what should have been deathly high fevers."

Lea couldn't breathe. She actually felt like she was suffocating as her heart beat rapidly in her chest. It was exactly what she had done for her birth mother the night Emmaline had been murdered.

"The oddest thing about it, though," said the king thoughtfully, "was that the magic did not match her essence."

"What do you mean, her essence?" Gray walked behind Lea, placing a hand on her back and pushing soothing energy into her chest. Her heart slowed a bit.

"Usually, one's magic feels as if it is a part of them. Ingrained wholly and completely within them as much as their blood and bone. But with your mother, it felt foreign in her body, as if she was controlling someone else's magic. I've never felt anything like it before." King Tanad took a long sip of his tea, then looked at Lea. "Not until I saw you today."

"Me?" Lea asked. "I don't have that power." But did she? Memories of ripping Queen Emmaline's baby from death's grasp flashed through her mind.

Lea shook her head, overwhelmed. It was as if the king could read her mind. "Don't you? I feel it in you now, just as I felt it in your birth mother all the years she lived within these walls."

Lea shook her head, overwhelmed. "I still don't quite understand," she said, rubbing her eyes and sending healing magic to the base of her neck where the beginnings of a headache thrummed. "So my birth mother, she was Fae?"

"Half. Queen Emmaline's mate, your grandfather, was human."

The shadows floating around Gray's body faltered. "Gregory was human?"

"He was," Tanad confirmed. "But with his life tied to Emmaline's, he lived and aged along with her until her death."

Lea fiddled with her hair. "If I really descend from Queen Emmaline, why am I human? It doesn't add up."

"It's possible your birth father was human as well. Your genes may simply have been diluted to be more human than Fae, my dear. It is no different than inheriting the color of your eyes or hair. But do not be mistaken. You do have Fae blood inside you. I can *feel* it."

Lea felt as if her brain was vibrating. She had Fae blood, if only a little. It was as if every question she asked pulled at the stray thread of a sweater that was her identity, unraveling the very core of who she thought she was.

"It changes nothing, Little Flower," Gray soothed. "Thousands of humans within the kingdom have Fae blood. Without being full-blooded, it's difficult to tell. Think of Emma. She is half Fae, and even then, you didn't know."

Lea took a deep breath, needing to move on with the conversation. Later, she could dissect who and what she was and wasn't, but not now. Not in front of everyone.

"It still doesn't make sense. If my birth mother grew up here, how did I end up with Adelaide? And what was that cottage across the border?"

"*That* is a question for Eudora. All I know is that I was instructed to bring you to Bearswillow and leave you with the village healer. Eudora said the fate of our kingdoms depended on it."

"You?" Lea asked in complete disbelief. "You're the one who left me there?"

"Only after I read Adelaide's power and confirmed she was capable of hiding your magic and keeping you safe. You are more like her than you might believe."

"My birth mother or Adelaide?"

"Both. The beauty and loyalty of your mother, Evangeline. The kind soul and gentle spirit of Adelaide. They are both a part of you, intertwined in a way that cannot be unraveled."

"That was her name?" Lea asked breathlessly.

Tanad's eyes softened as Lea's filled with tears. "It was. Chosen by Delphine."

"Was I born here?" Lea looked out at the sea. Had she come from another kingdom? One so very different from the one she'd called home for so long?

"No. Your mother disappeared one day, crossed the border back into Desia and did not return for years. Not until the day she showed up, just as Delphine had, with worry on her face and a tiny baby in her arms. I didn't know you by the name Azalea back then. I called you the name given to you by your birth mother. Hope."

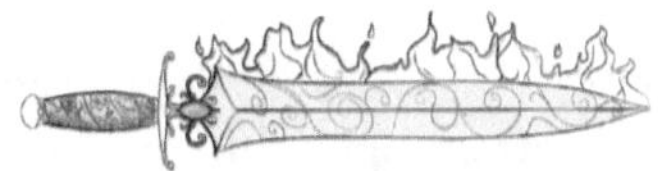

Lea sat in shock as they finished the rest of the meeting. She wasn't sure when it had happened, but at some point she'd ended up in Gray's lap, leaning against him with her head on his shoulder, completely numb. Gray's feelings and constant reassurance pulsed through their bond, *almost* as if he could speak directly into her mind—*You are the same person you've always been. You are mine. You are loved*—even so, she couldn't help but feel like a stranger in her own body. Long ago, she'd had a different name and lived in a different kingdom. It was no wonder

Bearswillow had always felt so small. She'd traveled the continent and lived a different life before she'd even left infancy.

Lea heard Gray, Erik, and King Tanad discussing building their armies, combining them, where to post their troops, how many to post, and where they thought they might find the biggest advantages for battle. They talked about how to prevent the Lonely Death from spreading between their soldiers, and on and on they went until their conversation became complete background noise.

She was pulled from the enormity of her own thoughts when King Tanad waved his hand over the table and it flattened. Shiny golden plates appeared on ornate pearl place settings, one for each of them. In the middle of the table, several large platters and bowls appeared. There was some sort of citrus-crusted fish, the heads still attached with orange slices laying on top as a garnish. An octopus sat on a large wooden plate, and next to it was a bowl that looked suspiciously like seaweed. As platters of colorful roasted vegetables and fresh fruit were passed around, Gray filled her plate.

He leaned over and spoke quietly in her ear. "Please, Little Flower, eat something. You need your strength. It's been days since we've had a real meal."

Lea knew he was right. When she'd looked in the mirror after changing into her new clothes—a soft cropped shirt and pants set that matched Janelle's except for its white color—she'd noticed how thin she looked. Her ribs were now pronounced and her cheeks hollow. She needed to eat in order to have the energy to train as much as possible before they returned to Bearswillow.

Offering Gray a tentative smile, Lea took a few bites. The food was delicious, but it didn't sit right in her stomach, turning to rubber in her mouth as she chewed. Continuing to push the fish around her plate, she listened to Gray ask Tanad questions while Janelle made fun of Erik for shamelessly requesting for a fourth helping. When dessert was offered, Gray placed a hand on Lea's shoulder and stood.

"If you don't mind, King Tanad, I think my mate and I will retire for the evening. If we're to leave in the morning, I'd like to spend some time with her." Gray reached forward to shake Tanad's hand. "I appreciate your hospitality."

The king rose, clasping Gray's hand and shaking firmly. "Of course." Tanad reached for Lea, his wrinkled fingers wrapping around hers. "I hope I didn't upset you, Azalea. The truth is a difficult thing to hear, especially when it's hidden itself for so long. But remember, my gift is reading people. Their abilities. Their powers. You are capable of so much more than you know."

"Thank you," Lea said softly, though she didn't feel very thankful at the moment. She felt overwhelmed. As if she'd said it out loud, King Tanad squeezed her hands tighter.

"You may be the strongest among us, but there is no shame in feeling weak." Tanad lowered his head to meet her eyes. "Allow your mate to help you. That is why you were given to each other, you know. You weren't meant to face this life alone. Let him take your pain, if only for a little while."

He leaned forward and kissed her on the cheek, a surprisingly grandfatherly gesture that made Lea yearn for the comfort of family. It had been so long since she felt true familial affection, and she hadn't realized just how much she'd missed it.

King Tanad gave Gray a long look. "Take it from an old man, Commander. Do not take your love for granted, nor the bond. We are on the verge of war. I cannot think of a single soul who doesn't yearn to know that they will never be alone again, whether in this life, *or* the next."

CHAPTER 51

GRAY

King Tanad's words echoed through Gray's mind with every step he took as he led Lea back to their room. *Never, alone, in life, or death. Never, alone, in life, or death:* a taunting cadence that threatened to make him consider he was being foolish. Even if Azalea was sent into the flaming pits of the underworld when she died, Gray intended to follow her there. There was no scenario, not on this earth or beyond the veil, that he would allow himself to be separated from her.

He flinched at the thought, his heart kicking into an abnormal rhythm as he imagined being without her. It was as natural as a star crashing to earth when it belonged in the sky. That is to say, it wasn't natural at all. It would be like living without his own heart, his own lungs or brain. It was impossible. He could no longer live without those vital organs than he could live without his mate.

Tonight had been another night of revelations, more truths that stacked on Lea's already heavy shoulders, the weight threatening to crush her completely. It was in the way Lea carried herself, as if her bones were made of rubber, no longer hard enough to support the weight of her body. Gray could feel the doubt threatening to consume her, that intrusive thought that she wasn't sure who she was anymore. He could sense what she was thinking. *Was she Hope? And not just by name, but the last hope for her kingdom?*

Why had Evangeline asked the king to take her away and abandon her in a tiny village to never be seen again? It didn't seem as if she'd been in imminent danger or on the run. No. She had shown up and asked a king to deposit her infant child on a hill in a small town, never to be heard from again.

Gray knew it wasn't fair that he was now taking yet another choice away from Lea: the choice of whether or not to fulfill the mate bond and attach their lives permanently together. Did they not share the same bond? Was it not the same tether that linked their souls together?

It was unfathomable to Gray to think that anyone could love another as much as he loved his mate, but it wasn't fair to think that Lea didn't feel the same way—that the thought of living on without him would not be a life worth living at all. He was certain that she wouldn't want to go on without him, either. Was there any way to justify taking that choice away from her?

And still, the idea of cementing her premature death, of tempting fate during a war unlike this kingdom had ever seen before—that risk terrified him. Utterly and devastatingly. The skin below his collarbone warmed, pulsing and burning as if telling him the answer. He had never felt so torn before. Not when he had to decide between keeping his mate safe and giving into what his soul longed for.

Gray opened the door to their quarters and Lea moved onto the balcony almost mechanically, as if she was so lost in thought that her feet were moving without her permission. Or maybe the sight of the ocean gave her some clarity. Gray wasn't sure, but what he did know was that he needed to make a decision. He couldn't keep Lea in the in-between of waiting to see if he would consider her words from earlier, or if he would change his mind.

"Lea, we need to talk about—"

"What else happens when you seal the bond?" Lea's voice came out stronger than Gray expected, but her question took him off guard. Is that all she was thinking of right now? Was that what was the heaviest on her heart after everything she had learned from Tanad?

"Well, our bond would become stronger. We'd be better able to sense what the other is feeling. I'm sure you've noticed right now that the farther we are away from each other, the harder it is to read my emotions?"

Lea nodded, chewing on her lip.

"We would also be able to speak directly into each other's minds. Distance would affect how easily we could communicate, just like it does now, but we would be able to be further apart and still feel each other. You'd live as long as I do, age as I age. Essentially, we would be one person. I could lend you my strength, and you could pull power from me if you needed to without touching me. "

"Could you take away my emotions?" Lea asked, tears welling in her eyes that she wiped away quickly with the heel of her hand. Her nose was red, and her lip trembled, but Gray felt the way she swallowed down the desperation rising up her throat.

His heart shattered in his chest, crumbling into a million pieces. "Oh Azalea." Softly and tenderly, he trailed his fingers along her cheek before placing his palm firmly against the side of her face. "I wouldn't be able to take them away completely, no. But I *could* ease them for you. Share the burden, just like Tanad said."

"Please?" Lea's voice broke, the heaviness of that sound piercing through Gray's willpower to deny the one thing he wanted more than anything in the world. The one thing that his body and soul had been begging for him to do since the moment he'd realized Lea was his mate. The urge that only got stronger once she confessed her feelings for him as well.

"Please," she said the word again, less a question and more of a plea. "Do it. Take the pain away. I'm so tired, Gray. Please. Where you go, I go. You told me before that I need to ask for help when I need it. I'm asking." She closed her eyes. "I'm *begging*."

"Okay," Gray breathed, his shadows waking up and reaching for her. It was as if that one word gave permission to his primal desires, his magic bursting from his chest, trying to bury itself inside of his mate and join with hers.

"Okay?" Lea's eyes snapped up to meet his, pure shock in every line of her tired face.

"Watching you hurt like this might be worse than you following me beyond the veil." He tilted her head back and threaded his fingers through the hair at the nape of her neck. "I love you. Wholly and desperately. So... Okay."

Lea sagged into him, collapsing in relief against his chest.

In one fluid motion, Gray lifted her beneath her shoulders and legs and carried her onto the balcony, where a bed had replaced the couches and chairs that had been there this afternoon. He'd known it would happen. It was the same every time he stayed at this castle. He imagined that many people liked to sleep outside in the fresh air to get some relief from the stifling heat of being indoors. But still, looking at the plush, king-sized bed, he couldn't help but feel that it was put there by the gods just for them.

He imagined it was their blessing, and a promise the gods would help protect them. Without breaking eye contact, Gray laid Lea down on the bed, raising one hand above his head, and swiping sideways. Immediately, every cloud from the sky vanished. Every tiny wisp, every bit of fog. Never in the history of the universe had there been such a clear night. Millions of stars winked at them as if announcing their approval.

They reflected back at him from Lea's blue eyes, and Gray brushed the hair back from her forehead so he could see them completely. He wiped the remnants of a tear from her cheek before kissing the trails of salt away until he reached her mouth.

A sigh fell against his lips, slipping between them and into his lungs. It was a plea, a prayer. *More.* And his control snapped. Now that he'd made up his mind to seal the bond, there was nothing he wanted more.

His body craved it in a way he could barely comprehend as he grew thick and hard, his muscles taut and desire heating his blood.

As his lips trailed her neck, sucking and nibbling, he ripped away the thin scraps of fabric the people of Calir called clothes until there was nothing covering Lea's skin. Gray stood, drinking in the sight of his mate naked before him, her hair glowing in the moonlight and her eyes dark with need. Her chest rose and fell rapidly as her gaze followed his fingers as they deftly unbuttoned the top button of his shirt.

It wasn't fast enough.

Quickly and fluidly, he reached behind his neck and pulled the shirt over his head as he ordered his shadows to unlace his boots. He kicked them off, then removed his trousers.

Lea began to sit up, reaching toward him, but he pushed her back down with a long, inky black trail of darkness. He wanted, needed, to look at her. He needed to be in control, to give her every part of him, body and soul. His shadows caressed her body up to her chin, gently holding her head against the bed before sliding down her chest, her stomach, pinning her down.

Lifting her leg and pulling her to the edge, he knelt on the stone balcony, glancing up at the sky once more to ensure that not a wisp of clouds remained. He pressed a kiss to the inside of her calf, just above her ankle, and the moan that left Lea's throat made him almost lose all restraint.

Slowly, tenderly, he worked his way up, kissing a path up to her thigh. Lea reached for him again, grabbing his face and trying to pull him higher, but he wrapped his shadows around her hands and raised them back above her head.

"I've dreamed of this moment for years." Gray rasped as he continued to kiss his way up her thigh. "Gone through every scenario in my mind of exactly how I would make you mine. I *will* take my time. You will not rush me, Little Flower." His eyes darkened as he lowered his chin once more and resumed kissing her soft skin, starting at the top of her other leg and working his way down. Teasing her, tasting her.

And gods above, did she taste sweet.

Lea didn't argue, her breaths turning to pants as she writhed beneath his touch. His palm splayed across her stomach, joining his shadows to hold her down as his lips reached the back of her calf.

"I want you, Gray," Lea urged, her arms pulling at the shadowy restraints pinning her down.

It was too soon. He wanted to taste every inch of her skin, spend hours building up her pleasure before finally giving in and pushing inside her.

"I need you," Lea moaned. "Please," she cried out, arching her back.

Whatever semblance of control Gray was hanging onto snapped, his eyes darkening and a growl ripping from his chest. He couldn't deny her. "Whatever you need. Forever," Calling more shadows, he spread her legs wider as his tongue found her center, swirling firmly against her. Lea arched into his mouth.

"Gods!" she cried out, throwing her head back.

"I do not share a bed with the gods," Gray said as he slowly pushed a finger inside her.

"Gray," she moaned as he swirled his tongue and crooked his finger.

"Better," he growled, adding another finger as he began to push in and out, trailing kisses up to her navel, then her breasts.

Electricity crackled in the air, his skin becoming impossibly warm. Gray raised his head to meet Lea's eyes.

What—

"Don't stop," Lea cried out, love and need flooding the bond so strongly it would have taken his breath away if it hadn't already been stolen by the sight of his mate.

Shadows surrounded her body, twisting and floating through the air and along the ground between the flames that flickered from her skin. Jet black fire filled with ash and soot mixed with red and orange sparks, warming the cool air blowing off the sea. And inside of the tornado of magic, his mate arched and moaned, her eyes closed tight, completely unaware of the display of magic she was creating.

Gray smothered the flames beneath her with his darkness, forcing a layer of shadows between her skin and the singed bedding below.

"You are the most stunning creature," Gray breathed, his heart thumping erratically at the display of pure power and raw sexuality. He lowered his lips to her throat, needing to feel the intensity of the heat of her fire. He wanted all of her. Every last piece of what made her who she was, but as his mouth touched her skin, the flames moved for him, warming his lips but not burning them. Everywhere his hands wandered, the flames parted, allowing him access to every inch of her glowing flesh. It was as if the very essence of her power knew that he belonged to her and refused to hurt him.

It was wild and beautiful, intense in a way that made him vibrate with need. Her magic was right. He was hers, wholly and irrevocably. And she was his. Gray was unable to restrain himself as he lined up his thick, impossibly hard length against her entrance, staring into her eyes as he pressed inside his mate slowly. Lea cried out as a groan ripped from his throat, the mate bond becoming so taut it was *almost* painful.

The balcony shook as Gray began to move. He released Lea's arms from his shadows as her nails drug down his back, meeting him with every thrust, her own shadows wrapping around them like a gentle breeze.

Their movements quickly became frenzied, teeth clashing and lips swollen as Gray moved faster, deeper. He lifted her leg, angling her to allow him to fill her completely, and gods—he could feel the very center of her.

Gray couldn't tell where he ended and his mate began, their bodies so entangled that he felt as if they were merging into one.

The ground shook, small pieces of sandstone cascading from the walls of the castle as the bed crashed to the ground, the legs collapsing as shadows and flames exploded out from their joined bodies. Gray barely even noticed.

The blanket caught on fire, and Gray ripped it off, throwing it onto the stone of the balcony as he rocked back onto his knees, pulling Lea along with him.

Her legs wrapped around his waist, straddling him as he pulled her against his chest. She began to rock, sliding up and down, but Gray pinned her hips to his. He needed more. Impossibly more.

Lea threw her head back as he continued to thrust, her breasts sliding against him as the wind blew harder. Enormous, powerful gusts that ripped the curtains from the rods and put out the fire now trailing from beneath Lea and Gray's bodies across the balcony floor.

Lea's words became nonsensical, professions of love turning into moans of pure pleasure as he moved in and out of her, increasing his speed. He couldn't stop. Couldn't slow down. Nothing had ever felt so perfect, so *right*.

Gray's magic felt as if it was going to snap, escaping from his body and wrapping around them, his shadows mixing with Lea's shadows and flames, swirling and combining with them in an enormous, swirling mass of darkness.

As Lea's walls tightened around him, her back arching, Gray stilled, spilling himself as he cried out Lea's name. His mate's name.

Their magic detonated, exploding outward in a flash of sparkling light that made the rush of day and night magic look like nothing more than a sunset on a cloudy day.

A searing pain burned beneath Gray's collarbone as absolute ecstasy pulsed through the rest of his body. It was unlike anything he had ever felt before, not just physically, but in his soul.

Thunder roared above the ocean, and the ground continued to tremble. Joy and love and pain and confusion crashed through the bond, and Gray pulled everything but the happiest emotions into himself, sharing the burden of his mate's pain as the wind finally slowed and the earth stilled.

□Lea's eyes opened, and Gray laid them back down onto the mattress, bracing his elbows on either side of her head as he claimed her mouth. "I love you," he whispered, regret churning in his gut as he realized that he had wasted too many days, *weeks*, squandering away this gift out of fear. But it no longer mattered. They belonged to each other, never to be separated. Not even by death.

CHAPTER 52

GRAY

Getting out of bed that next morning was the hardest thing Gray had ever done. They had come together again as the sun began peeking over the horizon, touching and exploring each other as if it was the first time. He'd ensured every cloud in the sky was gone, and as the mating bond finally snapped fully into place, the earth beneath them had once again rumbled and the wind had rushed across their skin. And as they found their release, the sunrise had exploded in the most vibrant display of beauty he had ever seen.

The pink sky had rivaled that of any rose that had ever bloomed, the red and orange streaks as saturated as fruit picked directly from the tree. It had bathed them in a golden glow, causing the mate mark beneath Lea's collarbone to almost shimmer. A moon and stars. *His* moon and stars, marking her as his for eternity. She would live as he did. Age as he aged. And that mark was proof. The sight was so beautiful and the thought so reassuring, Gray couldn't help but lean down and kiss it.

It's beautiful. He spoke directly into her mind. *Almost as beautiful as you.*

Lea jumped, lifting her head to meet his gaze. "Did you say that out loud?" she asked with a smile so broad and full of joy that Gray now considered that moment the most beautiful sight he'd ever seen.

I did not, he said, once again into her mind, and Lea sat up, almost urgently. She closed her eyes and scrunched her nose.

We did it. Lea's sweet tone resonated in his own head.

"Yes, we did," Gray laughed with an equally enormous smile as he pulled Lea back down and kissed her forehead. He turned her to face the sunrise and laid behind her, wrapping her firmly in his arms with her head tucked beneath his chin. Instinctually, Gray knew they'd never see another sunrise like this, and he wanted them to savor it, to remember every moment. He'd been so wrong—so utterly foolish. Now that the mating bond was complete, he felt whole, thoroughly at peace with his decision. He'd only been half a man before, had only seen in muted colors and felt the world as if through scratchy gloves.

But now? The fresh air smelled like a block of salt mixed with a cool breeze and clean water. His heartbeat was different—steadier, and perfectly in tune with the pulse of the woman lying next to him. The stars were brighter and the sunrise more saturated and his soul at peace. The restlessness that he hadn't even realized lived in his bones was gone, leaving him content in a way he had never felt before.

"How do you feel?" Gray asked into Lea's hair.

"I feel different. Like I'm someone new." She closed her eyes again, and a fire appeared, floating in the air. It was the size of her fist, and it bounced around the balcony like a ball. "My light feels easier to access. Like it's buzzing closer to the surface."

"And what about your shadows?" Gray prodded. It hadn't escaped his notice that she'd avoided using them as often as her fire, only calling on them when it had been absolutely necessary.

"I can't quite explain my shadows." Lea chewed on her lip. "There's a darkness in there that feels like it belongs to me, and then there's something in there, mixed in with my shadows, that feels foreign, like I'm not meant to wield it. And then, even deeper, hidden beneath everything else, there is pure, black power. I think that's the primary magic King Tanad mentioned. It feels wild and electric—almost painful. Like nothing and everything all at once. And the more I use my shadows, the more that magic seems to seep into my chest. That's what I used when I saved Queen Emmaline's daughter." Lea looked off into the sunrise. "Do you think Eudora will have answers?"

"I think she will. For a price, of course," Gray grumbled. He didn't want to talk about her right now, didn't want that manipulative, secretive witch to taint this moment.

Lea rolled over abruptly, pushing him back excitedly so that she could examine his chest. "I can't believe I forgot about the mark!" Her eyes crinkled as she leaned down and kissed just below his collarbone. "I thought it was supposed to be a sun?"

Gray's eyebrows lowered. "Well, you do have both day and night magic. I guess it could be either, or both."

He tilted his head down to look at the spot just above his heart, wondering what mark he'd been given to show the world who he belonged to. But to his surprise, it wasn't a sun, or a moon, or the stars, or even the wind. No. In place of the small flower that had sat within the tattoo of Lea's mountains was a moonflower, one that matched Lea's birthmark perfectly. It was the exact same size and an identical shape, as if they had been cut from the same pattern before it had been imprinted upon their skin. Though Lea's coloring was different, more the typical brown of a birthmark rather than the dark black of ink, they were a perfect pair.

"What does it mean?" Lea asked breathlessly.

"I'm not sure. Maybe it's because of what King Tanad said? Maybe it's the primary magic? That it can create *and* destroy, just like the moonflowers are fabled to be able to do?"

Lea's forehead scrunched. "I don't know why, but this feels like an omen. You're marked with the flower that I've failed to grow and use. The cure for your father's greed that I can't seem to master."

"I'm sure it's nothing, Little Flower. I think it's an appropriate mark, considering everything. It's unique, just like us. Maybe it's saying we're the key to defeating my father. Maybe we'll be the cure." Gray tucked

Lea's tousled hair behind her ear and gently pulled her lip from between her teeth with his thumb. "Hey—no more worrying. Not today. We've had enough days full of fear and uncertainty, and even more to come."

"Okay," Lea agreed, pressing her lips together. "Today we'll just be happy." They laid together for another several minutes until the last of the pink disappeared from the sky. Gray sighed, disappointment stabbing in his gut.

"You have to go now, don't you?" Lea questioned reluctantly.

"Unfortunately, I do," he agreed. "The only thing that could get me out of this bed this morning is making sure that the Lonely Death doesn't spread further into the kingdom. King Tanad is very powerful. With both of our magic combined, I believe we can make the barriers strong enough to delay the Lonely Death breaking through, if not stop it completely."

"What more could your father want? Why spread the disease to another kingdom? He doesn't even use the power he has now. Not really," Lea said.

"Absolute control. He wants the world to fear him. And he's getting his wish."

"Then I guess you should go." Lea sat up. Scrunching her nose again, Lea grabbed his hands. Gray felt a tug at the bond, something taking root in his consciousness. He tilted his head, waiting.

But I'll be checking in, she finally said in his mind. She beamed, and Gray couldn't help it. He had to kiss her, to feel that smile against his lips and cement it into his memory.

I'd expect nothing less, he answered.

Lea started to get up with Gray, but he gently pushed her back down. "Rest. We didn't get much last night. Erik will be training with you today, and you'll need your strength," he said. It didn't take much convincing for Lea to lie back down, closing her eyes and glowing with contentment in the early morning sun.

Gray quickly washed himself under the rain shower ceiling and grabbed his weapons, adding a second sword across his back. With only one thing left to do—check in with Erik and inform him he wished for the girls to start their training today—he left the room and knocked on his door, but there was no answer.

He knocked once more, louder. But all that met him was complete silence.

Where could he possibly be? Unless... Turning on his heel, Gray walked directly to Janelle's room, pounding his fist against the golden entrance. "You better be in there, Erik!" he shouted, leaning against the doorframe.

A shuffling sounded behind the door. "Give me a minute!" Erik's booming voice called before the door swung open, his body blocking the room behind him. Every other time Gray had ever knocked, Erik invited him in without hesitation. Gray smiled cockily. "I guess we have a guest?" Gray leaned to the side, trying to see into the room. "Or actually, *you* are the guest?"

"This better be important," Erik grumbled as he took a small step sideways, blocking Gray's view once again.

"It is. But before I tell you why I'm here, I'm going to warn you. Treat her well. If you mess this up, or hurt Janelle in any way, my mate is going to be furious. And I'd rather not disturb her after the long night we had." Gray pulled the collar of his shirt aside, showing the moonflower mark on his chest.

Erik almost glowed with joy, and Gray didn't think that his friend would be happier even if he had found his own mate.

"Congratulations, Brother," he said, with a nod before embracing him firmly and slapping him on the back several times.

Gray used the opportunity of Erik's distraction to peek into the room, and was pleased when he saw a blonde and purple head peeking out from underneath the thick comforter.

Erik pulled back and shook Gray's hand. "It's about time you listened to me. What changed your mind?"

"Lea was hurting, and I realized I could help take away her pain," Gray stated matter-of-factly. "I'm ashamed I didn't do it sooner."

"It came from a good place." Erik shrugged.

Gray turned serious, his smile fading. "I'm leaving with Tanad to help reinforce his magic at the border. I trust that I don't have to tell you that you're in charge of Azalea's safety while I'm gone."

"That goes without saying." Erik crossed his arms in front of his chest.

"In addition, I'd like you to begin her training. And it wouldn't hurt for Janelle and Emma to train as well. Noah should train with Tanad's men."

"Got it. Anything specific you'd like me to focus on?" Erik asked.

"Controlling her magic. Lea's willingness to use her shadows, as well as physical strengthening and hand to hand combat. They all need to get stronger and learn how to use weaponry effectively. Also, shielding and competency on a horse. As soon as the borders are reinforced and King Tanad and I agree on the best strategy to prepare to fight my father, and as soon as Eudora will see us so I can learn how to reverse the spell I asked her to perform, we will return to the rebels in Bearswillow. I'd like them to be as prepared as possible before we make that journey back."

"I understand. Anything else?"

"No. That will be all," Gray said curtly, with a firm nod before he turned to walk away. The door had started to close when Gray stopped abruptly and turned around.

"Erik?" Gray said warmly. "I'm happy for you."

CHAPTER 53

ERIK

Despite what Gray seemed to believe, Erik and Janelle had done little more last night than talk well into the morning hours with casual touches and tension-filled proximity to one another. He had thought, at one point when Janelle had scooted closer to him and their faces had only been inches apart, about leaning in and seeing if her lips tasted like the berries that had colored the ends of her hair, but something inside had told him to wait. It was a feeling he'd never experienced before, but somehow he knew with certainty that now was not the time.

It was as if he'd known exactly what she needed without her having to tell him, and so he had simply laid there for hours with his arm curled under his head, talking to her about whatever crossed her mind.

As morning grew closer and Janelle's eyes grew heavier, Erik suspected that her rambling had been her way to try to avoid sleep and, along with it, the nightmares that had haunted her for the past several days. Wordlessly, he'd turned her around and tucked her against his front, pulling the covers snugly around them. It amazed him how quickly she relaxed, neither of them saying a word as they both drifted off to sleep. Looking at her now, Erik hoped that there would never be a day that she would wake anywhere else.

Erik got dressed, wanting to allow Janelle as much rest as possible before they needed to start their training. Breakfast appeared on the table, fruit and various types of bread with jelly and butter, and Erik made a plate, bringing it to the bed and setting it next to Janelle.

"Good morning." He brushed her hair away from her face, and Janelle moaned into the pillow, rolling over and pulling the covers up over her head higher. "I thought you might like to eat before we trained."

With a huff, Janelle struggled into a sitting position, her hair sticking out erratically.

"Train how, exactly?" Janelle asked as she tried to smooth her hair behind her ears.

"Running, combat, and we definitely need to work on your healing magic. Lea will need to work on her magic as well."

"Did you just say running?" Janelle groaned as she laid back down and threw the blanket over her head.

"Why, yes, I did." Erik pulled the covers off of her and popped down on the bed, grabbing a roll and stuffing it into his mouth. Sometime in the night, Janelle had kicked off her pajama bottoms. Her curvy legs were bare, and the hint of something lacy peeked out from the oversized shirt she'd borrowed from him.

"Eat up," he coughed before standing and walking to Emma's room. Needing a moment to calm himself, he left Janelle alone to fume in peace about their upcoming exercise.

Emma looked far more rested when she answered the door, but her eyes were still haunted. The shadow of something otherworldly and tragic seemed to push down on her shoulders. But despite the fact that she was obviously still struggling, she gave him a warm welcome.

"Erik! Thank you for sending dinner to my room last night. I filled my belly and then slept the night through. Except, was there an earthquake this morning?" She tilted her head.

"I guess you could call it that," Erik said nonchalantly, not wanting to ruin Lea's surprise. "I came to tell you to prepare to train. We need to get you all in shape for battle. And I need to assess your magic, figure out how to best help you recharge."

"Well, actually," Emma walked to the table where her own breakfast sat and began picking at a croissant anxiously, tearing it into tiny pieces and avoiding Erik's eyes, "I searched out King Tanad last night, before you all met with him. I wanted to find out more about my abilities. He said that he doesn't know of anyone in his kingdom who can see what I do, but he's granted me access to his library. I'd like to spend my time while we're here researching, seeing what I can find out."

"I'm under strict orders from Gray to train you all in combat." Erik walked over to the table, placing his hand on Emma's trembling fingers.

Emma looked up at him with big eyes and allowed him to see the full extent of her inner turmoil. Her face looked far more gaunt when she stopped smiling—her skin more sallow, and the shadows beneath her eyes far more pronounced. "I can't fight with you," Emma confessed.

"What do you mean? You don't want to be part of the rebellion?" Erik grabbed one of her croissants.

"No, it's not that. I absolutely want a better kingdom, and for the king and prince to be overthrown. But I can't *fight* with you."

Erik suddenly understood. "You don't want to kill."

"I can't." Emma placed her head in her hands, taking several slow, deep breaths before continuing. "No one else has to look at the soul of the person they killed once they're dead. No one else has to hear them cry for their mothers or scream for help. I can't take people's lives. Not when I have to see the aftermath. But maybe, if I can find out more about my abilities, I can find a way to use it to our advantage."

"I still think it would be wise for you to learn how to defend yourself. Not to mention being able to heal yourself." Erik understood. He really did. But regardless of Emma's fears, she would be safer with a basic understanding of how to use all aspects of her magic.

"Erik, I can't be there, not during the battle. Not when the souls of what will probably be hundreds of men and women are wandering around, begging for help that I can't give them. I need to find another way to be valuable."

Erik very rarely felt sad. Of course, when he lost his mother, he had grieved, or when he heard about another town infected with the Lonely Death. But looking at Emma, Erik felt true sorrow. He couldn't imagine her burden, and he wasn't going to make her face it today. If Gray had a problem with it, he could take it up with him once he returned.

"Then, I hope you enjoy the safety of the library," Erik said warmly, grabbing another few rolls from her plate before turning to the door. "Hopefully you don't see my soul later this morning after I make Janelle and Lea run to the sea and back with me," he joked as he threw a roll in the air and caught it between his teeth.

"Oh, if you wouldn't mind, while you're in the library, it would be great if you could figure out how to get the stick out of Gray's ass. Lea's been trying to figure that one out for months." Erik's laugh bounced around the hallway as he closed the door behind him, walking to Lea's door and knocking four times. Despite Gray leaving with Tanad and the impending war, he couldn't help his good mood. It was amazing what a few hours with Janelle in his arms could do to him.

"Hey Sunshine!" he called. "Care for a little jog?"

CHAPTER 54

LEA

Lea had answered that *yes,* she was ready to be trained. But gods, had she been wrong. They changed into athletic clothing that magically appeared at the foot of their beds: thin, breathable leggings and cropped tank tops for Lea and Janelle, and hilariously tight linen shorts for Erik, as well as stretchy blue fabric to tie back their hair.

As ready as they could be, Erik led them to the back of the castle to face the beautiful sparkling ocean.

"Why doesn't Noah have to train?" Janelle whined as she stifled a yawn.

"Because Noah has already had training, and will be preparing with Tanad's army for the time being. So unless you'd like to train with them also, and I can promise you, they will be far less pleasant—not to mention significantly less handsome—then I suggest you stop asking questions and start stretching."

"Actually," Lea chimed in. "I heard my mom telling one of her patients once that it's not good to stretch cold muscles. You need a warm up first."

Erik groaned, wiping a large, calloused hand down his face. "Fine. No stretching. The first one who touches the water gets to watch during the first round of sparring," Erik told them before he started jogging through the shimmering golden sand.

What looked effortless for him felt like agony to Lea. She couldn't seem to catch her breath, and her legs burned as if fire was eating her alive. The sand was so fine that her bare feet slid and sunk into it, making it almost impossible to move forward. Lea had never run for fun in her life, not really. It was probable that the night she'd sprinted to fight the fenrir was the farthest she'd ever run, and the only reason that she'd even made it was because of the adrenaline pumping through her body.

Janelle didn't seem to be having a much easier time of it, despite the look of determination in her eyes that showed that she refused to admit it. She would *never* let Erik know that she was struggling. Lea tried to follow her lead, putting on a brave face and focusing on slow inhales through her nose and exhales out her mouth, but after about thirteen minutes of running, she collapsed to her knees at the top of a small dune, throwing up into the sand.

Overheated and so nauseous she could hardly see straight, she continued heaving.

Erik circled back to her and crouched down to her level. "Your healing magic, Lea. Make it cool you down and slow your heart."

"Easy for you to say." She spit into the sand, wishing desperately that she had some water to wash out the taste of vomit. "You're Fae. Freakishly strong and fast. Oh, and not *human*." Despite her agitation, Lea tried to use her magic to help cool her body, but she could barely focus as she retched again.

"Are you okay, Lea?" Janelle asked, bending over and placing her hands on her knees, sucking in deep, gasping breaths.

"I think so," Lea groaned as she rocked back and sat with her head between her knees. "I just need a minute," she said.

"Great, then I don't feel so bad for doing this." Janelle stood back up and sprinted toward the water, leaving Lea and Erik behind as Lea tried to collect herself.

"That best friend of yours sure is something." Erik rolled his twinkling eyes, rather unconvincingly, Lea thought, as he offered her a hand and pulled her up.

"Best friend of mine?" Lea said as she wiped her mouth. "Don't think I don't know what's going on with you two." She placed her hands on her head and took several more deep breaths. A grunt of acknowledgment was all she received from Erik as she focused her healing energy on her lungs and her legs. Forcing her heart to slow, Lea ordered her magic to sink into her muscles and relax them. After a few moments, she didn't feel good necessarily, but she felt like she could resume the torture.

"Ready?" Erik said, as if sensing that Lea had figured out how to help her body recover.

"Sure I am," Lea said sarcastically. "Never felt better."

"You're a terrible liar. But it doesn't matter. What you just did, do it as you're running. You can heal your body as it fatigues. Let's go," Erik said over his shoulder as he took off toward the water.

"Guess we're running again," Lea muttered under her breath as she took long strides. She breathed in through her nose and out her mouth once again, finding the light inside her chest. With every inhale, she focused on sending energy to her lungs, and with each exhale, she healed the burning fatigue in her legs. Letting her day magic flow through her veins, she sent it outward, forcing away the pain. It added another layer of concentration to her running, but as she gritted her teeth, forcing her mind and magic to obey her will, it *worked*.

Lea lowered her chin and picked up her speed. After a few more minutes, the white-capped turquoise of the ocean appeared as she crested over a significantly larger dune. Janelle stood shoulder deep in the water, spinning in a joyous circle, but whether from the relief of standing in the cold water or happiness that she had won the race, Lea wasn't sure.

What she was certain of was that the way Erik looked at her friend as she whooped and hollered about her victory was something more-than-friendly. Lea had seen that look before, but rarely. Only on

Gray's face as he'd observed her in moments he'd thought her attention was elsewhere.

She finally made it to the ocean and collapsed onto the sand, right where the water broke. It wasn't frigid, but it wasn't warm either. It was cool enough to lower her body temperature almost immediately, but not enough to make her want to get out or to send her teeth chattering.

Lea rolled onto her back, allowing the waves to rush around her. Watching a blue heron dive to dip its wings in the sea, she relished in the feeling of water splashing on her face. Sand and salt mixed in her hair, tangling it, but she didn't care. She'd made it. Not just in the race, but she made it from Bearswillow to Auropera. Then from Auropera to Calir. She made it from her birth mother's arms to the king's, where he had dropped her off on the hill outside of her parent's house. And she had survived it all. Just her existence was a miracle. And she would do everything she could to use that gift to help right what had been done to her kingdom.

"Five more minutes," Erik called from the sand, trying to hide his smirk as Janelle shouted something about praying more to the gods if she never had to do that again. "Finish cooling off, and then we run back."

Janelle groaned, trying to splash him. "You're not serious."

"Serious as the Lonely Death," Erik shrugged.

Lea rolled over in the water and looked at him pointedly. "Seriously?"

Erik grimaced. "Yeah... That wasn't funny, was it?"

"You're never funny," Janelle called from where she still splashed in the waves.

"Just for that, I think we'll go straight into hand-to-hand combat once we get back. I hope you girls ate your breakfast," Erik taunted, turning to run back to the castle. "Last one there does extra squats!"

CHAPTER 55

LEA

Lea was lying on her bed, staring up at the ceiling and wondering if there was any way she could get out of tomorrow's training, when there was a soft knock on the door.

"Come in," Lea moaned, absolutely positive that there was no way that her legs would be able to support her weight to get her to the door. After the jog, they'd done squats. Thousands of them. At least, it had felt like thousands. Followed by push-ups and pull-ups—even though what Lea and Janelle did definitely could not be considered a pull-up. To top it off, Erik had then asked Tanad for several of his best stallions, on which Janelle and Lea were forced to practice their riding skills, despite the fact that their legs were so overworked they could barely make it into the saddle. She'd healed herself as much as she could, and while the fatigue had eased significantly, she was so *sore*.

"It's your muscles rebuilding. Even magic can't get rid of that." Erik had laughed, ensuring her that it would still ease sooner than if she didn't heal herself.

He'd lied.

The door didn't open, and Lea called out again, assuming it was Erik or Emma being too polite to enter without her explicitly allowing them in. "I can't get up and let you in. I'm dying."

"Um," a male voice she didn't recognize cleared his throat. "I'm looking for Azalea?"

Heat crept up Lea's neck as her cheeks colored. "One minute!" Lea tried not to sound embarrassed as she forced herself to her feet, hissing as her sore legs attempted to carry her forward. Opening the door, Lea placed a confident smile on her face. One of King Tanad's soldiers, a tall man with deep brown skin and a dimple in his chin, stood behind the door with his hands behind his back. He peeked into the room as if looking for danger.

"I wasn't actually dying. I mean, obviously." Lea laughed nervously. "I had to train today, and everything hurts. Did you know your toes could hurt?" They did. Her poor toes were just as tired as the rest of her body from running barefoot through the sand, as well as the hour of trying to grip into the mat as they'd performed balance exercises.

"I can't say I did," he pressed his lips together, trying not to smile.

"Oh. Well, they can... Anyway, how can I help you?" Lea tried desperately to change the subject.

"I was instructed to summon you. The moonflower seeds you requested have arrived." He held up a satchel with a twisted, green-black vine peeking out of the top.

"Already? That's amazing!" Lea would have jumped for joy if her quads could have handled it, but instead she cringed in pain at the thought.

"If you follow me, I'll show you where you can plant them." The soldier turned and walked away without waiting for a response, his leather sandals slapping against the floor. Lea hobbled after him, wincing with every step. Nothing else could have convinced her to leave her room. But for the moonflowers? It was worth the pain.

The soldier led her outside through the same back exit they'd left through to run this morning, but instead of going straight toward the ocean, they turned left down a thin sidewalk with chipped and broken seashells embedded within. They ducked beneath a trellis with odd, deep purple vines climbing up and across it, providing shade.

"This shed isn't locked, so you can enter any time you want," the soldier said as he led her to a squat, round stone structure with a wooden roof and several arched windows, pushing open the door and beckoning her inside.

Several more sacks of vines sat beneath a cracked window, all with dark tendrils peeking out from the cinched tops. Hanging on the wall beside the vines were an assortment of gardening tools: shears, shovels, watering cans, trowels, and spades.

Lea's heart skipped at the sight. "You said I can come here anytime I want?"

"Day or night," he confirmed.

"Thank you..."

"Andy." The soldier smiled broadly.

"Andy." Lea returned the smile. "Were you the one who retrieved them?"

"I was," he confirmed, puffing out his chest proudly.

"I can't thank you enough. You're a brave man, entering the Wicked Wood."

The soldier was silent for a moment, crossing his arms and chewing on his lip before speaking. "I fled here with my mother, years ago. The Lonely Death had come to my village. We gathered our things and fled in the night. She was so afraid we would be exposed to the disease, she uprooted our entire lives. King Tanad accepted us with open arms. If he's committed to stopping the Black King's rule, then I will do *anything* to help him."

"That's admirable." Lea could feel Andy's passion filling the shed, kicking her heart into a faster rhythm. So many people wanted change, all across the continent.

"I guess that also means," he interrupted her thoughts, "that I would do anything to help you, Daughter of the Sun and Stars. It's an honor."

Andy finally met her gaze, some long-ingrained emotional pain shining in his eyes.

"The honor is mine." It felt ridiculous hearing a stranger call her a queen and look at her with so much hope and desperation, and yet to tell him that felt cruel. "Now, if you'd really like to help me," Lea said kindly, "then will you please show me to the gardens and help me with these bags?"

CHAPTER 56

EMMA

Emma had never seen anything so beautiful in her entire life. The king had granted her access to his library without hesitation, and though Emma had been expecting something grand, her wildest dreams could never have predicted what she would find behind the nondescript gold door. Even now, several minutes after entering, she stood in the center of the room, looking around in an attempt to take in the sheer immensity of the space.

How do I possibly get books off the top shelves? Emma wondered as she looked at the soaring bookcases rising at least a hundred feet high, only stopping when they met a domed, stained-glass ceiling in shades of blue and white that filled the room with dancing light, making it look like a churning sea. There were no staircases, no ladders. Nothing to indicate how she could gain access to the soaring shelves wrapping around the curved room. Emma turned in circles, deeply inhaling the scent of old, time-worn parchment and wondering where she should start.

When she'd told Erik that she had slept all night, she'd been lying. Emma had hardly slept at all, but not for the lack of trying. There was a buzzing in her head, a constant reminder of the gruesome faces of the dead that had followed them throughout the Wicked Wood. Emma had tried to describe it to Janelle at one point on their journey, but it hadn't been possible. There weren't words in their language that could possibly convey how horrific the sight of the bloody, mutilated bodies had been.

Once the dead had abandoned them and she'd been able to think more clearly without their constant presence, Emma realized that she had to figure out a way to either use her gift to help them, or get rid of it all together. She refused to let her power control her instead of the other way around. With a deep exhale, Emma finally walked toward one of the shelves, determined to figure out how the books were organized.

"Just think of the topic you want, and it should fly to that table right there." A gruff, male voice echoed through the room, startling Emma. "I'm sorry," the man said. "I didn't mean to scare you."

In Emma's periphery to the right, a man strode forward out of a door that she hadn't noticed. As the man cleared the doorway, she realized why. The door disappeared as the man walked away from it, sinking back into the wall. The area was quickly replaced by shelves upon shelves of books, filling the round room once again with all types of reading.

"Oh," Emma whispered in awe. She'd never seen such casual use of magic in her life before. "Um, did you say the books would float down if I needed them?"

"Yeeesss...?" the short man said abnormally slowly, as if she was completely daft. "Have you never used a library before?" The man was balding and stood a full head shorter than Emma. His round spectacles sat low on his nose, laying against his chubby, wrinkled cheeks. He was older, appearing to be at least in his seventies, but Emma wasn't sure if that was a reliable estimate considering so many more Fae lived in Calir than in Desia.

"No, actually." Emma straightened her shoulders and raised her chin, not appreciating his condescending tone. "Considering the Black King has outlawed any and all texts concerning magic, I haven't had the luxury of going to a library before."

The man's eyes popped open wide, and Emma felt his shock bounce around the circular room. "You're from Desia? And they *really* don't have books there? I'd heard it was so but, well, the absolute horror of it." He actually paled, as if the lack of access to books was the embodiment of his worst nightmare.

"I am," Emma answered, kindness softening her tone as waves of apologetic energy burst off the squat stranger. "And there are books there. Novels, and things to read for enjoyment. But nothing so grand as this. And certainly no magic to help you navigate what books go where, or books that will teach you anything at all, really."

The man stared at her with raised eyebrows, speechless.

"I'm sorry, your name was..."

"Oh, yes. How rude of me. I'm Bartholomew, keeper of the scrolls. Basically a fancy name for the head librarian of the kingdom. Is there something I can help you find?" he asked, pushing up his sleeves and adjusting his glasses.

"I'm looking for books on the dead." As if on cue, the shuffling of pages and groaning of wood cascaded through the library as hundreds of books moved forward from their homes on the shelves to float mid-air. "Specifically, on people who can communicate with or see them." Most of the books slid back into place seamlessly, however, roughly twenty still hung above her head..

"Are you able to narrow it down any more?" Bartholomew asked, scrunching up his face. He took a small step back as if afraid of her.

"I'd like to know if there is a way to get rid of magic. Or even just turn it off."

"You're an empath," Bartholomew stated rather than asked. "Such a burden, but also a gift," he tsked, shaking his head knowingly.

"How did you know that?" Emma crossed her arms, feeling exposed.

"You're not the first to come to this place searching for a way to find peace from the souls wandering this earth."

Emma's chest tightened dangerously with hope. "There are others like me?" she whispered in disbelief.

"Only one. A long time ago. I have not seen a gift such as yours in at least four hundred years."

So he is Fae, Emma thought. "And did they find their answer?"

Bartholomew shook his head slowly, and Emma physically deflated, her shoulders hunching forward. To have not been alone, to have had a friend who has experienced the same thing that she did... It would've changed everything. Made it tolerable, somehow.

"She did not. Not that I'm aware of, at least," Bartholomew said sadly. "Though at the time, I was not the keeper of scrolls, but an apprentice."

"Do you mean that she might have found it, and you just didn't know it?"

"No, my dear." Bartholomew gave her a wink and bounced on the balls of his feet. Energized, it appeared, from having a challenge. "It means that she did not have *me* to help her." With a snap of his fingers, all the books still hanging mid-air, as well as at least thirty new ones, gracefully floated down and stacked themselves neatly on the table. The texts were old, with cracked spines and worn leather in every color and size.

"How long will you be our guest here at the castle?" he questioned, a severe line appearing between his brows as his eyes raked over the enormous stacks in front of him.

"I'm not sure," Emma admitted, her stomach twisting into a knot. There was so much to get through. "Days? Maybe a week, I would guess?"

"Then we have no time to waste," he threw over his shoulder as he turned and hurried toward the table and pulled out a chair for her. "Even with two of us, it will be difficult to get through all this." He waved his hand at the books.

"Thank you so much," Emma said earnestly, her heart squeezing in gratitude.

"No, my dear. Thank *you*. It's been many years since I've had a new challenge. The answer to the Lonely Death has escaped me. As has how to defeat the Black King. But this," he gestured toward the table of books, "This is a riddle that I think we can crack."

"If you like a challenge," Emma said, the beginnings of a question forming in her mind, "there's something else I need your help with."

CHAPTER 57

LEA

Golden light beamed through the alcove window as Lea rubbed a finger across the worn leather journal—Evangeline's journal. She'd glanced at it back in the cabin, but she hadn't opened it since. It wasn't a lack of motivation that kept the book closed on the driftwood table in her room. It was more so that she'd learned so much new information in the last few days that she wasn't sure her mind, or her heart, could process it.

Cracking open the cover, she took a deep breath of salty air. The alcove was open to the sea, tucked near the back of the corridor that held their rooms. Lea hadn't even been sure she was emotionally prepared to look at the journal today, but she needed a distraction. Days had passed since Gray had left to help reinforce the wards at the border, and she *missed* him.

The feeling was nearly all-consuming, and Lea suspected that it had been amplified by the mate bond, along with her love, respect, and devotion to him. To her *mate*. Lea smiled. Gods, she loved him. It was a thick, heady feeling that flooded her veins and never left her, a warm blanket wrapped firmly around her shoulders. She felt like she could breathe deeper than ever before. Her power was easier to access, and a little easier to control.

I miss you, Lea sent down the mate bond. She'd probably told him a hundred times since he left, but she couldn't help it. It was all consuming.

I miss you more, Gray's rumbling voice replied, a whisper in her mind. It was faint, like listening underwater, but it was there. It didn't quench her need to see him, nor the way part of her soul was missing from her being, but at least she knew he was okay. She could feel Gray's love with every thump of her heart.

She'd tried to distract herself, spending hours each day in the gardens, unsuccessfully trying to grow the moonflowers. But the only time she had moments of reprieve from missing Gray was during training, which had continued daily just as Erik had told them it would.

It was hard to think of your mate, or anything else for that matter, when your enormous, secretly sadistic friend screamed at you to run faster until you emptied the contents of your stomach onto the sand. Though somehow, by the fifth day, Lea had miraculously made it without vomiting.

Her legs still felt like rubber, but she practiced what Erik had taught her. With every slow breath in, she sent healing magic to her lungs, forcing them to open wider and use her oxygen more efficiently. With every exhale, she focused on healing her legs, easing the intense burn and fatigue that made her limbs feel like gelatin. She still hated running and would much rather spend her time sparring or practicing her day magic, but she also knew that their morning jogs weren't just about the running. Though she needed to be able to perform physical activity without retching, she also needed to learn how to use small bits of her magic while doing other tasks and control it.

After their run this morning, Lea had needed to escape. To have some time alone, if only for a moment. Pulling her knees to her chest, she placed her birth mother's journal next to her, opening to a random page. Inside, a beautiful pressed flower was glued to a slightly stiff, time-aged page. It was a deep pink, with diamond-shaped petals that ended in a sharp point. It was beautiful, menacing and stunning and dangerous all at once.

Lea wasn't familiar with the plant, but scrawled next to it in a loopy, flourished cursive was a name: *Altranior Misciefoh. Most effective when planted with intent.*

Odd, Lea thought, flipping to the next page where a flower as big as her palm and as black as her shadows was pressed. *Mash into fine powder and mix into drink. Best if placed in bottom of glass prior to pouring. Use sparingly. Will kill in seconds.*

Lea flipped from page to page, reading the descriptions of the flowers in Evangeline's handwriting. There was a small, golden flower for luck and a silver vine for truth. *Plant at dawn, when truth comes to light. Must interrogate immediately. Lasts less than one hour.*

Poisons, Lea realized. Had her birth mother grown all of these? Was Lea's ability to nurture the earth inherited from her? Sure, she preferred to grow things that could heal, nourish. But all the same, Lea was certain that these flowers had bloomed with the help of magic. She swiped a tear from her eye. Though she would never meet her birth mother, maybe she had gotten *something* from her. Maybe a part of Evangeline lived inside her.

Lea paused. What other answers hid within this book? She swiped to the next page. It was blank, but a deep blue-violet residue dusted the parchment. *Autolycus: Thief of magic. Last remaining flower.*

"My Queen?"

Lea jumped, and Noah raised his hands in front of him. "I'm sorry. I didn't mean to scare you."

Laughing, Lea closed the journal. "Noah. I've told you. It's Lea, please."

"Lea, then." He smiled, but his cheeks colored as he dipped his head. "Are you okay?"

Shifting to give Noah room to sit, she patted the bench next to her. "I'm fine." She held up the journal. "It's been a lot to process, you know?

I wasn't over losing my mom, and now it feels like I've gained and lost another parent all at once."

Noah sat, keeping a respectable distance from Lea. It made her smile. He was so kind, so *honorable*. He never cursed, rarely teased. And above all, he was loyal, both to Gray and herself, even though Lea felt as if she'd done nothing to earn that kind of allegiance from him.

"I can understand that. To a point, at least." Noah held out a hand, raising his eyebrows. "May I?" he asked, looking at the journal.

Lea nodded, handing it over. "How'd you get through it? Losing a parent, I mean."

Noah promptly opened the notebook, flipping through the pages. He studied them for a few seconds before answering. "I have three younger sisters." Noah didn't look up from the pages. "My mom fell apart when Dad died. She couldn't get out of bed. Couldn't take care of any of us. It was... scary."

Tilting his head, he studied a deep blue flower, so dry from its time between the pages that it was crumbling into dust. "We received a generous gift from a stranger. It was enough money to feed and clothe us." Noah looked up, searching Lea's eyes. But for what, she didn't understand.

"That sounds like a godsend," she said, thinking about how much more difficult navigating her grief would have been if she hadn't been able to afford to eat.

"It was. Because my mom never recovered. Not really. I started staying up late to rock Lily to sleep and getting up early to change her diapers."

"Is she your youngest sister?"

Noah's lips tipped up at the edges. "Yes. She was only eight months old when my dad was killed. My mom couldn't care for her like she deserved. Or for Kaeli or Suzie. But I didn't want them to suffer even more. So I stepped up."

The sound of pages flipping filled the air until they abruptly stopped. Noah traced the words on a page, then lifted the book to show Lea.

Potion for peace from grief. Unsuccessful. There was no flower on the page. Just several rows of notes on different plants and herbs that had failed.

"Grief is a lot easier when you have a purpose. When it asks something of you," Noah said, his eyes sad. "I had people who depended on me, and I wasn't going to let them down."

"That's admirable," Lea whispered as she traced her mother's handwriting again, a wave of sorrow flooding her veins. Maybe it would have been easier if she'd had siblings, some other family member to hold on to through her grief.

"It's still what gets me through, Lea." Noah placed a hand gently on hers, stilling her nervous tracing. "My sisters *still* depend on me. Not for comfort anymore, but to help defeat the Black King. To give them a chance of living in a kingdom that values peace over power. It's why I sometimes guard Emma when she's alone in the library. Why I watch over you, and help where I can." He pulled his hand away. "I know I'm young, and Gray likely doesn't need my assistance. Not really. But I *have* to help. I busy myself with ways to be of service, both to him and the cause. Firewood, hunting game, helping his mate build and maintain a fire." Noah winked at her, and Lea's heart warmed. He reminded her of her friend Solomon back home. He was so good natured, and it made Lea's chest ache with homesickness. "I owe him *everything*. Not just for the gold he left for us when my mother died."

Lea's jaw dropped. *What? Gray had been the stranger who left them money when his father had died?*

"But also for being the one brave enough to help me continue to protect my sisters. Without him, there is no war. There is no chance for peace. Whenever I feel sad about my dad, that is what I think about. What can I do? Who needs me?"

Lea couldn't help but smile. "Well, if my opinion matters, you're very good at helping. Especially me. Especially when Erik is being a pain in the ass about my magic."

"I don't think you're hearing what I'm saying, my *queen*." He emphasized the word, and Lea's eyes snapped up. "Lea, of course, your opinion matters. This is how you deal with your grief. You have a purpose. You have power that until now, no one has even dreamed of. Gray may have the armies and the strategy and the plans in place to defeat his father and brother, but *you* are the one who can finish it. You have an entire kingdom of people depending on you. So you use that pain and grief and you turn it into a way to *help*. And in return, it will help you through it."

"I just don't feel—"

"Respectfully, Lea," he paused, "it doesn't matter what you *feel*. That you feel like you aren't enough, or that you're undeserving, or whatever it is you're worried about. You have the potential to be the most powerful weapon at our disposal. So it's time you believe it. Because we all believe in you."

Lea was speechless. He'd somehow smashed straight into the heart of her fears. Right into the center of all of her doubts. But he was right, wasn't he? As much as she didn't want her primary magic, that wild and unruly power continued to slowly leech from the crack in her chest. She was a descendent of the most powerful queen in Desia's history, and had magic of the day and night. Maybe it was time she started believing in herself after all. The thought made her want to vomit, but she shoved the feeling away. If Noah could be so brave as to join the Royal Army as a child, just hoping to find Gray and somehow make a difference, she could force herself to find some courage as well.

"Anyway," Noah stood. "Thank you for letting me help you all. The fact that I'm here, actually part of saving the kingdom... It's the greatest gift I could be given." Nodding solemnly, he turned to walk away.

"Noah." Lea stopped him. "We're going to need a court, you know. Gray and I, once we've won the war." It was true. Once the war was over and they had a kingdom to run, they would need honorable, honest people to help them. "Erik, Janelle, and Emma will be part of it. And you. If you'll have us, that is."

"Me? I—" Noah swallowed, his eyes practically sparkling with joy. "Of course. I'll prove myself worthy of this. I swear it."

"You already have, Noah," Lea said with a warm smile. "I'll try my best to prove myself worthy as well."

Noah nodded, a smile tugging at his lips as he bowed, then spun on his heel to leave. "Oh, I almost forgot," he said, stopping and looking over his shoulder. "Erik is looking for you. He said he'll meet you outside your room. But I'm warning you. He looks suspiciously excited."

CHAPTER 58

LEA

"Oh, Sunshine!" A jolly voice called as Erik came sauntering merrily up the hallway, a mischievous glint in his eye.

"I thought we were meeting after lunch for more training," Lea said, pausing and turning her head warily. "And why are you smiling like that?"

"I've changed my mind. I spoke to the king's top general, and he agreed to lend us a special room and the use of his soldiers for training purposes. They're waiting for us. Let's go," Erik ordered, and Lea marveled at how quickly Erik could flip between treating her like a friend and acting like an overbearing drill sergeant.

There was a skip in his usually heavy steps, and he was clearly excited about whatever he had planned based on his rosy cheeks and not-so-subtle smile. "You've been doing remarkably well in your training with your day magic," Erik said.

It was true; she had. Over the last several days, she'd been able to control the size and intensity of the heat of her fires. She'd also practiced latching her fire onto other objects as she had in the Wicked Wood, such as Erik's sword, or arrows flying through the air. She was beginning to understand that her magic was just like another muscle. With discipline and repetition, it had started to obey her, just like using a limb.

"You need to keep practicing, but I'm not sure there's much more I can teach you there."

"Then what are we working on?" Lea nearly had to run to keep up with Erik.

He didn't slow down his pace as he looked over his shoulder with a quirked eyebrow. "It's time to work on using your shadows."

Lea stopped dead in her tracks, her heart thumping in her throat. "Are you sure that's a good idea?" She had *just* decided to believe in herself, but doing it right now felt like too much. "Maybe we should wait until Gray's here so he can help me."

Erik sighed and hung his head dramatically before turning and closing the distance between them. He placed a hand on her shoulder and lowered his eyes to her level. "I don't know why you're so scared to use your shadows, Sunshine. But I *do* know that you will need to use them. Like I mentioned in the woods, night magic is really only useful during combat on moving targets. That's where the king's men come in."

"Can't we practice first on like, I don't know, sticks again?" Anxiety caused a cold sweat to break out on Lea's skin. Her night magic still felt wrong. Partly because the more she used it, the more her primary magic seemed to seep into her chest, and partly because of the something *other* that was mixed in with her shadows. It felt foreign and difficult to control, and it *terrified* her. "I'll do it. I know I need to practice, but not on people. Not yet."

"No." Erik crossed his arms. "Using your shadows in that way is the exact same as using your day magic. You can do that already. I have no doubt about it. We likely only have a week or two left here, assuming Eudora comes to find you soon. It's better to train here where we're safe and in a controlled environment."

Lea knew he was right, but she couldn't help but feel unsure.

"Are you afraid of hurting someone? Is that it?" Erik scrunched his forehead up as if desperately trying to understand her hesitation. "Because you're far less likely to accidentally injure someone with your shadows, you know. You'd have to be a lot more intentional about that."

"Yes, I'm afraid to hurt people! But it's not that," Lea replied. "It's more like... like the shadows might consume me whole. I'd feel better if Gray was here. The power feels bigger than me. And I'm worried that if I dig too deep into it, I might be trapped in the darkness forever."

"Good thing you can create light with your fingertips," Erik joked, wiggling his fingers, but he stopped when Lea's face fell. "You're really worried about your shadows consuming you?" he asked, his voice brimming with concern.

"I don't know why, but it feels like they're connected to my primary magic. They feel so much stronger and deeply tied into who I am than my day magic does. This power inside me—" Lea placed a hand against her sternum. "It feels dangerous. Like, it shouldn't belong to only one person."

"That's all the more reason to practice controlling it." Erik nodded at her seriously.

"I know you're right. But it still scares me," Lea admitted, pushing the tears away that threatened to wet her eyes. She wasn't sure why she felt this bone deep terror about using her night magic, but she'd never been more afraid of anything.

"I'm scared all the time, Sunshine. But we still have a war to fight, and I plan on helping you survive it. I'll be there with you the whole time. If it gets out of control, I promise I'll stop you."

"Okay." Butterflies beat their wings wildly in Lea's stomach. She still didn't feel like she had fully searched the depths of her power. But Erik *was* right. She'd be more of a liability during battle if she wasn't able to control her magic. She trusted Erik. Not only because Gray trusted him so completely, but because he'd proven himself to be a kind, thoughtful, and selfless friend. Noah's speech earlier, as well as the fact that Gray and Erik believed in her so completely bolstered her hope that maybe they were right.

"You promise you've got my back?" Lea rolled her shoulders, feigning confidence.

"Always." Erik placed a hand over his heart, sincerity shining in his eyes.

Lea took a deep breath and resumed walking, grateful that Erik had listened to her concerns instead of telling her she was overreacting.

"But, I am a little offended you even had to ask me that," he grumbled as he continued on toward Lea's worst nightmare.

CHAPTER 59

GRAY

The last several days of riding had been remarkably uneventful. Even so, Gray was exhausted. They'd started at the westernmost edge of the border and had inspected every inch of the magical wards protecting the kingdom from the Lonely Death. As they had ridden, he'd added his own magic to King Tanad's; intertwining and weaving threads of his darkness to the already existing barrier, fortifying it and making it significantly stronger.

It was a bit alarming how strong the boundary already appeared. How had the Lonely Death crept through it to begin with? It should have prevented not only the disease from passing through, but also anyone attempting to cross the border without King Tanad's explicit permission. Still, a village had fallen since he'd constructed the wards. How had that been possible?

The evidence of his father's greed was in the ghost towns that King Tanad had taken Gray through as they passed. The once prosperous villages had been reduced to bones and skulls on a map. The first two had made Gray feel physically ill. The smell was horrific. Not the bodies of the victims of the Lonely Death. No, those had been burned by Tanad's men to prevent infection. But it had taken weeks for anyone to learn that those villages had fallen. The animals had starved, and now flies and other bugs buzzed around the carcasses of horses and cattle.

Gray wished that he had day magic, just so he could burn the evidence of Brennus's malicious thievery of magic to the ground. These villages stood as stark reminders of his failure thus far. They were getting closer to the answers they needed to break the curse he'd set upon their family, but still, they needed more time to train. He knew the rebels had been working on their part back in Bearswillow, and Gray completely trusted that Vincent was taking their training seriously. But against his father's magic, they stood no chance, not now. Not until he spoke to Eudora.

The night grew a little darker as he thought about her, his shadows pulsing and writhing along the stark border that divided the forest and the desert, Desla and Calir, in quiet anger.

"Is there a problem?" Tanad asked, sliding off his horse and grabbing his water skin. He didn't wait for an answer as he walked to a crystal clear spring bubbling out of the golden sand.

The pool of water was massive, big enough to swim in, had they wanted, and Gray wished that he was here instead with Lea. He would strip her down to nothing, allow the cool water dripping off her breasts to quench his thirst. The thought made him grow hard, and he shifted, hopping off Obsidian to fill his own flask. "No, I'm sorry. Just thinking." Gray shook his head.

"And what, may I ask, were you thinking about that made your shadows react in such a way?" Tanad tilted his head curiously, taking a large swig of spring water.

Gray thought about his answer for a second. He hated that witch. She'd known exactly what she was doing when she'd granted his wish to make it impossible for his father or brother to kill someone else within his family. Just as she knew what was at stake here, what hung in the balance as she kept them waiting. But for some reason she was dear to Tanad and had resided in his palace for at least as long as Gray had known him. He didn't wish to offend his host, but he also worried that she would make breaking the curse far more difficult than it needed to be. And even further, he worried about what she would ask of him in return for her help this time.

Gray decided to be honest. After all, King Tanad was his friend, and they shared the same goal. Maybe it would help him if Tanad would speak to her on his behalf.

"I worry that Eudora is wasting time refusing to speak to us. She has to have known for years that I would someday come to break the spell. She knows about the Lonely Death, and according to you, has known about Azalea and what she is capable of longer than anyone. Does she not want this violence and reign of death to end?"

The king's face remained neutral. "You know as well as I do that Eudora has little interest in the problems of the Fae, *or* the humans. Her magic is different. It is similar to your mate's in that it belongs to nothing and everything. She is near limitless, but in a different way than Azalea is. While Lea has the sheer power to blow open the door, to bring the walls of the Black King's castle tumbling to the ground, Eudora has the knowledge to learn how to slowly pick the lock. She has pieces of the puzzle none of us understand, has seen things so far into the future that our problems seem insignificant to her. She helps the universe maintain balance."

"So she doesn't care that thousands of innocent people are being killed?" Gray retorted, his words coming out sharper than he'd intended. "How is that balance?"

Tanad cleared his throat and took a deep, calming breath. "She cares, of course, just as she cares that Brennus's soldiers will be slaughtered as well if we meet them on the battlefield. She does not see good and evil the same way that we do." Tanad held up his hand as if sensing that Gray was about to argue. "I know you assume she only wishes to take. You see her as similar to your father, gaining power in bargains made in blood for her assistance and knowledge. But it is Eudora who can be credited for keeping your mate alive."

Gray's mouth cracked open in shock. "Why are you just telling me this now?" Gray tried to calm his temper. He didn't believe that the king wanted to hide things from him without good reason, but it was frustrating only getting small bits of information as he found it necessary.

"There's more Azalea does not yet know, but the other night I felt her powers start to grow restless. I worried that learning even more might be harmful to her," Tanad said.

Gray bristled at the insinuation that his mate wasn't strong enough to handle whatever it was Tanad was keeping from them. "I'd never let anything happen to her. Lea deserves to know the truth."

"She does. But what she deserves and what her soul is ready for are two different things. I don't think you understand the immensity of what I feel inside her." Tanad pressed a hand to his sternum. "It is pure power, Commander. One can easily get lost within it, overtaken by the allure of the oblivion that comes with complete surrender to it."

Gray considered his words before responding. "My mate did not ask for her powers, nor did she want them. I would even guess that given the chance now, she would give them up to someone else who she felt was more worthy to wield them."

"Which is why she is the one among us who has them," the king agreed. They continued on in silence for a few moments before the king stopped his horse. "Eudora had a vision."

"Yes, the prophecy." Gray knew this already, as did Azalea. *Evil will fall at her feet, and death will follow where she commands.* But *how?* It explained almost nothing.

"Not only the prophecy. The prophecy, as you know, was spoken at the moment of the Queen's death. But the next vision? It was the night of your mate's birth."

Her birth? How did he not know about this? There was no justifying hiding anything about his mate from him. Gray's shadows tried to break free, but he held them at bay. "What did she see?" He asked, his words careful and controlled as he fought against a surge of rage. "And why, even if you don't believe Lea to be ready, have you not confided in *me* about this?"

"Eudora has stressed that the future's not set in stone. The ending of Lea's story could change. She insisted that for the good of our kingdoms, her vision was spoken of as little as possible."

"And I insist you tell me exactly what that vision entailed," Gray demanded.

Tanad sighed. "She saw many things. Many possible outcomes to what we're now facing. But one thing was certain. The Black King was coming for Evangeline, and he *would* find her. But there was a way to save her daughter."

"To give her away, without anyone ever telling her who she really is?" Gray's darkness pushed uncomfortably against his ribs.

"To send her to an isolated place where she would be protected, with no information about her true identity. Eudora saw Adelaide giving Azalea the potion that dampened her magic. When Eudora allowed that version to become the truth, it showed Azalea growing up. Living. *Thriving*. But not only that. Her vision showed your mate being the one who could change everything."

"It showed her defeating my father?" Gray ran a hand through his unkempt beard.

"In one reality, yes. In another, chaos and bloodshed, all in vain. It depends on the choices our dear Azalea makes."

"I don't understand." Gray rubbed the scruff on his face. He knew his mate to her very core. There wasn't a malicious drop of blood in her body. There wasn't a single part of her that wasn't good.

"All I know, my friend, is that your mate has the power to become the Queen of Flame and Shadows, a kind and merciful ruler, but also a warrior. *That* queen changes the world for good. Restores peace and magic, and defeats the Black King. Or," the king turned his horse, preparing to begin traveling again, "she has the power to cast the world into darkness and destroy everything that we are fighting for."

CHAPTER 60

LEA

Instead of leading her to the large, bright training room open to the sea air—a common design choice for the entirety of the castle—Erik took her down a winding set of sandstone stairs. It reminded her of when he'd led her into the depths of the Black King's castle in Auropera, the first time he'd ever tried to teach her about using her magic. But this time, they went even deeper.

The natural sunlight that had lit the halls on the ground floor of the castle disappeared as they continued further into its depths, and Erik created a small flame that floated in the air in front of them as they walked, reminding her of the shadows Gray had sent to show her back to her room. The darkness called to Lea's magic, twisting in her chest like it was trying to break free and join the blackness all around her. It made Lea feel uncomfortable in a way that was almost painful, and the further they went into the dungeons, the winding driftwood stairs seemingly never ending, the more her shadows scratched at the inside of her ribs to be set free.

Erik finally stopped in front of the broad, golden doorway. There were no fish swimming along the beautiful metal of this door. Instead, there were weapons: axes, swords, daggers, arrows, scythes, and several other things that she couldn't even recognize or name, but that looked completely barbaric.

"Where are we?" Lea asked.

Erik turned around, cocking his head as he took in the anxiety in her posture. Lea relaxed her hands, attempting to cover up her nerves.

"Now Sunshine, do you really think I would take you somewhere dangerous? Not just because I love you, but also because Gray would kill me, and I love *me,* too."

Lea laughed, warmth filling her chest at his brotherly affection. "As do I, Erik. What is this room, anyway?"

"It's just another training room. But," his eyes twinkled, "this one is enchanted."

"Enchanted to do *what* exactly?" Lea's throat squeezed tighter. Nothing good could come of this.

"I'll be the one in charge of the room today. Essentially, it will create any enemy I instruct it to. Whatever challenge I want, the room will make happen." Erik bounced on the balls of his feet as if he couldn't wait to imagine all sorts of terrifying monsters to make her fight.

"How is that possible?" Lea watched an engraving of an axe spin and fly across the door and imbed itself into the handle as if warning her away.

"King Tanad is far more powerful than he lets on. His warriors are some of the best trained I've ever seen, and it's because he prepares them so thoroughly." Erik crossed his arms. "I plan on preparing you just as well."

Lea gulped down the lump of nerves settling in her throat.

"Remember, while it might feel real, nothing in that room can hurt you. Not really." Erik smiled at Lea as if that made it any less scary.

"You mean not fatally," Lea muttered.

Erik threw his head back in his signature booming laugh. "Yes, not fatally. Stop worrying. The goal here is to use your shadows on moving targets, that's all."

"And what are the king's soldiers helping us with? I don't want to use my shadows on them." The memory of Lea's fire burning Janelle's arm back in Auropera flashed through her mind.

"They're here to be decoys, to help simulate battle. They'll be fighting as well, and you'll need to control your magic to make sure that you don't harm them."

Lea opened her mouth to argue, but Erik held out his hand. "Before you start, they can't be fatally injured either. Everyone is safe behind this door. That's why it was created. And I'll be there, too. I can stop you if you need help, or if it gets out of hand."

Lea shook her head and turned to face the door, taking a deep breath and steeling herself for what she would find behind it.

"They're waiting for us inside. Are you ready?" Erik asked.

"As I'll ever be." Lea held her hands in front of her as if they could protect her. Wordlessly, Erik opened the door and extinguished his fire. The pitch black was startling, and Lea lost all sense of where she was. She'd anticipated at least getting to see how big the room was, how it was laid out, and how many soldiers waited in there. Now? She couldn't even see how far in front of her the doorway was.

"After you," Erik said, giving her a small push. Lea stumbled forward, her shoulder brushing against the side of the door frame. After a few seconds, Lea felt like she was going to faint. The darkness around her pushed firmly against her and dug into her skin as if trying to rip her magic from her body. She could hardly breathe from the pressure in her chest.

"Calm yourself, Lea," Erik encouraged from somewhere behind her.

"I don't want to do this anymore." Lea fought against the urge to throw up. The dark power inside her pressed against her chest wall and surged through her arms as it begged to be released.

"One step at a time. First, control your breathing."

Lea had no choice but to obey. She took a four-second inhale through her nose, then exhaled for the same amount of time. It took about five cycles of slow breathing until her heart began to calm enough for the roaring in her ears to ease.

"Good," Erik said. "Now, the darkness in this room is under your command. Use it. Order it to search out your surroundings."

Lea continued her slow breathing, closing her eyes to help herself concentrate. She pictured running water in her mind and began stacking branches in front of it until only a small portion of the water could run through. She imagined that water was her power, and allowed a small stream of shadows to flow from her hands. With false confidence, she ordered her shadows to grab hold of the darkness around her, forming it into a weapon. Following the shadows, she mapped the room out in her mind, noting where they butted up against people and walls. As if someone turned the light on, she suddenly knew in her mind's eye exactly what the room looked like.

Oddly, it was an enormous, triangular chamber, at least eight times the size of the hall where the royals had eaten their meals back in Auropera. Over two dozen men stood scattered throughout the room, as motionless as statues. It caused an uneasy prickle along her skin to see the men standing so completely still. If Erik hadn't told her that the king's soldiers would be assisting today, Lea would've assumed they were dummies meant to practice sparring against.

"Do you see it?" Erik asked after several moments.

"Yes," Lea breathed, still inhaling and exhaling slowly in an effort to control that dark power inside her.

"How many men are there?" Erik asked, and Lea knew he didn't want an estimate. She began counting them.

"Twenty seven," she said confidently. She couldn't actually see them, not really, but she could feel them, map them out in her head based on where her shadows found them. It was as if someone had painted the room and placed it next to her, where she could reference it whenever she wanted.

"What else is here?" Erik sounded proud, and Lea smiled in the dark.

"Weapons. On the back wall." Lea traced the sharp edge of a sword with a long, shadowy finger.

"Anything else?" Erik prodded.

Ordering her shadows to spread out further, Lea pushed them up the wall and across the ceiling. "There's something up here." Lea continued wrapping her darkness around the object hanging above them. Somehow her shadows knew that it was long, cold strips of metal. "A cage." Her shadows continued to explore. "With locks. A bunch of different kinds." It was extremely odd, but there was no mistaking what she was feeling. There were padlocks and key holes, locks with combinations, and deadbolts.

"Excellent. Now I'm going to create enemy soldiers. They'll have magic, and they will be battling our fellow rebels. Your goal is to help our soldiers while incapacitating the enemies. Is everyone ready?" Erik's thundering voice echoed through the room, and a rumble of acknowledgment responded through the dark. Without warning, chaos erupted around Lea. In the blink of an eye, she was standing in the middle of a battle. Swords clanged while fireballs flew into shields and walls. Lea ducked as her shadows warned her of an arrow coming straight at her chest.

"Focus, Lea!" Erik yelled.

This isn't real, Lea said to herself. *Just try.* Lea commanded her shadows to explode around her, taking in as much of the fighting as she could in her mind. The soldiers Erik had created looked different from the king's. They were slightly larger, and while whatever magic being used made them firm to the touch, evident by the way they were able to physically fight, she could feel that they were slightly fuzzy around the edges and not completely solid.

A soldier to her right cried out as his sword was knocked from his hand. The imaginary soldier he was fighting pressed the blade to his throat, and Lea focused on the metal weapon. She reached out with her shadows, wrapping them around the hilt and ripping it from the man's hand before turning the sword on him and stabbing him through the stomach. He disappeared instantly.

"Amazing, Lea," Erik cheered her on as if he was watching a game of quoffist.

The clang of arrows bouncing off a shield met Lea's ears, and she searched the space for them. Where the triangular wall in front of her turned into a point, a man stood firing arrows off at a rapid pace. She heard the grunt of one of the king's soldiers as he was hit, landing with a thud on the ground.

They can't die, Lea reminded herself. Raising her chin, she built a wall of shadow in front of the man, angling it, so that the next arrow he loosed hit the shield and bounced back toward him, impaling him in the eye. Just like the soldier before him, he disappeared into thin air.

Lea allowed more shadows to escape her chest, their long fingers reaching out and snatching weapons, becoming weapons themselves. She wrapped her shadows around another soldier's neck, squeezing until he simply was gone. At the same time, she pulled the legs out from under another soldier about to deliver a death blow with a dagger, positioning his hand underneath him, so that he landed on his own weapon.

The more Lea used her night magic, the more her shadows called on that raw, dark, primary power, begging it to seep from the floor of her chest. It was intoxicating, like a shot of hard maple liquor. It prickled in her chest and buzzed along her skin, begging for her to destroy. *Maybe I can actually do this,* she thought as she lifted a man by his hair and threw him into a wall.

In the recesses of Lea's mind, she realized she should be concerned by how good it felt to be this powerful, to cause this much destruction. She should stop, call on her light to counteract that deep, black power. But she didn't *want* to stop, reveling in the intensity of her darkness until every last imaginary soldier had disappeared.

Her blood ran hot, and her body vibrated with the thrill of allowing that deep well inside of her to drain, just a little. There was so much more bubbling under the surface, and she yearned to unleash it all and see how deep her abilities really ran. A loud warning bell echoed somewhere inside her that told her she wasn't ready for that, but her wild, unruly power screamed back as if it could cover the sound of her conscience.

With every ounce of self-control she could muster, Lea called back her shadows, summoning them home like a child to its mother. They nestled snugly together inside her chest, and Lea swore that the darkness inside her actually sighed in contentment. The room brightened, torches lighting along the walls one by one with the flick of Erik's fingers.

He walked directly toward Lea, grabbing her by the shoulders and beaming with pride. "I knew you could do it! People really should listen to me more. I was right about the mate bond, and I was right about this. Your shadows are no different from your flames. We just need to work on controlling them, and you'll be unstoppable."

Lea smiled and allowed him to embrace her, but a tug of worry in her gut nagged at her mind. Erik didn't understand. Being unstoppable was exactly what she was afraid of.

CHAPTER 61

ERIK

Janelle was restless. When Erik returned to her room after training with Lea, he found her pacing. There had been a subtle change in Janelle ever since the tirror attack in the Wicked Wood. Since that day, she hadn't seemed quite able to settle her body or her mind.

"You weren't in the training room this afternoon." Janelle shoved a finger at him as he closed the door, stopping briefly to glare before continuing her pacing. "I need to train. You said we needed to work on combat *every day,* and then, when I showed up, assuming you would be there, the room was empty."

Every single afternoon since they'd arrived, Erik had been forced to almost drag Janelle kicking and screaming to combat training after their run. Erik's mouth cracked open. She had been in the shower when he'd returned before grabbing Lea for their lesson, and he hadn't wanted to disturb her. He'd assumed she would enjoy having an afternoon off. It wasn't like they'd made plans specifically to train and he'd failed to show up.

"I know Lea is the one who's gonna save us all and everything," Janelle continued pacing, "and that's great. I'm glad she's getting the training she needs. But I need to train. I need to be safe, too."

Erik felt like he had been punched in the gut. "Of course you need to be safe. You *are* safe."

"Then why didn't we train today?" Janelle threw her hands up in the air, the pitch of her voice rising higher and higher. Erik walked over and grabbed her gently by the upper arms, stopping her frantic movement.

"I thought you hated training. I thought I was being kind, giving you a break." Erik ran his hands down her arms, needing to ease the anxiety radiating from her every pore. "Do you really not feel safe?"

"I don't know." Janelle's lip trembled, and she cleared her throat to try to cover it up.

A painful mix of guilt and protectiveness lodged behind his sternum. "I would *never* let anything happen to you," Erik said firmly, willing her to believe him with the intensity behind his words, to feel it as deeply as he did and know he was speaking the truth. "Never."

Janelle looked down at her feet. "You might not always be with me, and I will *not* let myself get hurt—" she cut off abruptly.

Erik had the sinking, gut-wrenching suspicion that she had been about to say the word "again," and a fire exploded inside his chest. "Let's go train. Right now." Erik removed his weapons and jacket, stripping down to his undershirt and pants.

"Well, I didn't mean we had to do it at this exact moment," Janelle said almost guiltily, softening her voice and looking away as if she felt like she was being a burden.

"Yes, we do." Erik tried to push down the uncomfortable feeling in his chest telling him to gather her in his arms and take away all of her fears. "You need to feel safe? I need you to feel safe, too."

"It's so late, though," Janelle said, "and I don't wanna wake the others."

"The others don't need to train with us. Not tonight. Are you ready to go?" Erik walked over to the door, but Janelle shuffled her feet.

"You're sure?" she asked softly.

"I'm positive," Erik said like he meant it, and he did. The thought of Janelle not feeling safe filled him with a rage that he had never experienced before.

"Well, if you're sure," Janelle discreetly wiped her eyes with the heel of her hand, "then prepare for me to kick your ass." She squared her shoulders and elbowed him in the ribs as she walked past, clearing her throat.

The castle was completely silent as they walked to the training room, which, like their bedrooms and King Tanad's office, was completely open to the sea. The breeze flowing through the opening was refreshing, now that the sun was resting for the evening. Lea and Erik had trained straight through dinner, and what he'd seen had astounded him. The power Lea had—there was nothing like it. Not that he had ever seen, at least. Now he just needed to get her to work on her confidence, but he would never again focus on instructing Lea at the expense of Janelle's training.

Hurrying ahead to open the door for Janelle, Erik allowed her to enter and walked straight to the mat without a word. They both kicked off their sandals and walked onto the soft black pad, and Janelle raised her hands in a defensive stance.

Erik spent a moment observing her. She had gotten significantly better at defending her face and neck, but remained somewhat timid about going on the offensive, as well as with protecting her flank. There was a hint of definition beginning to emerge on Janelle's arms from the drills they'd been practicing, and she stood lightly on her feet, proof of her improving agility.

Every day they did push-ups and core exercises, as well as learned various punches and maneuvers that they repeated on a leather bag that was filled with sand and hovered a few feet off the ground. Every training session, Janelle had put up a fight, complaining and using colorful language to describe what she would do to him if he made her do another repetition, but Erik knew it was all an act. He'd observed how hard she worked every single day with every single exercise.

Janelle's knuckles were cut and bruised from her effort, but not once had she stopped an exercise to ask for healing, or even a break.

"What are you waiting for?" Janelle asked as he stood, silently assessing her.

"I'm waiting for you to attack so I can block you." Erik crossed his arms.

Janelle gave him a look that suggested she thought that he was trying to trap her.

Erik cocked his head. "Why do you think you need to be on the defensive?"

Janelle lowered her hands with a huff. "Because you're six foot four, and I am five foot three? Maybe that has something to do with it? Because you're a warrior, and I'm just learning how to not get myself killed?"

"*You* are a warrior," Erik walked toward her, grabbing her hands and pulling them back up to protect her face. "You're not just training to prevent yourself from injury. You're training to fulfill your potential, to improve what you are already capable of."

Janelle shuffled her feet and looked away.

"You found your way into the castle when Lea was taken, despite the fact that the king was very selective about who is allowed to work there because of the whispers of the rebellion. You are the one who led your friends to safety after fleeing the castle. They wouldn't have made it through town without you using your powers to guide them. You are every bit as capable as myself or Gray or Lea. So *that* is what I am waiting for. For you to realize what you're capable of. Now attack me."

Erik widened his stance and bent his knees slightly, raising his hands in front of him to prepare to block. Tears glistened in Janelle's eyes, but she simply nodded her head and resumed her fighting stance, not even bothering to blink them away.

Her stoic response made Erik's chest swell with a mixture of pride and sorrow. He hated seeing her this way, but she wasn't letting it rule her or destroy her. She was ready to fight through it.

With a tentative step forward, Janelle jabbed toward Erik's shoulder.

"No. Aim for the face, the throat, or the gut. Again."

Janelle followed with another half hearted jab.

"Harder." She wasn't trying, wasn't allowing that anger simmering inside her to fuel her movements.

"Do *not* pretend to be weak," he demanded. "It's insulting. Harder."

Janelle's jaw clenched, and she struck again, slightly harder.

"What are you doing?" Erik began stalking in a circle around Janelle, putting her on edge as he tried to rile her up. "You said you wanted to train. Then train. Harder."

Janelle launched at him, taking him by surprise as she dropped low with an uppercut to the stomach.

"Good. Again." Erik ordered.

They continued, Janelle jumping close to Erik, punching or kicking and then quickly backing away. Her strikes were fast, and though she was hitting harder, she was still too timid.

"You have to take me down. Get the upper hand." Erik dodged a punch.

"And how exactly am I supposed to do that?" Janelle snapped at him, growing more agitated by the minute.

"You're scared of something," Erik stalked closer. "Use it."

"I'm not fucking *scared*." Janelle shoved him backward.

"And I am not a fool. You're afraid, and you're lying to yourself about it. Fight me, Janelle. Prove to yourself that whatever haunts your nightmares has no hold over you."

"Shut up! You don't know what you're talking about!" Janelle shouted, her face turning red.

"You want me to shut up?" Erik yelled back. "Make me, Janelle!"

Janelle let out a cry filled with what seemed to be years' worth of pent-up pain and rage as she launched herself at Erik, driving her shoulder into his abdomen while hooking her right leg behind his and attempting to sweep it out from under him. Erik allowed it, crashing to his back with an echoing thud. It had been a good move, and one that she would have been successful with on her own, had she had a bit more time to work on strengthening. Erik made a mental note to make that an area of focus in training over the next few weeks.

Janelle climbed on top of him, straddling his hips and began throwing punches at his face, tears now streaming from her eyes. He blocked her blows gently, allowing her to take out her frustration on him.

"Good. More," he urged.

With a look of fury in her eyes, she reared back and punched again, this time smashing her fist into his lip. Janelle froze. "Oh my God, I'm so sorry." Janelle covered her mouth with her hands, her eyes wide and brimming with remorse.

Erik reached up and touched his lip to find blood on his fingers. "You do *not* apologize for learning to defend yourself."

Janelle tried to climb off Erik, but he grabbed her hips and pinned her against him, flipping them over. "And you definitely do not apologize when you throw a good punch." He turned his head to spit the blood filling his mouth onto the mat.

Janelle nodded, her chest rising and falling as her breaths became shallow.

Erik continued to pin her against the floor, his proximity to her causing his mouth to water and for him to grow thick and hard where his manhood pressed against her stomach. Janelle's eyes opened wide, and she squirmed, but she didn't push him away.

"Erik?" Janelle whispered breathlessly, "What are we doing?"

"We're training," he rumbled, every inch of him taut as he tried to keep himself from leaning down and tasting her lips.

"You know what I'm asking," she whispered breathlessly.

Erik's nostrils flared as he took a deep breath. "I'm waiting for you to decide what you want."

"I don't understand." She finally met his eyes, letting her tough facade drop and showing more vulnerability than she'd ever let him see.

"I think you know exactly how I feel about you, Janelle." Erik raised a hand to gently stroke her cheek. "I know what I want. But something's holding you back," Janelle tried to interrupt, but he continued talking, "and that's okay. I can wait until you know what you want. I want you to feel safe with me."

"I do," she said without hesitation, then paused as a hint of a smile pulled her lips up. "I do feel safe with you."

Erik bent down, resting his forearms on the ground on either side of Janelle's head and pressing his forehead against hers. The relief he felt at hearing those words was the greatest thing he had ever felt. He wanted to be her safe haven, her protector, her biggest fan. He wanted to be her everything. The feelings had snuck up on him over the past few weeks, but now they were all-consuming to a point that was maddening.

"Then, what do *you* want, Janelle?" His chest heaved with his effort to restrain himself.

Janelle bit her lip, taking a deep breath and exhaling slowly. With a trembling hand, she reached up and cupped his cheek. "I want you."

It was all the permission Erik needed before his lips crashed into hers, his hands tangling into her hair as her arms wrapped around his neck. Months of pent up tension fueled their movements, their kisses bruising in their intensity.

Janelle rocked herself against him, and Erik groaned, sliding his hand down to cup her breast.

"Erik," Janelle whispered, his name a plea and a promise.

Erik rose to his knees, pulling his shirt from behind head and throwing it to the floor before laying back down and brushing soft kisses along Janelle's jaw. He lowered his hand to the hem of her shirt and his fingers skimmed against her milky white skin, skin that he'd craved to explore every night since they'd begun sleeping wrapped around each other.

Janelle had taken to sleeping in his shirts since they'd arrived in Calir, the sight driving him to near insanity with need, despite the fact that they hung down to nearly her knees. He'd controlled himself, but now? He needed to see her, all of her. Feel her. He began pressing kisses between her breasts, lifting her shirt, and continuing down, kissing lower and lower. Erik needed to taste her, had waited so long to explore every inch of her body.

Something inside him demanded he show her what true pleasure felt like, what a man could do for a woman he loved. What a man *should* do for the woman he loved. He hooked his thumbs in the waistband of her pants, sliding them down slowly as he took in every inch of her exposed flesh. His fingers brushed against something hard and raised, and Janelle stiffened.

Erik searched her eyes for permission, and she nodded slightly before he pulled the side of her pants down further to expose her hip. A thick, jagged scar ran from her pubic bone across her hip bone, branching off and wrapping down her thigh and around her side to nearly her back. Erik's eyes darkened. He'd seen Janelle rub her hip subconsciously at times when she was nervous, but he had thought it was just a mannerism. But this? The scar *screamed* of violence and pain.

"Who did this to you?" Erik could hardly speak through the fire in his chest, the room suddenly stiflingly, unbearably hot.

"It doesn't matter." Janelle grabbed her pants and tried to pull them back up.

"Do *not* tell me it doesn't matter. This is why you're afraid, isn't it?" Erik traced the scar with his calloused fingers.

Janelle nodded silently.

"Is he still alive?" Erik's nostrils flared as he tried to control his magic.

"They are," she confirmed, looking away.

Erik felt his flames licking just inside his skin, threatening to explode out of him in his absolute rage. *They?* How many men was he going to have to kill? Because he would. He would kill every. Single. One of them. His rage became white hot, almost *painful* in his veins. Before his fire could hurt Janelle, he sent it outward, the torches in the room growing so tall the flames caressed the stone ceiling. Erik could see his reflection in Janelle's eyes, orange and red sparks flying around them.

"They won't be for long," Erik growled as he stood on shaking legs, helping Janelle rise from the floor and leading her out onto the balcony to escape the heat of his need for vengeance.

CHAPTER 62

LEA

After her evening with Erik, Lea couldn't settle. They'd trained until the sun was about to set, and Lea had returned to her room hoping exhaustion would pull her into a deep sleep. But as the rush of night magic had cascaded through the open wall, bringing in a gust of salty sea air, Lea's restlessness had only grown.

The more she'd accessed her shadows earlier, the more they'd seemed to multiply, eating up the darkness in the air and growing until she couldn't fully tuck them back down into her chest. Even now, tiny dark wisps emanated from her body, flickering like pure black flames.

With Gray gone and all hope for sleep lost, Lea wandered to the garden. It had filled her with hope to be given an opportunity to attempt to grow the moonflowers again, but that hope had quickly morphed into frustration as she found that the challenges of harvesting them hadn't changed with her increased magic.

The moon glowed softly and waves crashed in the distance as she slid off her shoes and stepped into the plot of dirt surrounded by sand. It was exceedingly odd, seeing such fertile ground sitting as an island in a barren seascape, but as Gray had told her before, magic wasn't controlled in Calir, and she was finding that the different abilities in the kingdom were far more diverse than she'd ever dreamed.

As soon as Lea climbed over the driftwood barriers to the garden and her feet touched the damp soil, her heart rate slowed. She took a deep breath, exhaling slowly as she savored the sweet scent of the various flowers growing all around her. In another life, or if she had more time, Lea would've explored this garden and everything growing in it. The tropical flowers were far more vibrant than the ones that she'd grown back home, and while she recognized a few, most of them were completely foreign to her.

Someday, when the king was defeated and the kingdom was once again living in peace, Lea would come back and learn all she could about these plants. But not today. Today, she had one singular mission. The same one she'd nurtured for the longest time. If the moonflowers could "defeat death himself," as her mother had told her, then Lea needed to learn how to grow and harvest them, and *soon*. There would never be a time they'd be more needed than now, with the Lonely Death spreading and war on the horizon.

She pulled a handful of seeds from the pocket of the skirt hanging loosely around her waist. It was once again white and flowed in soft folds all the way to the ground. The warm sea air blew it around her ankles, and she knelt down into the dirt, not bothered by the fact that she would get it dirty.

This was where she was meant to be, in the garden, connected to the earth. She'd already spent time here learning the differences in the soil and climate between her kingdom and Calir. The moonflowers grew differently here. Instead of tall, climbing vines, the moonflowers here seemed to prefer to bush out as they matured. They fared somewhat better in the shaded corner of the garden underneath a large foreign tree with bright pink flowers the size of her hand hanging from its branches, but still, even without the harsh direct sun, the small white flowers died off even before the petals fully opened. Yesterday, Lea had thought that maybe she would have some success when she planted three seeds beneath a large canvas sheet that blocked out all the light, but even in the shade, the flowers seemed determined to die.

It would have to be at night, she'd decided. Without the sun to burn the petal's edges, or the intense heat to dry out the vines, maybe she would be able to do it. Lea knelt down, cupping her hands and digging a small divot into the earth. She placed a seed inside before smoothing soil back over the hole and patting it down gently. Grabbing a watering can, she saturated the area, then watched with anticipation as the watering can magically refilled itself. *Amazing*, she thought. Lea would never get over how freely magic was available here. It almost made her giddy, and she hoped that her own kingdom would someday be the same.

Placing her hands on top of the small mound, Lea gathered the light in her chest and sent it to the seed. It only took a few moments before it sprouted, a small green shoot tickling underneath Lea's fingers. It snaked along the ground, growing so much faster than it ever had in Bearswillow. Lea allowed that energy to flow into the entire length of the plant, down into its roots and through the small tendrils branching off the main stem. The sight of white petals emerging from tiny buds caused her chest to squeeze, but after a moment, she sensed the creeping chill of death surrounding them.

It wasn't so different from what she'd felt as Queen Emmaline's baby had been struggling to survive. Powerful, black fingers closed around the flowers, pushing inside them and trying to pull away all evidence of life. More concerning was that it felt all too similar to the darkness Lea now felt inside herself—that raw, terrible power that had exploded within her as she'd fought to save the baby and had only grown today when she'd used her night magic. She tried to push it away from her moonflowers, but death's grip held firm.

She forced more light into the roots, urging them to take in more water, to fight against their own demise, but soon the plant's growth stalled and the petals turned into dust.

"Gods Dammit!" Lea hissed as she dropped her hands to her sides, flexing and extending her stiff fingers in frustration. It was the same thing, every damn time.

Lea tried again, once pushing the seed deeper into the soil, another time simply laying it on top of the ground. For what felt like hours, she attempted to change every variable she could think of. She'd planted one seed in the sand, given them differing amounts of water, had even tried to use her fire to chase away death, but that had left her only with incinerated flowers and growing desperation.

Sitting down in the dirt, Lea pulled the last moonflower seed from her pocket. She would need to ask the king's men if they'd return to the cottage and get her more. Pinching the small, crescent shaped seed between her thumb and forefinger, she held it up to the sky to get a better look. It was nearly identical to the current phase of the moon, slightly more slender, but the curvature was the same.

Maybe it's based on moon cycles? Lea pondered.

"It has nothing to do with the moon, Daughter of the Sun and Stars."

Lea jumped, dropping the seed as she spun around. Standing between the castle and the ocean against a starry backdrop was a small, frail woman.

"How did you..." Lea trailed off. Had the woman read her mind? "Who are you?" she asked instead, her shadows bursting to the surface of her skin on instinct.

"Who am I?" The woman remained still as stone as she looked Lea up and down. "I am the seer of all. I am the instrument of the gods; their voice and their will. I am the answer to the questions you seek." She nodded slowly at the ground behind Lea, where a large vine of moon-flowers was spreading across the ground, small white flowers blooming every several inches.

The woman hobbled to Lea, her movements slow and painful. Her long black hair was streaked with gray and pulled into a low bun, curly tendrils hanging around her face haphazardly from the tie holding it back. She was breathtakingly beautiful, despite the wrinkles etched into her face and the forward curve of her spine. Her eyes were *silver*—eyes that had seen too much—and were the most unnaturally stunning thing Lea had ever seen.

"You know how to grow the moonflowers?" Lea breathed, the hopeful energy flooding through her causing her to almost vibrate. This woman could help her. She could feel it in her very marrow.

"That is one of the answers you search for. But there are many more. Is that *really* the question you wish to ask?" The woman lifted her hand, and a moonflower plucked itself from the vine and slowly floated through the air, stopping just above their heads. "I know who you are," the old woman continued, spinning the flower in small circles as Lea watched in awe.

"The orphaned queen, giver of life, and servant of darkness. A young, naïve girl turned woman through trials of fire. A beautiful flower hunted by the Prince of Flames. A sun scorched bloom, fighting to survive just like these flowers you wish to master." The old woman snapped her fingers and instantly, the flower turned to ash and floated back onto the dark dirt like snow.

Lea shivered, taking a step back. This woman could help her, but without a doubt, she wore misfortune like a shroud. "Who are you?" she asked once again, already certain of the answer but needing to hear it from the crone's own mouth.

"You know who I am, girl," the woman said, a challenge in her eyes.

"Eudora," Lea breathed.

The witch tilted her head, narrowing her eyes. "I believe it's time we spoke."

CHAPTER 63

GRAY

As they neared the seventh village that had fallen to the Lonely Death, Gray's resolve strengthened. They hadn't run into any danger along the border so far on their travels, nor had he sensed any danger from his mate. They were so far away at this point that he couldn't speak into her mind, but still, with the mate bond sealed, Gray was able to feel Lea far more acutely. There was a constant undercurrent of light energy, skipping just next to his heart, his own rhythm thumping along with it.

The village they were approaching had only fallen the morning they'd entered Calir, just days after the sixth village had been decimated. Magic was so rampant within the kingdom that Calir had only seven men and women born without magic who were willing and strong enough to collect the bodies of the sick. It was far too big of a risk for King Tanad to allow his soldiers who had power to help, even if he tried to enchant his own protections onto them.

The cleanup had taken some time, King Tanad had explained a few days prior when they'd encountered the fourth village, where the seven selfless men and women were collecting bodies and respectfully stacking them in a large pyre to burn.

The fifth and sixth villages had almost broken Gray. He'd seen enough death, and certainly didn't need the reminder of seeing the bodies of families huddled together, embracing each other in their final moments. Still, he had looked, allowing the sight to fuel his fury. He memorized every face, let his darkness observe every ounce of horror and rage he felt. That was why, as they approached the seventh village, Gray felt a sense of relief. It was almost over.

He pulled a thick piece of cloth from his pocket and wrapped it around his nose and mouth. Tanad had been so kind as to bring lavender oil to drip onto their nose coverings to attempt to mask the smell of death and decay. Breathing in the calming scent, he straightened his shoulders. After he looked upon the bodies of the dead here in this final, cursed place, they could finish reinforcing the border against the Lonely Death and return home. Gray took what he could only assume was his last breath of fresh air for the time being and slid off of his horse, stretching side to side to loosen up his tight muscles. He couldn't help the tension that was creeping into his shoulders as he looked toward the final village.

"Our duty to the deceased, to acknowledge them and their inexcusable loss of life, is difficult, is it not? And yet it is a good reminder of why we are willing to sacrifice our own lives to stop it," Tanad said from behind him.

Gray exhaled sharply at the thought of dying, now that Lea's life was linked to his. And yet he knew that, if that is what it took, it was a sacrifice they were both willing to make.

"Respectfully, I don't need the reminder. The thought never leaves my mind, what my father has done to our people," Gray responded.

"Nor mine," Tanad said with a sad sigh before looking at the setting sun. "Let's go then." Tanad walked toward the rickety wooden gate to the small village. "We will soon lose light, and I wish to complete sealing the wards this evening. I'm sure you are eager to return as well."

Gray followed behind the king silently, flinching at the moan of the rusted hinges rotating as the gate opened. They walked to the first house, and Gray covered his nose with his sleeve, preparing himself for the awaiting stench, even through his scented nose covering, as Tanad opened the door. How many bodies rotted within these walls, just waiting for the king's men to come and give them a proper burial by fire?

The king paused as he entered the house, raising his hands in front of him. His gift was different from Emma's in that he couldn't see the dead, but he would still be able to sense the powers they'd had in life.

"There's no one here." Tanad turned around slowly, his eyebrows creased in concern. There was no sound in the home other than the pounding of blood in Gray's ears. No buzzing of flies or rustling of scavengers as they consumed the bodies of the dead. Something was wrong. He looked over Tanad's shoulder through the doorway at the blankets haphazardly thrown on the couch, and cups sitting stacked on the wooden shelves in the kitchen. Pushing his way inside, his heart picked up into a rapid, thundering rhythm. There was a kettle sitting next to the hearth, and a baby doll propped in a nearby chair. Someone had lived here, and recently. Dust had not yet settled on the floor or mantle. It was as if the inhabitants had simply disappeared into thin air.

But wasn't the kingdom on lockdown? No one was supposed to leave their homes. Without a word, Gray turned and ran to the next house, tearing open the door and barging inside.

Gray's shadows shot from his body, floating through the air and sliding along the floor to search the remainder of the house—but he could feel it, the emptiness. "They're gone!" He called to Tanad. A bloody rag laid on the ground, and Gray had a flashback of the rivers of crimson that had trickled from Lea's nose, and the sores that had dotted her chest and arms. He stalked back out onto the dirt road, ordering his shadows to disperse throughout the rest of the homes. He felt them twisting up stairs and climbing ladders, sliding beneath closed doors, and through keyholes. But there was not a single soul remaining.

"You said they were killed," Gray said, his words accusing. "Every one of them. Did you not investigate that?"

"Every man and woman safe from contracting the Lonely Death has been working around the clock, making their way east to collect the bodies and burn them. I couldn't spare a single one of them to confirm the village had fallen, and I am not willing to send someone with magic who does not have our protections to investigate when they themselves could be killed or bring the Lonely Death back with them. We received a heron with a message tied around its leg. It had the official seal of the village representative. He informed me of the first case of the Lonely Death. I knew it was only a matter of days before they were all killed. They already would've been infected by the time their message was received."

"Is there any possibility they escaped before that happened?" Gray closed his eyes, praying to the gods that this was the case, but a nagging feeling in his gut told him that he already knew the truth. He'd seen the bloody rag... The evidence of the disease.

"You know better than I do, Gray, that once the Lonely Death has been introduced to a household, it is too late. These communities are small. They are unable to avoid each other. There is only one baker, one butcher... Their lives are too interdependent for true isolation."

"Then where are they!?" Gray roared, clenching and unclenching his hands as his shadows spread even further.

"As I told you before, we have closed the borders. While I feared that the king's spies may have still been infiltrating the villages by sneaking through a break in the wards somewhere, I do *not* believe that more than a single man would be able to avoid detection. There must have been a hundred people living in this village. It's impossible that enough wagons crossed back-and-forth to take the bodies back to Auropera. My magic would have sensed something that big."

"Do you think they fled?" Gray asked.

Tanad looked toward the south, where several days' rides away, countless other towns dotted the landscape. "If they did, they would've infected other villages."

Gray pushed down the nausea rising up his throat. "The Lonely Death could be spreading throughout the entire kingdom as we speak."

"I don't know whether to pray they fled, or that they disappeared," Tanad said, closing his eyes and kissing a medal of the sun god hanging around his throat. "Both would have dire consequences."

"We need to return to the castle, send word to every other village to close their own walls and not allow travelers to enter." Gray stalked back toward Obsidian.

Tanad followed behind him. "No. We only have an hour's ride left to complete the border. We've come too far to leave that stretch undefended. Especially when it's so far from the capital. If there is any place the king is likely to sneak in, it would be there, where it's further from detection."

"Then let's go *now*." Gray looked at the sun's position in the sky, indicating it was late afternoon. "We'll quickly finish what we set out to do and return directly to the castle. If we push the horses, we should be able to make it back far more quickly than the infected would be able to walk to another village. They're rather isolated out here."

Gray jumped on Obsidian's back with ease, turning him straight north to resume enchanting the border. They'd been forced to move slowly, using up their magic and then waiting for it to replenish. Once it was done, there would be nothing stopping them from returning home as quickly as possible.

They worked even more efficiently this time, Gray adding his magic little by little, his arms cramping from holding them up in front of him. They rode until Gray once again saw the sea in the distance, the moon reflecting off the serene waters. The ripple of small waves floated toward them, along with a fresh breeze carrying the scent of salt and—a shockwave zinged through Gray's chest. "There's magic here, Tanad. Dark magic. Can you feel it?"

"I can." Tanad closed his eyes, concentrating as he raised his hands and walked toward the rocky cliffs bordering the beach. Gray dispersed his shadows, allowing them to follow the darkness emanating from the direction the king walked on their own accord.

"It isn't magic of the Fae." the king scrunched his face in concentration.

Tanad was right. Whatever it was felt foreign to Gray, unlike any magic he had encountered.

"It's the work of a witch." Tanad gritted his teeth as he pushed out more power. "It feels like—No that's not quite right. I can't place it."

Gray's ears began to ring, a sharp, high-pitched sound that made him squint and cover them with his hands.

Tanad did the same, taking a step backward as he looked at Gray with fear in his eyes. "This might not be safe. If you want to turn back—"

"This is without a doubt the work of my father. Even if it was his witch who performed the spell, he was the one who forced her to do it." Gray tried not to think of the witch his father kept enslaved; a broken woman, tortured and tormented until she had bent to his will. She might have been beautiful once, but scars marred her face and neck, her eyes so mutilated that her eyelids had fused together. "I will not abandon you, Tanad."

"Nor I you." Tanad lowered his chin. Gray was certain that they were both promising the same thing to one another, though in fewer words. They were complete allies in this war. One kingdom could not succeed against his father without the help of the other. They might not even succeed united. This was only one of many dangers they would face over the course of this war, but they would not face it alone.

Together, Gray and Tanad walked down a curving pathway, the sandy shore becoming rocky and uneven. The ringing grew louder, almost painful, but they continued on. Waves washed away their footprints, soaking their feet and trousers.

Gray's shadows abruptly halted, blocked by something solid that prevented them from moving forward any further. "Whatever it is, it's just ahead," he informed Tanad. With cautious steps, Gray crept forward, sidestepping a large uneven rock jutting out toward the ocean.

As soon as he turned the corner, he saw it; the magic that had caused his heart to quicken and his magic to revolt. Before him, just inside a small cave carved into the cliff side by thousands of years of waves crashing against it, was a doorway. At least, it was shaped like a doorway.

A perfect arch glowed from within the rock of the cave itself, illuminating it in a soft, gold and blue light. It rippled like water, reminding Gray of a time he had gone for a swim on one of his trips to Calir. He'd dove to the bottom of the ocean floor, holding his breath to swim for a shimmering shell he'd spotted. He could still see in his mind the way the sun's beams had danced as they reflected in the water. He'd wanted to stay down there forever, basking in the beautiful, dancing light and cool, calm water.

Now, looking at the blue and gold rippling water, he wanted to turn away and never return. Unfortunately, just like the last time when his lungs had begun to scream for oxygen, he'd had no choice but to go toward the surface.

With tentative steps, Gray moved in front of the doorway.

"A portal..." Tanad whispered.

"Can you sense where it goes?" Gray asked, praying that the king did, that they wouldn't have to enter without a clue as to where it would take them.

Tanad stepped forward slowly, using his powers to try to discern what lay beyond it. As he approached the portal, the king squinted his eyes and tilted his head, getting so close that Gray worried he would be sucked through at any moment.

"Do you have any idea where it leads?" Gray asked after several moments, unable to wait any longer.

The king turned around, sorrow and pain evident in his glistening eyes. His face was ashen, and his jaw tight. "I think this is something you need to see for yourself," he replied.

Gray ground his teeth, pushing down the warning bells that were so loud in his mind they almost drowned out the ringing that still made his ears hurt. He took slow steps forward, moving as if sudden motion could cause the portal to reach out and grab him. As he approached the liquid-like substance, shapes began to appear behind it, warped and distorted. It was more like water than Gray had first realized, and it looked like he was peering through a shallow stream. He could make out shapes and colors, but they were misshapen. Concentrating, he forced his eyes to absorb what he was seeing.

"I know exactly where this is." Gray's voice shook despite his determination to remain calm. Beyond the shimmering veil of the portal were bodies, stacked haphazardly with little care or regard to the fact that they'd once been living, breathing beings. But it wasn't just bodies he recognized—men, women, and children, all dressed in the clothing style of Calir. This was the damp, waterlogged dungeon of his father's wing of the castle, the lowest point, where he had been forced to watch as his father stole the magic of the innocent.

"Your father?" King Tanad asked, his face draped in despair.

Gray nodded, his fingernails cutting into his palms as he squeezed his hands into fists. "Yes. This is his work. The missing villagers... This must be how he removed their bodies." He could barely stand to speak as bile creeped up his throat, but Gray forced the words from his mouth, anyway. "Can you tell without entering if he has already taken their magic?"

Tanad raised his hands, his palms hovering only a centimeter above the portal. After several moments, as if he was searching within the soul of every single body in that room, King Tanad hung his head. "It is already done."

Gray wished desperately to retrieve the bodies, to give them a proper burial at sea, as was the custom in Calir. But it was too dangerous. Not to mention that it would tip off his father of their location. But still, the Black King could not have access to the kingdom. "We can't leave the portal here," Gray stated matter-of-factly.

"What do you suggest?" Tanad stepped back, analyzing the doorway.

It had to look like an accident. An act of nature. Gray let his shadows float from his hands, wrapping around the sharp rocks jutting out from the cave wall and holding tight. He let them spread outside of the cave, sneaking into small cracks and pockets, while firmly encircling the large rocks that supported the bottom of the bluff.

"We return to our horses, and we bring the cliff side to the ground."

It took immense concentration for Gray to maintain his hold on the dozens of jagged bits of stone as he walked back to where Obsidian waited, and yet it was as if his shadows were just as angry as he was, helping him maintain control.

Once Gray and the king were safely on top of their horses, Gray tore his shadows back with every bit of force he could muster, clenching his jaw as sweat trickled from his hairline. He kicked Obsidian's sides, directing the horse to Tanad's side and racing away as the caves and cliffs containing the portal disappeared into the ocean with an ear-shattering rumble.

The horses stumbled as the ground shook; the sand shifting as an earthquake more immense than anything Gray had ever felt before rocked the earth. As their horses jumped over the cracks forming in the ground and they shielded their eyes from the sand blowing wildly through the air, Gray hoped that his father felt it all the way in Auropera, and that he took it as a warning.

A warning that even the very earth was against him, and the gods would bring the mountains and sky crashing down to destroy everything he loved just as violently as the cliffs they raced away from.

CHAPTER 64

LEA

Lea's fingers trailed the thick, irregularly shaped stones of the circular tower as she climbed what had to be her hundredth stair. She'd stopped counting at fifty and had begun cursing whoever had designed the stairwell for not including a handrail instead. Her legs *burned*. Almost as much as her lungs.

Eudora kept a steady pace, diligently putting one foot in front of the other in a continuous rhythm. *Did her limp disappear?* Lea thought as she pushed on her thighs with her palms. The witch's strides looked too fluid, too easy. But the moment the thought passed through Lea's mind, the limp returned, a shuffling sound scraping from the stone floor with every step of her left foot.

If Lea had to guess, she would say that Eudora was intentionally misleading her about how much difficulty she had walking. Paying closer attention as they continued to climb, Lea watched Eudora's movement. *There!* Three more easy steps! *Why would she lie about something like that?*

They didn't speak as they came to the top of the tower. Not that Lea would've been able to with how out of breath she was. With a flick of Eudora's fingers, the door swung open with a groan. The witch led her to a chair inside a massive domed room, the walls covered in a violet, textured fabric that billowed loosely from ceiling to floor. The material bunched oddly in places, giving Lea the eerie feeling that someone could be hiding somewhere within them and she would be none the wiser.

One wall was filled to the top with bottles and vessels of every shape, size, and color. A tall, slender vial held a bubbling navy liquid, and next to it, a squat, square bottle swirled black and green. There were jars with feathers and jugs with different animal furs. Lea stopped examining them when, on the bottom shelf, she observed a large clear jug containing something that resembled human ears.

Rough, unpolished crystals in various shades of green, purple, and pink hung from the ceiling, and books were thrown haphazardly around the sitting area—which was simply two plush midnight blue chairs on either side of a scuffed wooden table atop a shaggy maroon rug. In the very back of the room was another winding staircase. *A bedroom?* The space gave every indication that Eudora lived within these walls.

Lea sank down into the chair in front of the window overlooking the moonlit ocean and a breathtaking display of stars. Her heart skipped a beat. There were thousands of them. Tens of thousands of them! The tower was so high Lea felt as if she could *almost* reach out and pluck one to keep in her pocket.

The suspicion settling in the back of Lea's mind grew. Without a doubt, Eudora was playing her. It was impossible for her to live this far up in the sky, to take those stairs day in and day out, at her age. *Something* wasn't adding up.

"You don't trust me," the witch said, taking a long sip of her tea. She set her cup down, then deftly rotated her fingers in the air. A second cup appeared on the table along with a shiny silver kettle, and Eudora poured the steaming water over the loose tea leaves, placing the intricate blue china in front of Lea.

Lea pondered her answer, not quite sure what to say. "I haven't de-cided yet," she said honestly, sniffing the tea and finding nothing amiss before taking a small sip herself. It was bitter, and Lea wished desperately for some honey or sugar to mix in to make it more palatable.

"Good. You shouldn't trust anyone. My kind are tricky, you know." She settled back into her chair, her piercing eyes sharp and alert. "As I'm sure your mate told you, we do not give information without receiving something we want in return."

"Is saving thousands of lives and overthrowing a murderous, evil dictator not something you want?" Lea took another sip of tea.

Eudora waved her hand in the air. "It's not a matter of caring about those lives. War will also take lives. Just as many, if not more."

"Then what *is* it you care about?" Lea's heart continued to flutter. *No,* she decided, *I most definitely do not trust this woman.*

"I care about my dear friend Tanad, and helping him protect his kingdom." Eudora clasped her hands in her lap, looking at Lea as if waiting for a challenge.

"Respectfully," Lea met the witch's gaze without flinching, "if you don't care about what the Black King is doing in Bearswillow, then why would you care about what he's doing here?"

"Because it saddens my black heart to see my lover in pain." Eudora's lips twisted into a disingenuous smile, the profession of love not quite meeting her eyes.

Lea's jaw dropped. "Your—"

"Lover, yes." Eudora placed her teacup down on top of the matching blue saucer. "He doesn't tell many people. Something about not wanting his rule to be questioned. It would destroy him to think that his subjects might believe him to be corruptible. But do not be mistaken. He secured his throne all on his own. The man is far too honorable for even an ounce of my corruption, despite my best efforts." Eudora winked, but Lea's shadows pushed against her skin, a warning to not believe the witch's attempt at camaraderie.

"He's been preoccupied lately," Eudora continued. "Staying up all hours of the night and worrying constantly about his kingdom and the safety of those who reside in it. I do not care about many people, but I do care about him." The witch's eyes softened, just enough to make

Lea believe she was witnessing a moment of sincerity. "That's where you come in."

"You're asking for *my* help?" Lea leaned back in her chair, her hands coming to rest on the arms as her eyebrows raised. In no way, shape, or form was this how she had expected this conversation to go. "What? You want me to put you and your friends in grave danger? Or maybe grow you some cucumbers?"

"Humor doesn't become you, girl," Eudora snapped, her lips tipping into a frown for a split second before clearing her throat and schooling her face into a bored mask. "I think that our relationship can be mutually beneficial." The witch crinkled her nose and sat up straighter, as if personally affronted by the way Lea slouched in her chair. "Is it not your wish to kill the Black King?"

Lea nodded her head, unable to stop herself from correcting her posture, pushing her shoulders back and raising her chin. "Of course I do."

"Well, *I* want the cure to the Lonely Death. And based on what I saw this evening in the garden, that is something we have in common. And yet, only you have the tools required to grow the moonflowers."

"That's all you want from me? For me to give you the cure to the Lonely Death once I learn how to grow the flowers?"

"That, and one small favor." Eudora picked at her nails as if disinterested. "The Black King has stolen something from the witches. In return for my help, I would ask that you retrieve it."

"Ask?" Lea raised an eyebrow, and Eudora looked her up and down before tilting her head.

"Ask. Demand. It is the same thing, my *dear*," she said, the word coming out like a poisoned dart.

"And where is this object that has been stolen?" Lea's stomach sank at the witch's tone. She was hiding something.

"Hidden in the depths of the Black King's castle. Don't worry. You'll be prepared for what you have to do. I've been waiting for that large, silly man to take you to the room of horrors."

Lea's eyebrows furrowed. *Silly man? Does she mean Erik?* "Is that what you call the training room Erik took me to? The one where you can make anything appear?" Was Eudora confused? That room had been scary, sure, but horrors?

"You haven't heard the wails of grown men, their cries for their mothers as they see before them the atrocities that riddle this world so they may learn how to defeat them. It appears your insatiably hungry trainer took it easy on you." Eudora cackled at her own joke.

A chill slithered down Lea's spine. Had he really taken it so easy on her? "What does the room have to do with what you want from the Black King's castle?" Surely Gray would know what it was if it was something of such significant value to both his father and the witch who had granted his curse.

Eudora's eyes snapped up as if she'd heard her thoughts. "It is of no use to your mate. Nor would he know why I seek it."

Lea placed a shield of shadows around her mind like Erik had been teaching her during training, seriously uncomfortable with the idea of Eudora poking around in her mind.

"In the depths of the dungeons, there is a cage. I assume you noticed one in the room?" Eudora asked, going back to picking her nails.

Lea nodded. "The one with all the locks."

"It is a replica. One that I requested Tanad create for me, and for his soldiers to train on. It is the one task that has escaped the abilities of my magic. I, unfortunately, am not able to break through the locks to retrieve what is inside."

"And you think I can?" Azalea shook her head slightly, her eyebrows scrunching. If a powerful witch couldn't do it, why did she think Lea would be able to? They were here to get *her* help, after all.

"You forget, I know what lies inside you." Eudora stared directly at Lea's breastbone as if she could see the magic swirling in her chest. "I know about the dark power threatening to consume you. *That power* is the only thing capable of opening the cage. Agree to help me, and I will give you the information you need to successfully grow the moonflowers."

"What about killing the king? And Prince Alaric? Gray still can't kill him without breaking the spell." Lea's head spun. What was she promising by agreeing to Eudora's bargain? It clearly wasn't an easy task if the dark magic beneath the crumbling floor inside her was the only way to obtain it.

"But you can, my dear. You have the power, if you act quickly," Eudora said cryptically.

Lea's fingers trailed the skin around her throat absentmindedly where the oozing black welts had marred her skin. "I'm part of their family now. I can't kill them anymore than Gray can."

"You are mates, not blood. There is nothing stopping you." Eudora patted her hair, rolling her eyes dramatically as if ensuring Lea knew she was agitated.

Lea leaned forward, calling her shadows to her fingertips as she placed a palm flat on the table between them. "We are married. He is my husband."

Eudora's eyes flashed, and her lips twisted into a snarl. "Impossible," she snapped, her wrinkled, blotchy hands shaking.

"I assure you, it is very much possible." Lea relaxed back, making no attempt to hide the satisfaction on her face at surprising Eudora. "It's the only reason I'm sitting here now. While we traveled here, I contracted the Lonely Death. It was the only way to save me."

Eudora gripped the arm of her chair, and Lea's eyes locked on her hands. Young, smooth skin wrapped around delicate, perfect fingers. Eudora looked as if she would spit fire with the next words she spoke, but Lea could only focus on her hands. She stood slowly, *easily*, as the crystals hanging from the ceiling began to rock back and forth, the long sleeves of her robe cascading down to hide her fingers. "I have watched your future unfold a thousand different ways, your path changing with every choice that could possibly be made. I know how your life ends, girl. Are you telling me that my visions were wrong?"

Lea struggled to remain seated, unwilling to appear afraid as she strengthened the shadows floating around her hands and unlocked the cavern where her dark magic swirled. "I'm *telling* you that is what happened. If your visions did not show it, then yes. I am saying they were incorrect."

Eudora's piercing silver eyes—eyes that looked so much younger than the frail body they inhabited—stared into her, so deeply Lea felt the need to place a shield in front of her. The faintest black fog appeared between them.

After several furious, deep breaths, Eudora returned to her seat, her movements appearing difficult again as the crackling energy in the room died off to a faint buzz. She picked up her tea, pulling a green vial from her sleeve and uncorking it. A single drop of gold liquid fell into the cup. With a swirl of her wrist, Eudora lifted it to her lips and drank deeply before flipping it upside down on the saucer in front of her. The witch settled back into her chair, pushing up her sleeves again to reveal discolored, wrinkled arms and hands.

"It doesn't matter." Eudora waved a palm over the cup. "This doesn't change that you need my help. And I need yours."

"If I agree to your terms," Lea lowered her chin, "then you'll tell me how to grow the moonflowers? *And* how to break the curse to allow us to kill Alaric and the Black King?" She was skeptical. It felt like a trap, like she was giving too little for information that would change absolutely everything.

"I will teach you how to find success with the moonflowers. But as for how to break the spell? That is a conversation I wish to save for your mate. Drink your tea," Eudora ordered, her fingers tapping impatiently against her knee.

Lea raised the cup to her lips. The tea was awful, but she needed a moment to think. It didn't seem like a coincidence that Eudora had waited to speak with her until Gray was far enough away that she couldn't communicate mentally with him. But at the same time, it was clear that the witch needed something from her. It wasn't as if what she requested went against her own goals. If the Black King and Prince were going to be killed, what would stop her from bringing Eudora whatever it was that was locked away in the dungeons? Gray would be the ruler of Auropera. Logistically, it sounded easy.

Lea took the final sip of tea, and Eudora stood fast as lightning, snatching the empty teacup from her hand and flipping it on top of the saucer. Lea reached for the cup, but Eudora grabbed her wrist, her grip so strong Lea was certain she would have a bracelet of finger shaped bruises in the morning.

"My offer expires in ten seconds. Make your decision." Eudora squeezed harder.

Lea yanked her arm away, stumbling backward. She didn't want to make a deal with this awful woman. But to be able to grow the moonflowers? Save thousands of people? Lea felt as if she had no choice. "I'd like to agree..."

Eudora's eyes twinkled.

"But make no mistake—" Lea's shadows slithered around the table, wrapping around Eudora's arm and up to her neck, pushing up her chin and holding her in place as Lea stared straight into her unnatural eyes, her darkness begging for release as the sting of pain fed their fury— "if you touch me again, I will kill you. You think I am the only one strong enough to break through the locks? That means I am more powerful than you. You think I am a sun scorched bloom? That might be true. But when someone is burned to their very bones, that fire never goes out. An ember remains—burning, waiting for retribution. Place your hands on me again, and you will be on the wrong side of my revenge."

It was a challenge, and Eudora clearly knew it. Her silver eyes flashed black, and for just a moment, Lea saw a beautiful young woman before her, but when she blinked, Eudora was only a frail, wrinkled witch.

"Understood," Eudora hissed.

"Then we have a deal." With Lea's words, the room flashed in a burst of light, the candles flickering and wind whipping her hair around her face. Eudora smiled broadly, closing her eyes and reveling in the elements erupting around the room. Lea could do nothing but watch, her heart pounding erratically. *What did I just agree too?*

As quickly as it started, the room calmed, the wind stopping and the flames of the candles growing low.

"What the fuck was that?" Lea snarled.

"It was nothing but a bargain. Fulfill your end of the deal, and there will be no consequences." Eudora eyed Lea's overturned cup.

"And if I don't?" Lea had every intention of keeping her word, would do anything at all to grow the moonflowers, but still, she needed to know.

"Then you forfeit your life." A wicked smile spread across Eudora's face, showing cracked, yellowing teeth.

"That wasn't part of the deal—"

"It is done." Eudora cut her off. "I believe in you. I know you'll deliver what I seek." With a snap of her fingers, Eudora's teacup flew into her outstretched hand, and the witch examined the leaves. "Mmmmm. As I thought." Her eyes flicked to Lea's. "My instructions will allow the moonflowers to grow."

Lea bit her lip, silently cursing herself for not questioning what would happen if she failed. Were the leaves telling her how to use the moonflowers, or were they simply telling the future? That if she followed Eudora's instructions, she would have success?

"They must be grown at night, after the setting of the sun and the rise of the magic of the night." An image of a moonflower appeared between them, floating in the air just as it had in the garden.

"That can't be it. I've tried that before, tried every possible time of night." Rage boiled in Lea's stomach.

"Quiet!" Eudora glared. "That is not all."

Lea took a deep breath and opened her hands, allowing the witch to continue.

"The moonflower's magic was stolen with the death of your grandmother."

"Queen Emmaline," Lea breathed, the memory of her vision flashing through her mind. The king had taken her blood, and as the moonflowers had dropped into the growing puddle beneath her, they had turned black and disintegrated, just as they did every time she grew them.

"Yes. Her blood was used to create the Lonely Death. It is a funny name, don't you think?"

"I don't think there is anything funny about the slaughter of innocents." Lea's shadows reached toward Eudora, itching to wring her neck.

Eudora waved her hand in the air as if wafting away smoke. "But you see, that is where the humor lies. Those who die of the Lonely Death, are not *dead*. Not until the king steals their magic, sucks out their very souls, taking what he wants and discarding the rest."

"What do you mean? They are gone. All of them. My mother..."

"Adelaide, yes. The disease is gruesome, appears to take the lives of those infected, but the soul remains. That is how the king can steal their magic. Their heart continues to beat. Slow and soft, but a beat nonetheless. He can only steal magic that is alive, but weakened. A brilliant spell, really." Eudora's eyes sparkled as if in admiration.

"That can't be true." Lea's hands began to shake, and she squeezed them into fists, her fingernails cutting into her palms.

"Would you have gone near someone with the disease? Had someone only bothered to check for a pulse, they would have realized the dead weren't really dead at all." Eudora smiled, and Lea felt the urge to shove her shadows between her teeth and down her throat.

Anger wasn't an appropriate word for what Lea felt. It was sorrow and rage and an all consuming urge for revenge. A dark, wicked fire flickered beneath the floor in her chest, its smoke floating through the small crack and escaping to wrap around her heart as the room grew darker, the flames of the candles only suggestions of light. Smoky gray shadows floated into every crevice of the room, pulsing with her own heartbeat.

"There it is, girl." Eudora's voice deepened. "Embrace the darkness. You will need that fury to do what is required of you to grow the moon-flowers."

Her dark magic skipped in response, thumping against the floor in her chest. "Tell me what I have to do." Lea would do anything. Absolutely anything to save the lives of those infected.

"It was lifeblood spilled from your grandmother's throat to create the spell. To break it, blood must be given back to the flowers. It must drown the soil where they grow, and the seeds must consume it. Only one with the blood of the wronged in their veins may pick the petals. They are owed to you, and you alone."

The right person, at the right time, with the right intentions... Her mother's letter grew warm in her pocket.

"Just water the soil with blood, and as long as I am the one to pick the petals, it will work?"

Eudora tilted her head, as if she wanted to say more. "With enough blood, yes. That will allow them to grow."

"And have your visions shown you this? Have they shown us success-fully killing the Nestruirs and growing the flowers?"

"In one reality, yes. You must be careful with the decisions you make. There are many possible outcomes." Eudora reached for Lea's cup, still overturned on the table in front of her, but Lea snatched it with her shadows, placing a finger on the inside and swirling the leaves.

"I will make the right choices," Lea said, standing and commanding her shadows to open the door to the stairwell. "And I will decide my own fate. Not you, and certainly not your gods' damned tea leaves." Lea placed the cup back on the table with a thud, the china cracking near the handle as Lea walked calmly from the room, her shadows swiping the small green vial hiding in Eudora's sleeve.

CHAPTER 65

JANELLE

Janelle's body was on fire, but she wasn't certain if it was from kissing Erik or from his explosive anger when he'd seen her scar. It wasn't exactly how she'd planned on telling him what had happened to her, the reason she stayed emotionally detached. Actually, she would have preferred to never have told him why she chose to stick to the physical aspect of relationships, but he'd felt the jagged lines on her skin, and she'd had no choice. Janelle had known what he'd find as he slid her pants down, and she'd let him do it anyway. That's how much she wanted him—enough for him to know the truth.

She was broken. Scarred. Not only on the outside, but deep inside her soul as well.

The cool sea breeze kissed Janelle's skin and blew her hair around her face, the heat at her back from the inside of the room almost tolerable now that she was standing in the open air. Janelle looked up at Erik who was staring intensely out at the ocean, his hands gripping the thick railing so hard, Janelle feared it might shatter.

"Say something," she urged, the silence causing her skin to itch and her scar to burn. The muscles of Erik's jaw bunched. He ground his teeth together, and with a heavy sigh, he turned to face her, pulling his eyes from the reflection of the moon dancing along the waves.

As he met Janelle's gaze, he almost looked like a different person. His eyes usually twinkled, and the dimple on his right cheek normally peeked out with the hint of a smile he wore at all times. Erik was always so happy, so different from her... From everyone she knew, actually.

"Will you tell me what happened?" His voice sounded deeper, rougher, as if he'd had to force the words from his throat.

"It doesn't matter." Janelle grabbed his hand. "It's in the past."

"It matters to me," Erik said, pulling her closer. "It's not in the past if it follows you when you sleep. If you don't feel safe. If whoever hurt you is still breathing."

Janelle's gut twisted at the pain on Erik's face, and she wished desperately that she hadn't said that. The truth was, she did feel safe; she knew that Erik would protect her at any cost. But when he hadn't shown up to drag her to training, it had sparked some deep insecurity inside her. It had been irrational, but the feeling that she wasn't important enough had been all consuming.

She was just a human, and not even the one who was going to save them all from the Black King. It didn't bother her, really. She loved Lea, and was proud of her friend for embracing her fears and trying to make the world a better place. Janelle was fine with being the sidekick to the future queen of Desia. But not to Erik. To Erik, she wanted to *matter*. "You asked me if I've ever been loved before. Years ago, I thought I was. I was only seventeen. I met a boy on Fire Night—a soldier."

Erik stiffened, his eyes flashing with red hot fire. Letting go of his hands, Janelle placed herself between him and the balcony railing, bringing his arms to rest on either side of her so they could both look out at the water. It would be easier for him if he couldn't see the pain she knew would be in her eyes—and easier for herself, too, if she was being honest. She wouldn't be able to hide the sharp, stabbing agony. Not from Erik. He'd always seen right through her.

"We were... together, I guess. Jakob found a way to always be among the soldiers sent to Bearswillow, and he would come see me whenever he could. We kept it a secret." Janelle's hand traced the scar on her hip.

"If you were *together*," the word sounded like poison slipping from Erik's clenched jaw, "why would you keep it a secret?"

"Plenty of girls in the village have a little fun with the soldiers on Fire Night, but to actually start a relationship with them? With a man who serves the Black King? A soldier who helps keep our village hungry and our men working to the bone? It wouldn't be tolerated. Not to mention that not everyone is so accepting of relationships between humans and Fae."

Erik leaned down and pressed his forehead to the back of Janelle's head, and she sensed him trying to control his breathing as she continued on with her story.

"One day my parents were gone, and Jakob came to see me. We were, um, being intimate." Smoke began to twist up from the railing, Erik's hands leaving scorch marks that spread from beneath his palms on the stone, but Janelle ignored it. If she didn't get it out now, she never would.

"His brother had found out about us, and he was furious. He came to find Jakob, and when he saw us together, he flew into a rage. They took turns beating me, Stefan and then his friends, and Jakob just stood there. He couldn't even look at me, fucking coward." Janelle swallowed down the bitter recollection of blood in her mouth, wincing at the painful memories. "Stefan threw me into a table with a clay vase on top. It was my mom's. My dad made it for her when I was born. I can still picture the little flowers that he painted along the top rim."

Janelle sniffled. For some reason, the devastated look on her mother's face when she'd seen the pieces of the vase in a pile by the fireplace was always what she pictured when she thought of that day.

"It shattered and cut my hip." Janelle swallowed, wishing she could keep the last bit of the story to herself, but knowing that she needed to tell Erik the complete truth. "Stefan took a large, pointed shard and—he pinned me in place as his friends held my arms above my head. I was just laying there, naked and bleeding," Janelle felt Erik's ragged breaths and the heat from the fire flickering across his skin that he was somehow preventing from burning her. His hands were now consumed with flames, but for some reason the heat against her back was reassuring.

"Did he..." Erik couldn't say the words, but Janelle knew what he was asking.

"No. They didn't." Janelle took a deep breath, knowing that what she was about to say could change everything. "He said I was human filth, unworthy of his brother, and unworthy of mothering his child."

"You were pregnant?" The railing of the balcony cracked, fissures spreading in long irregular crevices from the burned surface. "He hurt you, while you were pregnant!?" Erik seethed.

"No!" Janelle said hurriedly, shaking her head. "No, I wasn't. But we'd..." Janelle trailed off, clearing her throat. "Stefan said he wouldn't allow his brother to risk it. He stabbed the shard into my stomach, starting from the cut at my hip and twisting and ripping my insides to pieces. I think he wanted to make sure that not only could I not carry his brother's child, but that I would never be able to carry a child at all." Her voice cracked at the confession. She'd never told a soul, not even her closest friend. Admitting it out loud made it feel real.

Erik opened his mouth to speak but Janelle continued, needing to get the rest out. Needing it to be finished.

"He left me there, bleeding. Jakob told me that he'd come back for me someday, that he'd get me out of Bearwsillow and we'd run away together, but I told him if he did, I'd gut him. I never saw him again."

Erik exhaled slowly, and Janelle swore she saw smoke from his nose dispersing into the air.

"Somehow, I made it to Lea's mom. Adelaide healed me as much as she could, but the damage was done. I swore her to secrecy. She's the only one that knows what happened to me—besides you, now." Janelle hung her head. "I was doing okay. I'd moved on, and then the tirror in the woods showed Stefan to me. Showed me all of them. They beat me, again, and now I can't get them out of my mind. I'm broken," Janelle admitted with a sob.

Erik slowly turned Janelle around until she was facing him and caged between his large body and the balcony railing, his hands still crushing the fissured stone. "Are you finished?" he asked gently, a severe juxtaposition between the fury in his eyes and the softness in his voice.

Janelle nodded, unable to speak. She worried if she opened her mouth, years of pent-up screams would come rushing from her throat.

"You are *not* broken." Erik lifted her face, holding it firmly in his scalding hands and refusing to allow her to look away. "You are a survivor. You put yourself back together, so much stronger than you were before. You are *everything* that I want, and so much more than I deserve."

"Weren't you listening, Erik? I'm damaged. I can't have children, and—"

"You are *not* damaged," Erik interrupted. "From the moment you stole that dagger of mine as we walked back from the gardens in Auropera, I knew I had to have you, in whatever way you would let me. *You* are what I want. Not children. Not *anything* else. Only you." Erik was shaking her, and the passion in his voice almost made Janelle believe him.

"You don't mean that," she sobbed. He couldn't.

"I have never meant anything more. For months, I've tried to understand why you refused to let me in. But I told you, I'm a patient man. I knew that someday, when you felt safe, you'd tell me the truth. And I knew that whenever that time came, nothing you could say would make me change my mind."

"I'm scared Stefan will try to find me again, finish what he started," Janelle admitted, blinking away the image of his cruel face as he'd plunged the shard into her belly. The image that followed her into her nightmares.

"He won't have the chance," Erik vowed, the heat from his hands on her arms almost unbearable. "They can count their days, every one of them, because their deaths are *mine*. When I find them, I'll incinerate them inch by inch until they beg for death. And I will look them in the eyes as I tell them that I am here because I love *you*, the human they deemed worthless. The woman they *thought* they broke." Erik's words held a sense of finality to them, as if fate was sealing them in the stars as he spoke them.

Janelle had no doubt Erik would follow through with his promise, and then, it would be over. The nightmares, the memories. She would never have to worry about them finding her again. Relief filled her lungs as she shared the burden of her pain, her past. A weight lifted off her shoulders as she realized that even though she was broken, Erik *loved* her. He loved *her*.

Janelle's heart raced, and wings the size of the heron's she watched soaring over the ocean beat in her stomach. Janelle didn't often cry, and yet she was, a sob working its way up her throat. It had terrified her to be vulnerable, to confess her deepest insecurities, but Erik had somehow made it easy. And even with her soul and past laid bare, he loved her anyway.

Nodding through her tears, she pressed her forehead against Erik's chest. He folded his arms around her as if it was a reflex, engulfing her in heat, but Janelle didn't care. For the first time in over five years, she felt at peace, completely whole.

Janelle wanted to kiss him, to feel his hands exploring her body, but she couldn't force herself to pull away from his comforting embrace. She'd had plenty of physical affection in her life, but this emotional connection? Never once since that day had she allowed it.

She couldn't stop it as a cascade of love and belonging filled a hole inside her that had been sitting empty, waiting. As if Erik sensed her thoughts, he gently lifted her in his arms, cradling her against his chest as he returned them to their room. He placed her on the bed and silently climbed in behind her. Pulling her firmly against his chest, Erik tucked her head in the crook of his neck.

"Thank you," Janelle whispered, grabbing his arms where he held her.

"I meant what I said, Janelle. I love you. I would do anything for you. Whatever you need, I will be it."

Janelle was unable to bring herself to say the words back, not yet. She'd opened up enough tonight, and she sensed Erik knew that, knew how she truly felt. And so they simply laid there together, Janelle soaking up every bit of love that she could and wondering if maybe she actually was enough for someone after all.

CHAPTER 66

LEA

It was nearly impossible to focus on training the next day. In the early morning hours Lea heard Gray speak into her mind. Once again, instead of just feeling the presence of the bond and faint muted sensations of what he was feeling, his voice was clear and his emotions strong. *I'm coming, Little Flower.* As she opened her eyes and sat upright, shaking away the remnants of sleep, she was hit with an overwhelming sense of trepidation. Something was wrong.

What is it? Lea asked him.

King Tanad and I have news. We should be back by sunset. Gray's voice sent a zap of electricity through her chest.

I've missed you. Promise you're safe? Lea knew that physically, at least, he was fine. She couldn't feel any injuries or pain from him through their bond, but still, she needed to hear the words.

I've missed you too, and I'm fine. Are you?

Lea's heart raced. *I'm okay.* Lea paused, wondering how much she should share with him right now. *I spoke to Eudora.*

A lightning bolt of fury crashed in her chest. *I knew she would wait until I was gone. Tell me you didn't promise her anything.*

Lea hesitated. Gray wasn't going to be happy with her, but she couldn't lie to him. *Nothing that we can't handle. We can talk about it when you get here.* She sent a reassuring pulse of calm through the bond.

Lea swore that she heard him growl, but he didn't argue with her. There was no point, now that the deal had already been made.

Fine, Gray finally answered. *Go back to sleep, Little Flower. I love you.*

Lea finally gave up on sleeping after about an hour, her excitement about Gray's return making it impossible. Even after she dressed and ate her breakfast of colorful, tropical fruit, the day moved exceptionally slowly. Their morning run seemed to take twice as long, and now, after an afternoon in the 'room of horrors,' as Eudora called it, and then dinner in their rooms, they had returned to the training room to work on combat and weaponry.

Lea's eyes darted to the doors every few seconds, waiting for them to open and for Gray to enter. Hints of purple were beginning to float above the ocean, the bottom of the sun diving down for its evening swim. *He said by sundown,* Lea thought, trying to swallow her worry. She hadn't felt anything wrong, could still feel his heartbeat and his magic mixing with her own. Still, it was impossible to focus. Wordlessly, Lea sat down on the mat, folding her arms across her chest, waiting.

She sensed him before she saw him, that undercurrent of electricity that always warned her of his proximity, and she jumped to her feet and was out the doors even before Gray got there. Launching herself into his arms, she wrapped her legs around his hips. It felt like coming home, like sliding into the comfort of your familiar bed. Pressing her face between his neck and chin, Lea inhaled deeply, and the scent of the wind that carries in a summer rainstorm flooded her senses.

"I missed you so much," Gray whispered into Lea's hair, kissing her just above her temple. He held her tightly against his chest, the tension in his shoulders melting away.

"I missed you, too. Next time you need to leave, I'm going with you," Lea insisted. Being apart from him wasn't natural. Not at all.

"I absolutely agree." Gray's shadows folded around her body, assessing her.

"I'm fine. No injuries to report here, Commander," Lea joked as she ordered her shadows to do the same.

Erik appeared behind them, clearing his voice. "You're back sooner than I expected," he said, his voice brimming with concern.

Gray placed Lea's feet back on the ground, but kept her firmly tucked against his side. "We found something that warranted us rushing back. We rode through the night and day as fast as we could to get here."

Reaching out, Lea stroked the dark circles under Gray's eyes, taking in his messy hair and open collar. He looked completely exhausted. Lea closed her eyes, suddenly feeling faint. Was Gray really feeling this weak?

Grabbing her hand, Gray kissed her fingers softly before turning to Erik. "We need to talk, all of us. Erik, get the others and meet us in Tanad's study."

As soon as they were alone, Gray lifted Azalea back into his arms, wrapping her legs around him and pressing her up against the wall. His lips found hers immediately and his kisses were almost bruising as he tangled his hands through her hair.

"Never again," he rumbled against her mouth. All Lea could do was moan as she rocked herself against him, and Gray let out a heavy sigh.

"There's nothing I want to do more than bury myself inside you and forget the last week and a half. But there are too many things we all need to discuss. King Tanad is waiting." Gray leaned his forehead against the wall above Lea's head.

"We should go, then," Lea said breathlessly.

"We should," Gray parroted, but remained still as stone. After several long moments, he moved back, sliding Lea down his front and grabbing her hand. Without releasing one another, they walked to the war room, and Lea was unsurprised to see the king already waiting for them. Once Erik and the others joined, Gray wasted no time reporting on their journey.

"We learned how my father was able to get the Lonely Death into the kingdom. He created a portal." Lea's eyebrows raised as a wave of dizziness washed over her. She'd never heard of such a thing outside of fairy tales and bedtime stories.

"It's true," King Tanad said softly, a slightly dazed look on his face as if he couldn't believe it himself. "Gray destroyed it."

"I think our efforts reinforcing the border bought us some time, but our wards won't hold forever." Gray's shadows danced along the floor as if reliving the memory.

"This moves up our timeline," Erik piped in.

"It does," Gray pressed his lips together grimly. "My father could create another portal at any moment, and even if we sent soldiers to patrol the border constantly, I doubt any of them would be powerful enough to overtake his magic."

Lea opened her mouth to ask a question, but no words came out. *What was I going to say?* Lea was lightheaded, her vision going fuzzy at the edges and her head swimming. She closed her eyes and pressed her hand to her forehead, willing the sensation to pass, but when she opened her eyes again, she was no longer in the war room. Instead, she stood back in Auropera, her vision partially blocked by the corner of a rough stone wall. The sense of being out of control of her body was startling, but unlike her vision in the garden, this time it didn't feel real.

Lea couldn't feel the cold stone or smell the damp air of the castle. Instead, it felt as if she was in a dream. *Did I pass out?* she thought as she tried to focus on the sliver of room she could see around the wall. The scene unfolding before her was odd. The Black King laid in a large four-poster bed, his skin sallow and his chest rhythmically moving up and down. Most startling of all was that standing above the king, leaning over the bed and staring at him so intensely he wasn't even blinking, was Alaric.

The prince was so still that were Alaric's nostrils not flaring with every inhale, Lea would have thought she was looking at a painting. His lips began to move, but within seconds, his face turned a deep shade of red. Veins bulged in his forehead as he coughed, and a trickle of blood ran from the side of his mouth. Wiping it on his sleeve, the fabric staining a deep red, Alaric stopped, sucking in several deep breaths before his face returned to its normal, pale pallor.

Alaric glared at the king for what felt like an eternity before leaning down and speaking in his ear. "You'll be at rest soon, I'm sure of it," he finally said, and while the words were caring, his tone of voice was not. He sounded angry, each syllable dripping with bitterness. Alaric tilted his head to the side as if considering something before abruptly swinging his head toward the door.

The image in her mind shifted, and all at once it was as if she was running, paintings and curtains rushing past in her periphery as she sprinted toward a wooden door. Her vision faded into wisps of black before returning to the now silent war room. Gray was kneeling before her, his hands squeezing her thighs and the muscles of his jaw bulging.

"What just happened?" Lea asked, shaking away the foggy feeling in her head and her still blurred vision. Gray and Tanad shared a look.

"What did you see?" King Tanad asked, his voice gentle but his eyes piercing.

"I saw the king. The Black King, I mean," Lea rubbed the back of her neck where a cold sweat had broken out. "He was laying in bed, and he looked sick."

"Sick how?" Gray questioned, he and Erik looking at each other as if a silent conversation was passing between them.

"He was pale, and had lost weight, like he hadn't eaten in weeks. Um..." Lea blinked several times, trying to make the room stop moving. "He was asleep, and Alaric was standing over him, just *watching*." The picture in her head made her shiver. "Wait, how did you know I saw something?"

"Eudora gets the same look in her eyes when she has a vision," Tanad explained, speaking slowly and softly as if he thought his words might frighten her.

Lea shook her head. "It didn't feel like the vision I had of Queen Emmaline. It was different. Like I was watching it through someone else's eyes. I wasn't *there*. I couldn't look around or move... only see what I was shown."

"I don't like this." Gray stood, the candles in the room dimming as his shadows smothered their light. "If someone found a way to access Lea's mind, who's to say my father isn't planting visions, using that damned witch of his to feed us false information?"

"The vision tells us little, anyway. But you're right, the thought is alarming," Erik agreed.

"We need to know what that was before we return to Auropera." Gray turned to face Tanad, placing his palms flat on the table. "Summon her." He ordered, his eyes flashing with shadows. "Now."

"Eudora will call on you when she feels the time is right. You know this, Commander," King Tanad chewed on the side of his lip, and Lea thought he looked anxious for the first time since she'd met him.

"We don't have time for this!" Gray threw up his hands, sending shadows crashing into the ceiling. "While she sits in her tower, taking pleasure in making us wait, treating us like little pawns in her game, people are *dying*. Innocent people."

"She'll do it for you, King Tanad." Lea stepped in front of Gray, placing a calming hand on his forearm. "If you ask her to, she'll help us. She cares for you."

"She cares for me because I do not demand things of her before she is ready." Tanad raised his voice, and Lea paused. He was always so controlled.

"She doesn't want your people to suffer," Lea said more gently. "Tell her that King Nestruir has found a way into the kingdom, and we need to know how to allow Gray to kill his father. She'll do it for you."

"No one calls on Eudora. Not even me." Tanad clasped his hands in front of him as if closing the matter.

"I know where she lives." Lea turned back to Gray. He was right. They needed answers, and after speaking with Eudora last night, Lea had no doubt that it was nothing more than a sadistic need for control that caused Eudora to decide whom she spoke to and when. "I'll take you." Lea lifted her chin and looked Tanad directly in the eye, refusing to back down.

The king exhaled in a sigh, leaning forward and placing his palms flat on the table. He held Lea's stare for several moments before he shook his head and walked onto the balcony to face the sea.

CHAPTER 67

LEA

Climbing the hundreds of stairs to get to the top of Eudora's tower was no easier the second time around. Lea set the pace and Gray followed behind her while she focused on using her training to help her endurance, sending healing energy to her lungs and her legs with every inhale and exhale. As they trudged higher, Lea told Gray about her meeting with the witch, what she'd said about how to use the moonflowers and the fact that she'd refused to tell Lea how to break the curse regarding Gray's family.

Gray looked furious; his shadows twisted and grew with every word she spoke, his eyes darkening with wrath. Over and over he clenched his hands into fists, his shoulders raising toward his ears. While he didn't chastise her for making a bargain with Eudora, it was obvious that he wasn't happy about it.

"She's *going* to tell us everything we want to know. Tonight, if she wants to live," he grumbled. "We need to return to Bearswillow. Something doesn't feel right. I'm not sure what, but first the portal, and now your vision? Something's coming."

Lea nodded in agreement, unable to speak as she struggled to breathe.

By the blessing of the gods, they made it to the top of the tower, where the plain wooden door sat at the end of the stairs.

"Are you sure about this?" Lea asked. Smoke rolled from the small crack beneath the door as if a dragon was waiting to cremate them upon entry.

"You said she wants to help Tanad, and she's not powerful enough to kill us. Not the both of us together, at least. We have no other choice." Gray lifted his hand to knock, but before he could touch it, the door cracked open, an eerie *creak* echoing from the hinges.

"Did I not say when the tides were right and the stars were willing, I would find you?" Eudora's voice slithered into the hallway. It was full of warning, but Gray wasn't deterred as he shoved into the room.

"You'll still get whatever it is you want from our deal, Eudora. But I'm done waiting."

The witch stood by the window, turning and narrowing her eyes as the door slammed against the wall with a *crack*. "You're here because of the portal?" she guessed, and the room grew darker instantaneously as Gray's shadows spread into every corner of the space.

"You *knew*? I thought you wanted to help the king!" Lea stepped forward, her blood heating in fury.

Eudora wiped her hand through the air as if shooing away a bothersome fly. "I saw your mate destroying it. There was no reason for concern."

"You could have saved that village!" Gray seemed to grow larger, along with the shadows around him.

"I could have. And maybe lost the war," the witch said slowly, deliberately. "If you want my help, I suggest you reevaluate how you speak to me." Eudora stalked to a large cauldron in the corner of the room, the source of the smoke. She stirred the potion four times clockwise, then twice counterclockwise. The bubbling liquid hissed and spat frothing, deep red sludge as Eudora uncorked a black, jeweled glass bottle and pulled several dried petals from inside of it.

"If you'd like to keep your tongue," Gray retorted, enunciating every syllable with controlled rage, "I suggest you use it to tell me how to break the curse."

Eudora's silver eyes narrowed, and in the blink of an eye, she was standing only inches from his face. She trailed a finger from the corner of his ear across his throat to his collarbone, circling him with fluid, easy steps.

"What do you know of sacrifice, King?" Eudora asked, her voice as sweet as honeyed wine, but laced with an undercurrent of something wicked that Lea couldn't quite place.

Lea couldn't help the anger that flared through her chest. Gray knew nothing *but* sacrifice. He'd all but damned his soul as he'd watched his father destroy the kingdom, waiting for his chance to act. He lived a life that wasn't his own, one in which he dedicated every second to trying to save his people—a life he was willing to surrender for it.

"I think you know the answer to that question," Gray said coolly, his face as impassive as if it had been carved from stone.

"When I granted your wish for the spell I so graciously cast for you after your sister died, it was forged in equality. Your father could not kill you or your mother or brother, and in turn, you could not kill them. Undoing the spell only for your sake would disrupt the balance of the universe. Unless, of course, something of value is given freely."

"What is it you demand?" Gray strolled to the shelves of bottles, studying them like they were the most interesting thing he'd ever seen.

"Would you sacrifice anything at all? Your mate, for example?" A slow, vicious smile spread across Eudora's face.

Gray froze, as did his shadows, just for a moment before he raised a hand and lifted a golden jar with a black tendril, then sent it crashing to the ground. "You are alarmingly close to sacrificing your own life just by uttering those words. This is your only warning. She lives. No matter what," Gray seethed, tilting his chin up in a challenge.

Eudora paused. "Would you really do *anything* for her to live?"

"If you valued your life, you would know the answer to that question. Gray pushed Lea protectively behind him with a thick, black mass of shadows.

Eudora's grin only widened. "I was hoping you would say that. You'll be surprised that in this instance, the cost for your answers is not something I demand at all. I will break the spell, but a sacrifice will have to be made."

"You will not trick me this time, Eudora. You cannot have her. I'll give up my magic, my throne—"

Eudora stopped him. "The sacrifice will not be made today. I will break the spell in exchange for your word. You will sacrifice what is demanded of you. You will know when it is time."

"And she will live?" Gray's voice crackled like thunder in the distance.

Eudora's eyes flashed silver, and Lea once again saw a flicker of a young, beautiful woman standing in front of her, so quick that she questioned if she'd seen it at all. "I have seen the future. She lives, but only if you make the right choices. If you willingly sacrifice that which means the most to you."

"Lea's life is what matters most to me," Gray spat.

"Is it?" Eudora said, her eyes full of mischief.

Don't trust her, Gray, Lea whispered through their bond

We have no choice, Little Flower.

Eudora's lips curved up the smallest bit, as if knowing exactly what they were saying to each other. "If you make the sacrifice demanded of you, your mate lives. Fail to make the correct choice, and the spell will change. Your father and brother will become untouchable, and you and your mate will be vulnerable. Neither of you will survive."

Gray studied Eudora, his hand subconsciously tracing the hilt of his sword as he weighed her words. "How will I know what the gods demand as a sacrifice?"

Eudora's eyes glazed over, her posture stiffening. She was having a vision.

Lea stepped around Gray, coming to stand at his side. She grabbed his hand in both of hers as they waited for the vision to finish.

Eudora shook her head slightly, her eyes focusing once again. "You will know. I have seen it."

"And if I agree, the curse will be broken immediately?"

"You can kill your brother and father tonight," Eudora said, despite knowing that traveling that distance in such little time was impossible.

"Then I agree to your terms." Gray pulled his dagger from his belt, preparing to draw blood to bind his oath, but Eudora snatched the dagger away.

"Do not waste precious blood, Commander," she taunted. "A war is coming, you know."

With those words, a rush of magic blew through the room, parchment flying and bottles crashing to the ground. The candles flickered and Eudora's black and gray hair blew about her face. The mate bond twitched in her chest, pulling uncomfortably tight before calming along with the room. Unbothered, Eudora sauntered to a locked cabinet, opening the door and pulling a small burgundy vial with a wooden stopper from the shelf. She carefully ladled some of the potion she'd been working on into the container before corking it and dipping the top in melted black wax. Eudora handed the vial to Gray. "Your friend Emma will be needing this. She'll know what to do with it."

"Have you seen the king's death?" Lea questioned. She knew with certainty the witch would never tell her something that would reveal so much, but something inside her needed to ask anyway.

"I have seen death." Eudora met Lea's eyes. If Lea had believed Eudora had a heart, she would have thought she saw pity in her eyes. "You should go. Time is running out." Lifting her chin, Eudora morphed into a beautiful blue heron and flew through the open window and out across the sea.

CHAPTER 68

LEA

After packing their things and a sleepless night, they left at first light, riding directly from Calir to Bearswillow with as few stops as possible. King Tanad had been kind enough to lend them extra horses, as well as sending a few soldiers along as a sign of good faith. Among them was the same man who had gathered the moonflowers for Lea, and to her absolute delight, he showed up ready to leave with an extra satchel full to the top with vines from the clearing.

Janelle had argued when Tanad offered them the additional horses, saying that she needed to ride with Erik "for safety purposes." It had been complete bullshit, but it had made Lea smile. They'd spent enough time on horses over the past few weeks to be able to ride by themselves, especially since Erik had spent hours one day training them in combat while riding bareback. Add in a comfortable saddle and a broken horse, and Lea was certain Janelle would be absolutely fine.

Emma had spent the entire night before they left in the library and looked absolutely exhausted the next morning. She'd given Bartholomew a tearful hug goodbye with a kiss on the cheek and a sincere thank you when he'd walked her to the stables with several bags full of books. Emma had been quite tightlipped about what she'd been spending all of her time researching in the library, but it seemed to be helping her process her gift. It was comforting to see the light flickering in her eyes again, and anything that could bring a smile back to Emma's face, Lea was in support of.

The dead told Emma once again that Lea had an aura about her, one that frightened the demons and would keep them away. And they'd been right. They'd traveled through the Wicked Wood without a single incident, the forest completely silent as if Lea was the predator and every monster inside it hid for their own survival.

Gray and Lea had spent a lot of time on their journey discussing everything that had happened while Gray was gone, and Lea wasn't surprised when her mate turned rigid and surrounded them with shadows when she'd told him about her deal with Eudora.

He hadn't been aware of the cage Eudora had spoken of back at the castle in Auropera. As Lea had described it, his eyes had lost all their color, shadows completely consuming the green of his irises. As far as Gray knew, the cage did not exist. His father had shown him the darkest sides of himself, had flaunted his most evil deeds right under his nose his entire life, and Lea could tell that the idea that there was something potentially worse that he hadn't known about, even through his years of spying, made him anxious. But it couldn't concern him any more than Lea worried about the "sacrifice" Gray had promised to Eudora.

At least she knew her task. Find whatever was locked away in the cage in the castle, and bring it back. Gray's sacrifice could be *anything*. Well, anything but her life, and his, she guessed, since they were connected. Lea's chest warmed as she thought about when they'd sealed the mate bond, had tied their lives together. He couldn't die without her following him beyond the veil, and Eudora had given her word that Lea would live.

Despite being on different horses, Lea and Gray stayed so close to one another that the outside of their legs touched as they rode. Their time apart had been too much, and even though they'd both busied themselves with important matters that had done a fair job of distracting them, Lea never wanted to be away from him again, and she could feel through the bond that Gray felt the same way.

Every chance that Gray found, he ran a finger across Lea's cheek or played with her hair. Any time they were off their horses, eating a meal or resting, Gray lifted her and sat her in his lap, wrapping her in a protective cocoon of shadows. It was as if any physical distance was too great. He had to be touching her, and Lea felt the same.

The scenery grew more familiar the closer they got to Bearswillow, and a sharp jolt of homesickness wedged itself between Lea's ribs. The trees were no longer foreign, but sturdy oaks and maples with luscious green canopies. The ground was becoming rocky again, just as it did when entering or leaving the Torres, and the smell of fresh mountain air that always reminded Lea of home filled her lungs. She could sense the same excited energy in Janelle, who sat herself higher in her saddle as she tried to look through the trees to catch a glimpse of home.

Not too long ago, their small village had seemed suffocating, minuscule in a way that had made Lea long for adventure. But as they neared it now, she only felt comfort. They wouldn't be going into the town itself. The village had been evacuated once the rebellion had positioned themselves within the cavern hidden in the mountains. But even to be near home, to be able to peek out and see glimpses of the houses she'd walked past her entire life, it made her feel closer to her mother.

Her *mother*. Lea wanted to return to her cottage, to search through all of Adelaide's possessions for any clues she might be missing. She knew now that she was the queen's granddaughter, that King Tanad had taken her himself and left her up on the bald near her home. But was there more?

When the Torres mountain range came into sight, a tiny, rocky skyline still miles and miles away in the distance, Lea's heart sighed. A mixture of sorrow and belonging filled her chest. She'd thought that she would never see those peaks again. The peaks where she'd grown up, found her friends, and lost her mother. Just the fact that she was looking upon them made her feel like the gods were on her side. But her joy was short-lived.

Nausea filled her stomach as Lea's vision went fuzzy. She leaned forward in the saddle, bracing herself against her mare's neck as dizziness clouded her mind. The world tilted, turning hazy at the edges. Gray shouted her name, grabbing onto her reins as Lea's vision once again shifted, just as it had previously.

Alaric once again stood by the Black King's bed, his eyes full of frustration.

He took a dropper from a red bottle and tilted the king's head back, forcing a stream of thick liquid onto his tongue. The king mumbled incoherently, but the potion soon took effect, forcing him back into a deep slumber. Bracing his hands on the footboard, he began to chant, closing his eyes and focusing solely on his spell. The words were nonsensical, something from another language that sounded harsh and guttural. Alaric squeezed his hands into fists, but like the flip of a coin, his demeanor changed.

As words continued to tumble from his lips, Alaric's eyes popped open. He leaned over the bed, his eyes twinkling as a malicious grin spread across his face. He was *happy*. Not just happy—overjoyed.

Realization and horror crashed through Lea like a white-hot knife between her ribs, stealing her breath away. Alaric knew that Gray would seek to break the spell. Had he been trying to kill his father the entire time they'd been gone? Was that why he hadn't attempted to follow them? Because he'd been biding his time, waiting for the opportunity to kill the Black King himself once Gray broke the curse?

Lea was filled with terror, but it wasn't just her own. That *other* darkness in her chest rose and strained, begging for release. Was this a prediction? A possibility of what could happen? Or was she seeing a glimpse of something that had already happened?

Several agonizing moments of waiting passed, and Lea allowed herself to hope for the best. Surely this wasn't what Eudora had meant when she'd said that breaking the curse would allow harmony and balance to be restored.

Alaric was even more evil than his father, and if he stole the king's power? It was over.

Lea heard a woman's voice in her mind, one she recognized, but couldn't place. *Gods help us all,* the phantom voice said before Lea's vision morphed back to her own.

Lea saw Gray's concerned face, only for a moment, before he was blurred by the thick, salty tears running from Lea's eyes.

CHAPTER 69

GRAY

Gray was vibrating, struggling to keep his composure. Lea's vision was his worst fear come to life. Alaric had known Gray's first priority would be breaking the spell, and so he'd bided his time. But to actually kill his father? To steal the enormity of his power? He'd underestimated his brother. It made Gray's skin crawl, knowing that he hadn't seen this coming or prepared for this contingency.

Gray pictured his brother standing at his father's bedside every day since they'd left, casting his spell over and over, just waiting for the night that it would finally be successful. Alaric had gone completely mad, and Gray wondered if there was something that he could've done as they'd grown up to help him, to steer him away from this path of complete wickedness. Logically, Gray knew that he'd been raised by the same father, in the same household, under the same conditions, and that it was only his own conscience and choices that had saved him. But still, how could he be related to not one, but two men who were such monsters and not have become one himself?

If Lea's visions were true, then Alaric had somehow poisoned his father to subdue him until he could successfully cast the spell that would infect him with the Lonely Death, allowing him to steal his magic. It was the worst-case scenario, for while his father had been hungry for power, his aspirations had ended there.

Alaric had a vendetta, a need for vengeance against him and his mate that was buried in his very marrow. This was no longer only a war about helping the people of his kingdom and ending the rule of his father. Now, it was personal, and Alaric would not only attempt to take over the kingdom and continue to steal magic, but also try to ensure that everyone Gray loved was destroyed in the process. And he wouldn't stop until it was done.

But Lea's vision wasn't the only thing that was worrying him. Even more than what she'd seen, it deeply bothered Gray that Lea was having visions at all. From how she described it, it was as if she was in someone else's body, watching through their eyes. Whoever it was could potentially be an asset—after all, it appeared that they'd helped by warning them. But what if they weren't?

How was it possible that Lea was infiltrating someone's mind without even trying? Or was it the other way around? Had someone found a way into his mate's consciousness somehow?

Gray was glad to be returning to Bearswillow so he could discuss with Vincent what was happening. There were too many unknown variables for him to make plans on the best way to proceed without knowing how the army was doing with their training in Bearswillow.

They rounded a sharp cliff edge and Lea's shoulders sagged in relief as she noticed the large, tall crack in the mountainside. Exhaustion pulled at the skin beneath her eyes, and the urge to stop right there and make her rest itched against his skin. Foolish, when they had finally made it to a place with a soft bed and any comfort she could need.

The entrance to the cavern was well hidden by design. He'd known when he'd used his shadows to form it years ago that someday, it would be home to the rebellion. Unless you knew what you were looking for, one would think it was just a break in the mountainside, maybe the remnants of a rock slide from long ago. But it was so, so much more.

Gray led them through the crack, which was only about eight feet wide from side to side. It was pitch black, but Obsidian knew the way by heart. He'd traveled through this walkway hundreds of times over the years, and Gray suspected that the horse could find his way even if he wasn't there to guide him.

After roughly fifty feet, the tunnel opened into a large stone room, a chamber shimmering with his own enchantments. No one could enter without his, Erik's, or Vincent's approval. Inside these walls, they were truly safe, and Gray fully exhaled for the first time since they'd left Calir.

After sliding from his horse, Gray walked Obsidian to the far wall, where buckets of water and piles of hay waited. Normally, he would unsaddle Obsidian himself and reward him with cubes of sugar or sweet apples after such a long journey, but he needed to see Vincent as soon as possible. He would have to have one of his men take the horses to the stables he had built within the cavern and reward them there.

Erik finally broke the silence as he tied off his horse next to Gray's. "Would you like me to retrieve Vincent?"

"No," Gray grabbed Lea's hand. "Show Tanad's men to their quarters, then meet us in my office."

Gravel crunched beneath their feet as Gray led them to a nondescript iron door fitted into the rough, rocky walls. Their hushed whispers and clanking swords echoed throughout the chamber, bouncing off the high ceilings.

Pulling his dagger from his hip, Gray swiftly sliced a cut several inches long into his right palm, then placed his hand flat against the metal. With a long groan of gears turning and then a short *pop*, the door clicked open. He ushered them through the door, passing through a shield of magic so intense that Lea sucked in a sharp inhale.

You okay? Gray asked, squeezing her hand.

Lea squeezed back. *Just fine,* Lea answered with a reassuring smile as they entered a large living area. It had been built as a common room for the rebellion, a massive stone cavern with soaring ceilings and enough tables and chairs to serve meals or gather together for meetings. To the left, through a large rectangular opening, was a training room equipped with all types of weaponry, as well as mats and bags for sparring. Through an identical door to the right, carved from the stone of the mountain itself, were the sleeping quarters. There were three dozen small rooms, as well as four large barracks. And straight ahead through another, smaller door, were offices for himself and his most trusted soldiers as well as storage rooms for food and a kitchen.

It was late, and the common room was empty, but Gray knew that Vincent would have been alerted of their arrival and would likely be waiting for them in Gray's office. The others looked around in awe as they walked, Janelle and Lea muttering to each other about their shock that something this large could've existed so close to their homes without their knowledge.

It wasn't anything fancy, just cavern after cavern that he had whittled away one room at a time, but he was proud of it all the same.

"I'll give you a tour later," he said, his words clipped. "For now, this is the way to our meeting rooms."

Gray was unsurprised when he walked into the chamber that he used as his main office to strategize and found Vincent sitting behind his broad stone desk. What did surprise him, though, was that Thomas was also present, casually leaning against the far wall with his arms crossed in front of him. As Gray moved to shake Vincent's hand, Thomas stood up straighter. His eyes were focused on Lea, and Gray guessed from the intensity of his stare that he desperately wanted to get her attention.

A possessive growl rumbled in Gray's chest, and Gray's shadows begged to be set free, but he held them in. Now was not the time.

"Do you have news?" Vincent asked, leading them to a large sitting area in the corner of the room.

"Eudora's curse is broken." Gray wasted no time getting to the point. "Our plan is working, except," Gray looked at Lea, wondering once again how much of her visions were true. "We think Alaric has plans to kill my father and steal his power, or more likely, has done so already."

Vincent exhaled harshly, but maintained his composure. "That changes things."

"It does," Gray agreed. "Which is why we need to be prepared sooner than we thought. What progress has been made here?" They'd initially thought they'd have months, if not more, to prepare the rebels. They were well hidden, after all, and they had been more than thorough with keeping their intentions—and his involvement—a secret. They had taken care to be subtle, to thoroughly plan for every contingency. But if Alaric had been successful in stealing his father's power, it indeed changed *everything*. The two of them separately would have been a challenge. But Alaric holding their power combined? It seemed insurmountable.

Vincent straightened his shoulders.

"We relocated the residents of Bearswillow to Pelar, but many remained to fight with us. Scouts have been deployed throughout the kingdom, and more rebels have appeared from all over Desia. They're showing up every day. Many cite your father, Henry, as their deciding factor for joining us." Vincent nodded his head to Lea. "Our numbers have more than tripled since we left Auropera."

"Good." A bit of Gray's worries eased. Henry was staying true to his word and recruiting more men and women for their cause. They needed as many people as possible if they were to stand a chance.

"We've identified those with strong fighting skills, as well as those with magic, and have assigned them to duties that complement their abilities. For those without magic or experience in combat, we've been training every day and assessing where they will be most useful."

"Excellent job, Vincent." Gray rubbed a hand across his scruffy face, suddenly so very tired. There was nothing more they could do tonight, not with everyone asleep. Tomorrow he would get to work helping assess the new arrivals, as well as strategizing for how to best utilize everyone's skill set.

Emma stood up abruptly. "I'd like to speak to those with magic." She cleared her throat. "And my mom." She bounced on the balls of her feet. "Um, please."

Gray quietly observed her posture. Emma stood tall with her chin raised in confidence, but he didn't miss the way her fingers nervously tapped her thighs. Emma had been nearly silent for weeks, and when Gray had given her Eudora's potion, she had simply taken it from his hand with a thank you and turned away.

"I've been learning about different abilities, and I think I might be of help," she continued.

"Of course," Gray answered. It was obvious Emma was hiding something, but his gut told him to trust her. He was confident that she would confide in them when she connected the rest of the dots of whatever it was she was planning. "Vincent, will you make the arrangements for Emma to meet with all those with magic in the morning? And bring her to Elise. She'd wring my neck if she found out that I brought her daughter back and didn't tell her straight away."

"Consider it done." Vincent rose. "For now, I think it's best if *everyone* rests."

"I agree." Gray didn't miss the way Vincent's eyes lingered on the shadows he was certain darkened his eyes. "It's been a long journey."

With the mumble of agreement, everyone stood and turned to leave, but Thomas stepped forward.

"Lea, I'd like to speak with you. If that's okay with you, of course." Thomas looked to Gray, his face flushing slightly. Gray's shadows twisted inside him, but once again he held them back. If he believed that Thomas would hurt Lea in any way, he would be rotting in the ground already, not here with them, preparing for war. While he wanted nothing more than to take his mate away, bring her to their room, and explore her body in the comfort of his own bed, in the safety of his own home, he wouldn't stop Lea from speaking with her friends, even if he didn't particularly like *this* friend.

"It's her decision. Not mine." Gray tilted his head toward Lea, removing his sword from his back and rolling his neck from side to side.

"Of course." Thomas blushed, lowering his eyes. "Lea?"

"Sure." Lea said, leaning up to give Gray a kiss on the cheek before following Thomas into the common room. They settled at a nearby table, and Gray's shoulders relaxed a bit as Thomas positioned himself diagonally on the opposite bench, as far away from Lea as he could possibly sit. Good. The boy had some sense, after all.

Gray's shadows implored him for permission to drift across the floor and listen to the conversation unfolding just outside the room, but he trusted his mate and wouldn't betray her confidence by doing what his overprotective Fae urges demanded. Forcing his eyes away, he turned to Vincent.

"Find Noah a room, if you don't mind. As well as one for Janelle. Put them close to ours."

"Actually," Erik stepped forward, wrapping an arm around Janelle and turning to face Vincent. "Just a room for Noah will be sufficient. Janelle will be staying with me."

CHAPTER 70

LEA

Thomas looked older. He'd grown something resembling a beard since she'd last seen him, and had cut his brown hair a bit closer to his head. His arms and chest had filled out, clearly from the training Vincent had been running the rebels through over the last month that they'd been gone.

It was odd, sitting across from him now. So much had changed. Once, not too long ago, she'd thought that maybe she could love this man, but sitting across from him now, Lea felt nothing but the love of an old friend. Someone with shared history.

Where she'd once felt like she belonged to Thomas, and he had belonged to her, she now felt no ownership over him. She would always love him, of course, but the life she was living was almost unrecognizable. She no longer needed him to feel complete.

"I've had a lot of time to think since we've been here," Thomas started, clasping and unclasping his hands as he leaned his forearms on the table. "I need to apologize to you." He reached forward but stopped himself.

Lea was surprised at the pinch of hurt still inside her chest. He'd watched her be beaten. Had said things that were difficult to forget. But she still loved him as her friend. Nothing would change that, and she was certain that with time, the sting of those cruel words would ease away until they disappeared all together. "You don't. We've both made mistakes." Lea grabbed his hand in both of hers, squeezing tight.

Thomas sighed, squeezing back. "For twenty-three years, I trusted you completely. Never once in that time did I doubt a single word that you said. Not a single time." Thomas flinched at his own words. "But as soon as my feelings got hurt, I let that change. I'm sorry I didn't listen to you when you told me that Evander wasn't like his father and brother. I'm sorry I pressured you to choose between our friendship and your mate. I thought I was protecting you, but really, I knew how you felt, and I hated it."

Thomas took a deep breath and hung his head. "I should never have said that if you were with him, you'd be against us. I believe in this rebellion, but even if you wanted nothing to do with it, or if Gray hadn't been the Eclipsed King, I need you to know that I never would have let anything happen to you. You *never* could have been my enemy. I was jealous and angry and a coward. I'm so sorry. For all of it." Thomas sighed before standing, looking over Lea's shoulder to where Gray stood with Vincent. "I know things have changed, but you're still my best friend and—I just had to tell you that."

Lea stood and walked around the table, wrapping her arms around him in a tight embrace. "I've known all that for a long time, Thomas."

"I just want you to be happy," he said into her hair.

"I am," Lea smiled, pulling back. "Well, as happy as I can be, knowing that a war is coming and Alaric is probably going to come after us and try to slaughter me again."

She'd meant it as a half-hearted joke, but Thomas's eyes darkened and he clenched his teeth. "I'll *never* let him hurt you again. I swear it."

Without a doubt, Lea could tell he meant it. It was in the determined set of his jaw and the way he fisted his hands at his side.

"That's one reason I made you the sword. Wait—" he looked to her hip, then through the doorway to where Gray stood, his eyes scanning the room. "Where is your sword? Why isn't it with you?"

Lea's forehead scrunched up. She had no use for a sword here within the cavern, not unless they were training. "It's with my things. We left them with the horses."

"Bring it with you *everywhere* you go, Lea. That sword is special. I've never used more magic to create one weapon. It can only be used by you, and has the ability to become whatever you need it to be. It could save your life."

"What do you mean?" Lea wished she'd brought the sword with her so Thomas could demonstrate. While they'd trained in Calir, it had seemed like a pretty standard weapon. Lightweight, balanced, and razor sharp, but she hadn't noticed anything particularly magical about it. Honestly, she'd felt more capable using her powers than a sword, and hadn't even carried it much outside of training.

"I didn't have time to explain it all before," he said, "but the sword will absorb whatever power it senses. If you want to infuse it with shadows, it will take that darkness and amplify it. It can help you know where to strike, sense danger, and detect lies. Promise me you'll keep it with you."

"I didn't realize—yes. I'll keep it with me," Lea promised. "Thank you." A yawn pushed up the back of her throat. "Maybe you can show me how to use it tomorrow? I'm sorry. It's been a long few days."

Thomas caught her yawn, covering his mouth. "Right, of course. Sorry. I'm sure you're exhausted."

"I missed you," Lea said as she wrapped her arms around her friend again, relaxing into his familiar embrace. The distance between them was still there, but it was significantly smaller and less painful.

Thomas returned the hug, sighing. After several moments, he pulled away, rubbing the back of his neck and averting his gaze. "I've been wondering... How is Emma?"

"She's okay, I think. She's been quiet, spending a lot of time reading, but I think she's working through it. Any particular reason?" Lea raised her eyebrows.

His cheeks turned pink. "I've just been worried about her. You know, after what happened in Auropera. It's nothing," he said, turning toward the barracks.

"Thomas," Lea stopped him. "I think she'd be better if you checked on her yourself."

Thomas smiled, a blush creeping up his neck. "Do you think so?" he asked nervously, shuffling his feet.

"Yeah, I really do." Lea turned back to find Gray, craving a few hours of rest in his arms before the work of tomorrow began. "Goodnight, Thomas," Lea called over her shoulder. "Take good care of my friend."

CHAPTER 71

LEA

Lea didn't see Gray much over the next couple of days. He and Vincent had spent the mornings working through different strategies for where and when to attack, and Gray had spent quite a bit of time meeting and assessing the skills of the new rebels that arrived every day. Lea had been invited to work alongside Gray as he observed training and did whatever else an Eclipsed King does, of course, but she was too restless.

She tried to focus on her own training, but she couldn't seem to concentrate. The feeling of her magic pushing at her chest wall and bumping against her ribs, desperate to escape, had become almost unbearable. Her shadows felt like a rabid dog trapped in a cage, fighting with everything it had to be set free, but Lea wouldn't let it. Not yet. It was too much, so intense that she worried that were she to allow that raw magic slowly leaking into her chest to leave her body, it would consume everything it touched.

So instead she locked it away as best she could, using her shadows to seal off the crack allowing them to slither though. But that took focus, concentration that pulled her away from whatever other task she was performing to keep her magic in control.

Erik shouted every time she dropped a weapon or stumbled while sparring. He corrected her form over and over, finally yanking Lea from the ring when she failed to block a glaringly obvious punch from a tall, red-headed rebel with a crooked nose. After helping her up from the floor and allowing her to heal the bruise growing on her cheekbone, Erik pulled her outside the training room.

"You're not paying attention to your opponent's tells. You should have seen that punch coming from a mile away." Erik tilted his chin down. Even when scolding her, he had a slight smile.

Lea rubbed her sternum where her magic itched in her bones, scratching and pawing her insides as it begged to be released. "I think I need to practice less fighting and more magic. It feels like I'm going to explode."

"I should have realized." Erik patted her shoulder. "You're right. With as much magic as you have, you need to use it regularly so it doesn't build up inside you."

"Will it hurt me if I don't?" Lea asked, sparking small fires in both her hands.

"It could, if you wait long enough. It's more likely you'll hurt whoever's around you. After enough time, your power will detonate like an explosive, and you'll have no control over what it does. But first, it will distract you, pull your focus, which it already seems to be doing. You can't afford that, not around Alaric."

Lea looked down at her hands with new eyes, her worst fears confirmed. Had her fingers always been so menacingly long? "So," she dropped her hands to her sides, sighing. "Are we going to go burn some stuff, then?" Lea nudged her shoulder into Erik's arm.

Erik winked at her and began to pull her outside. "I'll do you one better, Sunshine," he said, his long, determined strides making Lea run to catch up with him. Erik didn't stop until he walked through the crack that made up the entrance to the cavern, and Lea blinked at the bright light. Warmth filled her arms and flooded through her body as the sun's rays kissed her face.

She'd thought her restlessness had been because of her magic, or maybe having nothing to do but train and sleep, but now she knew better. While those things had played a part, it had been the absence of sun and fresh air that had made her shadows feel so much stronger than her light.

After two minutes of walking in silence, Lea soaking up every ounce of sunlight possible, Erik stopped next to a ledge of jagged mountainside.

"We're here," Erik gestured with a flourished bow toward the wall.

"We're where?" Lea peeked around Erik, searching for what he could possibly be talking about.

"Come with me." A joyful, boyish grin spread across Erik's face. He grabbed Lea's hand and began climbing a series of irregular rocks jutting out of the wall. Lea wondered if he was taking her to see a beautiful view or an important vantage point, but as she took the final step toward the top, she'd never felt better about being wrong.

Her heart exploded into a million glittery bits, and she scrambled higher to get a better view. In front of her, hidden down within a ring of rocks, was a garden, right here in the middle of the Torres Mountains.

Lea's jaw dropped, her hands tingling. "Thank you," she breathed, turning to Erik with tear-filled eyes.

"None of that sappy stuff, now." Erik sniffled, covering it up with a cough. "You need to expend magic. This is a safe way to do it. And don't forget that I benefit if you grow some delicious food down here for me. I've been craving sweet honeysuckle jam on toasted bread." Erik looked as if he was actually drooling as he climbed down a wooden ladder that began just below the rim of the rocks. Lea scrambled down behind him, needing to touch the dirt more than she needed to breathe.

Her feet sank into the soft earth, and Lea sighed in contentment, kicking off her shoes and turning in a circle to examine every inch of her new paradise. It was a circular space surrounded by stone on all sides, the sun shining unobstructed by trees or rocks to bathe the dirt in the brightest, most beautiful glow. Hanging near the ladder was a pulley system, which Lea guessed was for when they needed to bring up the vegetables they harvested.

The garden was rather large, with moist, black soil. It was odd, seeing it here in the middle of the mountains, but Erik explained that Gray had planned for everything. They hadn't known how long the rebels would need to hide within the Torres and wanted to ensure they could grow food if their stores ran out.

It was obvious they hadn't needed to grow their own food yet. The beds were a disaster, full of weeds and grass, but among them grew tall bushes filled with vegetables. A cucumber vine ran along the ground to the mountain wall, where it began climbing up in curling tendrils. There were tomatoes and eggplants, and a patch that looked like the tops of potatoes. Somehow these plants were surviving even without care, and Lea considered how they would thrive if she actually tended to them.

In the very center of the stone circle was a large space occupied only with green and brown weeds.

After asking Erik to grab the vines they'd brought from Calir, Lea braided her hair and rolled up the short sleeves of her lightweight blouse, settling in to spend the next few hours pulling weeds from the soil until an area about eight feet by eight feet was completely spotless.

She was so engrossed in her task she didn't notice when Erik returned. Lea jumped when his laugh echoed through the mountains as he looked at her dirt streaked cheeks and neck, startling her.

"Prettying yourself up for our king?" Erik dropped the bags to the ground.

"Not brushing your hair again?" Lea retorted, not even looking up from the dirt, which only made Erik laugh harder.

After asking if she needed anything else, Erik left her alone to expend her magic. The temperature dropped as the sun lowered to the horizon. Lea wished she'd grabbed a sweater, but she couldn't bring herself to leave. She was too eager to grow the moonflowers tonight, now that Eudora had told her what was required.

Lea looked at the position of the sun, which was just beginning to set, so she busied herself picking the ripe vegetables, stacking them in baskets, and leaving them next to the ladder. There was no use in letting them rot away.

Once the magic of the night had spread across the land, her hair blowing around her face and the moon illuminating the ground in a soft glow, Lea pulled a small dagger she'd swiped from the training room and a tiny, crescent-shaped moonflower seed from the scratchy pocket of an apron she'd found amongst the tools. The hilt of the knife was cold in her warm fingers, its blade sharp, thin, and honed to a fine tip.

Kneeling on the moist ground, Lea pushed the seed down into the soil, just a few inches, then held her hand out in front of her.

Eudora's voice echoed in her mind. *Blood. That is the key.*

Before she could overthink it, Lea dragged the knife over her open palm. The moonflowers required an offering of blood, and so she would give it.

She hissed at the sharp sting of the blade against her skin and winced as she cut a clean line from one edge of her palm to the other. Sending up a prayer, Lea overturned her hand and allowed her blood to soak directly into the earth above the seeds.

With her wound still open and oozing, she pushed her blood-soaked fingers down into the soil, using her light to urge the seed to sprout. The seed cracked beneath her fingers, and it didn't take long for the deep green vine to poke out from the dirt. She pulled her hand away, avoiding healing her wound to allow blood to continue to flow onto the plant, and the vines began twisting around her hand, attempting to slowly grow up her arms.

Lea's entire body buzzed. *Is it working?* Gently, almost tenderly, she untwisted the vines from her body and watched as they trailed along the ground. After several long moments, dozens of small buds began to open, the white petals inside peeking out from their fibrous leaves. Electricity buzzed along Lea's skin, her mouth going dry in anticipation.

This was it—what she had sacrificed so much for. Her fingers hovered above a bud as the petals fully unraveled, and with a deep exhale, she used her uninjured hand to pick a single flower. Lea held her breath, afraid that even the slightest movement might cause the flower to crumble away into the mountain air.

The flower remained white and Lea cried out in a mix of shock and joy, a gasp breaking free from that small sliver of hope she held inside her heart. She picked another and another, closing her fists around the beautiful, whole petals. Her heart pounded and her hands shook. *I did it.* She would have shouted it from the mountaintop if her voice would work, but she couldn't speak. Could hardly think. *I did it!*

Lea jumped up, needing to tell Gray—no, *show* him. She put her foot on the first rung of the ladder, then opened her hand to look at the flowers once again, unable to believe she was actually holding plump, living flowers.

Her fingers uncurled from her tight fist, and—*No...* Bile rose up the back of Lea's throat, the bitter taste of failure making her head spin. In her hand, where the beautiful, pristine, white petals had been only *seconds* before, was a pile of black ash. *What went wrong?*

Lea tried to blink away tears as she ran back to the flowers, picking a few more, but this time she left her hand open, holding her breath as she stared without blinking. After about a minute, the flowers withered away and died. "Dammit!" *What am I missing?*

She had done exactly as Eudora had said! But maybe she had misunderstood. She'd said to water the seeds with blood... Did she need to mix her blood with water? Or maybe she needed more blood? She was close. She had to be! Lea had never gotten them to live for this long before.

Pulling another seed from her pocket, Lea pushed it down into the soil. The scab across her hand had begun to heal, but Lea followed the line of crusted blood with her dagger, digging deeper than she had before. Now bleeding profusely, she made a mirrored cut on her other hand, deep enough that blood ran down her fingers, dripping onto her apron.

She pocketed the dagger, then pushed her hands down into the dirt once again, completely saturating the soil with warm, sticky blood. *The blood must soak the earth*, Eudora had said. That had to be it. She just hadn't offered enough the first time.

Little Flower? A voice spoke into her mind, but she couldn't answer as she focused all of her light into the soil.

She kept her healing magic tightly coiled in her chest, continuing to water the ground until her eyelids grew heavy and her head swam.

Azalea!

Her vision blurred, and Lea placed a hand on her forehead, trying to steady herself.

"That's enough," Gray snapped from somewhere behind her, the moon suddenly obscured by dark storm clouds. Thunder crashed in the distance, and before lightning could even follow it, Gray was at her side. "What are you doing?" He grabbed Lea's hands, healing them immediately and pulling her tightly against him.

Lea pressed her face into the crook of his neck, taking slow, deep inhales to calm her racing heart. "I needed more blood for the moonflowers. It didn't work, and I—" The world tilted and she covered her mouth, holding back the nausea bubbling in her stomach.

"You could've killed yourself," Gray barked, his shadows wrapping around her body and searching her for other injuries. "Do you have any idea what I thought was happening to you out here? I called out to you, and you didn't answer!"

Thunder boomed and lightning flashed again, illuminating the garden, and Lea got a look at Gray's face in the darkness. Her blood ran down his neck and covered his hands, trails of crimson spreading across his shirt. *Shit*. She'd bled far more than she'd realized.

Gray lifted her in his arms and carried her toward the ladder. "Come on, you need to rest."

Lea nodded weakly. She needed sleep desperately, but a small gust of wind tickled her eyelashes. Cracking open her eyes, she suddenly wasn't so tired at all. Lea gripped Gray's arm as she craned her neck to look over Gray's shoulder. "Stop!" she ordered, and he obeyed, turning to see what she was looking at. Just feet away, hundreds of moonflowers grew from several long vines. It was the most vigorous plant Lea had ever seen. The moonflowers were creeping along the ground toward Gray, following him.

"Don't move," Lea ordered as they wrapped around his legs and climbed up his trousers. They circled themselves around his waist and up toward his shoulders.

Somehow, the vines maneuvered around Lea's body, consuming Gray alone. He gently set her down, narrowing his eyes and tilting his head. He removed the sword from his waistband, awkwardly slicing open his hand with the long blade. The vines immediately reacted, twisting and growing rapidly to get to the blood.

Gray held his hand out to the side, allowing his blood to drip into the soil. After enough blood had fallen to form a small puddle, he healed his hand. As soon as the blood stopped flowing, the vines began to unravel themselves from his body, moving away from where his hand no longer bled and pushing down into the bloody soil.

"They didn't do that for my blood," Lea almost whispered, confusion sending waves of shock through her body. "I've never seen them react like this at all."

Gray was silent for several moments, and Lea could hardly process the emotions radiating off of him in waves. Confusion, anger, then understanding.

"It was my father who took the queen's blood." Gray met her eyes. "It must be my bloodline to spill for the moonflowers to grow."

Lea pressed her lips together, fighting off another wave of dizziness. It made so much sense. How had she not seen it before? "Will you do it?" Lea breathed. In another life, she wouldn't ask. Wouldn't want her mate and the love of her life to hurt himself, to bleed, to help her succeed. But this was war. These moonflowers... They could save so many people. They could change absolutely *everything*.

"It would be my honor to be the one to help you grow the moon-flowers." Gray caressed her cheek, and Lea nodded into his hand. She was overcome with emotion, overwhelmed by his unrelenting love and selflessness. *Thank you,* she whispered into his mind.

With a steady hand and a quick kiss to her forehead, Gray moved the clouds from in front of the moon. "I would do anything for you, Little Flower. Now, hand me the dagger."

CHAPTER 72

GRAY

Kneeling with their shoulders pressed together, Lea pulled a moon-flower seed from her pocket. She gently placed it on the dirt, then slowly rocked back on her heels and called her magic into her fingers. They glowed silver-blue, ready to urge the flowers to grow.

Gray could feel her anticipation buzzing through their connection, her absolute terror that even with his blood, it wouldn't work. The agony of seeing her worry, of watching her throat bob as she waited to discover if the flowers would finally *live*, injured him more than any wound could. With a swift, forceful slice, Gray opened the cut on his hand once again, cutting deeper and letting his blood drip directly onto the seed.

The reaction was immediate. Vines shot out in all directions, spreading rapidly and instantly taking root. The evasive white flowers appeared within seconds, far more of them than when Lea had used her own blood.

It's working, Lea said into his mind, as if she was afraid she might scare the moonflowers with the sound of her voice.

Gray nodded, and Lea pulled a moonflower from its stem. The white petals almost shimmered, and they held their breath as they counted the seconds as they passed, but it didn't take long before the edges turned black, the darkness cascading across the petals far more slowly than usual.

It was as if a disease had taken hold, but the flower was trying to fight it off. It continued to spread until the whole flower was as dark as the night around them. Gray reached a tentative finger to touch it, but it disintegrated into a fine powder.

Lea cried out as if physically in pain, her shoulders falling as she wiped a tear from her cheek. Without hesitation, Gray opened another cut on his hand, even deeper this time, adding more blood to the already saturated soil. The moonflowers pulsed, every single one of them opening as one.

Lea looked up at Gray through her eyelashes, likely making sure he wasn't making the same mistake that she had. Her brow was creased in thought, and silent tears dripped from her chin. With shaking fingers, Lea picked another moonflower.

Gray's stomach twisted as the flower disintegrated to dust in her fingers. Lea ripped the dagger from Gray's hand, attempting to open a cut on her own hand again, but Gray stopped her.

"It won't work," he said gently as he sent a wave of love and calm down their bond.

"I don't understand!" Lea squeezes her hands into fists. "Eudora promised! She said an offering of blood!"

"What were her exact words?" Gray asked, his mind racing. *That fucking witch!* He should have known that there would be more to the instructions she'd given his mate.

Lea took a deep breath, closing her eyes. "She said it was the spilling of the queen's lifeblood that cursed the moonflowers. And that an offering of blood would be required to undo it."

Gray sat back on the cold ground, his blood chilling as he draped his arms over his knees. "Her *life's* blood... her life. The queen's *life* was forfeited when my father stole her blood to create the Lonely Death and destroy the only cure. How many times has Eudora said that magic demands balance? An offering of blood is not equal to a life."

Lea swallowed down a sob, sniffling as she squared her shoulders. Through the bond, Gray could feel her attempting to maintain control, to not give up and allow her raw, primary magic to feed off her emotions and overtake her. "Are you saying you would need to drain every drop of blood from your body for this to work?" Lea asked.

"I'm saying that I think the cost of the cure is a life. And not just a life, but someone from the king's bloodline."

"Balance," Lea breathed. "It was your bloodline that killed Emmaline. Now that same blood must spill for me to break the curse your father set upon the kingdom. I can wield the cure, but the cure is in your blood. Your father and brother's blood."

"The Lonely Death still spreads." Gray looked at the stars, the crushing reality of the consequences of his father's actions settling on his shoulders. "Unless we can ensure every person infected is eradicated, it will continue to spread, even if my father is dead. If Alaric is stealing magic..."

"Then we need to be prepared," Lea finished for him before standing up, wiping her eyes as a look of hardened determination washed over her features. Smoke rose from around her feet, and Gray's shadows squirmed uncomfortably as small, black flames appeared around her fingers, glowing soot and ash falling to the ground and extinguishing in the bloody soil. "Wherever Alaric falls, wherever his blood spills, I'll need to be there, ready to plant the seeds."

CHAPTER 73

LEA

The cool hilt of the sword warmed in Lea's palm, the beautiful pattern of vines and moonflowers replicated in the metal thrumming beneath her fingers. Her thumb absently traced along the empty locket soldered in the very center. *I want you to place a moonflower there, when you learn how to harvest it. Because I know you're going to do it one day, Lea. You're going to cure the Lonely Death,* Thomas had said the day he'd given it to her.

The fact that it was still empty made her want to vomit, as did the fragment of unease that still hung between them. They'd been best friends once—everything to each other. And while they'd made up, apologized and moved on, there was still a distance between them that felt unnatural and uncomfortable.

"Okay. How do I do this?" Lea asked Thomas, who stood in front of her in the vast stone training room.

"The sword was made for you, and only you. There should be a sort of—" he paused, "I guess *buzzing* is the word—against your skin when you touch it. Do you feel it?"

Lea closed her eyes, focusing. It was there, so subtle she hadn't even realized it. It almost felt like it was vibrating, but not exactly. It was as if the sword was *considering* vibrating. The feeling was nearly impossible to describe.

"Latch onto that power. Make it a part of you, an extension of your arm. Pull it into your chest, and then amplify and force it back out, just like you do with your shadows. It will tune in to whatever power is nearby."

Allowing the magic of the sword to push beneath her skin, Lea smiled. The energy felt familiar, comfortable. It reminded her of long summer days in the garden and Fire Nights lying with friends under the stars. It felt like Thomas, her once best friend turned... what? Enemy? Adversary? Turned friend again. After everything that had gone on between them, they were still Lea and Thomas.

"So it steals magic?" Lea asked, not wanting to take any of Thomas's precious ability. The rebellion needed it for the weapons Thomas was spending countless hours imbuing with his power.

"No. The metal essentially absorbs the power while it is being used, and replicates it. Once the magic wielder stops, the actual magic is pulled out and the copy remains." Thomas pulled a small dagger from his waistband. "Now, focus on how the sword feels once I start using my magic," he said as a pulsing, deep blue light engulfed the weapon, Thomas's eyes creasing in concentration as the blade doubled in size. "Direct it back to you and into the sword."

The moment the blue light appeared, Lea's skin prickled where it gripped the metal. The sword warmed in her hand, and as if on instinct, she reached out with the weapon's power, latching onto Thomas's magic and tugging it back into itself.

Thomas's eyes crinkled. "Amazing, right?" he said as the blue glow from his dagger faded. "Now, use it."

Lea reached inside her well of magic, shuffling through the different types inside her. At the very edge of her power was a tether, a long string that buzzed with the same electricity of the sword. Following it, she isolated Thomas's magic and latched onto it, forcing it to bend to her will. Blue light engulfed the sword as she focused on the slightly dull tip, which had been neglected since Thomas had gifted the weapon to her. Immediately, it sharpened to a deadly point. As the light faded, the swirling pattern of wind glistened as if the metal was freshly polished. It looked *perfect* again.

"Thomas! That's amazing!" Lea twisted the sword, watching the torch lights flicker on the shiny, perfectly pristine metal.

"Now put the sword down on the ground," Thomas said, gesturing to the sparring mat they stood on.

Lea obliged. The second the hilt no longer made contact with her skin, the buzzing tether and Thomas's magic disappeared completely.

"You can only use the magic when touching the sword. It's the conduit to everything. And it will only manifest other's power in the sword itself. You won't be able to make other weapons like I do," Thomas lifted the dagger that now looked impossibly deadly, "but you can always fix and sharpen this one. You can set the sword on fire, or mask it with shadow. But the sword won't help you see the dead or track animals."

"And I don't need to be near you?" Lea asked, picking the sword back up.

"No. Once the power is inside the sword, it will be there forever. But it will only work for you. Well—and me. I had to make sure it worked before I gave it to you."

"Thomas, this is amazing. Thank you." Lea twisted the blade in her hand, tracing a finger across the etchings. "This must have taken so much power to make. You shouldn't have exhausted yourself when you knew you'd be fleeing the castle the next day."

"It was nothing," Thomas said.

The blade warmed in Lea's hand, becoming so hot it was almost painful. She jumped, dropping the sword on the ground with a *clang*. "Shit! What was that?"

"Oh!" Thomas's eyes twinkled with excitement. "You'll feel the hilt warm when someone lies to you. I'm especially proud of that part."

Lea's eyes popped wide open, and she bent down to pick up the sword. "Thomas!" she gasped with mock horror. "Did you just *lie* to me?"

"It *was* nothing!" He laughed, holding his hands in front of him in a defensive position. "I promise!"

The hilt burned Lea's fingers once more. "You liar!" Lea squealed, raising the sword and chasing after him. A laugh bubbled from her throat as Thomas ran behind a hanging sack of dry grass they used as a sparring dummy.

"Okay, fine! Maybe it took a little bit of effort." Thomas shrugged. "But to keep you safe, it was worth it." The metal did not warm at his confession this time.

"And now? Do you think I'm safe with Gray?" Lea asked, squeezing the hilt tighter.

Thomas crossed his arms. "I do. And not only that. I'm truly, honestly, happy for you."

The sword remained cool in her fingers, and a lump formed in Lea's throat.

"Can you forgive me?" Thomas asked. "Really forgive me?"

Lea shuffled from foot to foot. She hadn't realized how much his words back in Auropera had hurt her. He'd implied that she was the enemy, but was that fair? So much had happened between them, but Lea knew that despite it all, Thomas would still die to protect her. Just like he would have before everything changed.

Meeting his eyes, she tossed him her sword.

"I forgive you, Thomas." The words were freeing.

Thomas's smile finally met his eyes, and they held each other's stare for a moment. Like a key turning over a lock, everything felt like it was back in place. "Glad to hear it," he said, handing the sword back and slinging an arm around her shoulders. "Do you have any more questions about how it works? Or what it can do?"

"Nope. I think I get it. Wanna grab some dinner?" Lea held her stomach dramatically. "I'm starving."

As if on cue, Thomas's stomach growled. "Let's go. Should we grab Janelle and Emma?"

"Emma, huh?" Lea teased. "Need to make sure your girlfriend eats?"

"She's not my girlfriend," Thomas rolled his eyes, but his cheeks turned pink.

"Why not? If you love her, tell her. A war is coming, Thomas."

"I don't love her. That's ridiculous," he argued, but his words lacked conviction.

Lea's sword warmed in her hand. A lie.

"Sure you don't—"

"Azalea!" Gray called as he rounded the corner of the training room, followed by two young rebels. "There you are." His eyes were dark and his hair mussed, as if he'd been running his hands through his chestnut locks in frustration. "I just received word from my scouts that we have an incoming visitor. Thomas," Gray said, spinning to face him. "Find Erik. Tell him it's urgent."

"Yes, Commander." Thomas nodded, striding away with determined steps.

"What's happening, Gray?" Lea asked, calling fire to her fingertips. "Who's coming?"

Shadows floated from Gray's hands and smothered her flames. "You don't need those. Not yet, at least. But we need to prepare. It's my mother. She's headed this way."

CHAPTER 74

LEA

"She was alone. Our men intercepted her a day's ride away and sent word ahead. She went further west than the village. According to your mother, she didn't want to lead Alaric here, and knew we would intercept her if she got close enough," Erik explained hours later in Lea and Gray's quarters. It was as nondescript as all the others within the cavern, with a domed, rocky stone ceiling and standard black metal bed frame and a small vanity. Attached to the bedroom was the sitting room they were now meeting in, standing among the tan canvas couch and chairs.

"Did she tell you what she wanted?" Gray lowered his voice as Lea stifled a yawn. They'd been waiting hours for Genevieve to get here, and she hadn't been able to calm her mind enough to rest.

"No. She said she'd only speak to you..." Erik paused. "And to Lea."

Gray's shoulders stiffened. "I will speak to her alone."

"No, you won't," Lea said gently. "We will speak to her together. Please, go get her Erik."

A protective rumble left Gray's chest as he sighed and leaned down to kiss her head. "Fine. Did she have any weapons?"

Erik shook his head. "Not a single one."

"Search again. If she's clean, you may bring her in."

Several moments later, the door opened again, and Erik walked inside, followed by Queen Genevieve. Lea wasn't sure what she'd expected, but it certainly wasn't for Genevieve to run to her and crush her in an overly enthusiastic embrace.

Immediately, Gray pulled his mother away with his shadows, wrapping them around her wrists to restrain her. He'd mentioned that he didn't quite trust her, that she had always remained so neutral that he wasn't sure whose side she was truly on, but as Lea looked into her eyes, she had no doubt where the queen's loyalties lay.

Tears streamed down Genevieve's rosy cheeks, her nose growing red as she stepped back and sniffled. Even crying, she was beautiful as ever, her waist-length brown hair windblown from riding. She tried to blink away the tears that trailed from her piercing green eyes before stepping back toward Lea. It was as if she couldn't stop herself from getting close. "You have no idea how hard it was not to talk to you at the castle." Genevieve said to her. "I knew it wouldn't be safe. For either of us. I can't believe you're actually here."

What is she talking about, Azalea? Gray spoke into her mind.

Lea pressed closer to Gray, feeling a little uncomfortable and confused by his mother's attention. *I have absolutely no idea*, she answered silently before looking back at Gray's mother. "I'm sorry, but I'm not sure what you mean."

"Of course," Genevieve laughed uncomfortably, "You wouldn't, would you?" She raised her restrained hands. "My arms, please, Evander. I hardly think I'm a threat to either of you."

"One step out of place, Mother, and this meeting will be over," Gray said, his shadows going slack, but not releasing her. Lea searched the bond and was surprised when she didn't feel worry or fear. It didn't appear that Gray believed his mother presented actual danger. Instead, Lea was assaulted with mistrust unlike anything Lea had ever felt before. It was mixed with resentment and anger, but a bright thread was woven in as well. It was longing—a tentative belief that maybe his mother was finally doing the right thing.

"Thank you," Genevieve said, wiping her nose with a handkerchief that Erik fished from his pocket. "I've gotten ahead of myself, I think."

"Why don't we sit?" Gray placed a steadying hand on Lea's lower back and led them to the couch.

"What are you doing here, Mother?" Gray's eyes were guarded, and Lea felt a gush of hope rippling against her heart. He wanted so badly to believe that she was on their side. That she was here to help. Lea hoped, for Gray's sake, that she was right about her own gut feeling.

"I want to help you," she said earnestly, leaning forward in her chair as if she wished she could jump out of it and embrace her son. "I know you don't trust me," she said, wringing her hands.

"Why should I?" Gray asked, lifting his chin. "You shouldn't. But I'll take a truth serum. Or swear it on the gods. It's a complicated story. But if nothing else, I am your mother. Please, let me try to earn your trust."

Gray, my sword. Thomas taught me how to use it today. It detects lies. Lea said, wrapping her fingers around the hilt but keeping the weapon sheathed.

Her mate raised his eyebrows, but didn't question her. *Tell me if she's dishonest,* he said before staring at his mother like he was weighing the sincerity of her demeanor. "I suggest you start at the beginning." He leaned back against the couch, pulling Lea almost onto his lap.

Genevieve audibly swallowed. "Well, I guess it started before you were born. I still don't understand it, but I need you to try to keep an open mind."

"I don't think anything could surprise me at this point," Gray responded. "Go on."

Genevieve relaxed, obviously relieved that her son was giving her a chance to explain. "I was there the night Queen Emmaline was killed. She was my very best friend." The queen's voice cracked. "I knew she'd gone to the gardens to gather moonflowers for a sick child. One of her maids' daughters had been suffering from a fever for *days*, but a storm hit. The thunder—it was unlike anything I'd ever heard before." The queen paused, her expression haunted. "I went outside looking for her, expecting to drag her by her cloak back inside so she wasn't struck by lightning. I had no clue she was already gone." Genevieve's eyes glazed over as if reliving the moment.

"She was cut open on the ground... both her neck and her stomach. The castle healer had sliced the child from her womb. They tried to warn me, but I looked anyway. That image will never leave my memory."

"Adelaide," Lea whispered, and the Queen's eyes snapped to hers.

"Yes," she breathed, staring at Lea as if she was a ghost.

"Go on, Mother," Gray urged, placing a hand on Lea's knee.

"Your father had killed her," the queen continued. "I'm sure by now you know that he's responsible for the Lonely Death." She looked at Lea, her eyebrows raised.

"She knows everything." Gray squeezed her hand, and Genevieve nodded.

"I knew he wanted power, of course, but at the time, I had no idea how far he would go to get it. Brennus was not a kind man, even then, but I didn't think he was capable of murder. I was naïve. So foolish. He took Emmaline's blood that night and—" Genevieve paused. "I didn't know. I didn't know that was the key to the spell. That damned bloody rag sat in a glass box on his desk for the longest time while he worked with that witch to get everything *just* right. I should have destroyed it. We wouldn't be in this position if I'd known what it was."

"Father's sins are not your burden." Gray looked away, as if the sight of his mother's tears were too much for him. The black shadows around her wrists finally unraveled, relaxing in long tendrils on the ground.

Genevieve gave Gray the tired look of a weary mother, and Lea noticed how, beneath her beauty, she seemed to have aged in the weeks since Lea had left the castle.

"I worried about what he would do to me after Emmaline died. I was fairly strong in my own right, and my magic of the night *almost* rivaled his. That's why he married me. He knew that by combining our bloodlines, our children would be powerful."

"I've always wondered how he took your magic without killing you, and why he didn't take Callie's the same way," Gray's hand fisted, and Lea grabbed it, rubbing her thumb across the bunched muscles.

Pain lanced through her chest from the bond as Gray said his sister's name, and Lea's own sorrow echoed back to him, mourning the young girl she never got to meet.

"That's the thing," Genevieve stood, her nervous energy leading her to pace. "Something happened that night. I ran toward Emmaline. I wanted to save her, and I raised my hands and called on my shadows and then, my magic was *gone*." The queen met Lea's eyes and held her stare.

"It looked like you were going to hurt my mother," Lea whispered, fiddling with the stones hanging around her neck, her fingers worrying the smooth jasper.

Genevieve froze. "*Looked* like? I knew it. You were there, weren't you?"

Lea nodded, her mind moving too fast for her mouth to keep up.

"I was going to try to help her," Genevieve's words were choked, "but my magic had disappeared. I never felt it again after that day, not until you walked into the dining hall. It sang out to me, and suddenly I could feel it again, calling from wherever you were."

That was it—the answer to what that sliver of darkness in her chest was that felt so foreign and *wrong*. "It's not my magic at all, is it? It's yours," Lea pressed her hand against her chest, that strange darkness twisting almost painfully now that Genevieve was standing before her, close enough to touch.

Genevieve knelt before her and squeezed her hands. "You saved my life that night, when you took my magic. There's no doubt in my mind my husband would have killed me as soon as he was able and stolen every last drop of my power. You are the reason I am here. You're the reason I am *alive."*

Well...? Gray asked through the bond?

The sword hadn't warmed. Not once. *She's telling the truth,* Lea responded.

Gray squeezed her knee. "Lea had a vision and was taken back in time. She saw my father kill the queen. The baby? *She* is the reason that child lived." He turned to Lea. "Do you know how you took her magic?"

Lea looked up at him with wide eyes. "No, I thought she was attacking my mother. I just called her darkness to me. It was the last thing I did before I woke up in the meadow."

The room darkened a bit, and Lea could practically see the gears turning and the plans rearranging in his mind. "How did you find us?" Gray's eyebrows lowered as he faced his mother, transforming from her mate into a soldier once again. "No one knows about this place."

"I saw you." Genevieve stood, brushing off her dress.

Gray's shadows spread out as if searching for whatever caused the breach in their location. "Explain. Now," he ordered.

"It started a few weeks ago." Genevieve said. "If I tried hard enough and followed the call of my magic, I could see you. Well, not exactly you, but I could see through your mate's eyes."

"It was you, wasn't it?" Lea's mouth went dry. "You showed me Alaric trying to kill the king."

"I'm still surprised it worked. I started trying to show you things when you were still in the castle. I'd focus on Alaric coming to find you. Once, I tried to show you him pulling some servant behind him with a bucket of water. But it never worked. Seeing through your eyes was so easy, but getting into your mind? It was almost impossible." Genevieve wrung her hands together. "I know it was a violation to sneak into your mind, but I didn't know what else to do. I was trying to warn you."

The queen's eyes darted to Gray nervously as if scared of how he'd react to her confession. "You were still in Calir and I knew you needed to return to ready your army." She paused. "The king is dead." The room was as silent as a grave and Genevieve looked up, not a single hint of sorrow in her eyes. "I always thought I would be happy to say those words, but I'm afraid his death has only made things worse."

The breath was stolen from Lea's lungs, her heart thundering in her chest. They'd known it was a possibility, a probability, even. But hearing it confirmed made her want to vomit as much as if she'd been told a meteorite was shooting toward them. Lea searched the mate bond, needing to check in on Gray's emotions. She braced herself for an assault of shock and worry, but instead she only felt steely resolve.

"I suspected as such," Gray answered, his shadows twisting around him and brushing against Lea's calves as if touching her could calm them. "My men in the castle said Alaric stopped requesting the poison. I assumed that meant he'd been successful in ending the king's life once I broke the curse."

"He poisoned him to make him sleep. Every night he cast the spell to give your father the Lonely Death. He knew it was a matter of time before you broke the spell yourself. And so he was ready. And now Alaric has his power. All of it." The queen sat down, holding her head in her hands while Gray stood, swapping positions as he began to pace.

Lea had never thought there was any resemblance between them, but Gray's mannerisms were identical to his mother's as he stalked back-and-forth on the light blue carpet.

"Do you know Alaric's plans? I know he's rallying an army. My latest reports say he has three battalions of five hundred men. But he's being tight-lipped, even amongst his most trusted advisors. I'd hoped we would have our army prepared and Lea in control of her powers, as well as Calir's forces ready to join us before we marched on Auropera. I've been in the process of attaining catapults and weaponry. But I worry we're running out of time." Gray paused his frantic pacing to wait for her answer.

"I'm sorry, but—you know everything I do. I fled as soon as I saw your father's body cooling." Genevieve twisted her wedding ring around on her finger.

"How long do you think we have?" Lea asked.

"A week." The queen bit her lip. "Maybe two, if we're lucky."

"My most recent reports support that theory," Gray added, turning to Lea. "I'm sorry I haven't told you yet. I was waiting on word to confirm my suspicions before worrying you."

A rush of shimmering day magic spread through the room, somehow finding its way throughout every inch of the cavern in a startling gust. Gray stood motionless for several minutes, his fingers flexing and jaw bunching. Lea could feel his nervous energy, his restlessness, but hiding beneath it was a shred of something lighter. Was it optimism?

"Lea, you took her magic. Mother could watch through your eyes because it was still a part of her, even if it was inside you. Do you think you could give it back?" Energy crackled through the room, Gray's shadows swirling as if in anticipation of something *big*.

"I don't know." Lea's eyebrows furrowed as she tried to remember exactly what had happened that night. "I don't really even know how I took it."

"Our original plan had us taking the castle and capital city. But if Alaric is bringing the battle to us, we could use it to our advantage. You know this village better than anyone. If we could position rebels throughout the village and give bits of your power to them, if you could somehow see through their eyes, it could change *everything*." Gray's words were animated, his spirit feeling lighter than it had in weeks. "It would be like we're everywhere at once. Janelle could help us plan the safest place to choose to fight. And if you could *take* magic..." Gray started pacing again, his shadows curling and filling every corner of the room as his eyes lit up excitedly. "If you could take Alaric's magic, even just some of it, maybe we could actually win this war and limit the casualties."

Excitement burst in the back of Lea's throat. Gray was right. If she could do this, they would have a clear advantage. Or at least a *chance*. "I'm not sure how it works, but I'm willing to try."

"Mother?" Gray questioned.

"Yes, *please*," she breathed, and the queen's magic in Lea's chest sighed in response.

Lea scooted to the end of the couch and patted the seat next to her. "Might as well get comfortable," Lea joked. "This could take a while."

"There's no pressure here, Azalea." Gray lowered his chin, waiting for her to acknowledge him.

"I know." Except, did she? She could feel the pressure like a crushing weight on her chest. She wanted to *help*. Lea felt a wave of love flow through the bond and took a deep breath, then held out her hand, palm up, toward Genevieve.

The moment their hands touched, electricity sparked between them, shadows immediately floating from Lea's fingers and wrapping around Genevieve's hand and up her arm. Both of them inhaled sharply, their eyes widening.

"Hello, old friend," Genevieve said with tears in her eyes as her magic fought to return home. Lea allowed the shadows to move of their own volition and snake out of her chest, giving them permission to go where they wanted. Within seconds, Genevieve was completely engulfed in black smoke-like shadows, so dark it was as if they were trying to consume her completely.

"I think it's working," Lea whispered as she cracked open an eye. The foreign feeling inside her that she hadn't understood was almost gone, and only the smallest bit remained between her light and her own night magic, as well as the darker, raw power she kept locked down deep.

Lea pushed out the last of Genevieve's magic and watched in awe as it filled the room. There was so much more of it than she'd thought.

"Call it back to you, Mother," Gray spoke from somewhere in the darkness.

"I'm trying," she stuttered, her voice strained.

Hesitantly, Lea pulled her fingers from Genevieve's grasp. Maybe without contact... The shadows screamed, roaring in protest as they were pulled away from their master and back against Lea's skin. Lea waved her hand in the air, trying to shake away their hold, but wherever her hand moved, the shadows followed.

"Don't let go, please," Genevieve gasped, clasping Lea's hand between both of hers. Lea allowed the shadows to once again wrap around Genevieve and squeezed her eyes shut. She searched through every inch of the cavern inside her, looking for whatever still remained that would not allow the queen's magic to leave her. She found the very center of her magic, where her light and her mate bond and her shadows combined, and, there! Swirling among her own magic was a wisp of a shadow that looked different, *felt* different.

She formed the fire inside her into a flaming dagger, red hot and deathly sharp, and with every ounce of strength she could find, she cut the queen's magic from her own with a single, clean swipe. The shadows around them, finally free, flew through the room in a large arc, breaking away from Lea completely before rushing toward Genevieve. The queen held out her arms, throwing her head back as the shadows crashed into her chest and disappeared, leaving only silence and startling darkness, every candle extinguishing at once.

Lea sparked the candles, and the room brightened as Genevieve slowly lowered her arms and opened her eyes, tears dripping from her eyelashes. "You did it," she whispered as she raised a slender hand. Long tendrils of deep, blue-black shadows drifted from her fingers, gracefully floating toward Lea and caressing her cheek. "You really did it. How can I ever repay you?"

"It was yours to begin with." Lea said, feeling lighter without the queen's magic, the discomfort behind her sternum suddenly and completely eased.

The queen's lip trembled as she nodded and turned to Gray. "I'm sorry I didn't save your sister. I'm sorry I let him hurt you. I was weak."

"You were a victim, too." Gray's voice was strained, but Lea could feel the strength of his emotions. He was brimming with love, the kind of love a child feels for their mother.

"Can you ever forgive me?" Genevieve asked.

Lea stood from the couch, walking toward the bedroom and kissing Gray on the cheek as she passed. *I'm tired. I think I'll go to sleep, but take your time,* she said into his mind. Genevieve and Gray deserved privacy, a moment to talk, to heal, just the two of them.

As she sat down at the vanity, Lea placed her palms flat on the smooth wood, the swirling grain pressing into her fingers. She looked at herself in the mirror, wondering if she looked any different now that she'd cut the queen's magic away. But her reflection remained unchanged other than the dark circles beneath her tired eyes.

Lea exhaled, wondering if she should go to bed or wait for her mate. She could only imagine how much Gray and his mother had to talk about, but Lea knew that Genevieve was already forgiven. Gray wouldn't blame her for being afraid of Brennus, wouldn't fault her for his sister's death. In her own way, Genevieve had protected them by not fighting the Black King and making them a bigger target for his anger, another way to hurt his wife.

No. All the blame laid on a single man's shoulders. A man who was now dead. Lea hung her head and allowed herself to mourn the fact that she wasn't the one who'd ended his life. Shadows swirled in her eyes as the raw, dark magic in her chest twisted. It yearned for vengeance, and without Genevieve's magic taking up space in her chest, it was harder to hold at bay.

Lea hung her head. She was so exhausted. From the blood loss and lack of sleep, sure, but also from the pressure of holding that darkness down. So for just a few moments, alone in the flickering light, Lea stopped fighting it. She allowed a tiny stream of that raw, terrifying magic to escape into her chest, filling her with fury and vengeance before pushing it back down with a deep breath and climbing into bed. It was as if nothing had ever happened. Or would be, if not for the ten perfect indentations in the wood where the black fire that had engulfed her hands had burned it away, leaving scorch marks behind. For just a moment, she'd been fire. She'd been destruction. She had become death herself.

CHAPTER 75

EMMA

There were thirteen books spread out across Emma's room. She'd made sure to take care with them, opening each one gently so as to not break their spines and avoiding folding corners of the old, but well-preserved pages. It amazed Emma how much she'd learned over the past few weeks; everything from different types of magic she hadn't known existed, to the history of the kingdom, even before Queen Emmaline's death.

There were still so many she hadn't been able to read completely, which was why, when Thomas knocked at her door, she didn't even notice. It wasn't until he opened the door and popped his head inside that she realized someone was in her room.

Emma jumped, squealing as she scrambled backward. "Thomas! You scared me!"

"I'm sorry." He took a step back, holding up his hands. "I figured you'd be lost in your reading, so I thought I'd check on you. See if you were hungry or needed anything. I brought you a muffin. But I can leave if you're busy," he offered, gesturing toward the door.

"No! Um, no." She lowered her eyes, feeling wholly uncomfortable with Thomas's undivided attention. It wasn't his fault. Emma disliked *most* people's attention. Everyone's really, except for her mother. But with Thomas, his eyes on her face made her nervous in a different way, one that caused butterfly wings to tickle her stomach. But it wasn't just that. She felt unprepared when it came to her feelings for Thomas. *Why didn't I search King Tanad's library for some sort of book on knowing if a man likes you?*

"What are you reading about?" Thomas approached slowly as if he was afraid he would scare those butterflies away.

Scooting to the side to give him room to sit, Emma pointed to the page she was reading. She'd read these words before, back in Calir. Thank the gods that she'd chosen this book to start with, because without it, she would have missed the opportunity to get Eudora's help.

The witch had called on her one night when she was in the library alone, exactly as she'd been reading this very page. "You'll need a potion for that." The old woman had raised her chin as if daring Emma to argue with her. "If you want it to work, that is."

Emma had been speechless, only nodding with an open mouth as Eudora turned with a flourish and closed the door behind her. A few days later, Gray had handed her the potion without expecting any answers in return, and she'd been grateful. She wasn't sure her plan would work, and had needed to find out more before giving her friends hope. But now? She was confident she could do what she'd been reading about all these weeks. Well, eighty-six percent confident.

"I've found a way to help us. At least, I think I have." Emma untucked the hair from behind her ear, hiding her face behind it.

"Will you tell me more?" Thomas's voice was gentle, a soothing balm against the anxious buzzing that always made her fingers need to fidget or her toes to tap.

"Well. It started as a way to control my magic. I don't want to always see..." Emma didn't even want to say the words.

"I understand." Thomas laid a hand on her back, and her skin instantly heated. "Did you learn something that can help with that?"

"Not about how to stop it. But something happened in the Wicked Wood. I watched one of the dead try to strike at a nabis and join in the battle. He wanted to help, but couldn't, and it made me wonder. Their spirits are still here. They can interact with me. What if there was a way for them to fight with us?"

"You mean join the rebellion?" Thomas sat up straighter.

Emma forced herself to make eye contact, her palms growing sweaty. "I mean soldiers who can kill without being killed again."

Something unrecognizable danced in Thomas's eyes, and it unsettled her. She was used to being able to sense people's feelings. So why couldn't she now?

"An army of the dead," he said, his words laced with awe. "Our army is half the size of the Black King's, if that. Emma, this could change everything! Could it save them, too?"

Emma shook her head. "No. Their soul would still be severed from their body. Once that happens, there's no way to connect it again." A lump formed in Emma's throat, and she swallowed. "I don't like to think about it too much. It almost feels cruel, asking so much of someone who just lost their life. But we have to ask them, right? Because if every soldier that falls is willing to keep fighting, it gives us a chance."

Thomas scooted closer, pressing himself against her shoulder to look at the page, and Emma's heart skipped. "I promise you, any soldier who was willing to risk leaving their home to come fight with us knows the likelihood of their death. I'm not doing this for a better life for me. I joined the rebellion for a better life for every single person living in Desia, for my family. If I could continue to fight after I died, I would do it without hesitation."

Emma closed her eyes and sucked in a breath as she rubbed her chest. The thought of Thomas dying in the battle was physically painful. "I know that, rationally. I do. It just feels like such a big thing to ask of someone."

"And it's a sacrifice we would all make," Thomas said firmly. "How did you figure this out? It's... It's nothing short of brilliant." There was that look in his eye again... The one that she couldn't quite identify.

"When I was in Calir, King Tanad let me use his library. Well... You knew that already." Emma felt a blush creeping up her neck. "It was very kind of him. He didn't have to do that." She began tapping her feet together. "Or allow his head librarian to spend all his time helping me. He was so kind. I don't think I would have been able to get through all this information without him. I'd like to visit him again. Once the war is over, of course." Emma gestured to the many books laid out around her, and Thomas stiffened.

"Sorry, I'm rambling again, aren't I?"

"No. You're perfect." He tilted his head, pressing his lips together as he hid a smirk. "Go on."

"When we were in the Wicked Wood and I saw the dead, the soldiers had the things that they'd carried with them when they were killed. I saw swords and arrows and shields, rope and cloaks. I thought that maybe since I could communicate with them, there could be a way for them to interact with the physical world as well..."

Reaching toward the head of the bed, Emma picked up a small leather-bound text. It was red, and completely inconspicuous. "This book has a story of someone else who had my same power. They discovered a way to let the dead connect with the world. Cora—that was her name—used the power for more noble reasons than what I'm trying to do." That familiar feeling of guilt that had followed her ever since she had the idea of the army of the dead gnawed at Emma's insides. "She used it to allow loved ones to interact with those who had passed. They couldn't speak, but they could touch them, hug them. Hold them one more time. And I wondered, if they could do all that, maybe they could do even *more*."

Thomas stared at her with an open mouth, his eyes shining with complete awe. "You're amazing, Emma."

Emma shook her head, trying to push down the bubbles of nervous energy working their way up her throat, wholly uncomfortable with his praise. "This power of mine, it feels like a curse. Not a gift at all. But, maybe it could be if I could use it for good? Maybe..." Emma trailed off.

"It would make it worth it," Thomas finished for her.

"Yes. It might make it easier to deal with the bad if something useful can come of it. At least I hope that it will." She planned on using her gift to allow people to get closure, and would offer that service to the families of soldiers after the war. It was entirely possible she wouldn't be strong enough to witness that much pain, but Emma hoped that the closure those mothers and brothers would get would be enough to get her through the hard days.

"Have you told Gray?"

"Not yet. I've been reading about how to do it, but Thomas, can I be honest with you?"

"Of course." He opened his arms, and Emma wondered if he was offering her an embrace or just being sincere with her.

"It scares me, opening myself up like that. What if I am a coward? What if I can't do it?" A drop of blood appeared where Emma picked at the side of her fingernail.

Thomas's jaw dropped. "First, you are stronger than you know, Emma. You *can* do it. I've never been more certain of anything. Second, you will see the dead either way." He trailed his knuckles down her cheek, turning her to face him, and her stomach tightened. "Won't it be a little easier if seeing them does something more than just torture you?" His stare made her heart thump erratically, and suddenly she was almost choking on the need to change the subject.

"Anyway. That's what I've been working on." She forced a smile. "You wanted to go get something to eat?" Thomas had been busy making weapons for the rebellion, working most nights until sunup, and then resting during the day. Muffins weren't nearly enough to sustain him with all the power he was using. Plus, she'd hardly seen him since they'd arrived. Not that she blamed him, of course. They all had a role to play in this war—all had sacrifices they'd have to make.

"Yes, well, I really just wanted to talk to you." Thomas seemed nervous, ducking his head and running his hand through his now-short hair. "I've been thinking about you a lot lately," he confessed, finally meeting Emma's eyes.

"Why would you do that?" Emma asked, her nerves making the words sound harsh and the butterflies in her stomach turning into massive birds whose wings were so big it felt like they were trying to crack her ribs. She tapped her fingers against her leg, desperate to get some of the anxious energy out of her body.

Thomas placed his hand on top of Emma's, stalling her fidgeting. "There's nothing to be nervous about. I promise. You're always safe when you're with me."

"I'm not afraid, I'm... I can't explain it. My body feels itchy sometimes. Tight, like my skin is stretching across my bones so taut they might pop through."

"How can I help?" Thomas's eyebrows lowered, and he started to pull his hand away.

"Wait!" Emma interjected, pulling his hand back. "Pressure helps." She took a few slow breaths.

Hesitantly, Thomas reached forward to grab her other hand, pulling them together and squeezing tight.

It grounded Emma almost instantly, and while she was still incredibly uncomfortable with Thomas's undivided attention, she forced herself to stop fidgeting. His touch felt good, and she thought that maybe if he pulled her into his arms and squeezed her tight, the whole world might go silent for the first time in her life.

Emma had thought that maybe there'd been something between them back at the castle, but at the same time, she'd known how much he loved Lea. She didn't blame him. She loved Lea, too. Not in any romantic sense, of course, but she could understand his feelings. Her friend was strong and brave, and outspoken in a way Emma almost envied.

"Look, I know that my timing isn't great. There's a war coming that I might not even survive, but I've made the mistake of not expressing my feelings before, and I don't want to do that again. I don't want to die with regrets."

"You're not going to die, Thomas." Emma shook her head, refusing to look in his eyes.

"I had a dream the other night, before you all came back. It made me think—" he stopped, swallowing his words. "I'm hoping for as few rebel casualties as possible. But it doesn't change the fact that I'm willing to sacrifice my life for the people I love. I won't go beyond the veil with anything left unsaid, Emma."

"What do you need to say?" she asked, her tongue heavy in her mouth.

"That you're beautiful." Thomas let go of one of her hands and cupped her cheek, caressing her skin with his thumb, but he didn't force her to meet his eyes. "You're the kindest person I've ever met. You're strong and soft, somehow at the same time, and the way you are handling your power... I'm just—I'm completely amazed by you."

Emma felt like she was glowing, was certain she had to be dreaming. In fact, she'd had several dreams very similar to this.

"I like you, Emma. So once this war is over, I'd like to see where this can go. That is, if you feel at all the same way." Emma finally looked up, and a boyish grin spread across his face the moment they made eye contact.

Her throat was so dry she could hardly swallow. *Is this actually happening?* "I think I would like that very much," she whispered.

Thomas scooted closer, their knees now touching and his eyes dropping to her lips.

"I think I would like to kiss you." He leaned closer, slowly, giving her time to stop him. Emma stared at Thomas's strong jaw and plump lips as he moved closer. If she'd been able to speak, she would have told him that she'd never wanted anything more. But her words were too thick to move up her throat. And so she leaned forward, closing her eyes and the last few inches between them.

A sigh escaped her mouth as she reveled in the pressure of his lips, soft and tender in a way that made her want to cry. The kiss was full of hope, of *possibility*. Yes, war was coming, but if she could help, if they could win, there could be so much *good* waiting for them on the other side.

Thomas pulled away, his breaths short and ragged, his eyes mirroring the possibilities that had laced his kisses.

Emma gathered up her courage. "I think it's time I talk to Gray." She cleared her throat. Committing to opening herself up for the dead to tether to, it terrified her. It would be painful, and emotional and all around just *hard*, but as Thomas nodded and grabbed her hand, lacing his fingers between hers, she knew without a doubt that it would be worth it.

CHAPTER 76

LEA

After a few restless hours of sleep, Lea forced herself to climb out of bed. Gray had joined her at some point, but she didn't think that he'd ever closed his eyes. Instead, he just held her, so tight it was as if he was counting down the days he had left to sleep wrapped around her.

As Lea pulled the blanket away, preparing to leave the warm cocoon of her bed, a *crinkle* of paper caused her to pause. Next to her pillow, where Gray had laid, was a folded note.

Little flower,

I hope you rested. I wish you would go back to sleep, but if I know you at all, I will see you only minutes after you finish reading this letter. I've sent word to Woodhurst for your father to return, and am meeting with Vincent to discuss how to best utilize him, should he make it here in time. I'll be in the training rooms. Find me when you're ready.

A bubble of excitement worked its way up Lea's throat until she was holding back a smile. She had missed training the past few days, had actually missed her morning runs with Erik and Janelle. Once again, working with the moonflowers last night had made her feel helpless, almost hopeless. But she wouldn't be hopeless for long.

Lea considered all the different ways she would like to kill Alaric as she dressed for training, donning tight black leggings and a matching black shirt that hugged close to her skin. She'd learned in those first few days of training that loose clothing only made her more vulnerable, so she'd taken to wearing tighter garments so her opponents had nothing to grab onto as she fought.

After she finished braiding her hair, Lea walked to the training room, stretching her arms as she went. Every mat was taken by fellow rebels sparring with varying degrees of success. A small group of women performed archery in the back, and Lea recognized the butcher's wife among them, while the butcher himself practiced small bits of fire magic nearby. The blacksmith appeared to be lifting rocks with just his mind, stacking them neatly in a pile as tall as he could until they toppled over.

Everywhere she looked, both strangers and neighbors she'd known her whole life were practicing magic. It was astounding, but also filled Lea with a sense of joy seeing others wield their magic so casually. It should have always been like this.

It took only a second for Gray to find her, his green, smoky eyes locking on her immediately. She felt that familiar zing of electricity across her skin, a sensation that she'd grown so accustomed to that it barely registered anymore.

Gray bent his head to say something to Vincent, then strode to Lea with long, confident steps. "I knew you wouldn't sleep for long." He frowned at her. "Are you rested enough? You lost a lot of blood last night."

"I'm just fine. Never been better." She bounced on the balls of her feet. "Where should I start?" she questioned.

"I thought we could try giving away a bit of your magic, testing to see if you'd really be able to see through someone else's eyes."

Lea's magic stuttered in response, repulsed by the idea. As if sensing her discomfort, Gray grabbed her hand and led her over to where he had stood with Vincent in the middle of the room. "We'll only give the smallest bit, only to a few people who we know would allow you to take it back."

Lea nodded, forcing her magic to calm down. If they could see the whole battlefield from different perspectives, it would be a clear advantage. "Who do you think I should try it on?" Lea asked, looking around the room.

"I already asked Janelle if she'd be okay with it." Gray gestured to where Erik sparred with Janelle, sweat dripping from his brow as if she was giving him a run for his coin. He paused their fight, and Janelle took the opportunity to slam her leg into the back of his knee, causing it to buckle. Erik's eyes went wide with a mixture of pride and surprise as he fell to the ground with a thud.

Erik raised his hands in the air in surrender, and Janelle stopped her attack, offering him a hand and pulling him up. Inclining his head to the doorway, Gray grabbed Lea's hand and lead her out of the training room, Erik and Janelle following behind.

"It will be easier to focus out here." Gray pulled out a chair for her at one of the tables in the common area. "Janelle, sit here next to Lea."

Taking her seat, Janelle reached out her hand and grabbed Lea's. It was so uncharacteristically affectionate of Janelle that it almost made Lea cry. She wasn't sure what exactly was going on with her and Erik, but whatever it was, it was good for her friend.

"Now, Lea," Gray sat down across from them at the table while Erik continued to stand, his hand on his sword as if he might need to use it. "I don't think you need to give much magic. If I were to guess, the key would simply be to have your essence inside someone else to where you could call upon it. Does that make sense?"

Lea nodded, remembering the pain she'd felt when she cut away the Queen's magic.

"Try whatever you did last night to give my mother her powers back, but this time, isolate a bit of *your* magic. Only the smallest amount."

Closing her eyes, Lea imagined the flaming dagger in her mind. It was far less difficult to picture this time, and as she delved into her chest, she separated her magic into a ball of light and dark, like rays of sun peeking out through storm clouds. Using the white-hot dagger, she pictured nicking away the smallest bit of magic and pushing it to the side, separating it from the mass of power next to it.

With slow, controlled breaths, Lea plucked away the tiny speck of magic and pushed it out of her chest and down her arms, through her hands, into her fingers, and then, with a deep exhale, she forced it beneath Janelle's skin.

Her friend gasped, pulling her hand away as a static shock zapped between them.

"I'm sorry!" Lea looked at her fingers. "Did I hurt you?"

"No, it's just—It was a strange sensation," she muttered.

"Do you feel it?" Gray asked Janelle, who closed her eyes as if searching for the magic. After a few seconds, her mouth twisted into a smile.

"I do. It feels like you, Lea. Like light and hope, with a pinch of stubbornness and bad decision making."

Lea reached out, biting back a laugh as she swiped at Janelle, who was trying to hit her in the arm. Gray caught her hand in the air with a pitch black shadow.

"There's no time for joking," he snapped.

"Who said it's a joke?" Janelle retorted without missing a beat. Erik leveled her with a look.

"What? I could have said much worse," Janelle argued.

"Enough." Gray held up a hand. "Lea, can you find it?"

Lea wasn't sure if it was because Janelle sat so close to her, or if it would always be easy to find that piece of herself she'd lent to her friend, but she knew exactly where her magic was. She could feel it, pulsing and calling to her. Without Gray needing to tell her to, she closed her eyes and followed it, allowing her power to wrap around her consciousness like a warm blanket.

Janelle's thoughts began banging around in her head, but Lea constructed a shield of darkness in her mind, silently thanking Erik for all the hours he'd spent in Calir forcing her to work on shielding, both physically and mentally. Her friend's innermost thoughts were none of her business.

With all the focus she could muster, she willed the magic inside Janelle to show her what she saw.

Lea blinked, and suddenly she was looking at herself through Janelle's eyes. She jumped backward, nearly falling on her ass as she scrambled away from the table. "Oh!" she gasped.

"What happened?" Gray asked, placing a steadying hand on Lea's elbow.

"It worked," Lea laughed, a small, joyous sound that caused a beat of pride to flash from Gray through their bond.

"You did it. You stunning creature." Gray lifted Lea off her feet, crushing her against his chest and spinning her in a circle.

"It'd help us even more if I could take magic," Lea said, raising an eyebrow at Janelle.

"Wait, mine? I don't even know how much I have? What if it's only a tiny bit, and you take it all?" Janelle asked, her eyes nearly bugging out of her head.

"One thing at a time, Little Flower. Let's see if you can show Janelle what you're seeing." Gray crossed his arms and leaned back.

Her friend's face relaxed, and Lea tried not to smile. She knew that Janelle would let her practice taking magic if she had to, but she also knew that having that magic, whether a sliver or a huge slice, made Janelle feel safer.

"Alright. We can start with that, then." Lea took a deep breath, not certain how to even start. With giving away magic, it started with finding her own power. She followed the phantom trail from her chest toward her magic, focusing on pushing her own thoughts into Janelle's head. Her magic wrapped around her friend's consciousness once again, and Lea focused on what she was seeing, but—*dammit*!

Once again, she was looking at herself. Pulling her magic back, she shook her head.

"Did it work?" Erik asked.

"No, I tried, but—I saw through Janelle's eyes again. You didn't see anything, did you?" Lea asked her.

"I'm sorry." Janelle winced. "I didn't see anything different."

Lea rubbed the back of her neck where her muscles met her skull, a headache forming and wrapping up into her temples. "Let me try again," she said with false bravado.

"Mother said it was difficult, Lea. If you need a minute—"

Lea held up her hand, already trying to push what she was seeing toward Janelle. She prodded at her mind, looking for a way to break through and force her own thoughts inside. Her vision began to transform again, blurry this time. "Anything?" she asked, her concentration faltering as her head started to pound.

"Nothing," Janelle confirmed.

Lea let go of the thread of power between her and Janelle, her vision coming back into focus. "I can't get through."

"We'll keep practicing. I'm sure you'll figure it out." Gray laced his fingers between Lea's. "The most important thing is that you'll be able to see throughout the battlefield. That's more than we could have hoped for."

"It doesn't feel like enough," Lea said, pressing her lips together, trying to hold her disappointment at bay. Gray was right. Being able to see the entirety of the battlefield was no small victory.

"We have to celebrate every victory, Little Flower. Before today, I wondered if it was even possible for us to win this war. But now?" Gray cupped Lea's face tenderly between his hands. "We have a chance. Our people might live. And it's because of *you*."

CHAPTER 77

ERIK

Erik had hardly seen Janelle since their conversation the other night, when she had opened up to him and he'd almost burned King Tanad's palace down with his fury. It had taken every last shred of his self control to not leave that night, to go find the soldiers who had assaulted her and make them pay. His daydreams were now filled with the different ways he would kill them.

The visions filled his mind every waking moment. As he ate, he dreamed of poisoning their wine. While drying off from bathing, he thought about the color their faces would turn and the panic he'd see in their eyes if he strangled them with his towel. Erik had accidentally come a little too close to splitting Gray's throat as he imagined an epic sword fight against Jakob, Stefan, and their friends while they'd been training.

He'd had to remind himself that Janelle was okay, that he could help put her back together. But that didn't mean he couldn't fantasize about cutting her attackers from ass to eyes, splaying them open like a duck on the dinner menu.

The past few nights, Janelle had been asleep by the time he'd returned to their room. Gray and Erik had spent hours every day discussing strategy, working with the rebels, assessing their magic, and maintaining their own training. In addition, now that Lea could give away little bits of her power that would allow her to see through others' eyes, they had been making plans for what vantage points were most advantageous, and who should be positioned where for Lea to gather the most valuable information.

Erik was exhausted, and frankly, quite crabby. He'd grimaced and ground his teeth more than laughed and smiled the past few days, and it hadn't escaped Gray's notice.

"What is going on with you?" Gray asked after he healed himself from the nick on the right side of his throat.

"It's nothing." Erik cleaned the blood off his sword and sheathed it. "I'm sorry I cut you. My mind was elsewhere."

"Don't be sorry. Just tell me what's going on. I can't have my second in command distracted. Not right now."

"Says the guy who acted like an animal until he stopped being an ass and sealed his mate bond," Erik grumbled.

Gray's eyes narrowed knowingly. "Is that it? Did something happen with Janelle?"

Erik's nostrils flared as he took a deep breath. "I guess you can say that. It was a long time ago. But she told me about something that happened to her, spineless men who hurt her, and now all I can think about is killing the bastards who did it."

Shadows escaped from Gray's fingers. "*That* is something I can understand. Is she okay?" he asked, frown lines bracketing his mouth.

"She will be." Erik forced his shoulders to relax, wiping the sweat from his neck. "Let's get back to training."

"No. Go be with her." Gray threw Erik a towel. "We might not survive this war, Erik. You're ready to fight. Make sure you're not so focused on the danger to come that you forget to live your life now." Gray strapped his sword on his back and walked away, giving Erik no time to argue.

Not that he would have. The moment Gray disappeared through the training room door, Erik stalked toward his room with determined steps. His friend was right. If they only had days or weeks left, Erik wanted to spend every one of them making Janelle feel loved.

Janelle wanted the physical? He would give it to her. But dammit if he wasn't going to show her the emotion behind it as well. Still sweaty and shirtless from training, Erik threw open the door, praying Janelle was inside.

The crack of the door against the wall rang through the room, and Janelle jumped, spinning around from where she stood flipping through one of the few books he kept on the bookcase carved from the stone of the cavern wall.

Erik's chest heaved as he drank her in, her curvy legs peeking out from one of his white shirts.

"You're back early," Janelle said breathlessly, her eyes trailing across his bare chest.

"I am." He began to take slow, decisive steps toward her.

"Is everything okay?" she asked, glancing behind him toward the door.

Erik grinned, closing the distance between them and pressing his body against hers, pinning her to the wall as his hand wrapped around the side of her waist, pulling her hips against him. "It will be, once I taste you and you're panting my name. I've always wondered if you'd taste like berries."

Janelle's jaw cracked open, her eyes widening as she sucked in a breath. "You have?" Janelle said breathlessly before averting her eyes. "Don't you have important second-in-command things to do?" She squirmed, but Erik grabbed her chin between his fingers, forcing her to meet his eyes.

"*Nothing* is more important than showing you how much I love you. Don't pull away because this is real."

Janelle's bottom lip trembled, and Erik rubbed his thumb across it. Her hand absently drifted to the scar on her hip, but Erik grabbed her wrist in his other hand.

"No one will ever hurt you again, and certainly not me." His words were harsh, his eyes never leaving Janelle's as he placed her palm against his chest and lowered his own to trail the raised skin crisscrossing her hip.

"I should have been with you every night. I could have prevented what happened to you." Erik leaned his forehead against hers. "I'm sorry I couldn't protect you then. But I swear to you, you're safe now."

Janelle closed her eyes, a single tear sliding down her cheek.

"Let me love you, Janelle," Erik pleaded, fire crackling along his skin.

Janelle tilted her head back, her lips hovering so close to Erik's that her breath twisted with his. "Only if you let me love you, too."

The words barely left her lips before Erik crushed his against them, swallowing her confession as if he needed to know if her love tasted like berries, too. Lifting her by her hips, he sat her on the bookshelf, spreading her legs to stand between them.

The candlelight reflected off her pale skin, and Erik followed the trail of light down her neck and chest and across her collarbone. Fire sparked on his fingertips and he set his shirt aflame, commanding it to burn the fabric while leaving Janelle's skin untouched. Ashes floated around them like snow, and a rumble escaped Erik's chest.

"Beautiful," he rasped as goosebumps dotted her skin. He warmed his body, his hands and lips with the fire inside him as he trailed kisses down her chest, across her peaked nipples to her belly button, then toward her hip.

Janelle tried to grab Erik's head and pull him back up to kiss him, but he pinned her with a stare. "Every inch of you deserves to be worshiped. Especially your scars."

She paused, running a hand across his cheek before leaning back and allowing him to do just that. He traced the lines with his tongue, whispering praises as he silently vowed to never allow her perfect skin to be marred again, to make the soldiers who had done this pay a thousand-fold.

Janelle sighed, finally relaxing, her hands bracing on the thick, stone shelf, and the sound went straight to his cock. Erik ran his hands from her hip bones down her thighs, stopping at her knees and spreading her wide before him as he fell to his knees. Janelle threw her head back, scooting closer to the edge of the bookcase.

It was all the permission Erik needed as his lips closed over her, sucking and swirling his tongue. The gasp that left Janelle's throat was the most beautiful sound Erik had ever heard, sending a jolt of desire that made fire trail along the ground where he knelt.

"More," Janelle moaned, grabbing the back of his head and grinding against his lips. He spread her legs wider as Janelle wound tighter and tighter. "Erik!" she cried, and it was his undoing. He had to be inside her, had to take her and feel her around him as she begged for release.

Erik stood, pulling his belt from its prison of loops with one swift movement and quickly unbuttoned his pants. Janelle lurched toward him, wrapping her arms around his neck at the same moment he thrust inside her, both of them stilling as he slid in to the hilt. Her ragged breaths caused her breasts to slide against his chest, and Erik grew impossibly harder.

As he began to move inside her, his fingers trailing her scar and hers raking lines down his back, Erik knew without a doubt that he was home. No matter where the war took them, no matter what dangers he faced, he would sacrifice whatever it took to protect this woman. He'd spent his life motivated by revenge, needing to kill the king for what he'd done to his mother. But in an instant, his motivation shifted.

The war was still coming, but he was no longer fighting for the memory of his mother alone. As Janelle tightened around him, his name on her lips like a prayer, Erik knew without a doubt who and what he was fighting for. He spilled himself inside her, kissing her deeply as she sagged against him, and promised the gods he would do whatever he could to keep her safe. Even without a mark branded on her skin, she was his, and he'd sooner burn the entire world than let her get hurt again.

CHAPTER 78

LEA

"Render Alaric powerless, and it will change everything," Gray said with stars in his eyes. He'd emptied out the training room, sensing Lea's discomfort with practicing in front of the rest of their army. Normally, Lea would be grateful for the privacy, but now it just made her feel more vulnerable.

"What if I take too much?" Lea asked. When she had taken Genevieve's power, she'd taken every last drop. But Gray was far more powerful than his mother, and she worried that her chest might actually explode if she accidentally stole all of Gray's power. Giving Genevieve's magic back had been easy. She'd simply sent it home to where it belonged. Even giving away her own had been less difficult than she'd expected. But stealing it? Carving someone else's power away from its master was as unnatural as stealing the light from the sun.

If Lea was being honest, being overwhelmed by Gray's magic was only a small part of what worried her. She was painfully aware of how that dark, primary magic inside her hungered for more. Without Genevieve's magic taking up space in her chest, keeping that raw power locked away down deep had been even harder. It wanted release. It begged for *more,* yearning to consume everything it touched. It was in the way the magic pulsed and thumped along with the rhythm of her heart. What if she started taking Gray's magic, and couldn't stop herself? What if she hurt him somehow?

"That's why you're practicing with me. With the bond, I'll be able to feel what you're feeling. If you're getting weak or overwhelmed, I'll know to stop you."

"Right. Okay." Lea wiped her sweaty palms against her thighs. "I can do this." Closing her eyes, Lea prepared her magic.

Gray widened his stance and crossed his arms, standing casually on the mat as if he had no concerns. "Start by using the bond to find my magic. Once you learn how to cut some away, we can try again on someone you're not bonded to."

Lea did as Gray said, her magic following every loop and twist of the tether between them in her mind as she tried to find the very center of him. When she gave her magic to others, that searing hot blade of fire cut through it easily, and her magic obeyed, moving wherever she wanted it to go. But as she severed away a piece of Gray's night magic, it refused to budge.

His eyebrows scrunched up as Lea continued to tug at the small bit of power, but it wouldn't budge. "Pull, harder," Gray said. "I can feel it. You're close."

Lea pulled, wrapping her magic around Gray's and imagining it going taught as rubber before snapping. She tugged until her head pounded and her body shook.

Gray sent a wave of calm through their bond. "Take a break, Lea." Gray urged. "There's no rush. What was different when you took my mother's magic?"

Lea dropped her hands, thinking back to the night she'd had her vision. "I thought my mother was in danger when I took Genevieve's power. It looked like she was about to attack her."

"Or maybe it worked because of the adrenaline? You'd just watched Adelaide cut a baby from the queen's stomach." Gray said, his eyebrows lowering in concentration.

Or maybe, Lea thought, *it's because you were accessing that darker magic. That place deep inside you, hidden away behind the cold floor in your chest.* "Maybe." She pushed the thought aside. "Let me try again." Lea squared her shoulders and took a deep breath, searching for her courage as she dove deep into her magic.

She pulled at the bit of primary magic that had seeped from the crack in her chest and mixed with her light and shadows. As the dark, raw power took hold, her throat constricted and her head pounded. Her heart raced erratically and fire danced behind her eyes. Somehow, she was freezing and consumed in flames simultaneously. It was as if she stood naked in the snow while fire burned her skin. She dug deeper, the burn intensifying as the room grew hotter. Lea burned from the inside out, and a strangled cry of pain burst from her throat. Gray was suddenly at her side, his hands rubbing her upper arms.

"You control your power." Gray's voice soothed the sting, and she breathed a little deeper. "Do you understand?"

Lea kept her eyes closed, fighting against the pounding in her head and taking a deep breath. It took several minutes for her to regain control—long, agonizing moments in which the dark, black fire inside her revolted against what she was trying to do. Gray continued to hold her arms, steadying her, grounding her. Finally, Lea forced her magic to submit.

"Good," Gray said, exhaling loudly, and Lea realized he'd been holding his breath. She forced herself to meet Gray's gaze, then froze. Reflected in his eyes, she could see that in her own danced red, blazing fire.

"It's okay. You're okay. Keep going." Gray maintained eye contact, refusing to let go. Lea watched the fire in her eyes as she reached into her chest and followed the tether to her mate. She found Gray's magic, but this time, instead of using a blade of fire, she formed one of unbridled power, made of both flames and shadow—black embers flickering red and yellow in the depths of darkness. She sliced away a small bit of his power and began to pull it toward her.

Gray's magic fought back, recoiling from Lea's presence. It was as if Lea was trying to steal away Gray's heart or lungs. His magic was just as much a part of him as his blood and bone, and to steal even the smallest bit felt impossible.

Lea grabbed Gray's hands and squeezed, grounding herself and ordering the magic to obey her. It started to relent, small bits of shadow mixing with her own, but it wasn't enough. Pain burst behind her eyes as the room spun.

"Stop, Azalea. It's too much."

Lea felt resistance as Gray tried to pull his magic back, his shadows untangling themselves from her and darting away.

"No!" Lea wouldn't stop. She was so close, she almost had it. If she could just pull harder. Allowing a bit more of that dark power inside her to leave her chest, she closed her eyes and demanded that Gray's magic bow to her will. Lea was vaguely aware of flames dancing along her skin, of shadows wrapping around her mate, but she couldn't stop. The magic inside her demanded she finish. She needed more: more magic, more power.

Gray hissed and pulled his hands away. "Lea control it! We're done. You're *done*. Stop!" But his words barely registered. Her magic fought harder against Gray's as her head swam and her chest ached. Lea was vaguely aware of something wet dripping down the side of her face and neck, but she didn't care. *Couldn't* care. She needed Gray's magic—wasn't sure she could breathe without it.

"Azalea!" Gray roared, thunder booming and shaking the walls of the cavern as he grabbed her once again. She could feel her flames singeing his flesh, and was vaguely aware of his hiss of pain as he shook her violently.

"Open your eyes! Look at me, Little flower, you are *mine*. You belong to *me*. Only me."

Her light responded, arcing toward Gray and wrapping around his magic. *Stop!* It seemed to call to her. Lea *wanted* to stop, but she was so hot, and it was agonizing. There was an inferno in her body, so hot that it blanketed her mind in smoke, making it hard to think. Every inch of her body hurt, each breath like knives in her lungs and each beat of her heart like it was pumping glass.

"Come back to me, Little Flower," Gray soothed, as if his words could ease the torment of the fire consuming her. Lea forced open her eyes, silently begging Gray to stop the pain. She looked down at his hands—blistered, charred skin wrapping up his forearms to the elbow. It was like a splash of cold water to her face.

As quickly as the magic had overtaken her, she forced it back down, closing it off and releasing Gray's power from its grasp. She dropped to her knees at the same time Gray did, and he pulled her into his chest, stroking her hair. She grabbed his hands and flooded them with healing light, his skin smoothing over and the wounds closing.

"I'm so sorry," she whispered, her whole body trembling. "I didn't—I couldn't stop it."

Gray rocked her back-and-forth, shushing her. "You can't go there again, Lea," he said. "That power isn't natural, not for a Fae *or* a human. Whatever it is... It will destroy you."

"I need to find a way, Gray." Lea didn't want to argue, but there was so much at stake. Guilt dug at her chest like a wild animal, and anger burned hot in her blood. This was why she hadn't wanted to practice back in Calir. She'd known it was dangerous. *Known* that she wouldn't be able to handle it. "If that's the only way I can take Alaric's power—"

Gray cut her off, shadows expanding and pulsing through the hall. "I'll think of another way." He grabbed her face between his now healed hands. "*We* will think of another way," he repeated, pressing his forehead to Lea's as he tried to control his rapid breathing.

Footsteps pounded just outside the training room, and Gray's shadows exploded around them. Noah stumbled through the doorway as the darkness flew toward them, but Gray stopped them at the last second. Noah's eyes were frantic, wide with utter and complete terror. Blood dripped from his arm and down his fingers. Without letting go of Lea, Gray called his shadows home.

"What's happened?" Gray reached for his sword.

"We're fine, for now." Vincent walked through the door. "Noah has news."

"Why are you bleeding?" Gray asked, his eyes darting between the two men.

"It's Alaric. I came as fast as I could, but I was a day's ride away. I fell running up the mountain trying to get back here to warn you." Blood dripped with a *pat pat pat* onto the stone floor.

"Calm down, Noah," Gray ordered, his tone firm and calm. "Take a deep breath, and tell me what happened."

He did as instructed, closing his eyes and exhaling slowly. "I was out scouting when I saw Ezra. He was—"

"Who is Ezra?" Gray's eyebrows bunched. "I'm not following."

"He's a friend of mine from back home, a guard with me in Auropera. He was fleeing here with news. Alaric killed his advisors. Every single one."

"Dammit!" Gray growled, the candles in the room extinguishing as one. Noah lifted his hand, and they ignited again, revealing a look of absolute and utter fury on Gray's face. His eyes were black, and shadows floated around him like a halo of vengeance as his shoulders heaved with each breath. "It took me *years* to get my men into Alaric's court. Without them, we have nothing! No information, no spies close enough to learn anything of importance."

"Ezra escaped to warn us. He was called to dispose of their bodies. Alaric killed anyone who knew anything other than that his armies have gathered. They're on their way." Noah rubbed his bloody hand along the back of his neck, his shoulders sagging as if carrying the weight of the world. "I'm sorry I didn't get here sooner."

"You did good, Noah." Gray's eyes darted to Vincent. "Go get Erik," he commanded. Vincent was out the door in less than a second, and Gray turned back to Noah. "Do you trust Ezra?"

"Completely. He wanted to find the Eclipsed King, too, but we left in such a rush, I couldn't get him. His brother was killed by the Lonely Death. If he says Alaric's coming, then it's the truth."

"Do you have any other information?" Gray's feet tapped out a furious rhythm as he paced back and forth. "How many troops?"

"I don't know. I don't think that information was disseminated among the soldiers, but we can ask him if he knows anything else." Noah gestured toward the hall outside.

"He's here?" Gray's shadows began to snake toward the doorway.

"He's in Vincent's office," Noah said.

"I want to speak to him," Gray said just as Erik walked through the door. "Now."

"What's happening?" Erik's hair was mussed and his shirt untucked.

Gray turned slowly, the room growing dark as shadows floated all around him. "We've waited for this day for over a hundred years, and still, it's here too soon. Ready our forces, Erik." Gray pulled Lea against his side, squeezing her tightly. "Tell our soldiers to make their peace and say their prayers. Alaric is coming."

CHAPTER 79

GRAY

After sending Erik to gather the others, Gray and Lea walked silently to Vincent's office. Gray tried to control his shadows, but they pushed at his skin and escaped of their own will, growing along with his fury. It didn't surprise him at all that Alaric had stolen his father's magic, but still, he'd at least hoped it wouldn't come to this.

Defeating both his brother and his father would be challenging enough if they each had their own magic, but if Alaric truly had stolen the king's powers, then he was, without a doubt, the most powerful Fae alive. He wasn't sure even Lea's power could match the immensity of the magic that Alaric now possessed.

He and his brother had always been so close to evenly matched, with Gray having just a slight upper hand due to his focus and control. But now? Alaric had stolen his father's death from him. And Gray feared he wouldn't have the strength to overcome the magnitude of his stolen power.

As they arrived at the office, Vincent standing guard outside the door, Gray got a strange feeling in his gut. Something didn't feel right, but he didn't know why. Maybe it was the timing of all of this. How would a soldier have known to head toward Bearswillow, and with enough time to get a word to them about the incoming attack? Alaric was playing some sort of game, and Gray intended to find out what it was.

"Vincent," Gray angled his head. "What do you think? Can he be trusted?"

"I interviewed both him and Noah when they arrived. He's just a boy, and a terrified one at that. He has no weapons, and only a small amount of day magic. I don't see any way he could be a threat."

Gray ran a hand across his scruffy beard. "I'd like to speak to him, then." Vincent took a step to the side and opened the door, swinging it inward to reveal a tall and lanky boy, not yet a man. Ezra sat, pale-faced, with wide eyes and his hands in his lap, his knuckles white from his tight fists.

"Ezra." Gray commanded the room instantly, the others filing in behind him. "Thank you for coming to warn us. You might have saved our lives by escaping. What can you tell me about my brother's plans?"

Ezra swallowed audibly. "I don't know much, other than that the entirety of the royal army has been called back to the capital and divided into troops. We were given four days' notice."

"And how was it," Gray stalked around the desk, "you knew to come *here*?"

"Alaric informed us we'd be marching on Bearswillow." He leaned back in his chair, his wary eyes watching Gray's shadows intently. "The army will travel as one until they get to the mountains, then split, half around each side. You'll be completely surrounded."

Gray's face remained passive, despite the turmoil churning inside his gut. "How does he even know where we are?"

Ezra looked away, pressing his lips together. "I don't know exactly. The way he spoke about it. It was... odd. He was so certain you were here, but I'm not sure he knows you're actually *in* the mountains."

Erik and Gray made eye contact. "Someone turned on us," Gray spat. "They betrayed our location. That is the *only* possibility. Vincent, I need a list of everyone who has left this compound since our return." He spun around to face Ezra again. "How do you know all this?" Gray crossed his arms, not backing down from his intentionally intimidating stare at Ezra.

"After he killed his advisors, Alaric addressed the army. He told us *everything*. All the reasons we needed to kill you. He said we needed to avenge your father. That it was your fault their king was dead. None of it made sense." Ezra rambled, scooting his chair back so far he hit the wall. "He's lost control completely, gone absolutely mad. It feels like there's no real plan other than for him and as many of his soldiers as possible to show up here and destroy every last one of you. I couldn't let that happen."

He's telling the truth.

Gray's eyes flicked to Lea, whose hand was wrapped firmly around the hilt of her sword." My brother is calculated. He has to have some sort of plan. Something that was worth killing his advisors for knowing." Gray leaned forward and placed his palms on Vincent's desk, his shadows floating to the floor and wrapping around the boy's legs. "How did you manage to get away?"

Ezra's eyes bugged out of their sockets, and the scent of urine floated through the air.

"I just ran through the gates. I thought it was suicide. I was positive Alaric would come after me. He was standing on the parapet as I left. It..." He rubbed his hand across his face. "It was like he knew I was going to flee. And he just held his arms out toward me, smoke and fire whipping around him. But nothing *happened*. I stole a horse from the stables, and I fled. I wasn't sure where exactly you were, other than that you were hiding somewhere near the village of Bearswillow. I headed this way as fast as I could, and by the grace of the gods, I stumbled across Noah."

The candles in the room flickered, and a stab of horror gripped Gray's heart through the bond.

"Get everyone out of here now," Lea whispered, running to the door and grabbing Janelle and Erik's arms. "Get out! Right now!" The panic in Lea's voice caused a cold dread to wash through Gray's entire body.

"Vincent, where did Noah go?" Gray took a step away from Ezra.

"He returned to the barracks on my orders." Vincent's deep voice was questioning. "What's happening, Commander?"

"Please," Lea begged her friends, terror filling her eyes as she opened the door. "Get out of here now." Janelle started to move to the door, but Erik placed a heavy hand on her shoulder.

"It's too late, Little Flower." Rage boiled in Gray's stomach, pulsing through his arteries and into every tiny vein and capillary.

"Too late for what?" Thomas asked, wrapping a protective arm around Emma's shoulders.

"Open your shirt," Gray instructed Ezra, who narrowed his eyes in confusion.

"I don't understand. Why would you need me to—"

Shadows wrapped up Ezra's body, coiling around his neck. "Open. Your. Damned. Shirt!" Gray's staccato words were bursting with fury. "*Now.*" He hissed through clenched teeth.

With shaking hands, Ezra slowly unbuttoned the jacket of his royal uniform. As he pulled his tunic to the side, the room stilled, going completely soundless—so quiet, Gray thought he might choke on the thick, cloying silence.

On Ezra's chest, beginning to creep up toward his collarbone, was a red rash giving way to tiny black dots. The Lonely Death.

"What is that?" Ezra stood frantically, the chair toppling behind him as he wiped at the rash with his hands as if he could wash it away. His wide eyes filled with panic. "Please, someone tell me. What is it?" The boy shrieked.

"You expect me to believe you didn't know?" Gray's shadows squeezed tighter, but Lea placed a hand on his arm, silently begging him to stop.

"Know what?!" Ezra was now sobbing. Lea walked to him, now immune to the disease, and pressed a palm to his chest, sending healing energy flooding into his skin. She whispered soothing words, explaining to him what had happened, that he was infected, but that she would fix this. Gray didn't hear the rest. He was blinded by fury.

It had been a trap. Alaric hadn't been out of control at all. He'd known *exactly* what he was doing when he'd told the entire army of his plans, when he'd waited on the parapet to see who would flee to warn his enemies. By allowing Ezra entry into their fortress, they had played right into Alaric's hands, and now, any rebel with magic would be dead within the week.

CHAPTER 80

GRAY

Hours had passed since Ezra had entered the cavern, breathing the Lonely Death into the air without knowing that in his attempt at helping the rebellion, he had probably doomed them all. It would only be a matter of time before black wounds would start appearing on the chests and hands and throats of all those with magic. Gray thanked the gods for the small mercy that the rebels who didn't possess magic would be safe, as would his mate. For now at least.

Gray had been unable to keep his hands from Lea's skin as they all moved to sit near the fireplace, caressing her fingers and tucking her hair behind her ear. With his army infected, Gray could feel death whispering at his neck. Alaric would wait until tomorrow, when the illness would begin ravaging the weakened bodies of the sick, to launch his attack. They'd had the numbers to have a chance, enough people with magic that could help them. But now? There was little hope. Shame oozed from every one of Gray's pores. He'd let his people down. He should have seen this coming. Why hadn't he considered this possibility?

If he hadn't been connected to Lea, if his life wasn't tied to hers so intimately, Gray would sacrifice himself and his blood to allow the moonflowers to grow. Even if Lea was willing to sacrifice herself as well, it would do no good. Alaric was too powerful, and the only one capable of matching him was Lea. To sacrifice himself would be to save an entire army of people just to leave them to be slaughtered by Alaric without anyone to defend them.

"You are not allowed to give up." Lea touched his shoulder, sending a wave of love so potent it ran through his body and collected as a lump in his throat.

It had been difficult to discuss strategy with the blood roaring in Gray's ears, but somehow, they'd persevered. Ezra was sent to an empty room to quarantine with Noah on the off chance the Lonely Death hadn't begun to spread, and word was sent for everyone to remain wherever they were until they were told otherwise. If they were lucky, only those in Vincent's office and the barracks Noah returned to had been exposed.

The room was almost pitch black as Gray's shadows writhed in every corner, smothering the light of the torches. They'd planned for years for this. It couldn't end this way. It wouldn't.

"We have to kill Alaric," Gray's breaths were ragged. "That's the only way out of this."

Lea looked up through her eyelashes at him, her soft, beautiful face creased with worry. "We spill his blood and grow the moonflowers."

Gray hated the weight that sank onto Lea's shoulders. He wished desperately that he could take it from her, that he could be the one with the burden of being the only person that could save them.

"I can do it." Lea looked around at her friends, pausing on each of them as if memorizing their faces. "If we can get to Alaric and kill him, I can grow them. We just need his blood, and we can save everyone."

"We need a new plan," Erik said confidently as he schooled his face into the epitome of calmness. "Our numbers and the courage of our soldiers won't be enough if our army is weakened with the Lonely Death, especially now that he has Brennus's power."

"Well..." Emma stepped forward with tiny steps, as if she was second guessing what she was about to say. Thomas placed a steadying hand on her shoulder, and Emma took a deep breath. "I've been studying a lot, and I was thinking, and, um... well, reading. I have some ideas, if that's okay."

"Eudora's potion..." Gray trailed off.

"That's part of it. Yes." Emma's voice was soft, and Thomas pushed her forward gently. "Um. So we've known from the beginning that you and Lea are our best chance of defeating Alaric. You're the most powerful, so we need to get you to him. Lea, if you can find Alaric through the rebels' eyes, Janelle can help lead you both to him safely."

Erik wrapped his arms around Janelle, pressing her back against his front protectively. "I'll stay with Janelle to protect her." Erik looked at Gray as if challenging him to question his statement.

"That goes without saying." Gray shook his head, his eyebrows lowering, slightly offended that Erik had felt he'd had to say it. "Just as I will not be leaving Lea's side during the battle."

"Right. Um... Of course. But that's not all." Emma wrung her hands together, her fingers turning white from the pressure. "I found a way... Well, I'm pretty sure anyway—"

"Emma," Thomas said, his voice soft. "You can do it."

"Right." Emma took a deep breath. "The dead can fight with us. I can make that happen. If any soldiers die with a weapon in their hand, that is. I can make it so they can continue to fight. Our numbers will never dwindle."

"Emma, that sounds—" Lea started, concern evident in the tension in her jaw.

"I've already decided," Emma said, uncharacteristically confident. "Eudora gave me a potion. If I drink it, it will slow my heart, bring me close to death. I can be the bridge between the physical and the spiritual. As long as I remain in that state, they will be able to interact with the world."

Thomas stiffened, his hands fisting at his sides. "You didn't tell me that part. No, Emma."

Emma held up a hand. "I've already decided. We will all die of the Lonely Death if we don't do this."

"And how do we know this won't kill you?" Thomas asked, and Gray didn't miss the way his voice cracked with fear.

"Because." Emma turned to Lea with tears in her eyes. "The moon-flowers will bring me back. You told me what your mother said, Lea. *Picked by the right person, with the right intentions, at the right time, the flowers from these seeds can stop death himself.* They will bring me back. Eudora confirmed it."

Gray expected to feel a jolt of anxiety or disbelief through the bond, but instead, all he felt was cold, steely determination.

"I need to give magic to more people." Lea said. "As many as we can. I need to be able to see every inch of the battle. I refuse to risk not finding Alaric." Black fire and smoke began to erupt from Lea's skin, ash and soot floating to the ground like snow. It was breathtaking—beautiful and terrible all at once. Lea looked at Gray, an unspoken plea in her eyes. She would be accessing her magic fully, every part of it. *Don't let me lose control,* she spoke into his mind.

You are mine. Do you understand me? I will not lose you to Alaric, and I refuse to lose you to your darkness, he promised back.

Lea nodded. "Erik, gather those with magic, the ones who haven't been exposed to the Lonely Death, and bring them to the training room. We'll start there, then ask for volunteers."

Gray's chest warmed at seeing Lea step into her role as queen—as his equal. "And bring me the latest reports. Whatever gives us our most recent information on Alaric's numbers," he said, dismissing him with a nod.

Lea placed a hand on the hilt of the sword strapped to her hip, the one she hadn't been without since Thomas had made her promise to keep it with her. "Thomas, finish as many weapons as you can. We need a sword or dagger in every rebel's hand."

"Of course." Thomas turned to leave. But Gray stepped forward, stopping him.

"There is a stockpile in a locked room behind the kitchens. Find Elise. She can show you. If you can't forge enough new ones in time, strengthen the ones we already have."

With a tight-lipped smile and a caress to Emma's arm, Thomas began gathering the weapons in the room. "I'll strengthen these first, then find Elise to attend to the rest."

The chamber grew warmer as Lea's shadowy flames grew, her pupils flashing red and black as if the fire was alive inside her.

Gray placed a hand on her lower back, grounding her. He could feel her magic churning, begging for release. "Vincent, I'd like you to show Janelle a map of the mountains and Bearswillow. Janelle, decide where we should lead the battle, what landscape will give us the biggest advantage. Then help Emma decide where she will be."

"Emma, what are the requirements for your plan?" Lea asked her.

Vincent walked to a cabinet, removing a large scroll and gesturing for Janelle to follow him to the sitting area as Emma looked at the books stacked on the shelves.

"I will act as a tether, a conduit between the dead and the physical world. I just have to drink the potion, and it will put me somewhere in the in between." Emma looked to Thomas, who froze in the doorway as he carried the weapons out. He turned to face them, his shoulders set in determination.

"Then let's pick a place that's isolated, away from wherever you decide we will make our stand," Lea continued, ignoring Thomas's concern.

"I will be guarding her," Thomas said as his gaze met Lea's, his eyes full of desperation.

"Done," Lea said without hesitation. "I'll need someone to gather my moonflower seeds from the wreath above my bed."

"I'll see to it," Vincent chimed in. "Once we're done here."

"Good." Lea took a deep, shaking breath.

"Let's go, Lea," Gray said, his voice far more calm than the fear flooding his lungs. But it was nothing compared to what he could feel from his mate. Lea's rage was building to what felt like a dangerous level. He needed to get her somewhere safe, to talk her down from letting that dark, raw power of her primary magic overtake her rational mind.

With everyone assigned to a task, Lea stalked from the room, leaving scorch marks behind on the stone floor with every step.

Gray followed, catching her arm with a shield of darkness between his skin and hers. "What are you doing, Lea? This is dangerous. You need to pull that power back."

"This is it, Gray. Either we kill Alaric tomorrow, or we *die*. I'm done fearing who I am, pushing down my magic. I will fight with *every ounce* of power I have." Lea looked away, as if unable to lie to his face.

"And what if it destroys you?" Gray rasped.

Lea met his gaze, the fire in her eyes horrifying and beautiful in equal measure. "If we're going to die, Gray, don't you want to go down in flames?"

CHAPTER 81

LEA

Lea had spent the entire day giving away little bits of magic to anyone who was willing to allow her access into their mind. Her fire had slowly dimmed until she glowed like an ember, exhaustion pulling her shoulders down and making her eyes heavy. Gray had carried her back to their chambers as the sun was setting, once the training rooms were emptied and their plans were in place. There was nothing left to do but allow the night to pass, pray for their souls, and await the morning sun.

But they hadn't been able to wait. Before the morning light was even peeking above the horizon, Lea and Gray had wordlessly risen and walked hand in hand to stand together in the rocky terrain of the mountains, their arms around each other and their eyes scanning the village she'd called home for so many years. It ached, seeing it abandoned, but there was no time to let that pain settle. There would be enough pain soaking into her soul by the day's end. She was certain of it.

The cold wind whipped at Lea's braided hair, stinging her cheeks and turning them a rosy pink. It would be hot once the sun fully rose, but right now she was grateful for Gray's warmth.

They'd found a few precious hours of rest, wrapped in each other's arms, before Vincent had knocked on their door with news: scouts had identified royal soldiers approaching from the North, splitting into two units to encircle the Torres Mountains and Bearswillow, just as Ezra had said. They would arrive by midday.

It's what they'd hoped for, thank the gods. Janelle had identified the least risky place to battle, and they'd counted on Ezra's reports of Alaric's plans to make that decision.

The rebel army would gather in the expanse of field on a tall hill just outside the town square. Once the fighting began, there would be no time for those on the other side of the Torres mountains to join the fight. On three sides of the field were dense woods. It would be challenging for a large group of soldiers to travel through them, and they certainly wouldn't be able to do so undetected. Alaric's forces would have no choice but to enter through the town square where the rebels would have the higher ground.

"It's taking too long," Lea whispered, her words flying into the wind.

"It takes time to get into place," Gray said calmly, though his eyes remained locked on the landscape before them. "They'll be there soon."

Lea exhaled a slow breath. "We should have seen something by now," she said. Her skin warmed, and as she shuffled her feet, Lea felt the crunch of charred earth from the black flames dancing around her legs.

"There." Gray turned Lea's head east with a gentle tug of her braid where a puff of smoke rose from a faraway hill. The sign they had agreed on.

Sagging back against Gray, Lea closed her eyes. "Thank the gods." Thomas and Emma had made it to Lea's house. It had been the perfect location. It was far away from where the battle would occur, almost on the opposite side of the village. There would be no reason for soldiers to come anywhere near it.

As she waited for a second puff of smoke to indicate that Emma had taken the potion and was tethering herself to the earth, shadows and smoke began to dot the town below them. Lea counted them off in her head, waiting for the final number: thirty-eight. Thirty-eight sets of eyes, in place and ready for Lea to use to find Alaric.

Because they *had* to find Alaric. Several rebels had started to show signs of the Lonely Death in the early morning hours, including Emma and Janelle. A pain as sharp as a shard of glass slid into her heart, and tears pricked her eyes.

"We *will* kill Alaric, Little Flower. And you'll save them all." Gray's voice was sad, thick and gravelly.

"Do you promise?" Lea asked, continuing to look toward the village as their soldiers assembled. She didn't need to look at Gray to see the truth, that he couldn't promise her such a thing—it was in the hands of the gods now. But still, she needed to hear the words, even if just to calm her pounding heart enough to allow her to think.

The sun pulled free of the horizon with a rush of day magic, rising into the sky and bathing the valley within the Torres in a shade of red that looked eerily like blood. It made Lea's magic revolt, her primary magic banging around in her chest, begging to be released.

"Not yet," Gray said, sensing her unease. "You have the seeds?"

Lea put her hand in her pocket where she had tied a small satchel of moonflower seeds into her fitted fighting leathers. Seven hid in the heel of her left boot, and several more were enclosed in the locket of her sword, which was strapped to her back. "I have them."

A final puff of smoke from her house appeared. Emma had taken the potion.

"That's our sign." Gray leaned his forehead against the back of Lea's head for just a moment, breathing her in. "If something happens to me—"

"It won't," Lea interrupted. "It can't." Her voice broke. She couldn't discuss it. Couldn't bear to think about it,

"I know. But just in case, if something happens to me, plant the moonflowers as fast as you can. Try to grow them before the bond brings you beyond the veil with me. You can save everyone, Lea. Even yourself." He turned her around. "It has been the privilege of my life to love you, Little Flower. If death separates us today, I will wait for you, however long it takes. I love you. Yesterday. Today. Tomorrow. It doesn't matter where I'm loving you from."

Lea could only nod, her throat too full of sobs to risk speaking and allowing them to escape.

Gray bent down and pressed a soft kiss to the corner of her mouth before taking her lips fully, kissing her slowly as if memorizing every curve and line of her mouth.

"I love you, too," Lea choked out, trying to push down the anxiety hammering against her ribs. It felt too much like goodbye. "But we are *not* dying today." Opening the crack in the floor of her chest a little wider, Lea stepped back. Shadows and flames drifted from her body, wrapping around her like a shield. She wouldn't let fear paralyze her. Not today. Not when so many people were counting on her. It was time for anger, for revenge for the things Alaric had done to her, and to Gray, and the entire kingdom. It was time to follow the darkness inside her, and unleash it.

"Alaric wants to come after us?" Lea stood up taller. "Let him." Black flames rose in an arc around her as she began to tunnel deeper into the fiery black pit beneath the floor in her chest. "I am the Queen of Flames and Shadows. I will scorch this whole damn earth, if that is what it takes. I will turn it into ash so thick, it will block out every ray of sunlight, until all that remains in this world is darkness. No one but Alaric will be going beyond the veil today. Not if I can help it."

CHAPTER 82

LEA

The sun was scorching, far warmer now than it had been when it had just begun to peek out through the mountains. Sweat dripped down the back of Lea's neck, trickling between her shoulder blades and causing a shiver to run down her spine as she stood hand in hand with Gray in the middle of the open field, their army behind them, waiting. Their intel from Vincent's scouts had told them that Alaric's army would arrive by midday, but once again, he appeared to be playing games.

Alaric's army stood just on the border of the village as they had been for hours, standing still as statues. A standoff. But Gray would not back down, refused to bring the battle to them. With so many sick, they needed the advantage of higher ground and refused to stray from their plan.

It was nearing six in the evening, based on the position of the hot summer sun. Gray had long ago instructed the rebels in the field to retreat to the shade and rest. Luckily, no one with the Lonely Death had started hallucinating, but the black sores on their bodies continued to spread, crossing backs and trailing down arms. A few had wounds on their tongues and the roofs of their mouths, and one unlucky soldier had begun to bleed from his eyes.

Lea had done what she could to help them, but everyone knew it was futile. She held the cure in her pocket, but the seeds were useless without Alaric's blood.

Every few minutes, Lea shuffled through the many different vantage points she could observe through their soldier's eyes, but the royal army was nowhere to be seen.

Through Thomas's eyes, she could see that Emma laid in Lea's old bed, tucked as far away from the battleground as possible. It looked like she was sleeping, or it would, if not for the gray tint to her skin and sheen of sweat across her pained face. How long would the potion even last? How long until it completely drained the life out of her without the moonflower to bring her back? The thought made nausea churn in Lea's stomach.

Lea grew even hotter as her magic crackled along her hands and arms, expanding in her ribs and begging to be let loose. The crack in her chest had widened, allowing more raw magic to seep out. The urge to destroy the floor all together and allow it to burst free was intoxicating, but the thought was overwhelming. Instinctively, Lea knew that to allow her primary magic to take over would be to surrender her reason and critical thinking. Even the small amount pounding inside her was enough to cloud her mind.

"Not yet," Gray said, clearly feeling the pull of her power through the bond. His tone was firm. "Not unless it's absolutely necessary."

Lea tried to push the magic down, but it refused. Instead it continued building, stretching as if it could rip through her skin and escape to wreak havoc on the world. Lea felt a sudden tug in her chest, distracting her. She reached her hand out to grab Gray's arm, grounding herself before following the tug of her magic.

Suddenly, she was seeing through Murray's eyes. Lea had never met the man before, but he was one of the soldiers that Gray had trusted enough to let hold a piece of Lea's magic. Her eyesight transformed, fading from looking out over the grassy, green field to looking through the dirty, cracked glass window of a bakery, witnessing a hoard of soldiers walking in perfect formation.

They were coming. But, why now? Had they won the standoff? Had Alaric really given up so easily?

The uniforms of the royal army had changed. Instead of a deep navy, they were now blood red, with thick leather breastplates and the royal crest embroidered on the left pocket. Except now, the crest depicted only a sun, surrounded by fire. The first six rows of soldiers were clearly Fae, with at least twenty men in each row. On their chests, stitched right next to the royal crest, were their insignias of magic.

"They're here!" Lea cried out in her mind, unsure if she'd spoken the words out loud back in the field or into Gray's mind through the mate bond, but hoping she had. Lea quickly gathered as much intel as she could before pulling herself back into her own body.

"They're coming. *Now*!" Lea shouted the moment she was back in control of her own vision, but Gray had already turned to signal Erik. Gray's eyes swam with darkness, his shoulders back and his posture confident. He looked like a warrior, almost like a god, as he barked orders, shadows stretching out around him in every direction.

"Get our troops ready!" Gray shouted to Erik, who rushed to assemble the army as Janelle scrambled to her feet from where she sat in the shade with her eyes closed, searching for danger.

"We need to split into two groups. I feel a threat coming from behind!" Janelle called out as she sprinted to Gray. She closed her eyes again, her face scrunching in concentration.

"Go tell Erik to station a third of our troops around the perimeter with Vincent." Gray ordered. "Put the sick in the middle. They fight as a last resort." Janelle nodded, sprinting to where Erik was assembling a line of young, wide-eyed soldiers.

Lea turned back toward town, searching for fragments of red between the old stone buildings. The clanging of weapons and the thunder of feet behind Lea told her that their army was almost in formation, just as another tug at her magic caught her attention, this time from a different direction. Her sight was now that of a soldier she had met in passing, Casey, who had impressed Lea with her ability to hit a target the size of a pea with an arrow from a hundred yards away. She was hiding behind a large rock near the stream Erik and Lea had walked by before the Fenrir had attacked, her bow and quiver strapped to her back.

There are soldiers here, the voice sounded in Lea's mind as Casey crouched further down behind the rock. *At least two hundred, maybe more.*

Lea pulled herself back, quickly shuffling through the rest of the open connections to her magic. Soldiers were splitting up and spreading throughout the village. There were some heading toward the cottages near where Thomas lived. Others approached the woods. There had to be thousands of them, and they were *everywhere.*

"They're surrounding us, Gray." Lea grabbed her mate's arm.

"We're still in the safest spot." His eyes were black, but his shadows were somehow even darker. "The woods are too dense for them to fight efficiently. Vincent's men will take care of it if they attempt to enter from behind us. The only other way they can approach is from straight ahead through town, and we have the high ground," Gray repeated the reasons they'd chosen this location as if convincing himself they'd made the right decision. "Do you see Alaric?"

Lea searched the images in her mind again, but she didn't see him anywhere. Panic immediately consumed her, her heart thundering and blood roaring in her ears. "No. What if he's not coming? What if he's not here, Gray?" If Alaric hadn't traveled with them... Lea couldn't even think about what that would mean.

"He'll be here." Gray's dark, gravelly voice was full of confidence and his jaw was set in determination. "He infected *hundreds* in our army. He doesn't have the self-control to let that magic go to waste. If nothing else, he'll be here to take their powers once they die."

Another tug—Janelle. *You only have minutes,* she heard Janelle say once she was in her head. *Be careful.* Lea wished she could speak to her friend, but she hadn't had success projecting her own vision to those with her power. Every time she tried, her head swam and her stomach churned before she was thrown into someone else's sight. So instead, Lea pulled back and focused on her task. Black flames burned the grass at her feet, and her shadows whipped around her along with her hair in the stagnant summer air. *This is it.* Lea grabbed her sword. She had imbued it with Thomas's powers the previous night, and it thrummed beneath her fingers, shadows and flames and death vibrating through the metal.

"It's time." Lea's voice sounded foreign as it left her mouth, and Gray grabbed her hand, intertwining his fingers with hers as he pulled his own sword from his back.

"To whatever end," Gray squeezed her hand tighter, "I will *always* be with you." His eyes never left the streets below him, and Lea wondered if it was because he was watching for the royal army, or because he couldn't bear to look at her as their probable death approached them in the form of thousands of blood-red soldiers. "Remember your ultimate goal, Lea. Grow the moonflowers, *no matter what.* You're the only one who can save us." Gray rasped as the first line of Alaric's men appeared from below, their bows pointed at the sky.

Flaming arrows rained down around them, dotting the darkening sky with deadly falling stars of fire. With an explosion of shadows, Gray gave the command to attack. A flash of gray lightning crashed in the middle of the soldiers closing in on them, throwing royal soldiers to the ground as pieces of cobblestone rained down around them.

With Gray's order, chaos ensued. All at once, both armies ran toward each other, the rebels stopping at the top of the hill to maintain their advantage of elevation. Lea had been correct that Alaric had placed his soldiers with magic at the front lines, and she dodged a small ball of fire that flew at her head.

Gray's shadows ripped from his body, wrapping around soldiers necks and plunging straight through leather breastplates and deep into their chests to rip out their still beating hearts. Lea threw a blast of fire out in a shock wave in front of her, and black, smoky flames incinerated the soldiers immediately, white shards of bone crumbling into piles.

Widening the hole in her chest, she finally allowed the magic that had once terrified her to escape. Death's grip overcame her, and now, in the midst of battle, Lea no longer feared it—she *became* it.

A battle cry tore from her soul as Lea turned to her left, shielding herself with shadow to protect her body from arrows. Her sword was as light as a feather in her hand, crackling black flames surrounding the metal. The sword tugged her hand left and she turned, listening to the way her weapon seemed to be trying to direct her movements. Metal hit metal, her sword vibrating with an intensity that made her arm ache as she blocked what would have been a fatal blow. Lea pulled the sword back, then stabbed forward into the enemy soldier's stomach.

Instantaneously, the soldier burst into flames, screaming as death's grasp pulled him under. Before he could take his final breath, Lea kicked the dying soldier's sword from his hand. Emma had been very clear; do not allow the enemy to die with a weapon in their hand.

Sweet agony filled her chest as she sucked more magic from deep inside herself in preparation to attack a group of royal soldiers who had broken through to their side and were approaching the sick, who stood weakly with weapons raised in their bloody hands. Every piece of her wanted to rain down death and destruction, but the enemy was too close to their own soldiers, so she held her darkness at bay.

Two of the sick, Sierra and Tiff, began to run forward, but Lea ordered them to stop, flashing lightning to catch their attention. "Stay where you are!" she ordered as the wind abruptly picked up. A strong gust threw her words across the field, and they paused.

Lea shot a thick stream of black fire into the grass. It spread like a spider web, branching out and twisting around her fellow soldiers while wrapping around her enemies. Their swords melted and their skin dissolved from their bones as her molten fire encased them, destroying them completely. Their screams of pain fueled her fury, as if her darkness fed off of the torment and suffering of the wicked.

But, unlike the last time Lea had witnessed battle, she felt no remorse.

Back to back with Gray, they fought in tandem, flames and fire, swords and shadows and smoke circling around them in a lethal waltz. Lea's weapon guided her movements as wave after wave soldiers were cut down, with only a few of Alaric's men breaking through their lines.

Their casualties had been minimal so far, at least that Lea had seen, and she sent up a quick prayer that Emma's plans were working. She raised her sword, preparing to incinerate a man in red approaching a young female soldier fighting valiantly with only a small dagger, when the man stopped in his tracks. It was as if the goddess of the moon had finally heard her. Red exploded from his chest, blood spurting as he fell to his knees.

It worked. Lea almost sobbed as another enemy soldier near her fell to the ground, holding his neck as blood bubbled from a clean slice across his throat. Emma had done it. The dead were with them.

Lea let the pain of the loss of their own soldiers and the memory of losing her mother fill her chest, spurring her anger and fueling her darkness as another tug nagged at her mind. She threw up a shield to answer the call of her magic, following the tether to a view of a mountain stream where the red backs of soldiers retreated in the distance.

They're retreating. I don't know why, but they're heading your way. Lea pulled back and quickly flashed through her other connections to see the same thing again and again—soldiers turning around and heading toward the middle of town.

Alaric's here somewhere, Lea thought, searching for him. He was commanding them. He had to be. Why else would they retreat?

More soldiers are coming. Lea resumed fighting.

Got it. Gray replied through their connection as he leapt through the air and sliced the hand off a soldier about to stab a rebel from behind before doing the same to his head. He turned to her, fury in his eyes, blood splattered across his face.

Find him, Gray commanded as the storm clouds darkened overhead. Thunder boomed, shaking the earth. *I'll cover you.* As Gray shrouded her in shadows and stepped in front of her, he forced a long tendril of darkness into the chest of an approaching soldier, his red uniform turning even darker as blood ran from his hollow chest. Gray threw his body to the side, summoning his lightning and striking a group of nearby royal soldiers as a fire wielding rebel melted their weapons.

Lea searched through Bearswillow, probed every possible avenue for Alaric. He *had* to be here, but she couldn't see him through Vincent's eyes as he picked off soldiers staggering through the woods, nor through Thomas's as he watched over Emma. He wasn't around where Erik fought at the edge of the field, staying close to where Janelle hid within an enchanted pocket of the woods to focus on what her magic was telling her.

Lea had *almost* given up and returned to fighting when she felt a pull of her magic—no, a yank. It screamed of danger and desperation, and Lea dove toward the tether, following it until she finally saw what she was looking for—the worst case scenario.

He's here. He's walking toward your house right now. Through Noah's eyes, Lea saw Alaric, dressed in a crisp, stark white uniform trimmed in gold and striding confidently up the side of the hill she knew so well. His blond hair was unmistakable, as was the arrogant posture in which he carried himself. Green eyes scanned his surroundings, full of fire and malice. *What is he doing?* Lea wondered. There was no way he knew that Emma was there. The soldiers hadn't been told the details of their plan. Only that if they died, to make sure they did so holding their sword.

Her vision began to move as Noah stood and looked down at his shaking hands. He pulled his sword from its sheath, a prayer falling from his lips.

"Don't!" Lea screamed. "Stop! We're coming!" Lea's heart stopped, her lungs seizing as panic filled every inch of her body. Dammit! She should have worked harder to make the magic tether work both ways. She needed to warn Noah, had to stop him.

Gray's voice was suddenly in her head. *What's happening?*

Alaric is here. He's walking toward my house, and Noah is going to fight him. Lea dug deep inside her chest, pulling and molding her powers into a molten ball waiting to detonate.

He'll be killed. Gray's panic was evident in his voice.

Lea threw a dark, soot-filled flame into the sky, and Erik's head snapped up, meeting Lea's eyes. His jaw clenched as he sprinted into the woods, emerging seconds later holding Janelle in his arms.

"Lea!" Gray roared, pulling her attention back to him. "I'll go after him. I'll save them. *Please*, just stay here. Help our soldiers. I'll call a storm when Alaric is dead, and you can join me and plant the seeds—"

"I will *never* leave you to fight alone again. *Never!*" Lea grabbed Gray's arms and shook, but his strong frame was immovable.

The moment Erik and Janelle reached their side, Lea plunged into her darkness. She felt like she was burning from the inside out, but she didn't care. There were too many royal soldiers to kill, and so many of Alaric's men were still running through the streets to join the battle.

With a scream of determination, Lea stomped her foot, throwing her arms out and her head back. Black flames erupted in front of them, dividing the majority of what remained of Alaric's forces from the rebels in the back with a wall of fire. She reached for the ends of the flames and grabbed them in her mind, forcing them to encircle the town square completely.

Behind them, a few rebels still fought against Alaric's men, but with them separated from new attacks, and with the help of the fallen, they at least had a better chance of survival.

Lea pulled Erik and Janelle close, then encased them all in a shield of shadows. For just a second she parted her flames, pulling Gray and the others with her to the edge of the woods before closing the gap and sealing off the rebels once again. With an order to run, they darted through the dense forest, avoiding the town square as they circled around the village to get to Lea's house. Why had they decided to place Emma so damned far away?

Sensing her urgency, Gray lifted Lea to his chest, increasing their speed and sprinting toward her old home. They flew across the ground, behind the courthouse, and past the Coughlin's until her cottage appeared on a hill in the distance, the sun just beginning to sink below the horizon behind it.

Lea screamed for Noah to stop as he emerged from behind the maple tree near her now overgrown garden, close enough to hear her, but too far away for her to intervene. Alaric's head snapped up, a sneer smearing across his face as his eyes met hers, then shifted to Noah.

The young boy who had never killed anyone, who had helped her with her fire and told her a hard truth when she'd most needed to hear it, who had shown his loyalty and bravery again and again, looked like a warrior as he ran with his chin high and his sword raised.

Gray dropped Lea on the ground, sprinting toward Noah with every bit of speed he had, but it wasn't enough. As Noah arced his sword over his head, preparing to slice through Alaric's neck, Alaric threw his head back with a cackle, fire exploding around him and encasing Noah until he became nothing more than a smoldering pile of bones.

CHAPTER 83

GRAY

Gray's first thought as Noah's skull tumbled down the hill was that he hated the smell of burned flesh. He had always hated it, but it was so much worse when the acrid, sweet scent came from the decimated remains of someone you cared about.

A stabbing anguish, so intense it took Gray's breath away, knocked him backward as Lea's scream echoed across the hill. Gray instinctively knew that his mate's pain was not of the physical kind, but the kind that cut deeper—the soul-shattering agony of losing a friend. Noah was gone. Just like that, he had ceased to be.

Alaric stood next to Lea's house, leaning casually against the stone as if he hadn't just incinerated a boy with his entire future ahead of him.

Gray had never seen anywhere near that much power from Alaric before, irrefutable proof that he had been successful in stealing their father's magic. Gray's stomach sank. Alaric exuded pure, terrible might. It would be nothing short of a miracle for them to defeat him now, not if he'd already mastered the power he had stolen.

"You fucking bastard!" Gray yelled, storming toward Alaric and summoning clouds to darken the sky. Lightning danced on Gray's knuckles, cracking around them and crashing into the ground. Shadows surrounded him like the black of night.

"Hello *brother*." Alaric looked at his nails, completely unbothered as he picked at a cuticle, then wiped a piece of ash from his sleeve. Gray held back the urge to vomit. It wasn't just ash. Only one thing had been burned here.

Lea was suddenly at Gray's right, deadly silent as black flames and shadows flicked around her feet and sword. Erik appeared on Gray's left, tucking Janelle behind him.

"You fucking coward!" Gray spat. "Sending all of your men to fight while you what? Explore the town?"

We need to get to Thomas and Emma, Lea said. *We can't let him find them.*

"They seem to be defeating you so effectively. I thought I might take a little tour of the place that grew your *Little Flower* here," Alaric said as he winked at Lea. Gray bristled, stepping slightly in front of her.

"Keep her name out of your mouth," Gray growled. "This is between you and me, Alaric."

"It does seem a fitting end to our story, does it not?" Alaric stood up straight, putting his hands in his pockets. "You broke the curse, hoping to kill me, believing yourself to be the more powerful Fae, just like you always have." Alaric threw his hands up in the air, and a fireball exploded in the sky, as large as the setting sun. Lea quickly threw up a shield of shadows to protect them from falling flames, her eyes lingering on the thatched roof where a spark ignited the straw.

"You're not the most powerful one now, are you, little brother?" Alaric raised his chin and tilted his head to the side. He didn't blink—didn't move. He was truly the monster Gray had always thought him capable of becoming.

From the corner of his eye, Gray saw Janelle move to Lea and whisper something into her ear.

Throwing a spear of flames into the ground at their feet, Alaric roared. "Stop it. Stop it!" His eye twitched and his whole body shook. "Stop talking!" Alaric shouted, spit flying from his mouth like a rabid dog, his voice raw from the intensity of his screams.

Janelle froze, and Alaric stared her down.

"It's not too late to stop this, Alaric." Gray shifted forward, trying to pull Alaric's attention away from Janelle and Lea. "You have Father's power. You're the king now."

"The king no one wants!" Alaric spat. "You were always Father's favorite! Mother's favorite! Even our sister preferred you until she got what she deserved. Perfect Evander," Alaric taunted. "I know what people said. 'Such a shame Evander isn't the crown prince.' You laughed at me. *Both of you!*" Alaric pulled a sword from his belt and gestured erratically between Erik and Gray.

"You thought I was *nothing*!" He tilted his head back and forced a harsh, humorless laugh. "Ha. Ha. Ha." Alaric paused, "And now, who will be laughing?" The horrifying smile on Alaric's face instantly disappeared, replaced by his bared teeth. "Me." His voice dropped to almost a whisper. "Because *you* will be *nothing*. Nothing but a rotting corpse. Nothing but the weak prince who failed to save the kingdom, who failed to save his *mate*." Alaric swung his sword at Lea, a stream of fire exploding behind her to prevent her from stepping back.

But Lea didn't budge, didn't even flinch as she ordered her black flames to detonate around her, consuming Alaric's flames within her own.

He cocked his head at her, his eyes raking over the hissing fire surrounding her. "You." Alaric pointed the sword at Lea's throat. "You and that fucking power you hid. No one believed me. You made me seem *crazy*, but I knew what you were, what you hid beneath your skin. You'll never know how much I savored burning it each night at dinner, chipping away at that armor of yours. I'll kill you last, I think. Make you watch as I steal your mate's power, then yours. And you won't even have your precious moonflower seeds to stop me." He sent another blast of fire at Lea's house.

"Do you want to know why I'm here instead of fighting with my army? Because I knew they could handle you without me. *You* are not a threat. Once your army falls from the Lonely Death, I will steal their power. I only bothered coming here to destroy the moonflowers myself." Alaric swung his sword around in a circle, forcing a laugh again.

He's completely lost his mind, Gray whispered to Lea through their bond.

"It's the only cure, you know," Alaric continued. "Father thought he'd eradicated them all. But *you*." He repeated, his voice dripping venom as he stopped his erratic pacing. "*You* fucked it all up. Fucked *everything* up!" Alaric's eyes slowly dragged up Lea's body, a sickening grin pulling his mouth into an almost sneer. Without blinking, he stared at the black fire surrounding her like it was made of pure gold.

"Will it never be enough?" Lea asked, her voice shaking.

Alaric slowly tilted his head as if possessed, his voice changing, echoing—the sound of thousands of voices mixed together, slithering from between his perfect white teeth. "Only your death," Alaric hissed. "*That* will be enough."

"Your fight is with me, Alaric," Gray's shadows lashed out at him, forcing him to take a step back. *When he attacks,* Gray said into Lea's mind, *run and get Emma and Thomas out. Take Janelle with you, Erik and I will fight.*

I'm not abandoning you, Lea argued.

"The mate bond is so convenient is it not?" Alaric's macabre grin returned. "Kill one, kill both." He stepped forward with his right foot. His tell.

Gray felt Lea's reluctance, her absolute refusal to leave him for even a second. But if Alaric found Emma and Thomas, or the fire spread to where they couldn't escape...

It will be okay, my love, Gray whispered in her mind.

He didn't get the chance to feel her response. Just as Gray had predicted, Alaric lunged with his sword out, slashing wildly.

CHAPTER 84

GRAY

Lea raced to Janelle, and Gray heard her order her friend to get Emma and Thomas out as Gray dodged Alaric's blow. He angled his body toward the house, pulling his brother's attention away from his mate. Gray was no fool. Lea was the only one who could defeat Alaric. But he could provide a distraction.

Janelle disappeared through the front door and Lea returned to Gray's side. His heart was pounding, his stomach filled with apprehension. He'd hoped that his mate would flee to save her friends.

They needed Emma to hold her tether to the dead—needed them to be able to fight if Lea's fire faded back in the meadow. Who knew what was going on back there, but if the whole field of soldiers had been slaughtered and he hadn't done everything he could to protect them, Gray would never forgive himself.

But that wasn't the only reason. Despite her magic, her power, he didn't want her anywhere near Alaric. It was obvious that he was losing his mind, that any bit of rationality or sense had deteriorated as he'd stolen their father's magic. He was unstable, more of a threat than Gray had ever imagined.

Alaric spun, his sword an extension of his arm as he moved with inconceivable speed. Even for a Fae, Gray had never seen someone move so quickly. Lea swung a flaming sword at Alaric's knees, but he jumped with the agility of an antelope. Erik pushed a wall of fire toward him as Gray sent arrows of shadow at his chest, but with a flick of his fingers, Alaric threw up a shimmering shield of thick, hard air.

The sword in Lea's hand began to glow, and Gray ordered a bolt of lightning to strike at Alaric's chest, distracting him. Lea was using the weapon Thomas had made her to absorb the power surrounding her, and Gray was grateful. He made a mental note to thank Thomas as he forced crash after crash of lightning down around Alaric, forcing him to strengthen his shield.

With a roar, Alaric shattered the shield with a blast of fire, each piece of solid air bursting into shards of flaming glass. A shield of air just like Alaric's burst from Lea's sword, wrapping around her as Gray and Erik ducked. Pieces of Alaric's fractured shield embedded into Gray's arm, and he hissed in pain. *Shit!* he cursed. *How many different types of magic has Alaric stolen?* He plucked the shards out with his shadows as Lea darted forward, swiping at Alaric's neck.

Without even looking at her, Alaric pushed a palm outward, a gust of wind like a tornado sending her flying to the ground.

"Azalea!" Gray shouted, searching the bond for injuries.

I'm fine. Lea coughed, struggling to her hands and knees as she sucked in deep breaths. Alaric had knocked the air out of her, but she was otherwise unharmed. *Help Erik!*

Gray turned just as Erik ran around Alaric's back, drawing his sword and preparing to strike, but he was thrown backward with an earth-shattering blast of fire, sending him crashing into the side of the house. Erik's head hit the stone with a *crack*, and the scent of blood filled the air.

Horror washed over Gray, and he risked a glance at his friend. His relief was mild, but sweet. His chest still rose and fell rhythmically. He was alive.

"You heard him. This is between my brother and me. Stay out of it," Alaric hissed. His words were pointless. With hardly any effort from Alaric, Erik laid unconscious.

In his periphery, Gray saw Lea crouching, her sword swirling with shadows as she creeped toward them.

"I *said*, this was between me and my brother!" Alaric roared, throwing his hands in the air as walls of flames at least fifteen feet high surrounded them, blocking Lea off. The fire began to spread, and Gray's stomach dropped.

The fire, Azalea! Pull Erik away! He shouted, gathering his shadows and attempting to suffocate the flames.

"No magic, Evander." Alaric raised an eyebrow and his sword. "I want to watch the blood drain from your throat."

Gray ignored him as he forced his shadows outward, aiming for Alaric's neck. He would use every last bit of his magic to defeat his brother. He refused to allow himself to be killed, not if he could help it, not if Lea would be killed with him. Silver-blue lightning crashed inches from his brother's feet as Lea tried to strike Alaric from behind the wall of flames. Gray's chest swelled with pride. His mate, his warrior. Gray ordered his own lightning to join Lea's, aiming to hit Alaric's sword, but he dodged too quickly.

"You never listen, do you?" Alaric screamed, spit flying from his mouth.

Gray ripped Alaric's feet out from under him with his shadows, then lunged with his sword. Alaric rolled, but not before Gray's blade sliced across his cheek.

Black-red blood trickled from the laceration that ran from Alaric's nose to the tip of his ear, dripping down his face and into his mouth. "Magic, then?" Alaric threw fire around him in an arc, so fast and so broad that Gray was unable to dodge it. His uniform caught fire, and he cried out in pain as he sent his shadows to smother his flaming sleeve. "If you insist. It's your grave."

CHAPTER 85

LEA

With trembling fingers, Lea reached out to touch Alaric's wall of fire. Her heart pounded, and she struggled to breathe, her lungs paralyzed by the distance between her and her mate. She winced, cursing under her breath as the fire burned her skin.

She could part her own flames, touch her own fire, but she couldn't get through Alaric's, couldn't control his magic.

The fire, Azalea! Pull Erik away! Gray's voice shouted into her mind. Panic flooded between her ribs and up her throat. As fast as her feet could carry her, Lea sprinted around the circle of fire to where Erik still laid unconscious, the flames creeping slowly toward his feet.

Lea dropped to her knees next to Erik, her hands cradling his head where blood leaked from a long, jagged gash. Flooding light into her fingers, she sent healing energy down his spine to stabilize it before focusing on the cut, watching intently to ensure it closed fully.

Erik moaned, stirring, but remained unconscious. As the fire licked at his boots, Lea ran behind him and grabbed his arms, dragging him backward with every ounce of strength she had until he was a safe distance from the growing inferno. With a groan of pain, Erik rolled onto his side. Lea pushed more light into his body, but still, he didn't wake.

He's breathing. He's moving, Lea reassured herself as she scanned Erik's unconscious body for anything she might have missed. *He's going to be fine.* There was nothing more she could do for him, except ensure the fire didn't get close enough to burn him. Her sword vibrated in her hand, and Lea latched onto the power, pulling it inside her.

As she pulled at that string of power that flowed from inside the metal, the wind stirred. She fastened onto it, commanding a gust to blow the flames away from Erik. The fire bent and bowed, submitting to her will. The fire flickered, and through the smoke, Gray and Alaric appeared. Blow for blow, they met one another, their swords moving so fast Lea could hardly keep up.

She pushed even harder, directing smoke into Alaric's eyes as his flames died off, unable to maintain their heat. Alaric stumbled, coughing on the thick, black fog, and Lea ran to Gray's side, arcing her sword overhead and bringing it crashing toward Alaric's neck.

He was too fast. With the wind still whipping around them furiously, Alaric's fire was unable to spark. He spun in a circle, dodging her blow while sending long daggers of ice shooting from his hands.

Gray cried out as ice embedded itself in his calf, and Lea threw a shield of shadows over them as he yanked the melting shard from his skin. Sweat dripped from his hairline, and ash spotted his face as he focused on healing his wound.

Lea leached Alaric's new power into her sword. Pulling moisture from the air along the blade, the sword cooled to near freezing. Lea raised it overhead, then swung it forward as hard as she could, hurling a spear of ice at Alaric.

As he covered his head with his arms, his concentration snapped. Calling on her wind again, Lea blasted him backward, raw magic crackling in her blood.

"Erik!" Janelle's scream broke through Lea's rage, her wind faltering as she tore her eyes away from Alaric and to the front of her house where Janelle was sprinting to get to Erik while Thomas carried Emma down the hill toward safety.

"No!" Lea screamed at her friend as Gray stalked toward his brother, his sword gripped in his bloody hand.

Alaric's eyes locked onto Janelle as she raced to Erik, throwing herself on top of his still-unconscious body. A smile that looked more like a snarl pulled at his hollow cheeks, and he raised his hands toward her friend.

He's going to kill them. Get Janelle and Erik out of here, Gray said into her mind as he sent bolt after bolt of lightning down in front of Alaric. He strode forward like the God of Death, his bloody arms bulging as shadows whipped around him in a fury. *And then help me finish this.*

Lea screamed again, her feet moving as quickly as they could toward Janelle and Erik. Lea pulled Janelle off him, shaking her violently. "You have to get out of here!"

"I'm not leaving him!" Janelle scrambled back, reaching out for Erik. "Wake up!" She patted his face, and his eyes cracked open.

"Where am I?" he rasped.

Lea wasted no time. Now that Erik had regained consciousness, she placed her hands on his head, easing whatever headache remained and pulling him to sit. "You're in the middle of a fucking battle, Erik! Get Janelle out of here. Now!" Lea looked over her shoulder to where Gray and Alaric fought in a swirling fog of fire, shadows, and ice.

As if a bucket of freezing water had been dumped on his head, Erik jumped to his feet, his eyes darting toward Gray as he ran to where his sword lay on the ground and picked it up.

"Janelle, if you've ever listened to anything I've asked of you, please do it now. Run," Erik begged. With a glance back at Janelle, his eyes full of things he didn't have time to say, Erik took off toward Gray. The second Janelle stood on shaking feet and turned, Lea sprinted back to her mate.

The world exploded in a violent flash of light and a sudden, agonizing scream ripped from Lea's throat as she was thrown backward. She rolled to her side, trying to breathe through the excruciating pain, certain that Alaric had snuck up behind her and stabbed her through her spine. Lea threw up, struggling to get enough oxygen as the pain in her chest intensified. Nothing she'd ever felt before had been even close to this torturous. She was dying. She *had* to be.

Lea pressed her hand against her chest to stop the bleeding, and Janelle was suddenly at her side, her hands trailing along her body. "What is it?" Janelle asked frantically, her eyes wide with terror. Lea couldn't speak through the pain.

"Lea! Stay with me!" Janelle pleaded as she lifted her hands from Lea's body to grab her face.

Her *hands...* They were clean.

CHAPTER 86

GRAY

Harnessing his fury, Gray struck his lightning again. But with a wave of a hand, Alaric blocked it as if it was *nothing*. The lightning ricocheted off the hard shield of smoke and air, causing the ground to erupt at Gray's feet. He dodged left, forming his shadows into a long, sharp tendril. If he could distract Alaric, maybe he could plunge it into his chest, wrap it around his heart and rip it out. He just needed to get close enough.

As Gray circled his brother, he sent more shadows and lightning, striking at random in an attempt to disorient him.

Alaric laughed, completely unfazed, his eyes manic. "Do you not understand the power I have in here?" He beat his chest like an ape, so hard that Gray was certain that he was bruising his own ribs. He was frantic, frenzied. Past all logic and reason. "I should just kill you now. I would. But I've fantasized of this moment for too long." He grinned widely, blood bubbling between his teeth from the wound on his cheek as he thrust his hand out toward the shadows Gray commanded. Instantly, they turned into flames.

Gray roared, cutting off his flaming shadows before they could incinerate him.

"I'll tell you what, little brother. Surrender, and I won't kill your entire army. I won't even kill your friends. Consider it a kindness," Alaric offered, spitting blood onto the ground.

"And you'll what? Take our power and become our father? A power-hungry monster who murders and steals until this kingdom has nothing left? I'll die before I surrender."

The fires froze, and Gray felt an energy buzzing in the air. Something was building, something terrible. It reminded Gray of when he gathered his shadows and darkness inside his chest, honing them into a weapon to unleash in a sudden torrent of power—but whatever he was feeling was bigger. Whatever this was, it was sucking the very life from the world.

The grass turned brown beneath Alaric's feet and Gray's lightning crackling in the clouds overhead dimmed.

"If that is your wish," Alaric hissed, throwing his head back and his arms out to the side.

An explosion unlike anything the world had ever felt before detonated in a blaze of blinding, earth-shattering light. It was pure energy, erupting in a white hot flash of fire that burned Gray's skin and sent him flying. Gray was completely powerless to stop himself as he was ripped backward, his spine hitting the ground with a sickening *thud*.

The breath was stolen from his lungs and black dots appeared in his vision as flames ignited his pants. The fire rapidly spread higher, burning his chest and arms, his skin bubbling and turning black wherever it touched. Gray fought through the pain to find his shadows, using them to suffocate the fire before shooting them toward Alaric. His shirt fell apart as he lifted an arm to order his darkness to grasp Alaric around the throat and rip him to his knees, but once again, Alaric was too fast. Gray tried to sit up, but he couldn't move below the waist.

Before Gray could heal himself, Alaric darted forward, plunging his sword just below Gray's chest with a howl. Gray cried out, grabbing the sword in his fists and attempting to pull it out. If he could just get up...

But he was too weakened, and his brother too powerful. Alaric placed his foot on the base of Gray's sternum just below the sword, then, with inhuman strength, ripped it upward, tearing straight through Gray's breastbone. Blood bubbled from his mouth as Alaric yanked the sword from where it now sat at the base of his throat and threw it on the ground. He bared his teeth, his face dotted with the crimson evidence of his hatred as he pulled a dagger from a sheath at his thigh and sank it between Gray's ribs. Once, twice, then a third time.

"I told you it would be my face you saw as you took your last breath. I hope it haunts you for the rest of eternity."

CHAPTER 87

LEA

Lea pressed a shaking hand to her chest again, then pulled it away to inspect her skin. *No blood... Why was there no blood?* Understanding crashed over her, stealing the air from her lungs.

"No!" she shrieked, somehow dragging herself to her feet through the pain and stumbling toward Gray and Alaric, rage pooling in her gut, so potent it almost blinded her.

The agony was too much—she couldn't think, couldn't process what this amount of pain meant. Lea began to tear at the remaining floor inside herself where her magic hid. She needed the darkness to consume her—needed something big and powerful to fill her until there was no room for anything else. It was her only chance to defeat Alaric.

She plunged deeper into the cavern of her power, ripping apart the floor until it shattered away into nothing but rubble. Her dark magic finally broke completely free, exploding inside her in a burst of energy that set every inch of her body aflame, clearing her mind and dimming the searing torment that had been spreading up her sternum. There was no space for pain, there was only pure, undiluted power.

Her vision darkened, or maybe the world around her did. She wasn't sure. Lea could feel death hovering just above her shoulders, but instead of fearing it, she *commanded* it. The grass beneath her feet turned to ash as black flames completely surrounded her, whipping savagely, waiting for instructions from their master.

Lea's eyesight sharpened instantly. The twists and swirls in the ash falling all around her looked like the intricate patterns of snowflakes, and the flames caressing every inch of her body glowed in shades of darkness she'd never seen before. The heavy scent of soot filled her nostrils as the crackling of fire overwhelmed her. Energy flooded her limbs, her muscles tightening and her body almost buzzing. She felt stronger, almost superhuman. Invincible.

As the thick, shadowy smoke cleared, Lea flung out her darkness, grabbing the back of Alaric's shirt and ripping him back from where he stood over Gray.

"Get away from him!" Lea hissed in a voice that sounded so different from her own, shielding her mate completely in shadow at the same time she threw her hands out, ordering her silver-blue lightning to crash into Alaric's chest. The blast threw him backward, and he flew through the air until crashing into the base of a tree at least twenty feet away.

"Heal Gray!" she shouted to Erik as he rose from where he'd fallen during the earth-shattering explosion, holding his head. His skin was slightly green, and he wobbled on his feet, but he would have to push through. He needed to help her mate, because she was the only one who could finish this.

Lea wanted desperately to run to Gray, to heal him herself and see how far his injuries went. But Alaric had to die. Only one brother could survive, and she'd be damned if it wasn't the man she loved.

Every fiber of Lea's soul begged her to incinerate him, to turn the monster into nothing more than embers in the wind that would blow away and never return, but she needed his blood. Without it, Emma would die. And Janelle and Thomas and Erik, along with half of the rebellion or more.

Erik dashed to Gray's side as Lea sent her shadows to wrap around Alaric's neck. He tried to burn them away, but Lea funneled more energy into them. She *would* be stronger than him. There was no other option.

Lea squeezed her sword tighter in her fist, the cool metal thrumming in her hand, pulsing as it absorbed her raw power, the primary magic she was finally allowing to escape after so long. Alaric fought against her shadows, struggling to his feet as he set the field surrounding Lea's house on fire. Red flames mixed with black ones, shadow and smoke swirling around them as the wind blew violently across the hill.

Alaric raised his hand and his sword flew through the air, the hilt landing firmly in his palm. With his lips twisted into a snarl, he threw fire straight at Lea's head, but it was absorbed by her own flames, only adding to their intensity.

Roaring in anger, his face turned red and his jaw clenched so tightly that Lea thought she heard the crack of his teeth. Wave after wave, Alaric attacked, but it only added to Lea's fury as she deflected his advances.

Alaric's attacks were becoming sloppy, his eyes wide with a hint of fear, as if in complete disbelief of Lea's power. Sensing his distraction, she struck Alaric with a spear of shadows, but this time, he was prepared. He threw a ball of fire above his head, sparks raining down as he lowered his chin and directed streams of ice at Lea.

She ducked, but Alaric didn't stop. Wave after wave, he threw fire and ice in her direction. "I'm not afraid of you!" Alaric shouted with a sneer, *almost* convincing her, but the sword in Lea's hand warmed.

Lea's darkness sang out to her, a mesmerizing melody that demanded she listen. It burst from her soul of its own volition and latched onto Alaric's flames, pulling his magic into her very marrow. The feeling of his power flooding into her chest was overwhelming—intoxicating and horrifying all at once. Her head began to pound and her body ached. Rivers of something wet trickled from her nose and ears, but Lea didn't falter as she called his vile power into her body. Pain turned to agony, but Lea didn't stop. *Couldn't* stop. They were too evenly matched. She needed to get close enough to spill his blood, something she would only be able to do if Alaric was powerless.

Lea's black flames grew higher as Alaric's magic followed her direction. She felt herself growing stronger, but as her powers grew, so did her wrath. Alaric's fire felt different; full of hatred and jealousy, and it spread like poison through her blood.

His eyes blazed with something akin to fear as black fire overtook his own. Alaric's flames shrank, and he screamed in rage, his eyebrows raising and his face going white as he took a step backward. He knew what she was doing. *Hurry,* a voice urged in her mind.

Lea raised her sword in the air, the metal blade turning as black as midnight as shadows burst from the etchings of the wind and snaked up his body, slicing and ripping at his skin, pulling him closer.

Alaric roared, digging his feet into the ground, resisting her magic's pull. "You think *I* crave power? Here you are, wasting your time stealing mine as your mate takes his dying breaths! And for what?! Once his heart stops, so will yours!"

His words were like arrows embedding directly into her soul, the black haze controlling her mind fading as the reality of what was happening shook her to her core. She'd asked Erik to heal Gray, so why wasn't he here fighting beside her? Lea glanced over her shoulder, her hold on Alaric's magic faltering when she saw Gray. He was still as stone on his back, Erik's face and hands red as he struggled to stem the bleeding from his chest. *Oh gods, his chest.*

"I'll fucking gut you for this!" Lea screamed, ripping away his power with everything she had. Alaric shifted as his flames dimmed. Pure, unadulterated rage overwhelmed Lea as she consumed Alaric's magic, the expression on his face shifting from murderous to that of a cornered animal.

She had to end this. Killing Alaric was the only way to save Emma, the sick rebels—maybe even Gray. Tanad's words circled in her mind. *Magic that can create just as it can destroy.*

On instinct, Lea isolated her primary magic—the wild, wicked power that the goddess had said was only evil if that is what she chose it to be. Well, if embracing that evil was what was required to save her mate, then it wasn't a choice at all.

Pulling as much raw, dark magic as she could into a dense ball in her chest, she forced it through her arms and out of her fingers. Alaric stumbled back as black flames crashed directly into his sternum, burning a gaping hole in his shirt instantly. Lea watched the skin above his breastbone turn black as she demanded her magic slice through it like a razor, twisting between his ribs and wrapping firmly around his heart.

"You fucking *bitch*!" Alaric spat, collapsing to the ground, his face going pale as sweat trickled from his hairline. He coughed, holding his blackened skin as he spit out blood. "I'll kill you," he said through bloody teeth. "All of you!"

Lea branched the magic out, spreading a poison inside him made of every horrendous, awful thing that had ever happened to her—the pain of his torture and assault, the agony of losing her mother, the rage she'd felt watching Queen Emmaline's murder. She commanded the reaper to seep into his blood, to rot him from the inside out.

Alaric tried to speak, tried to roll to his knees and rise, but Lea pointed her sword back at his shaking, sickly body, funneling his power into her chest as quickly as she could.

Lea saw the moment Alaric accepted his fate in this battle, watched in horror as he clenched his jaw and, using the last of his energy, slammed his palms onto the ground in a flash of red hot fire that made her eyes water and her skin flush. In less than a second, before Lea's magic and sword could completely drain him of his power, life, and blood, Alaric was *gone*, leaving only smoldering grass where he had been standing only moments before.

CHAPTER 88

LEA

The crown prince turned king was gone, and along with him, the only way to cure the Lonely Death, but as Lea took in Gray's bloody, broken body, it no longer mattered.

Lea collapsed onto the ground next to Gray, her shaking hands immediately pressing against the horrific wound running from his abdomen to his chin. "No, no, no..." Lea muttered in shock, the pain in her own body growing.

Shards of bone protruded from the open gash, barely distinguishable from the shredded muscles and blood pooling in the crater where his sternum used to be.

Crimson trails ran from Gray's eyes and ears, from the corner of his mouth as Lea turned his head and forced him to look at her. "Wake up! You *will not* die. Do you hear me?" She pressed her hands inside his gaping chest, flooding him with healing magic, but there was so much blood, so many places he'd been wounded, she could hardly tell where it was all coming from.

"Alaric?" Gray sputtered, his lips turning a grayish blue as he raised a weak, trembling hand to Lea's face.

"I tried... I... I'm sorry. *Dammit!*" She tried again to heal him, but the wound was so big, so deep. "Erik! Help me!"

Erik placed his hand on top of Lea's, Gray's blood squirting between their fingers with every erratic, slow beat of his heart. "It's a fatal wound, Lea. Not even you can heal him. Without the moonflowers..."

"He will not die! I can heal him!" she sobbed. "Fucking *help* me!" Black flames erupted around them in her anger, and Erik flinched. "Open your eyes, Gray!" Lea sobbed, filling him with healing energy, every last bit of light that she could find.

"His spine is broken. And his ribs...He's lost too much blood. Lea, listen!" Erik grabbed Lea's shoulders, shaking her. "He's lost too much blood," he repeated.

Blood. With fumbling fingers, Lea pulled the satchel of seeds from her pocket, ripping it open and dumping them onto the blood-soaked earth. Lea pushed them into the wet soil, scooping the red liquid from the surrounding ground and forcing it onto the seeds. "Keep healing him, Erik!" Lea demanded, pushing her hands into the saturated dirt and flooding her magic inside. They had to grow. *It has to be enough.*

"Little Flower," Gray croaked, his eyes struggling to remain open as he fought to take short, wet breaths.

Lea raised her head to look at Gray as she continued to funnel every bit of magic she had into the moonflowers. "I just need one. Just one petal. And then you'll be fine."

"Lea," he whispered, his voice so weak she hardly heard him.

"No!" Lea wept. "Please don't leave me, Gray. You can't." She focused back on the ground, where small vines had only begun poking up from the soil. "Why isn't it working!?" she screamed, snot running from her nose, her tears adding to the flooded soil.

"It requires"—cough—"every... drop," Gray croaked, choking on a clot of blood. "I will *always* love you," he whispered, his fingers threading through the hair at the nape of her neck.

"I'm going with you," Lea threw herself on top of Gray, his arms wrapping around her as warm blood coated her chest and face. Gray pressed a kiss to her forehead, his lips trembling. Somehow, his hands already felt cold as they rested against her skin.

"I will always love you," he repeated as he weakly turned his head to look at Erik, "but you have to live."

Erik's callused, stained hands wrapped around Lea's arms as he pulled her away from Gray, who immediately shielded himself with shadows.

"No!" Lea screamed, kicking and fighting as Erik lifted her from her mate. Lea set her skin on fire, black flames shooting up Erik's forearms, but he held firm, wrapping his arms more securely around her and hissing in pain as Gray summoned the strength to grab Alaric's dagger from beside him.

"A sacrifice..." he whispered sadly, blood gurgling from his mouth. "I'm sorry, Little Flower. Forgive me," Gray begged as he raised the razor sharp tip to his chest. Lea threw her shadows out, reaching for the dagger and throwing Erik back into the house as Gray dug the edge of the blade beneath his collarbone, roughly carving the mate bond from his skin with shaking hands.

The pain was paralyzing. Lea's back arched as the mark was seared from her chest, the bond violently ripping itself from around her heart and shattering into a million tiny pieces, the remnants turning to ash. Her connection to Gray disappeared completely, and her vision went black as she fell to the ground, her lungs struggling to expand. Lea fought to crawl toward Gray, reaching out a hand and screaming a scream that made her throat bleed and the mountains tremble. As Gray's head fell to the side, a jagged hole where his promise of forever had been, he took one final rattling breath. "Forgive me," he exhaled.

Lea felt the last beat of Gray's heart in her soul, a soul that withered and turned black, as if Gray had been the only light inside her. Darkness tore across the hill, blocking out the moon and stars as Gray's body stilled and his green eyes glazed over, reflecting back the world as it erupted in an explosion of flames and shadows.

ACKNOWLEDGEMENTS

To everyone who read this book, THANK YOU from the bottom of my heart. I hope it took you on an adventure, and I hope you look forward to the final book of the *Magic of the Wildflower Series*, coming Fall of 2024.

If you enjoyed this book, consider helping me get the word out by leaving a review on <u>AMAZON</u> and/or <u>GOODREADS</u> and follow me on Facebook, Instagram, and Tiktok @meganshadeauthor

Preorder book three of the Magic of the Wildflowers Series—A Petal in the Crown— <u>HERE</u>

To the greatest beta readers I could ask for—Brittany O'Barr, my fabulous book club (Molly, Bethany, Tammy, and Mindy), Shannon, Kerrie, Randal, Jenessa, Kenzie, and Lindsey.

Lisa Tulp and Sarah McFarland, thank you so much for your proofreading expertise.

Sara, thank you for reading and rereading until we thought everything was just right.

Lindsey Staton (@honeyy.fae on IG), thank you for your beautiful art, support, and friendship. You're the real MVP.

To Stef, my cover designer, thank you for nailing it every single time and being an absolute joy to work with.

To my husband, my number one fan and biggest cheerleader. You'll never know how much your support has changed my life.

To all my family, especially my mom and mother-in-law, who have done so much to help me as I've navigated this new stage of parenthood.

To Molly, because I love you. Your support means the world, even if it takes you months to finish a book.

To my friends, both those who have read my books and those who have been my cheerleaders, thank you so much for everything you've done to support and encourage me. I love you all.